POWER

Borgo Press Books by S. FOWLER WRIGHT

*Arresting Delia: An Inspector Cleveland Classic Crime Novel * The Attic Murder: An Inspector Combridge & Mr. Jellipot Classic Crime Novel * The Bell Street Murders: An Inspector Combridge & Mr. Jellipot Classic Crime Novel * Beyond the Rim: A Lost Race Fantasy * Black Widow: A Classic Crime Novel * The Blue Room: A Novel of an Alternate Future * The British Colonies: No Surrender to Nazi Germany! * The Capone Caper: Mr. Jellipot vs. the King of Crime: A Classic Crime Novel * Crime & Co.: An Inspector Cleveland Classic Crime Novel * Dawn: A Novel of Global Warming * Dead by Saturday: An Inspector Cleveland Classic Crime Novel * Dream; or, The Simian Maid: A Fantasy of Prehistory* (Marguerite Cranleigh #1) * *Elfwin: An Historical Novel of Anglo-Saxon Times * The End of the Mildew Gang: An Inspector Cauldron Classic Crime Novel* (Mildew #3) * *Four Callers in Razor Street: An Inspector Combridge & Mr. Jellipot Classic Crime Novel * Four Days' War: The Alternate World War II, Book Two * The Hanging of Constance Hillier: An Inspector Cleveland Classic Crime Novel * The Hidden Tribe: A Lost Race Fantasy * Inquisitive Angel: A Novel of Fantasy * The Jordans Murder: An Inspector Combridge & Mr. Jellipot Classic Crime Novel * The King Against Anne Bickerton: A Classic Crime Novel * Megiddo's Ridge: The Alternate World War II, Book Three * The Mildew Gang: An Inspector Cauldron Classic Crime Novel* (Mildew #1) * *Murder in Bethnal Square: An Inspector Combridge & Mr. Jellipot Classic Crime Novel * The Police and the Public: Some Thoughts on the British System of Justice * Post-Mortem Evidence: An Inspector Combridge & Mr. Jellipot Classic Crime Novel * Power: A Political Fantasy * Prelude in Prague: The Alternate World War II, Book One * Red Ike: A Novel of Cumberland* (with J. M. Denwood) * *The Return of the Mildew Gang: An Inspector Cauldron Classic Crime Novel* (Mildew #2) * *The Rissole Mystery: An Inspector Combridge & Mr. Jellipot Classic Crime Novel * The Screaming Lake: A Lost Race Fantasy * The Secret of the Screen: An Inspector Combridge & Mr. Jellipot Classic Crime Novel * The Song of Songs and Other Poems * Spiders' War: A Novel of the Far Future* (Marguerite Cranleigh #3) * *Three Witnesses: A Classic Crime Novel * Too Much for Mr. Jellipot: An Inspector Combridge & Mr. Jellipot Classic Crime Novel * The Vengeance of Gwa: A Fantasy of Prehistory* (Marguerite Cranleigh #2) * *Was Murder Done? A Classic Crime Novel * Who Murdered Reynard? A Classic Crime Novel * The Wills of Jane Kanwhistle: An Inspector Combridge & Mr. Jellipot Classic Crime Novel * With Cause Enough?: An Inspector Combridge & Mr. Jellipot Classic Crime Novel * Wyndham Smith: His Adventures in the 45th Century: A Science Fiction Novel*

POWER

A Political Fantasy

by

S. FOWLER WRIGHT

THE BORGO PRESS

An Imprint of Wildside Press LLC

MMX

CHAPTER ONE

A TALE, like a journey, should begin at one end, and conclude at the other. But it is sometimes advantageous to look well at a distant landmark, before commencing to reach it in a pedestrian way. In this spirit we listen to a conversation which is proceeding in Lady Crystal Maitland's own apartment, where she is entertaining Mr. Israel Goldstone, the editor of the *Morning Standard*, to dinner.

There are two others at the small, luxuriously-appointed table, Lord Rigby Stilton at her left hand, and her sister, Lady Jehane Norchester, opposite.

Mr. Goldstone is getting a good dinner, which he likes, as many editors do. But he has not come here for a meal, nor for the attraction of Lady Crystal's really beautiful eyes. Neither has she invited him because of any personal intimacy.

Socially, Lady Crystal recognises four strata of the race to which she belongs. There is her own exclusive and exalted circle; there is a large number of gentlepeople with whom she can consort without derogation, though it would be rather impudent for them to expect to consort with her; there is the large number of persons who are "Well, my dear, not *quite*...."—and there is the general body of the proletariat who are dearly impossible.

If she did not place Mr. Goldstone decisively in the third stratum, it was only because his fitness for the fourth was too obvious to be overlooked.

Mr. Goldstone had no idea that she held this opinion concerning him, because, though each of them was much cleverer than they thought the other to be, neither was a very good judge of character.

Mr. Goldstone looked upon her as an exceptionally fine young woman who had made a conspicuous social success with the help of her birth, her dressmaker, and her physical attractions. She had married Stanley Maitland, rather to the surprise of her friends, as he had been unequal to herself both in birth and fortune, but he was recognised as a man who might go far both in the profession of the law and the political career that he had subsequently chosen, and her own ambitions were obviously in the latter direction. No one among her own circle had discredited her with the assumption that she had allowed her affections to overrule her discretion.

Mr. Goldstone, looking at the matter from the Fleet Street angle, which is shrewd but shallow, thought she had done well for herself; but he would have hesitated to congratulate Stanley Maitland upon the wife he had gained.

She might be a gracious and clever woman, with an appearance gratifying to a connoisseur's eye, but he considered that other attributes in a wife are at least equally necessary. A woman's thoughts should be concentrated on her husband's comfort, and, next to that, on a filled and flourishing nursery. Those were the ideals which had maintained his race, even in scattered exile, for two millenniums. He doubted whether she considered her husband's comfort to be as important as her own, and he would have classified her as a shy breeder, in the language of the horticulture to which his leisure hours were devoted, and with the coarseness of the stratum to which he belonged.

She had invited Mr. Goldstone with the express purpose of giving him the official view of the recent Nigerian troubles, as she had had them from her husband, the Colonial Under-Secretary, and with the promise that she could add some authentic details which he would be unlikely to obtain elsewhere. Actually, she cared little for the Nigerian complication, nor was Stanley particularly concerned about the Press attitude thereto. She intended to use the occasion for a calculated indiscretion concerning the probable resignation of the President of the Board of Trade, which she would finally, and very reluctantly, permit him to use, on condition that its origin should not be divulged under any circumstances.

Mr. Goldstone was not greatly interested in Nigeria, and would not have accepted the invitation but that he had a different objective. He hoped to learn something concerning the disappearance of that brilliant young scientist, Mr. William Feltham, which had taken place about three weeks earlier, and which had so far baffled both the police and the press.

He knew that Maitland had been Feltham's closest friend. He had a strong opinion that he knew more about the matter than he had disclosed, even if he could not solve the mystery. But efforts to draw him out had proved abortive. To have a quiet talk with his wife, while he would be at the House, was an opportunity not to be missed, and it was an additional satisfaction when he found that

Lady Jehane, who was said to have been particularly friendly with the missing man, was one of the party.

But it had been no part of Lady Crystal's programme that Mr. Goldstone should occupy her younger sister's attention. She had invited Lord Stilton especially to fulfil that function. Rigby was known to be devoted to Jehane. He would be in every way a most suitable match. The sooner she forgot her unfortunate liking for the vanished scientist, the better it would be for herself and others. Lady Crystal's private hope was that Mr. Feltham had gone to a place from which he would not return; on which condition she was content to remain in ignorance of its address.

It was an unsatisfactory dinner for all of them. Jehane resented the too-obvious purpose with which Rigby had been placed beside her, in which, indeed, her sister had shown less than her usual competence. She gave him no reason to enjoy the meal.

Lady Crystal found that her indiscretion missed fire, Mr. Goldstone's only recognition of it being a casual remark which showed he knew more about the matter than she did herself; and Mr. Goldstone failed signally to obtain any information from either of the ladies concerning the disappearance of William Feltham, for the excellent reason that they had none to give.

The only mutter of importance which transpired—and that was an importance which he did not recognise—resulted from Mr. Goldstone's efforts to keep the conversation upon the Feltham mystery, or upon such topics as would enable him to resume it without difficulty.

This led him to mention the extraordinary quantity of letters which are received, in such cases, both by the police and press: letters containing theories which are often ingenious and sometimes fantastic, or giving dues which are almost always worthless.

"The difficulty is," he went on, "that one in ten thousand may contain an important fact, or a real solution; and it is therefore never quite safe to ignore them."

"I suppose," Lord Stilton suggested, having been baffled by the monosyllables of his left-hand neighbour, and being glad to open a more promising channel of conversation, "I suppose you can tell most of them are crazy without losing much time, even if you can't always spot the winners."

"Yes, mostly," Mr. Goldstone agreed, "though it's not always as easy as you might think. Of course, some of them are just raving nonsense. I was handed one as a curiosity, just as I was leaving this evening. I looked at it in the car. It's from a man who's going to destroy London in a year's time. To prove that he can do it, he's going to destroy part of Kensington Gardens ten minutes before opening time on Sunday next."

"You don't take it seriously?" Rigby asked. "We've heard a good deal about death-rays and heat-rays and destructive gases since chemists got on to those lines during the war. I suppose the governments won't let them stop."

"I shouldn't say it's altogether the governments," Mr. Goldstone answered, with his usual fairness. "They don't need any stopping. They go on of themselves. Very few scientists seem to have any moral sense. Very few chemists, anyhow.

"I always thought that Feltham was rather of that kind" (with characteristic persistence, he led the conversation back to the missing man); "even that last invention for seeing past days on the screen—he just let it loose on the world without a thought as to what consequences it might have."

"I don't think that's a very good illustration, Mr. Goldstone," Lady Jehane remarked coldly. "It was one of the most wonderful inventions of the age. Besides, what harm could it do?"

"I don't say it does any," Mr. Goldstone answered cautiously. "I only say that he may not have regarded that question, one way or other. Actually, there's no doubt it's being used politically, though the purpose isn't quite clear."

"I saw it once," Lady Crystal informed him. "Stanley wanted me to go. I wouldn't say it does no harm, Jehane. It almost bored me to tears. I never did care much for bucolic scenery. But it wasn't that. It's the pace that kills." (She smiled slightly as she used the proverb to a reversed meaning.) "The whole afternoon was occupied by seven cows and a dairymaid. Ten minutes—cow turns round. Seventeen minutes—cow turns back. Sixty-four minutes—enter dairymaid (sensation). Even Hollywood's better than that."

"I think it's fascinating," Jehane asserted. "It's knowing that it isn't faked, and what actually happened, and no one knowing what's coming next."

"Anyway, you're sure the letter's a fake?" Lord Stilton persisted. "I'm not sure of anything. But if we published all that sort of thing that comes into our post-box, we should have two scares a day, and no readers left before the month ended. You can see it, if you like. The man seems able to type, and that's more than most of them do." As he spoke, Mr. Goldstone pulled out the letter, and with no more than the glance which was necessary to assure himself that he had got the right document, he handed it across the table. Rigby read it aloud:

Jan. 23rd, 1934

THE NEWS EDITOR
THE "MORNING STANDARD"
FLEET ST., E.C.4

SIR,

I do not suppose you will publish this letter when you receive it, though, if you do, you will find that you have pulled off the greatest scoop of the century.

All I ask you to do is to keep it until the end of the week, in which case you will publish it on Monday morning without any further request from me.

I am in possession of an invention which will absolutely destroy any part of the world to which it is directed. I am applying it in such a way that it will destroy the London area at midnight on Dec. 31st next, within three miles of Charing Cross, in all directions.

My condition of withholding this sacrifice is that I be given absolute power of government from the 29th inst. until the end of the year. I require absolutely autocratic power, which will be used solely for the national good, as I am able to see it. On that condition, the destruction will not occur.

Should I die, however, in the meantime, from whatever cause, I can only advise that the whole area should be vacated, with all valuable property of a portable character, prior to the date and within the area mentioned, as nothing could then avert the catastrophe.

In evidence that this letter cannot be ignored with safety, I propose to destroy an acre of Kensington Gardens, as shown on the enclosed map, on Sunday morning next, ten minutes before the opening.

I will disclose my identity in due course.

Yours, etc.,

ONE WHO WOULD RULE TO SAVE

"Whatever else he may be," Rigby remarked, at the conclusion of this letter, "he isn't a fraud. If he can't do what he says, he offers to commence by demonstrating his incapacity. Unless he's a lunatic, he must be either a genius or a jester."

"They're mostly lunatics or jesters, about equally divided. The genius doesn't come our way," Mr. Goldstone replied unemotionally.

"Then you won't do anything about it?"

"I didn't say that. I shall probably send a copy of the letter to the L.C.C., or whoever's responsible for Kensington Gardens, about which I'm not clear without reference. It's just wasting a stamp."

Rigby returned the letter, and as it passed through Jehane's hands, her eyes fell upon it, and she started visibly. The next moment she regained her self-control. "May I?" she said casually, as she opened the sheet. She looked at the well-spaced lines, and at the quality of the paper. "It's a good letter," she said, in the same casual way. "He must be an educated man."

"May I see?" Her sister's voice was as casual as her own. Mr. Goldstone passed the letter across.

Lady Crystal gave it no more than a moment's glance. "Yes," she said, "it's typed well enough. It's hard to understand an educated man wasting his time on such nonsense." Definitely, though without haste, she turned the conversation to other things.

When her guests had gone, the sisters gazed at one another in a common doubt, though not with the same fear.

"You are quite sure?" Crystal queried.

"There's no doubt. It wouldn't be so certain if it were a vowel, because they get the most use, but a broken f...there wouldn't be two of those. He may be somewhere in the house now."

"I don't think that follows. All we really know is that the letter was typed on Stanley's Underwood, which only you and he use as a rule. If Mr. Feltham did it, it means he's gone mad. But whether he's mad or not, I don't see how he could have been in the house for three weeks without being seen."

She thought that Jehane was the only one, except Stanley, who could have given William Feltham access to that typewriter. Had she reacted to the letter in a different way it might have been a natural deduction that she had done so. Lady Crystal did not think that to be the explanation. At the back of her mind she had a more dreadful, but—no, it was an incredible fear.

CHAPTER TWO

THERE were two views of the way in which William Feltham took the sudden elevation to fame and fortune which resulted from the commercial success of the Pastographical process.

The press commented with approbation upon the fact that he did not relax the severity of his scientific researches. What use is money to the true scientist, what value has it, except as it may facilitate him in the more rapid pursuit of knowledge? His life is not for himself, but for all humanity. It was suggested that William Feltham was engaged upon experiments the result of which might be so stupendous as to make his invention of the Pastographical receiver seem but the recreation of an idle hour.

It was known that he had entrusted his financial interests entirely to the hands of his friend and lawyer, Stanley Maitland. It was said that the only personal use he had made of his sudden affluence had been to enlarge his laboratories, and to order delicate apparatus to be manufactured to his own designs, and without consideration of the expense involved.

What other use could money have in the true scientist's hands?

"De Vaux of gold had never need
Save to purvey him arms and steed."

In the pure scientific mind the ideals of a departed chivalry had come back to the world.

Actually, it was not only the manufacturers of scientific apparatus who benefited from Mr. Feltham's fortune. His orders for rare and difficult drugs were placed with what seemed to be an almost reckless freedom, and if his wealth were used in any illicit way, it was in overriding the regulations which restrain the traffic in these incalculable poisons.

But his continued concentration upon his scientific researches was a fact beyond question. In the first weeks following the sale of his patent rights for a cash payment of half a million pounds, and royalties which might prove to be of much greater value, his attitude had been a puzzle even to Stanley Maitland, who has been described as his closest, and was actually his only friend.

The invention of the Pastograph (to use the commercial name by which it afterwards became popular, rather than a more accurate scientific description) gave the world the benefit of one of those novelties which seem so wildly impossible before their demonstration, and so simple afterwards.

It was already known in theory, though it may not have been demonstrated, that the vision of all earthly happenings must be carried outward into the wastes of space, as far as the reflected light of our planet may be able to penetrate, which, it is immensely probable, cannot be limited, except by the curvature of the light on which the vision is carried. Now a regular curvature, however slight, must have one certain result, that it will return to the place from which it began. And the extent and limit of the vision of all that has taken place on the earth since it became a solid planet may be determined by the gradual curve of the light-rays on which they are carried, which must bring them back, at however great an interval, to the place at which they began.

That had been the theory which William Feltham had expounded to his friend's sympathetic but somewhat sceptical attention many times in the last three years. He had admitted that there were some mathematical complications. The heavenly bodies move, both relatively and absolutely. There are possibilities of light-rays being deflected from the exhibition of a perfect circle, or that they may return to, and be absorbed by the sun from which they came, before they would reach the earth again. But, in spite of these difficulties, William Feltham had convinced himself that light-rays were actually repassing the earth, bearing visions of that which had occurred upon it in remote periods, and that they could be seen by man, if an apparatus could be constructed which would filter them successfully on to a receptive screen.

And in the end he had proved his point. It was useless to dispute his theories, or question his mathematics. The vision itself was there.

And yet—amazing as its success, and great as its wonder had been—it had definite and exasperating limitations. The scenes which were recovered were much more recent than had been anticipated, being those of about three-and-a-half centuries ago, and (as might have been anticipated) they could only be observed at the rate at which the actual events had occurred. There were great difficulties also in regulating the exact place which could be observed; and as to the period of observation, there was no question of regulation at all. It simply could not be done. You had to take what the light-rays gave.

The period which was borne upon the rays which were now returning to the earth, after their three hundred and fifty years of distant wandering in the wastes of space, was the later part of the reign of Queen Elizabeth, and the scenes which were first given to the public were those of the early summer of 1588.

By setting up sufficient receivers, a practically limitless number of different pictures might be obtained, each showing the incidents of field or street or village as they had occurred in that year, with a wealth of fascinating and often surprising details of the dress and occupation and habits of men and women, and of the animal and floral life, both wild and domestic, of that period.

The exasperating limitations were that the pictures were soundless, that nothing could be seen of the interiors of the houses, but only the outdoor happenings, and that a change of scene could only be obtained by moving the very elaborate apparatus and receiving screen. The last difficulty was a very serious one. It appeared to be the normal natural law that the light-rays should return to the actual scene of the original portraiture, but some disturbance had caused a southerly deviation of about fifteen miles.

If therefore, it should be desired to observe the main street of Stratford-on-Avon, it would be necessary to calculate a position about fifteen miles to the south, acquire the site, at whatever cost of compensation or demolition, erect the necessary apparatus in a suitable building, and then discover that the scene portrayed was no better than a meadow into which no one might enter for a month of watching, or a river where no one fished.

Yet it was felt that, with all these limitations, the records obtained were of an incalculable value, both historical and social, as well as of an absorbing interest; and while the commercial interests which had secured control of the world patents were busy in experiments by which they hoped to quicken the pace of presentation and to increase the human interest—in other words, to fake the records they were obtaining—there were many who were content to sit hour by hour watching the slow unfolding of a past scene, with its unexpected moments, its infinitely varied possibilities. The screen which was recording for the first time (and which would be potentially eternalised by a simultaneous photography) had, to many, the fascination of a perpetual first-night. This was particularly the case in England, where the temperament which can watch a cricket match for a slow-moving hour in anticipation of a moment's crisis, found another gratification for its particular tempo. In Boston, it had a similar popularity. But the people of New York rejected it with decision. They might reconsider the matter when someone had injected a little more pep; but, as it now was, they said briefly that it bored them stiff. Why, they asked very reasonably, should you waste your day watching a New Jersey woodland for a Red Indian who never came, and perhaps miss the latest comic turn that Jimmy Walker was performing, as a very popular alternative to providing New York with a decent government?

It may have been with a shrewd eye to this comparative slowness of the English character, or (as was rumoured) with some undisclosed political purpose, that a guarantee fund of £50,000 had been provided from a secret source to secure that rural scenes should be taken, and continuously exhibited in various parts of England.

It was about six months after the sale of William Feltham's patents had brought him the golden reward which so few inventors are ever destined to see, that he sat with Stanley Maitland one January evening in his own room, in a state of hardly-suppressed excitement such as Stanley had never known him to exhibit before, even when he had announced the first successful experiment of his great discovery.

He was a young man, still under thirty, with sandy hair that inclined to red, large, rather prominent grey eyes, high cheekbones, and a freshness of complexion which he owed primarily to an excellent constitution, complicated during recent years by the absorption of whisky in considerable quantities.

He was not a man who was lightly confidential, but he and Stanley had been friends from college days, with one of those curious attractions that seem to be based rather on difference than similarity of character or interests. Though he might trust no one else, he had good cause to trust Stanley Maitland. It was Maitland's money—not always easily spared—that had rendered possible the experiments of the last five years. It was Maitland's abilities as a lawyer and negotiator that had secured him the full value of his invention. With a generosity which he did not always show, and which even then may have been less than excessive when all the circumstances are considered, he had insisted on his friend accepting ten percent of the fortune that he had realised. And then he had returned to work in his enlarged laboratory with a tireless, sleepless intensity, supported now by all the resources that had previously been no more than a useless, maddening dream.

"I had Young on the phone this afternoon," Stanley said, "and I took the opportunity of asking him how the royalty account would be coming out for the first six months. He didn't think there'd be much to draw—the accounts have to be made up to next Saturday— as most of the period they were busy with preparatory work, but there'll be a good bit coming for the next half-year from contracts already made. He said he didn't suppose you needed the money, but if you did, you could draw anything up to £50,000 against what's accruing due. I didn't say anything to that. There'd probably be some question of interest allowance when it came to signing the cheque, and I didn't suppose you'd want it before it falls due in six months' time."

Feltham looked at him with vacant eyes. "Oh, yes, I expect there would," he answered vaguely. And then, after a pause, "It doesn't matter. I've got it all now."

"All what?"

"All the wealth in the world."

Stanley said nothing. He looked doubtfully at the half-suppressed excitement of the speaker, and at the glass which he had seen filled up more than once already.

"Oh, you don't believe me, of course! You didn't believe that little thing about the screen, not at first. Now I'll tell you just what you think." He was standing on the hearth-rug and he turned to Maitland, who was on a low chair at the side, in an almost menacing way. "You think I'm half-drunk and half-mad. But you'll find you're wrong for the second time! I'm not William Feltham now, I'm the world's king. I've been that for a week past, and I've only known it for three hours. Curse those damned maps!

"What do you think I've been slaving here for, for the last six months? You didn't think I should do that. You know you didn't! You thought when I got that money I'd go on the burst. You thought it would be just drink and women—the women I've never had!

"But I meant something better than that. Something bigger than that, by a good way! It's what I've always meant from the first. *Knowledge is power.* That's the one true word in a world of lies. I've said that every morning when I've waked, and every night when I've gone to bed for the last five years, while I've been earning four-pound-five a week analysing those beastly electric dyes all day, and doing my own work for half the night.

"And today I'm the world's king! I've meant to get the power, and the power's mine. There'll be no need to say that, when they know where they stand in a week's time. I've got to have one friend, so I'm going to tell you the lot. You're the only one I can trust. But God knows there's enough for both.

"You know I've had a new lock put on that door."

He stopped suddenly, as though, even now, he hesitated about making a confidant. His eyes went to a newspaper portrait of a very beautiful woman, which was pinned over the mantelpiece.

"You know who this is?" he asked abruptly.

"Yes, it's the Countess of Blaire. You've told me that before."

Feltham swung his arm round in a savage exultant gesture, pointing to the unmade bed which was in a corner of the untidy room. "*I tell you in three weeks I'll have her in that bed.*"

He took another gulp of whisky, and refilled the glass.

Stanley wondered whether he believed himself to have surprised some scientific secret, such as that of the transmutation of metals, which would enable him to create wealth at his own will. Well, perhaps it was excusable for him to be a little unbalanced at the first moment of such a discovery. And he knew that Feltham had always brooded fiercely over the carnal pleasures of life from which his poverty shut him off, as no higher obstacle would have done. But he had never seen him like this. He felt that it was no time to argue. He said simply: "I don't think I'd be too sure of that. I don't think she's the sort of woman you could buy like that, even though she was on the stage."

Feltham laughed shortly. "You don't understand yet. You won't talk like that when you do. I'll have what I like, and when. I tell you the world's mine. You think it's just money, and lots of people have got all they want already, and some care for other things more! *It isn't money; it's life.* What won't a man give for that?"

He bent down toward his auditor, and said in a tense whisper, as though it were a secret too great to be spoken aloud, even in the privacy of that room: "*Suppose they knew that London could be destroyed in a night?* I don't mean gassed or bombed. I mean just *gone*. Just some fine ash. I know it sounds too great to be true. But it was sure to come. It would have been someone else, if it hadn't been me."

He was erect again by now, speaking aloud, and refilling a just-emptied glass.

Stanley wondered whether over-study had crazed his brain. He said: "You can't expect me to understand till you tell me a bit more."

"I'm telling you just as fast as I can. See this bottle?" He held up a little phial which had been standing on the mantelpiece filled with a substance rather like condensed milk. "I thought I'd done something when I found this out three months ago. I'll show you what you can do with that. With a single drop. But it's nothing now. You just come into the next room."

He took a bunch of curiously-shaped keys, and worked for half a minute at the mechanism that fastened the heavy door which he had fitted to the entrance of the laboratory rooms, to which the one in which he ate and slept was a mere vestibule.

He swung the door open, and led the way into the room. It was of moderate size, and had the usual fittings and atmosphere of a chemist's laboratory. Stanley had been in it before that massive door had been fitted. He saw no change, except that two doors, of similar solidity, were in the opposite wall, where there had only been one before of a more ordinary pattern.

"There's nothing here," Feltham said abruptly, as though answering his thought, "except I said I'd show you this."

He pointed to something on the table. "What should you call that? Look at it, but don't touch. It's a bit brittle."

Stanley looked at a repulsive object which it was not easy to classify. He said: "It looks like the mummy of a cat, only it's more wrinkled than mummies usually are. More shrivelled somehow. And, of course, it's too small. It's only about a quarter the size. Still, I should think that's what it is. The Egyptians did make mummies of cats, didn't they? It's not a thing I know much about."

"You've not made a bad guess. But there's nothing Egypt there. See these scratches?" He showed the marks of a cat's claws along his wrist. "That was what made them yesterday. It was a black cat then. I gave it one drop from that little phial in the next room. You know we're almost all water? Well, when you get any of that in your body the water goes. I can't put it more simply than that. And in thirty seconds there's not much left. But that doesn't matter now. I thought a lot of it till yesterday, but I couldn't see how to use it. I haven't got any rich uncles to dose. But it doesn't matter now. Just look here, and don't touch."

He crossed over to the left-hand door, and opened it with manipulations more elaborate than those which had effected his previous entrance.

He pulled it open to show nothing more than a black ebonised wall less than three feet away. The door opened into a tiny black cabin, the opposite wall of which had a number of switches and discs and dials, and there was a seat before it, a mere stool fixed to the floor, on which one might sit while operating the keyboard before him. As the door opened, an electric bulb glowed from the roof.

"Well," Feltham exclaimed, with an exultation that seemed excessive for what he showed, "what do you make of that? I'll tell you these controls have cost me more thought, ten times over, than the thing itself. That was simple when I'd once got the formula right. That was only a matter of putting two things together, both of which every chemist knows, but no one's thought of them in combination, and then electrical direction, which isn't difficult, and the thing's done."

Stanley looked at the indicators and switches which faced him. He saw a disc bearing the numbers 432113. There were studs below by which the numbers could be changed at will. He raised his hand carelessly toward them as he said, "I suppose these studs change the numbers, but what it's all about's a bit more than...."

The sentence broke off as his hand was struck roughly down. "Didn't I tell you not to touch anything?" Feltham asked savagely

"I wasn't going to touch anything."

"Well, I thought you were. Sorry, of course. Wonder if you can guess what those figures mean."

Stanley studied them for some time. He observed that there was no figure above a four, and he felt that there must be significance in that fact. He saw that there were four switches connected with a row of dials below them.

"Yes," he said, "I think I can guess. It's the order in which these three switches have to be manipulated."

Feltham looked pleased. He said: "No, it's not that at all. But it's what anyone might guess. It's a date reversed: December 31st, 1934.

"That controls the time that it acts. This left-hand switch gives the centre from which it radiates. It's set for Charing Cross. It might be a hundred yards wrong. The maps are dreadful. A hundred yards, but not more. The second switch controls the radius. It operates for anything up to five miles. It's set at three. The third switch can be set to electrocute anyone who enters the next room. It's a bit complicated to explain how that has to be used to get the current on or off. I'd be sorry for anyone who tried it without knowing."

He drew back from the black chamber, and closed it again. He pointed to the other door. "That's where the real show is, but we won't look at that now. It's not good to breathe it too much."

They went back to the fireside again, in the untidy living-room. Stanley said: "I wish you'd tell me just what you reckon that thing does?"

"You'll see that," Feltham answered, "if you'll go down to Ditching Green. I adjusted it to deal with an acre of the common there one night a few days ago, using the best large-scale maps from the last ordnance survey, and I went down in the morning, and nothing had happened, and I thought the whole thing must be a dud, though I couldn't see how. And then I thought, suppose those maps aren't quite right, and I went again today, and made a thorough search. There's a little wood—perhaps five or six acres—on the south side of the common, and I found that it acted there. It's on the east side, but not close enough to show till you get among the trees. Somebody'll have a surprise."

"You mean you've destroyed trees at Ditching by an apparatus in these rooms?"

"That's the word. I don't know exactly what there was on that acre, but you can form a pretty good idea by what's all round it. There's nothing there now."

"Suppose someone had been in the wood at the time?"

"It wasn't likely at night. Besides, I hadn't meant it to be the wood. Anyway, it wouldn't matter. We still hang murderers, because it's an old habit we can't break, but we've dropped the silly idea that there's any value in human life. Look at the hundreds of thousands we kill and wound for the sake of speed. They simply don't count. It's the same with the breeding of children. Any excuse's good enough for avoiding that. The scientific mind doesn't accept the old superstitions. You ought to know that by now."

"And you mean that that device in the next room could destroy London in the same way that you've destroyed an acre of Ditching Wood?"

"Yes. Up to a radius of five miles from any set point. That's the extreme limit, with the apparatus I've made. Of course, it could be increased. It's just a question of the first expense...."

Feltham glanced at his friend as he said this, and caught something of doubt, even of horror, in the gaze that was fixed upon him. It was controlled in an instant, for Stanley was on his guard. His mind fluctuated between the belief that he was in the company of a super-criminal or a dangerous lunatic. Fortunately for himself, he had both coolness and courage to meet such an emergency, and the fact that he had known William Feltham from boyhood, and regarded him with the confidence of familiarity, may have helped him to control the situation.

But he saw now that he had been incautious for one doubtful second. He saw the sudden light of suspicion in his companion's eyes. He was about to ask some casual disarming question, when Feltham advanced upon him, raising a clenched hand. "If I thought—," he began, and stopped, as though he could not articulate the sudden rage that possessed him.

Stanley looked up quietly. "Thought what, Bill?" he asked casually, as though blind to the menace in his friend's attitude.

Feltham's manner changed. He sat down. "I'm a bit excited tonight," he said apologetically. Then he chuckled to himself. "There's one thing I haven't told you. I'll not only be the king of the world when it's known what's in that room, I'll be the safest man too. If anyone tries to break into that room, the thing will go off at once. It's set for the end of the year, and if it's to be set forward till the day before that, or disconnected, I'm the only one who knows how. If I go, London goes too."

He looked at his friend with a cunning which was no longer entirely sober. Stanley took it for a hint that suspicion had not entirely left his mind.

He answered: "You seem to have planned it out well. The curious thing is that I've been thinking quite lately that something of this sort would be sure to happen: that it could only be a matter of time. You see, I've been taking politics rather seriously since I found that I must go into them, or Crystal would give me no peace. Not that I was unwilling, but I'm not a popular orator, and I'd got enough to do with the legal practice I'd got. I began to think, and look round, and what I saw was a great civilisation drifting to destruction with no leaders at all. Of course, other civilisations have gone down before ours, though we don't always know how. I suppose they've been led into the abyss.

"But the curious thing about ours is that it's not being led at all. It's just stumbling on in a blind, leaderless self-slavery, and if anyone interferes to lead or guide it, it just shakes him off its back in a impatient irritated way. *All the force comes from below.* I entered political circles and I found that no one dreams of governing in England today. They listen with their ears to the ground.

"If any governing's done at all, it's in Whitehall, not Westminster. And you get the anomaly there that the men who govern are all controlled by the same fear—the fear of a blind force, a system to which they are slaves, and which no one dreams of defying.

"Democracy's got the bit in its teeth, and it dashes on like a bolting horse, boasting of its own speed, and proud of the fact that no one can rein it now. It hasn't the faintest idea of where it's going, or why.

"Look at some of the things you've mentioned yourself just now. Would any king worth the name have permitted the ghastly motor-slaughter that has stained all the roads of the world with blood? Would any king worth the name have permitted the open sale of the means of preventing life?

"We are looking on at a civilisation without control, and without the freedom that control gives. We are a nation of slaves, and slaves to a tyrant that we cannot kill, being beyond our reach. Our new rulers are the aggregate folly and the aggregate weakness of mankind. Comfort and cowardice are the new gods.

"I'm asked to go in for politics, but if I said that I don't feel fit to govern, people would think me mad. I'm not expected ever to govern anything. You couldn't reasonably be expected to run a fried-fish shop successfully on such lines as that.

"Well, I don't suppose you want to hear all this now"—he saw that Feltham was giving him a very divided attention, making restless movements, and half-articulate noises, as though finding it hard to control the excitement that possessed his mind—"but it made me think of two things.

"First, I wondered whether, if there were nothing but disaster ahead, there might not be a way back before it would be too late. I don't think there is. I don't think there could be. But I thought it might be good for people to see what life really was like a few centuries ago, before men mattered less than machines, and before freedom had left the world.

"That was what made me finance the continuous screens that are giving us records of what country farms and villages were like, and the lives of the people then."

"You mean it's you that have been doing that?"

"Yes, I used the commission you paid me. I'd no better use for the money, and I didn't reckon I was throwing it away. I reckon there may be a good profit before I've done.

"But that wasn't what I started to say. I said it made me think of two things. It's the second that's to the point now.

"I thought it wasn't natural for our civilisation to continue without control, whether it were going uphill or down, and I looked round for any power that might be rising in the world that might prove irresistible. And I could see only one. I mean the power that comes from the secret knowledge of physical forces. What we call science.

"In the Middle Ages, men held it down. They fought it with the gallows and the stake. They had the sense to be frightened. They couldn't stamp out every spark, but they kept the conflagration down.

"In the nineteenth century, they forgot their fear. They warmed the snake to a more vigorous life, praising its wisdom, and admiring its skin.

"Now they're afraid again, but it's too late.

"That was how it seemed to me. I thought that sooner or later science would put a power into the hands of someone who would use it for his own ends. I thought that, sooner or later, someone would hear what I have heard just now."

Stanley paused at this point. What he said had been true enough. He had had these thoughts. But he had been talking against time. He was inclined to think that he was dealing with an insane man. He might also be dealing with an insane imagination, or it might be that Feltham was unbalanced by the magnitude of his discovery, and the conceptions of power it gave. In either case, he must be discreet, both in words and actions.

As he paused, Feltham said abruptly, "That's what I told you before. If it wasn't me, it would be someone else before long."

"Yes," Stanley assented. "I expect it would."

"And what I want to know's this. Are you coming in with me, or staying outside? I'm not afraid that you'll give me away. No one could do that. You don't know anything that won't be public in a few days. But you've stood by me while I've been poor, and you're the one man I can trust. I don't want you to leave me now. And I only want the first pick, and after that the world's yours."

"Yes," Stanley agreed, "there'd be plenty left. We shouldn't quarrel about that." He wondered what it was that Feltham wanted to pick. Physical pleasures, he supposed, of the baser kinds. He saw that a suppressed stratum of physical passion had risen with sudden violence at the prospect of gratification. It must always have been there. More or less, it had been exposed before, at unguarded moments, contrasting with the practical austerities of a hard-working life. There had always been the fondness for alcohol. Controlled, it was true. He had never known him to be drunk—unless he were drunk now. But he had always drunk in a greedy way. So he had always taken any physical pleasure in which he indulged. It was as though he smacked his lips audibly. Probably, he would still take his pleasures in a controlled and yet greedy spirit. When this first excitement had died down. That is, if it were true.

And Stanley was disposed to believe that it was. William Feltham had already shown himself to be a brilliant chemist. He had not claimed anything previously which had not proved to be true. That he believed it himself was beyond doubt. That he was taking the power it gave in an ignoble way, that he proposed to put it to shameful use, was no evidence against the fact or magnitude of his invention. That such discoveries will always be made by men of noble or selfless minds is a baseless assumption. Probability is in the other scale.

"There's one question," Feltham went on, "that I can't decide. Whether it wouldn't be better to act first, and let people learn what it really means.

"Suppose we just wipe up London tonight, and leave people to find it out. Just let the world wonder how it had happened for a few days, and then come forward and say another area is marked out, but we won't say where, and nothing will happen while we're both alive, and everyone does what they're told. Wouldn't the devils jump when we gave the word! Suppose we said if anyone didn't please us with her behaviour, we'd wipe out her neighbours for half a mile round? Wouldn't they bring her in at a run? No, I don't know that it wouldn't be best to begin with showing what we can do. It might save a good deal of talk, and I dare say we shall have to do it in the end, to show we mean what we say."

He jumped up as he spoke, and began to pace the room again in an excitement of indecision. Stanley saw that, if he were not mad, if the power he claimed was a genuine thing, it might depend upon his own coolness and discretion to avert one of the most appalling catastrophes that the world had known.

He said: "I wonder you choose the middle of London. There's so much there that you couldn't replace, if it were once gone."

"We needn't worry about that. There'd be plenty left. Besides, we want something spectacular. Something that will leave everybody a bit *stunned*."

A whimsical thought came to Stanley's mind, at which he smiled, even then. Suppose they were themselves within a three-mile radius of Charing Cross? Suppose Feltham should destroy himself and his own apparatus in his demonstration? He did not know the exact distance which they were from that centre, but they must be very near the edge of the threatened locality, if they weren't within it. It was a quite possible oversight. It was just the sort of mistake that a madman makes.

And if that should happen, they would have taken the secret to destruction with them. London would be dust, and that stupendous catastrophe would be inexplicable forever.

"I suppose you're quite sure," he said, "that we're not within the three-mile limit ourselves?"

"Oh, yes. I'm quite sure of that. We're just on the edge. About a hundred yards clear. We should be as safe as though we were in Japan. And we should get a good view from the roof. I reckon we should just see the houses sink gently down. There wouldn't be any noise. They'd dissolve before they'd reach the ground. There'd be some fine dust. Not overmuch. Probably about two or three feet deep where the buildings are. Of course, there'd be nothing on the roads, except some little heaps of ash where the cars had been— perhaps a bit stretched out if they'd been going fast at the time. It was my idea to have it somewhere where we could get a good view." Stanley saw that the raising of these objections had done no good. They had been brushed aside, and the discussion of them had fixed Feltham's mind more upon an immediate experiment than it had been previously; Well, it might not matter. Probably it was no more than a madman's dream.

Still—if it weren't? He decided that he must seem to acquiesce, to agree. It would be the only chance. He was roused from these thoughts by Feltham's sharp question.

"Well, are you in with me, or not? You haven't said that yet?"

"Yes," he said steadily. "I'm in with you, if you're quite sure. I'd like to feel convinced that nothing can go wrong. You know I've got a good deal to lose. I don't want to end in Dartmoor, and, speaking as your lawyer, I don't want you to either."

The last sentence was adroitly worded to contain an indirect reminder of Stanley's past services. It may have influenced the cordiality of William Feltham's reply. "Yes. That's only fair. You've always been straight with me. I'll show you how the thing's done, and we shall start fair. I've said there's enough for both, and if you only take the same commission you did before—well, ten percent of the world isn't a bad fee."

He led the way back to the laboratories.

CHAPTER THREE

IT was nearly an hour later that Stanley re-entered the living-room. He was still in doubt as to the reality of the claims which his friend had made for the elaborate apparatus which he had inspected. But, if it were true, it was his secret also now.

They had talked during the inspection, and he thought that he had persuaded Feltham to do nothing that night, nothing till they had had more time to think it over, and could agree on a common plan. So he thought, but he was less than sure. Had not Feltham said, at the last, "Well, perhaps we'd better think it out a bit more. But don't forget and go into the city tonight. I might change my mind." And now he was closing up the great doors, and in a moment he would be back in the room.

Stanley's glance fell upon the little phial on the mantelpiece. After all, if these things were true, there was nothing which would not be justifiable. If they were no more than a madman's dreams, there could be no harm. That the merest drop from that phial would cause a cat to shrivel up to a little wrinkled mummy like that—it wasn't a very probable thing!

There was no more than a second in which a decision must be made. He picked up the phial. He looked at the whisky in the half-empty glass. There should be just time, if he were quick. If he were caught trying...!

It was a near thing. The cork didn't come out readily, and the liquid was too stiff to pour. He had to pick up a spent match, push it into the bottle, and then stir it round in the whisky till it was clean of the globule of white viscid substance which had clung to it. And it was no more than a drop. It was absurd to think that it could do any real harm.

And just as he withdrew the match, and put it down on the ash-tray, Feltham pushed open the door. It would have been impossible to put the phial back on the mantelpiece without being seen. It would come into Feltham's line of vision before the table beside which he stood. With a quick movement, he pushed the phial into his trouser pocket.

Feltham saw that he was by the decanter. "Fill up," he said genially, "there's another glass there." He knew that his friend did not usually drink, but on an occasion such as this...!

He had that curious delusion of most drinkers, that no one can really dislike what is a pleasure to them, even though they may say so a hundred times. He added: "You needn't mind robbing me now. We've got all that the world holds."

Stanley had a strong inclination to bolt. Suppose Feltham should notice that the phial was gone? Suppose it should change the colour of the whisky (but it didn't appear to be doing that), or alter its taste? What might not happen then? It would be past denial. The evidences would be too clear.

But stronger than the instinct of flight was the determination to see it through. He said: "No, but I'll have another cigarette before I go."

Feltham said: "Well, there are plenty there." The conversation had brought the whisky back to his mind. He picked up and drained the glass.

"Damned queer whisky," he said irritably. He sat down opposite Feltham. "I'll have another glass to take the taste of that away," he added. And then: "No, I won't. I don't feel any too good. I reckon I've had enough now."

Stanley watched him keenly. Any moment his eyes might be raised to the place where the phial should stand. If they did, he would have to say he had seen him carry it to the next room. He might believe it in the half-drunk state he was in. And while he was in there he could slip away.

He sat for half a minute watching Feltham, who was opposite to him, his eyes moodily on the fire. He seemed to have gone quiet and dull, which was not surprising after all he had drunk, and all the excitement he had had, but otherwise there was no change.

To Stanley, that half-minute seemed like an hour. Suppose the dose had no effect, which was the most probable thing, or produced some minor discomfort which would be less than death? How should he explain the fact that he had taken the phial? How should he put it back unobserved? He had been told nothing of the process by which the drug took effect. Suppose Feltham felt the first symptoms, and realised what had occurred, while still able to revenge himself upon the friend who had repaid his confidence in such a way?

He felt he couldn't stand it any longer. "Well," he said, "I suppose I'd better be going." He got up, throwing the cigarette into the grate. He was surprised to notice that it had scarcely been burned at all.

Feltham raised his head in a stiff way, as though his neck didn't work easily.

"No," he said, "don't go. Give me another drink. I'm feeling queer somehow." He spoke in a dry cracked voice that squeaked on the last word. His face, as he raised it, looked strangely drawn and dry.

Looking down upon him, Stanley knew that what he had heard that night was true—true, at least, so far as it concerned the thick white liquid, and the shrivelled cat. *William Feltham was drying up.*

It may have been the sudden horror of realisation in his own eyes that told the truth to the dying man, or it may have been the effort of speech and movement that carried the fatal message to a weakening brain.

Horror and bewilderment were in the lifted glaze that met the horror in Stanley's eyes. Then, with evident difficulty, the slow head turned toward the mantelpiece. The next moment, realisation came. A fierce flame of hate lit, for an instant, the hardening, glazing eyes.

The arms were half lifted towards his murderer with extended claws. But they fell impotently as Stanley stepped back, and realised that he had nothing to fear.

The man was visibly shrinking. His clothes sagged.

Vapour, having a faint, intolerable stench, steamed upward from his collar. The bones showed in his face. There was no expression now in the fixed stare of the dying eyes, which were contracting backwards within their sockets.

It was a high, straight-backed chair on which he had been seated, unlike the one from which Stanley had stretched his legs. Now, as though they ceased to contain a man, his clothes slipped emptily to the floor.

CHAPTER FOUR

STANLEY looked down thoughtfully at the heap of clothes on the hearth-rug, from one end of which projected the shrivelled mummy-like head which contained the brain of William Feltham: the brain which had contrived the horror by which it died.

Reaction might come, emotion might overwhelm him later. He could not tell. But at present he felt quiet and cool. Actually, his strongest emotion was surprise that he felt no other.

He was aware of the need for prompt action, but there was time enough. There was no need for haste or alarm.

Feltham never encouraged visitors, except himself. He was sure to be undisturbed. He looked up at the clock. It was thirteen minutes past seven. He had told Crystal that he would be looking in at the theatre. He wanted to see *The Barretts of Wimpole Street*. Well, there was no reason to alter his plans. There would be time for that.

He looked round for a newspaper, and found an old copy of the *Sunday Express*. He spread the sheets on the rug, around and under the heap of clothes below the chair. He did not want any mess. He thought that William Feltham would be brittle in his present condition. He began to unbutton the clothes.

The newspaper proved to have been a useful precaution. The legs broke so much that it was necessary to hold the trousers over the paper, and shake them out. William Feltham was brittle, but he burnt well.

It took longer than he had expected. There were the clothes to be put away in a natural manner. There was the little heap of articles which had been taken out of the-pockets to be disposed of in likely ways. There was the dried cat to be burnt. That may not have been necessary, but it seemed a wise thing to do. It had meant unlocking the door into the next room. That had been an anxious moment. If Feltham's confidence had been less complete than he professed, it might have been a "difficult" thing.

Stanley took nothing away with him except the little phial which was still in his pocket, and the keys which it was essential for him to have, including one of the outer door. There would be no concealment about having those. Already a plan was forming in his mind.

It was three minutes past eight when he walked out, not caring by whom he might be seen, and stood in the street until he succeeded in gaining the attention of a passing taxi. No one would be able to suggest that, on the last occasion when he had called upon William Feltham, he had left in a furtive way.

CHAPTER FIVE

WHEN Stanley arrived at the theatre, he telephoned Jehane, who, in addition to being his sister-in-law, acted as his private secretary, asking her to leave some data which she had been abstracting for him on his own desk. Having dealt with the subject of his call, he went on to mention that he had just come over from Bill Feltham. He said that Bill had been rather queer in his manner. He thought he was suffering from overwork. How had he been queer? Well, he had been talking wildly about inventions that would revolutionise the world. He couldn't say more on the phone. Jehane said she would be up when he came back, and he could tell her then.

She told Crystal that Stanley had been with Bill, and had thought he seemed queer—no, just overworked. She was staying up to see Stanley when he got back. Crystal was not surprised at that. It was understood that Jehane took a regrettable interest in William Feltham, and that that would account for her making excuses at times to accompany Stanley when he was meeting the inventor. Jehane did not admit it, of course.

Crystal said she had promised to look in at Lady Barford's. The car was ordered for twelve. Would Jehane say good night to Stanley for her, and tell him where she had gone? Jehane would.

On the way home from the theatre, Stanley debated with himself how much he should tell Jehane. He did not think of Crystal quite in the same way, perhaps because she would be less likely to ask. But he was confidential with Jehane as a man naturally is with an attractive sister-in-law, who is also a very intelligent and reliable private secretary. He was not used to deceive her. In the end, he decided that what he told should be true, and of a kind to prepare her mind for other things that must surely follow. But he would use truth with economy. There were several things that might advantageously be left out.

So when he found her in the library, as he had expected, and Crystal's message had been given, he said: "There's something queer about Bill Feltham. I've never seen him quite like he was to-night."

"How was that?"

"Well, for one thing he was making the wildest boasts as to some new discoveries he said he had made. Incredible boasts. For one thing he said that he'd destroyed an acre of ground at Ditching without going out of his laboratory. Done it quite casually by way of experiment in destroying the world. Just a matter of pulling a switch."

Jehane laughed. "It sounds the sort of thing that might be awkward if it backfired. Had he been having rather more than usual?"

"He did fill up once or twice."

"So it sounds. Anything else?"

"Oh, there was some wild talk about what he'd do when he possessed the world. Not particularly elevating. Bill can be rather a pig, when he gets like that." (If it were true that Jehane had cared anything for Bill—which he was inclined to doubt—it might be no unkindness under present circumstances to show him as he really was.)

"Yes," she said thoughtfully, "I should think he could be rather that way. But he's a clever pig, all the same."

"Yes, I think I'll go round to Ditching in the morning, and see whether there's any truth in the nonsense he was talking. I wonder whether you'd care to run me over in the two-seater, say about 9:30? I don't suppose Crystal'd care to come."

"Oh, she might. But I don't suppose she'd be up at that hour."

"Very well, if you will. And I'll go round and see him afterwards. He's given me a key, and told me to go in any time. It was all rather queer."

"What Bill needs is a few weeks hoeing turnips. Not that there'd be much doing in that line just now. But you know what I mean."

Jehane yawned, and went to bed.

CHAPTER SIX

THE next morning they went to Ditching. Stanley found the destroyed acre after a short search.

Jehane stood at his side. They had parked the car at the edge of the wood, which was a dense thicket of nut-bushes, with briars and brambles, and straying ivy in some places, and yews and close groups of hollies. There were no more than a few oaks or other of the larger trees, but the undergrowth was so thick that the blackened acre could not be seen, even at this season of fallen leaves, till they were close at its edge.

Jehane said: "What a fire there must have been! But perhaps there weren't any trees just about here?" She pushed the toe of her shoe down into two or three inches of blackened dust. She said: "It doesn't seem like a fire."

Stanley agreed to that. The dust wasn't quite like ash, and its quantity was too great. It was as though whatever had been there had just disintegrated and collapsed on to the ground, turning darker as it did so, but that not uniformly, for in places there were patches of lighter dust.

Jehane spoke again. "He must have seen this place, and made up that he'd done it himself." She spoke without conviction, for there was a strangeness about that dust, an abnormality which disturbed her mind.

Stanley said: "Look at that tree." Her eyes followed his to a silver birch which was rooted outside the destroyed area, but must have leaned over it, growing with a slanting bole. Bole and branch and twig ended abruptly as though they had been sheared off with a giant knife. No fire could have done that. What on earth could? Perhaps earth was not the right word.

Jehane had become very pale. She said: "What a terrible thing!" And then: "Do you think you ought to go there this morning? Do you think he's safe?"

She seemed concerned rather for Stanley than for the man she was supposed to favour, but perhaps that was not surprising, after what she had seen.

He answered: "Oh, yes. There's nothing to fear. But it seems a senseless thing to do, to destroy like that, even if you have found out how. I'll look in as we go back, if you don't mind driving me round."

"No, I don't mind. I think I'll come up with you."

"Well, come as far as the door. You needn't come in."

"Oh, I think I will, if you don't mind. I should like to hear Bill's account of that wood."

"All right, if you'd rather."

Stanley made no further objection. They ran back into the Bayswater Road, and when they came to Dawlish Mansions they went up the steps together.

CHAPTER SEVEN

DAWLISH MANSIONS had been the property of Sir George Dawlish (it was no more than Dawlish House in those days) until he had been taxed out of financial existence by the competitive exactions of a succession of Labour and Conservative governments. That was (of course) largely his own fault. His taxation returns had always been accurately rendered (had a burglar demanded to know where he had placed his pocket-book during the night he would probably have answered with the same simple rectitude). His income was derived from tenants whom his ancestors had neglected to bleed when they could have done so quite easily. He himself had neglected to profiteer during the war. He deserves no sympathy.

Dawlish House passed into the control, though not the ownership, of a speculative builder, who acquired the obligation of paying the rates and taxes upon it, which amounted to much more than its sane annual value; and he followed the prevailing fashion of his tribe, and complicated further the financial nightmare in which he lived, by converting it into a number of "mansion flats."

The work had been nearing completion when William Feltham came on the scene, and had been in time to acquire the whole of the top floor, with some modification of the builder's plans, so that that roomy solitude had been adapted to his peculiar needs. Its isolation was increased by the fact that the lift which had been installed was only carried (owing to certain structural difficulties) to the floor below, the approach to his outer door being by a spiral staircase, the commencing breadth of which had shrunk to narrowness in the course of its ascent. It was a position which was unlikely to be disturbed by uninvited visitors.

"Mr. Feltham in?" Stanley asked casually of the lift attendant who was also the caretaker of the premises. "Well, sir, I can't rightly say. I haven't seen him go out. But Mrs. Harper knocked there for a good ten minutes this morning, and he wouldn't open, if he was. But that's happened once or twice before. I suppose he's busy inventing something, and doesn't hear, or won't come."

"Well, I'll go up anyway," Stanley answered. "I've got a key, and he didn't seem quite himself last night. You'd better come too, Jehane. We won't stop if he isn't in."

Stanley knocked first, and then, after waiting a reasonable interval, inserted his key, and went in.

He felt no surprise, and affected little, on finding that the living-room was empty. He knocked at the inner door, and received no response.

Jehane looked round the untidy room with disfavour.

"Thinking he needs a wife?" Stanley questioned lightly.

"No, a keeper seems indicated," Jehane replied, with a slight asperity. She had never shown any sign of resentment when Crystal assumed that she took a feminine interest in William Feltham, but was curiously irritated if Stanley adopted the legend.

"Well," he said, "it's no use staying here."

"No," Jehane answered, "it's a smelly room." She led the way out.

He glanced back as he followed her. He had been studying the disordered room with some attention. He remembered the popular theory that the criminal always overlooks the little detail by which he is hanged at last. He couldn't see that he'd overlooked anything, but probably they never did. The fireplace was certainly rather full, and what an analysis of its ashes might reveal was beyond knowing.

"Lost anything?" Jehane asked.

"I was just wondering whether he might have left a note on the mantelpiece. Having asked me to call, and giving me a key, and then going off like this—"

"It does seem a bit dotty. But if he left a note he'd put somewhere where it could be seen without searching, wouldn't he?"

"Yes. It's no use staying. I think I'll look in again tomorrow, and see if he's back. I shan't have time again today."

They went out, and down the short flight of stairs, and Stanley rang for the lift.

"He's out right enough," he told the man. "I should tell Mrs. Harper when she comes again."

"She won't come till tomorrow now, sir. Nine o'clock's her time."

Stanley took no notice of the reply, nor did he allude to his friend's absence again on the way back. He did not wish to appear over-concerned.

He had been pleased to see how naturally the man had taken it when he said he had a key, though he had anticipated that attitude. He was a frequent, almost an only caller on that top floor, and his business and personal relations with the inventor were general knowledge.

His objects had been to make Feltham's absence known, and to lead up to the time when public enquiries would be natural, as promptly as possible; and he wished it to be in evidence that he had been the first to observe that disappearance, and had done so without concealment.

He wondered whether criminals were usually able to plan so coolly, and why it was that he did not experience any of the emotions that murderers are supposed to feel.

He did not even feel like a murderer. Not in the least. Perhaps that was because he felt he was so thoroughly justified in the decisive course which he had taken to arrest William Feltham's exceptional activities. Perhaps it was because he had done so little to secure that result. A mere drop of glutinous white matter, on the stick of a spent match! Perhaps it was because there was a poetic justice in the fact that Feltham had himself decocted the poison which was his end. Perhaps it was because those brittle ashes had been so easy to burn. He had read that murdering a man is a simple matter if compared with the private disposition of the resulting corpse. That is what causes murderers to grow grey at an early age. But he had had no such difficulty. He was tempted to wonder with a grim whimsicality how many scores of his fellows he might not be able to remove by the thorough method which had been placed in his hands, without it being possible to fix the guilt upon him. The very fact that Feltham had thought it worth his while to concentrate his efforts upon the production of a drug so deadly seemed a sufficient defence of his action in testing it on its inventor, as the Sicilian tyrant had once roasted its designer in the interior of his brazen bull.

No. He was not disturbed in mind as to the moral aspects of the drastic course he had taken. He felt assured that, if all the circumstances were known, it would have the hearty approval of his fellow-men.

Neither was he concerned as to any personal consequences of an unpleasant character. At the worst—at the very worst—he could say that he had found the dried shell of his friend's body, as the clothes that it no longer filled had slipped to the floor, with the fatal phial on the table beside him. Experiments with the drug would demonstrate its potency. What had he done but burn those dreadful ashes in an impulse of horror, or a foolish fear? No one would suspect him of having distilled such a drug. It would be an evident case, either of suicide, or of the death of one who had miscalculated the effects of his own invention.

No, he had little fear of the law.

His diplomacy was directed by a further foresight. He aimed to make public the disappearance of the scientist in a natural way, while avoiding any dangerous investigation of the secrets of those inner rooms. Doubtless, a time would come when the Court would allow him to presume death. But that was really a minor considera-tion. It was true that he was the sole executor of the missing man. But he also had a power of attorney as his lawyer and business rep-resentative, which gave him an even easier and less restricted con-trol of the situation.

The real problem that possessed his mind was that of the use (if any) to which he should put the sinister power which had fallen into his hands.

He knew, at least, that he should not use it as Feltham had pro-posed to. He was incapable of the coarse crudities of indulgence which had appealed to the inventor's starved and sensual body. He was incapable even of the less gross indulgences which come to the minds of many when they imagine the advantages which unlimited wealth confers. He was almost happily married. He was accustomed to find his pleasures in higher forms than Feltham would have easily understood. He had the imagination which is so frequently lacking in the man whose life is spent in the pursuit of chemical facts. But in all—or almost all—men, there is the desire for power, the belief that they could control the lives of their fellows better than is being done by the blind or conscious forces around them.

What power (he pondered) did this knowledge really give? Could it be securely and potently used? And, if so, to what end? With these speculations working quietly to fruition in the back of his mind, he went on with the preliminary programme which he had planned—that of eliminating Feltham from the expectations of men.

He went again next morning to Dawlish Mansions, and was suf-ficiently surprised that his friend was still absent. By these visits he felt that he averted the possibility that the caretaker might have be-come alarmed and broken into the flat, with unforeseeable conse-quences.

On the fourth day he suggested to the man, in a casual conver-sation, that Feltham might have thought that he had told him that he should be away for a time, and have given him the key so that he might watch over his effects in his absence. Acting on this theory, he arranged for Mrs. Harper to come the following day and reduce the dirt and disorder of the living-room, while he remained on the premises. He had the satisfaction of seeing the somewhat ambiguous contents of the grate, including some calcined fragments of bone which had not entirely disintegrated, removed without any suspicion being aroused. He remarked on the quantity of ash which she was shovelling up, and received the satisfactory answer: "Lor', sir, that's nothing! These sciuntific gents! You should see what I sometimes finds." William Feltham went down in the bucket.

CHAPTER EIGHT

THE next day Stanley telephoned Scotland Yard, saying that he was not quite easy in his mind concerning his friend, Mr. William Feltham, who had been absent from his flat for some days in an unusual manner. Scotland Yard sent Inspector Combridge to interview him.

The Inspector listened carefully to what he had to say, but did not appear greatly impressed. Had the absentee been a married man, the case would have been widely different. The fact that he had given Mr. Maitland a set of keys of his flat made it almost certain that he had planned to be away for some period.

Stanley said he realised that. He should not be so uneasy but that there had been something a little strange in Mr. Feltham's manner on that last evening.

The Inspector appreciated the point, but suggested that the object of his intended departure (whatever it might have been) might have occasioned some slight excitement. Might he not have contemplated private absence, and taken his friend into partial confidence just because he wished to prevent the possibility of any further enquiry being aroused?

Stanley said, of course, he might have been overanxious, but he thought it was always best to let the police know if anything unusual should occur.

Inspector Combridge approved this sentiment. Of course, if the absence of Mr. Feltham should be unduly prolonged. He shook hands and parted.

As he walked down the street, he reflected that if his department were to follow up all the bachelors who leave their flats for a few days after the acquisition of sudden wealth, they would be even busier than they were then, but it was less sure that they would be occupying themselves in a very useful or popular manner.

Seeing that it would be difficult to excite the police, Stanley mentioned William Feltham's disappearance in conversation at Sir George Donnington's dinner table in the presence of the editor of the *West End Tatler*, though without addressing that gentleman.

The next day, the *Tatler's* chief reporter was smelling round Dawlish Mansions at 8:30 A.M. Before his paper went to press on the following Thursday, he had discovered one fact which caused Inspector Combridge, when it came to his knowledge, to give the case a little further consideration. The keys which were now in possession of Mr. Maitland were the only ones in existence. Mr. Feltham had attached great importance to these keys, which were specially made to locks of his own design. He had ordered no duplicates, and had stipulated that none should be in existence. Even the lock of the outer door had been of this order. In the light of this information, the handing over of those keys, even to his lawyer and closest friend, acquired a graver significance.

Inspector Combridge realised this, though he still thought it the simplest and most natural explanation that Feltham had been engaged on some adventure of the underworld in which he felt that it would be unsafe to carry keys to which he attached such importance. What could he do better than entrust them to his lawyer's keeping? Why was he not more explicit in doing so? Well, perhaps he was reticent as to the reason of his projected absence. Perhaps he feared criticism, or that efforts would be made to dissuade him. Inspector Combridge knew that the simplest explanation is most often the true one. But he assumed little, and it occurred to an acute mind that one point might need explanation. If Feltham handed over the only key of the outer door, and Stanley had left him there, how did he afterwards let himself out, and lock it behind him?

Stanley had the same thought. For one brief second he wondered whether he had committed the oversight which the guilty are said to do so continually. Then he remembered that, however good the lock might be, it did not prevent it operating automatically when the door was shut. Inspector Combridge learnt the same thing in his own way, and put an absurd doubt out of his mind.

This was about ten days after the night when William Feltham had poured his whisky for the last time. It was the same evening that Stanley found himself alone with his wife in a mutual interval of unusual leisure.

Lady Crystal had started her adult life with the unusual advantage of knowing exactly what she wanted, and with clear plans as to how it should be obtained. She meant, both individually and through her husband, to be a power in the land. She had wealth, beauty, brains, and the prestige of a great name. She thought the emotions should be indulged in a controlled way. She chose her husband with care, and wooed him with such delicacy and charm that he had no doubt that the volition had been his. It was, indeed, a case of mutual attraction, and Lady Crystal had found it a very pleasant thing to ride her emotions with a loose rein.

Stanley could hardly doubt the sincerity or the strength of the love which surrendered itself to him, for it seemed that she had so much more to give than to take. He did not doubt this, even when he was to learn that that surrender was a somewhat qualified attitude.

He had means, but they were relatively narrow; a good name, but it was comparatively unknown; good abilities, but they had still to prove themselves in the highest spheres.

He gained a charming wife whom many men who seemed to have more to offer had coveted but could not win.

If she had ambitions for him which were somewhat larger than, or somewhat different from, his own, could he deny that she had some right to urge them upon him?

Besides, he responded readily enough. It was his strength and weakness that he had been interested from childhood in so many things. He had taken up the study of the law with avidity. It offered a form of mental gymnastics which he enjoyed, and in which he could engage with conspicuous success. But so, also, would a score of other occupations of quite different kinds. He had the quality of imagination which would have found novelty and achieved distinction in the activities of a wholesale grocer, or a market-gardener.

Lady Crystal's interest was in politics, which was a family tradition. Her ancestors had supported the Conservative Party as long as that name had been invented, and for some centuries earlier under other symbols. She believed in the established order, and that the stability of the British Empire and the welfare of the Conservative party were synonymous. In the British Empire she believed as the greatest and noblest of the works of man, with some Divine assistance thrown in. It is possible to doubt whether this may be an absolute truth. It is also possible to have an ignobler faith.

She had few ideas that were even tinged with originality, but no habits or beliefs of unconventional kinds. She had the enormous advantage of treading well-beaten paths, and of convictions undisturbed by any contending doubt.

When she proposed to Stanley that he should enter Parliament, he had agreed very easily, though it had not been his own ambition. When a seat was offered to him at a by-election which was safe enough, but not too safe for it to be felt that he had done the party good service when he proved a capable and popular candidate, and won it with an increased majority, he enjoyed the fight, and the sense of triumph which such a victory gives.

When, two years later, there was some reshuffling of the political pack, and he was offered an Under-Secretaryship, he was not oblivious to the fact that Crystal had worked both hard and skilfully to obtain it for him, nor ungrateful to her. But he was also aware that Sir Bardsley Clinton, the Premier, was not the man to offer it, on whatever solicitation, had he not considered him adequate for the duties which it entailed.

It had followed one of those intimate little dinners which Crystal was so expert to arrange and handle, after which he had found himself engaged in a political discussion with Sir Bardsley, which was apart from the hearing of others, and on which occasion, as he realised afterwards, he had expressed some of his private convictions with unusual freedom. He may have done less than justice to the adroitness with which Sir Bardsley had handled the conversation to draw them out.

He had said, among other things, that he failed to see any vital distinction between the Conservative and Labour parties, as they were both communistic in their actual legislative enactments, however differently they might talk. Perhaps the principal distinction was that whereas the Labour Party might threaten more loudly, the Conservatives could, and did, pass legislation of a greater stringency, owing to the fact that there was no opposition to face, and their own adherents were hypnotised into an astonished muteness. He suggested that a succession of Labour governments during the last twenty-five years would never have succeeded in increasing direct taxation to its present level; and, had such a government attempted to do so, the national outcry would have been too loud for it to endure; probably the House of Lords would have regained its popularity by finding some pretext on which to destroy it.

Sir Bardsley did not, in his heart, dispute the truth of these propositions, but he was not sure that it was to the advantage of his party that one of the most promising of its younger members should observe them so clearly. Most of them honestly believed that the policy of the party which he had the honour to lead was unchanged since the days of Palmerston, and this simple faith was worth at least a million votes. To realise that the Labour Party is no more or less communistic than its opponents is halfway to joining it on a sufficient provocation arising.

He considered the advisability of restraining this too clear-sighted young man with the blinkers of office. And it would have been difficult for himself to say how far it was this consideration, or that of Stanley's admitted ability, or the influence of his charming hostess, or the cheque which he knew would be on its way to the nourishment of the party funds before the week closed, which led him to make the offer of the vacant Under-Secretaryship. Probably, with the second allowed, any one of the other three would have prevailed.

However that may be, Lady Crystal drew a cheque for £10,000 to the order of the chief Government Whip, which she looked at with some hesitation, and then consigned to the flames. She drew another for £7,000, which she considered would do the trick. Liberal as she was in many ways, she hated waste with a characteristic fastidiousness, and she had not abandoned the previous cheque-stamp without a moment of irritation at the result of her indecision. But she felt that the difference in the amount was worth the sacrifice. She had not the type of mind that would readily recognise that a cheque-stamp has no intrinsic value.

Mr. Goodwin Pemberton considered the cheque next morning with a contented mind. He had hoped for more, but he had feared that £5,000 might be all that he was destined to get. It might have been worse.

Stanley did not know of this cheque. His wife did not offer her confidences as to her finances, and he did not ask it. Had he known, it might have annoyed him, which would have been unreasonable, for no one entered Sir Bardsley Clinton's government, even as an under-secretary, who did not deserve to do so. It might be too much to say that every one of equal merit met with a like reward.

Sir Bardsley might be incapable of a conscious job, but he could not be insensible to the potential political importance of the man who was Lady Crystal's husband. Since the death of her father, the Duke of Norchester, she had inherited his vast wealth, and become the mistress of the somewhat gloomy magnificence of Norchester House, which had been one of the social strongholds of the Conservative Party for generations, and in which it was her declared ambition to revive the political *salon* which had exercised so potent an influence both upon English and Continental politics during earlier centuries.

It was true that this form of political influence had been generally regarded as obsolescent, but Lady Crystal knew that while human nature remains unchanged, the influences of wit and beauty cannot cease, nor the effects of social exclusiveness fail.

Now Stanley had been in office for about three months, and even his chief, the Colonial Secretary, Sir George Donnington, who was not a man of easy disposition, or quick to praise, had said frankly that he had never had a more discreet or intelligent helper. Stanley did his work, and kept his thoughts to himself. He spoke occasionally in the House on departmental matters, with an efficiency which was generally recognised, and he answered questions adroitly. Clearly, a coming man.

Lady Crystal felt that she had no occasion to regret her choice of a life-partner, and was in a very friendly mood on the Sunday evening, ten days after the disappearance of William Feltham, when she sat facing her husband in the little private room to which he only was admitted in these hours of infrequent leisure.

As she looked at him, she even had a regretful hesitation over her discreet decision that the production of an heir to the Maitland name and the Norchester traditions, which she had recognised from the first as an essential part of the programme of a successful marriage, such as she intended that hers should be, was to be an incident of the fourth year of her wedded life. But there were other things to be done first.

The love that was in her heart, which was true enough of its kind, though it moved in a shackled mode, caused her also to have a feeling of compunction over a decision of the earlier day, about which she felt that Stanley would be annoyed, though he might be reluctant to show it.

"Stan," she said, and he looked up in a momentary surprise at the abbreviation which she seldom used even at their rarer moments of emotional intimacy, "I hope you won't mind, but I've let Simpson have the Home Farm. You know we can't be down there more than three months of the year, except sometimes at weekends, and you'll still have the Big Meadow, and all the land that's behind the house. I'd have asked you about it first, but Toller telephoned that we'd got to say yes or no, because Simpson'd got the offer of the Ringwood Farm, and was afraid he was going to fall between two stools, if we said no in the end."

Stanley understood the position, and recognised that Crystal was right. Simpson was a good farmer. He had made a success of Two-Ash Farm, which was next to the Home Farm, and which had been unprofitable in other hands. He would be always on the spot. He would do better than they would do with a bailiff, and their own irregular visits. Crystal was right, though she knew his reluctance to part with the Home Farm. But the fact was that he had other things on his mind, and even this question had become a comparatively trivial thing.

Very naturally, she misunderstood his slowness to answer. "You don't really mind?" she asked. She remembered that there would be questions of the sale of stock, in which Stanley took more interest than she was disposed to do. "I had to decide in a moment, and it seemed the wisest thing. Simpson's a good man."

"No," he roused himself to say. "I don't mind. I think I'd be happier farming all the time, but it's no use trying to carry on anything you can't do properly. Simpson's the right man. Besides, it's your matter."

"But I don't want to look on it like that. You know I always consult you about the estate, Stanley. But you can't farm in Nor'ster, and be in office here, and with your law practice as well."

"No," he said, a little wearily, "I see that."

Crystal was always practical. She faced facts. To admit her values was to allow that she was seldom wrong. She knew—they both knew—that he was tempted to deviate toward a hundred conflicting interests and occupations. In the background of her mind, when Toller's message came through, had she not had the thought that this irrevocable decision to give up the farm would hold Stanley more closely to the political career on which she desired him to concentrate? Did it not explain the half-apologetic faintly-guilty feeling of which she was conscious now? Was he not conscious of it in the same way?

Anyway, she wished he wouldn't look like that. It was unlike him to show annoyance, without saying straight out what he felt. She had expected him to smile, and say she had done rightly (as she new she had), even though he might feel disappointed; and she was prepared to be sorry and apologetic till his assurances that it was the right thing should have a satisfactory sincerity in their tone. She knew that it would be fatal for them to drift apart. When she had had her own way on any vital matter, she never left it at that. She did not feel that the incident was satisfactorily terminated till she was sure that she was forgiven, and the skies were clear.

"Stan," she said. "You know Simpson's the best tenant we've got. I didn't like the idea that we'd half lose him, as we should if he began farming on Cecil's land."

He roused himself to understand her mood, and respond.

"You've done the right thing," he answered, more heartily than he had done before. "I should have said the same if you'd asked me first."

That was more satisfactory. "I don't see that we need sell the Herefords," she suggested. "There ought to be land enough left for them." And then, when she saw that his attention had wandered again: "Stanley, is anything the matter? Aren't you well?"

"Yes," he said vaguely, "I'm well enough. Only a bit tired."

She did not see why anything should have tired him particularly, and these occasional Sunday evenings, which she planned that they should spend together, usually found him in more responsive moods. She would have liked to be kissed under the throat in a way he had which she approved, and which might lead to even more familiar intimacies. No one would disturb them here. But her pride seldom failed her. If he really felt like that…. "I'm sorry," she said kindly. "You'd better get to bed early, and have a good night's rest." She was seldom too tired herself to control the punctual proprieties of her conduct; to suit it to the occasion, however exacting; but she could make allowances for others in a fundamentally generous mind. She felt that she needed that self-control, that equality to the situation, now. Otherwise, she might have shown annoyance or disappointment in an ill-bred way, of which she would have been more ashamed than of a score of more serious delinquencies. Not that she was of delinquent habits. Her conduct, like her manners, was of the highest, most select brand of conventionality.

Stanley thought: "If I told her that her husband is a murderer, that I've sent Bill Feltham up the chimney, I wonder what she'd say? Under the circumstances, she might say I've done rightly, as long as it won't get found out. But suppose I told her about the invention that's in my hands? She wouldn't hear of using that as Feltham meant to do. Not for any purpose whatever. She'd say that such things aren't done. And yet, if I should do it, I suppose she'll have to know in the end." He didn't like keeping it to himself. They had their reticences, but they were such as are allowed by a mutual confidence and respect. They were of allied interests, and neither would lightly question the loyalty of the other. He would have liked to tell Jehane also, feeling that she would take it in a different spirit. He had confirmed a previous suspicion that her reputed liking for Feltham had no basis of fact. He thought she would be adventurously excited rather than repelled by the possibilities of the position. But his loyalty to Crystal made it impossible to tell Jehane while he was silent to her.

He felt the constraint of the moment. Was he becoming as unbalanced as Feltham had been, and from the same cause? Fortunately, he did not drink.

He knew also that there was a wide distinction in the fact that if he could not dismiss the idea of using the power that was in his hands, it was from no such selfish carnality as had excited William Feltham's mind. However vainly, however foolishly, he thought of it as a beneficent potentiality that might save the world from the aggregate folly of mankind, which was its captain now. Yet he asked himself whether he were not really actuated by a lust of power as fundamentally despicable as Feltham's physical appetites, and he found no assured answer.

If he should rule the world, it would be certain that he would not use his power to possess the Countess of Blaire, but, should he do it to constrain his neighbours in other ways, would not his actions be on the moral level of that vulgarly projected ravishment?

Well, there was the difference that he would be seeking the good of his fellows rather than a selfish pleasure.

But perhaps the better answer was that he might rescue them from a lower and less tolerable tyranny, from which they could be released in no other way.

They were ruled now by a counting of heads. Surely the wildest substitute for intelligent leadership which had afflicted mankind since it had developed gregarious habits! What was the phrase he had coined? The aggregate folly of mankind. That was exactly it. Or would the average be a juster adjective?

But he saw one danger, the existence of which he must have constantly before his mind, if he were to keep his own soul alive, or to be the saviour of a civilisation that stumbled toward its doom.

If he could gain the power he dreamed, the impulse to impose his own will upon his fellows would be a great, and might be an over-mastering temptation. He must remember always that the greatness of his opportunity would not be to substitute a personal for a collective tyranny, but to restore an almost forgotten freedom: the joys and perils and adventures of freedom, for the comforts and cowardice of the present slavery which hung over England like a shadow of relentless doom, enervating its citizens till they felt it better that their race should end than that they should be trained in hardship for the conquest of the empty lands.

He was roused from the labyrinth of these reflections to consciousness that Crystal was speaking to him again. She was looking at him with smiling eyes, and her languid voice had a half-laughing mockery, but there was a faint tone of asperity also, which he was quick to hear.

"No," he said. "I'm sorry. I'm afraid I'm not very good company tonight. Yes, I'd better go."

Crystal said: "I think I'll go too." She felt there would be no pleasure in sitting alone to reflect upon the fact that she had looked at Stanley with inviting eyes, and that he had looked back as though she were not there. Was he really ill? He had hardly seemed quite like that. She had a queer foreboding of some vague calamity, which her common sense should have put firmly aside, but found it hard to do. No doubt, Stanley would be himself tomorrow. There was no doubt, either, that he was very queer tonight.

CHAPTER NINE

THE next morning Lady Crystal came down and joined Jehane at breakfast, which she usually had in her own room. This may have been because she had gone to bed unusually early, or because she was more worried about Stanley than she could see any logical reason to be.

Jehane had a habit of retiring early, one of a score of differences of habit which kept the sisters from more than the casual intimacies of a real affection. Stanley had had breakfast, and left word that had gone out for a walk. The next night the House would resume its sittings, and his hours would be as irregular as those of his wife.

"Hallo, Crystal! Had a flea in the bed?" Jehane exclaimed at this unexpected appearance. Jehane had an occasional freedom of speech which would have approached vulgarity in anyone of less patrician birth, but vulgarity in a Norchester is an impossibility. What they do or say becomes the right thing as the words are spoken, or the act performed.

Crystal did not respond to the flippancy of her sister's mood. She said "Stanley didn't seem very well last night. Is he working too hard?"

"No, I don't think so. But I think he's worrying about Mr. Feltham. I don't see why he need. He may come back any day."

"I don't see that it's our affair whether he comes back or not."

"No, I don't know that it is. Of course, Stanley knew him rather well. I should say he was about the only friend Mr. Feltham had; and he did all his business for him."

"Do you know where Stanley is now?"

"I believe he's gone round to Mr. Feltham's flat. He often does."

"Not walking?"

"Yes. He does walk there sometimes. He told me he wanted to be alone to think something out."

Crystal looked at her sister in a thoughtful silence. She had no mind to suggest that there might be matters that Stanley was concealing from her, and which Jehane might know. Some things, of course, would come under Jehane's notice in her secretarial work. It was natural to ask whether Stanley was working too hard.

But Jehane's answers had given an impression that she was saying less than she knew. Crystal felt annoyance which she would not show. She turned the conversation to other things.

She was unjust in her thought, for Jehane had not been deliberately reticent. She could not readily explain matters which puzzled herself. She understood, to a point, that Stanley might feel a responsibility for Feltham's affairs during his inexplicable disappearance. She did not understand why they should require his daily attention, and cause him to be preoccupied continually. Actually, when she faced the question, she saw that it was no more than a presumption on her part that the evident worry that possessed his mind might not have a different cause. Yet she felt an instinctive certainty that it had no other. Besides, there was that acre of desolation in Ditching Wood. Had Stanley found something among the papers of the missing scientist which explained his conduct? Some sinister mystery which he was unable to solve?

So she wondered, getting somewhat near to the truth. But it was surmise rather than knowledge. She would have explained it to Crystal in reply to a more explicit question: a larger measure of offered confidence. As it was, they both withdrew to their own thoughts. The effect of the conversation was to give them both an increased uneasiness. Each thought that the other knew more than she had been disposed to say.

But two days later Stanley was more like his natural self. He appeared to be buoyant and confident, and though inclined to be preoccupied, and to discuss routine matters which Jehane brought under his notice in a somewhat perfunctory way, his manner was no longer such as to suggest that any doubt or trouble was on his mind. Both his wife and her sister concluded that they had suffered from a too-active imagination, and were contented in this belief up to the evening of Thursday the 25th, when Mr. Goldstone showed them the anonymous letter already narrated.

CHAPTER TEN

THERE are many of the oppositions of life which cannot be faced without fear, but the tremors of those who advance upon them are less than will be felt by others who attempt evasion or resort to flight.

Stanley Maitland experienced the relief of this natural law when his resolution hardened to accept the responsibility which fate and his own action had placed in his half reluctant hands. He would take the power which Feltham's sinister invention gave, and use it, if he could, not for his own gain, nor for the enslaving of his fellow-men, but to restore such measure of freedom as those may endure who have been born to the security of a settled bondage, and in whom the slave mentality is already dominant.

That he formed this resolution so definitely, and so soon, was primarily due to a remark by a County Court Judge in the East End of London, who certainly would not have uttered it had he foreseen what consequences might follow.

The old gentleman had had a poor woman before him, against whose husband her landlord was proceeding for arrears of rent. She said she had come in her husband's place so that he might not lose a day's work, and she asked for time to be given on the ground, among others, that she had a large family of children, and was expecting another.

The judge had listened to her narration of hardships with sympathetic patience until she had mentioned the size of her family, when he had interrupted her sharply with the exclamation: "Then you ought not have had them! You ought to know better than that. You ought to have been taught. And now, you see, you've had all these children, and you can't pay your rent!"

The incident was still sufficiently rare in England to be "news" in the journalistic sense (though it might be a poor third to the fact that abortion had recently been condoned by a popular Bishop and a High Court Judge), and it was widely reported.

Stanley read it when in the smoking-room of the House of Commons, sitting opposite to the Hon. James Shackston, popularly know as Jimmy by his friends, to which his political opponents added the adjective Jumping, in disrespectful allusion to the fact that he had changed his political faith with exceptional frequency.

Jumping Jimmy, a heavily-built man, with small twinkling eyes and a brain that moved more quickly than his ponderous body, was Chancellor of the Exchequer in the Coalition government, of which Stanley Maitland was no more than a star of the third magnitude. He was a smoker of black cigars, which the caricaturist would always project enormously from his moon-like face. He pulled one from his mouth to answer Stanley, who had passed the paper over to him with the query: "What do you think of that?"

"The old boy seems to have dressed her down a bit rough," he replied in a casual way. He spat comfortably, and the cigar resumed its position.

"He doesn't seem to have enquired as to the quality of the children," Stanley remarked, "nor worried himself particularly as to how they might be getting on in a home where the rent couldn't be paid."

Jimmy looked across at the speaker with more attention than he had done previously. He regarded Maitland as a coming man, and he had found in the past that his judgments were rarely wrong. It is well to understand such men at an early stage of their careers. He did not follow Stanley's line of thought very clearly. He said: "Oh, I don't know. They don't always report all that's said. I dare say he gave her some rope on the rent. He'd mean what he said for others more than for her. She's made her blunders." He drew his cigar for a moment. And then, as Stanley said nothing further, he added, half to himself: "The bitch needs sterilising."

Stanley deliberately controlled any outward sign of his reaction to his remark. He had been studying the men, his colleagues and superiors, who were the nominal rulers of the British Empire, during the last two days, in a way which he had never previously done. He was not concerned to urge his own opinions. He wanted to know what these men really thought of the vital problems which they must face or avoid.

He said: "We can't learn much from a six-inch report like that. But suppose the woman's got a decent husband and a healthy family; shouldn't you say they're more important than how the landlord gets his rent?"

The Hon. James Shackston thought the question to be a singularly foolish one, and he answered it with a lazy politeness.

"Well, you can't live rent-free in this country. It's more likely they're a scurvy lot." He was silent for a long moment. In imagination, he saw the possible circumstances of that slum-bred family in vivid and varied ways, which would have surprised Stanley had they been communicated to him. Jumping Jimmy had one of the best brains in England, and a gift of swift and sympathetic imagination which enabled him to use his sledge-hammer gift of oratory to the swaying of many thousands. But he did not allow his imagination to control a very shrewd and practical and selfish mind.

He added: "The trouble is the way these people will breed in the slums. You know, Maitland, you wouldn't do it yourself. They're not wanted here, and they're not wanted anywhere else."

"Australia isn't exactly full up."

"They wouldn't take them there. Not at a gift. They're not the sort they need."

"Isn't it rather a reflection on ourselves that we don't support our own children, and that they're not considered good enough for the empty lands?"

"It's 'can't' rather than 'don't.' We're overpopulated already. You can't expect city children to go out ploughing, where they mayn't even get a wireless set. There's too much to give up."

"Don't you think we could do a bit more to support them, if we felt it were worthwhile? Suppose we knocked £20,000,000 off our petrol imports, and bought food instead?"

"Of course, you could argue that. But, what's the good? I'm practical politician."

"And as a practical politician you think nothing can be done?"

"I didn't quite say that. We need more clinics to teach women while they're young. These things usually right themselves in the end. Get the population down by five or ten millions, and it'll simplify most of the problems that are worrying us now."

"And Australia for the Asiatics, and South Africa for the Blacks?"

"Well, we can't change the world."

Mr. Shackston got up, and strolled away. He had a doubt as to whether he might not have overestimated Maitland's abilities. You could never be quite sure of these youngsters. Still, he might outgrow it. He knew Donnington thought him a coming man.

During the next twenty-four hours, Stanley made himself a nuisance to about a dozen members of His Majesty's Government. He showed each of them the same cutting, and endeavoured to obtain their opinions concerning the problems which it raised in his own mind. They reacted variously. Some of them sympathised with the woman, and thought the judge might have expressed himself rather differently. Others thought she deserved all she got, and a bit more. One thought that that sort of thing would never stop till it should be made a criminal offence to have more than three children. As to producing children for which you could not provide, it ought to be punished as heavily as are the other major forms of dishonesty.

But on certain points they adopted a common attitude. None of them regarded children as national or parental assets. They were expensive nuisances, to be either partially or entirely avoided. None of them considered that there must be something radically rotten in a social organisation which produced such a position. None of them appeared to consider that the government had any responsibility. None of them appeared to consider the fact that a woman having the care of a large family might be in a state of constant anxiety as to the provision of their food and clothing to be an evil at least as great as that a landlord should be delayed in the receipt of his rent. They were sorry for the poor little brats (of course), but it was the woman's own fault. Such things ought to be stopped.

They took the suggestion that, if there were a real shortage of food, we might import more, and reduce our petrol purchases, either as an impracticable folly, or a senseless jest. They all agreed in the assumption that children cannot be too few, nor machines too many.

There was a time, Stanley reflected, when human life was held to have a supreme and eternal value. Perhaps man had exaggerated his own importance. Anyway, that time was not now. This was the machine age, the age of man had gone by.

He found also that they were at one in regarding it as a natural thing that men should require of life that it should give them comfort and security, and should otherwise have the right to reject it, if not for themselves, for their children. Their ideal of life, or that which they complacently regarded as satisfactory to English citizens, was that of a pampered dog which will be painlessly poisoned when its mistress dies. And the result of this basic vulgarity was to leave them wondering whether life was worthwhile, even if it could give them the good time which was its essential necessity, its substitute for the old ideals of noble living which seemed to have left the world.

What could be the fate of a nation, of a civilisation, so led or so leaderless? If there were any warning in the records of history, any truth in the teachings of Christ, any wisdom in the world's philosophers, it could but stumble blindly toward an ignoble and disastrous end. It was a subordinate issue that he was annoyed more than once by the assumption that he himself would avoid or limit his own parenthood. It was not suggested offensively. It was said in the spirit in which a toper will assume that his neighbours drink. And Stanley was not sure that it was unjust. He would not have chosen to commence his married life with such a condition, but he had accepted it without emphatic protest from the lips of the woman he loved. It was a bargain "just for the first year or two" to which he had assented as a condition of immediate marriage, and he was not one lightly to challenge a bargain made.

But in his present mood, seeking to stand aside and to look at things as they were, rather than as it was customary to represent them, it seemed to be a circumstance that unfitted him to criticise, and must make him impotent to lead. Could he remain in the old bondage, and call others to a freer habit of life?

Still, it was not by his own volition that he was the partner of a barren marriage. There was Crystal's point of view to be considered, as well as his. He remembered that a High Court Judge had declared from the English bench, and there was an actual legal decision in the state of New York, that a husband had no property in his wife's body, and that she had a right to decide whether she would have children at all. Yet the law of both countries still provided that, though she should fail, against her husband's will, in the vital obligations of marriage, so long as she should refrain from other intimacies, he must continue to keep her. Why?

Could the obligation remain, so illogically, so inequitably, when its foundations had been swept away? Might not women find at last that they had lost more than they had gained by this delusion of independence?

In older time, when life had less of disciplined routines and greater individuality, a man could not divorce his wife as easily as he could today, but he could beat her into submission should she decline the obligations of marriage while she ate the fruits of his industry. To observe that is not to suppose that such incidents were common to happy or normal marriage, but, should they occur, other men did not interfere with a domestic incident which they might be incompetent to decide. Was the woman whose chastisement was a preliminary to copulation really less happy, was she even less degraded, than one who took her husband's money in a marriage bargain which she did not keep?

Not that such a question had any personal application. His bargain with Crystal had been clear, and had been clearly kept. He had no doubt she would observe its later condition with a scrupulous and deliberate punctuality. Whether it had been an unholy bargain to make was a different matter, as to which he had an almost equal responsibility.

So his thoughts had wandered, and when they came back to the question of the use, if any, to which he should put the power which Feltham's invention had placed in his hands, he found that his decision was made. For good or evil, for life or death (and he saw that his own death would be a very probable consequence), he would do what one man could, even by the menace of this dreadful weapon, to bring the spirit of freedom, of noble living, of daring, of adventure, back into the hearts of men. Life might be harder or more precarious, but it must become valuable once again. More valuable than a machine. Not something to be yawned over, or despised, or dreaded. He believed in England with a great confidence and a great pride. No cost would be too great which would redeem it from decadence. No deprivation, no toil, no hardship, even to the ordeal of disastrous war.

CHAPTER ELEVEN

ON the night on which Lady Crystal entertained Mr. Goldstone to dinner, Stanley came back from the House shortly after midnight, and went straight up to his own room, where he was somewhat surprised to find that she was waiting for him. Crystal rarely came into his private apartment, though she knew that she was free to do so. Less often still did he invade hers, except by her own invitation, though it might sometimes be no more than the implicit one that a glance can give.

He was in good spirits, as he had been each evening since he had made his decision. Doubts might come in the hours of darkness, or with the morning light, but courage rose as he thought and planned and worked in the laboratory which had become his own, and in which he dared to do no more than to observe, with a blind obedience, the instructions that William Feltham had given him, a few minutes before the brilliant brain had dried and shrivelled, and the bare soul returned to the Ultimate Responsibility from whence it came.

This morning he had posted the letter which chance had brought back so promptly to his own house. This afternoon he had set the machinery of which he knew as little—the machinery so impossibly intricate to understand, so dangerous to approach, and yet so simple to control by the devices which Feltham had designed and left ready to his hand—he had set it to provide the demonstration in Kensington Gardens which was to proclaim his power. After that, at question-time, he had answered a foolish question on the Nigerian trouble in a manner which had startled a listless House. "In view of the unfortunate incidents which had occurred recently between the Buntu and Sunshu tribes in the Nigerian hinterland, and the evident inability of Sir Malcolm Robertson to control the situation, could assurance be given that he would be recalled and replaced by a stronger governor?" Such, in substance, had been the question, and when the House had expected listlessly that he would reply that the answer was in the negative, he had startled it with the blunt retort: "No, we're not such fools."

The Honourable James Shackston, in a supinely sprawling attitude on the bench beside him, his eyes half-closed, and his mind idly alert, was confirmed in his suspicion that something was wrong with Maitland. Probably some woman at the bottom of it. Or had he gone mad with conceit at having won a wealthy wife and being appointed an Under-Secretary of State in his twenty-eighth year? It's astonishing how few men can stay the course. Or was it a calculated indiscretion? Was Maitland playing for publicity with some audacious project of forcing himself into a more influential position? Jumping Jimmy, who had watched and plotted for twenty years for the moment when he could seize the premiership, as patiently as a cat will sit at a mouse's hole, opened his eyes to regard Stanley, who had resumed his seat in apparent indifference to the sensation he had created, with speculative eyes. Was there another danger here to be watched and thwarted? Maitland didn't look like a troubled man. He had the look of assurance which is half the battle on the political arena, where men are assessed and feared at their own valuation—if they can make it good.

On the way home, Stanley had considered how and when he should tell Crystal. He felt that it was a position which would need careful presentation. He saw also that it was expedient in itself, and due to her, that she should learn it first from him, rather than from the event or the talk of others. But he did not want her, because he did not want anyone, to know it prematurely. He owned to himself that he could not foresee how she would take it. She might prove a most useful ally. It seemed more probable that she would endeavour to dissuade him. He didn't want to spend the next two days in a fruitless controversy. He had too much of which to think. Suppose she should even decline to keep the secret, if he should entrust her with it?

No, he would not tell her tonight. It would be best to do so on Sunday evening, midway between the time of the demonstration of his power on Sunday morning, and the announcement of his identity which he had planned to make in the House on Monday night.

Sunday evening was the usual time for their occasional intimacies. He had let Crystal down rather badly on the last occasion. Well, he would ask her to keep Sunday evening free, and then he would tell her all, and perhaps make amends in other ways for his previous rudeness.

As he entered his room, he waked from the wisdom of these plans to the knowledge that he was still something less than omnipotent, as Crystal said: "Stanley, I had Goldstone, the *Morning Standard* man, here this evening. He showed me such a queer letter that I thought you ought to know about it at once, if you don't already."

He saw that there must either be explicit deception or absolute frankness now, and chose the latter alternative without hesitation. He said: "Yes, I know. Is he going to publish it?"

The quiet and ready admission rather stilled than stirred the absurdly disturbing doubt in her mind. She answered: "No, he said it was too silly for that. But Jehane thought—we both thought—that it might be Feltham's doing."

"What made you think that?"

"We thought it had been typed on your Underwood."

"Wouldn't that make it more likely to be mine?"

"Yes, perhaps it would. But we knew it wasn't the kind of thing you'd be likely to do. It wasn't a very good joke, and it couldn't have been written seriously, except by a crazy man."

"Well, it wasn't written by Feltham. Feltham's dead."

Crystal showed no interest in the scientist's end. She held to her point: "Then who did?"

"I was going to tell you about that. There's a good deal to tell, and I shall want your help. I meant to ask you to keep Sunday evening clear, but perhaps it will be better now. For one thing, I want you to give Goldstone the tip to publish that letter. I was afraid he'd be too dense."

"Of course I'll do that, if you wish, but it sounds silly."

"Then I'll tell you now, if you're not too tired. And we'd better have Jehane in. She's got to know, and it'll save saying everything twice."

"I'm not too tired. I shouldn't trouble about Jehane now. She's gone to bed."

"Well, I suppose she'll wake. Tell her to put on a dressing-gown and come along. It's quite important enough for that."

"You mean because Feltham's dead? Do you think she'll care that much?"

"No, I don't think she'll be overmuch surprised, and I don't think she'll care at all. It isn't that. There are other reasons why she'll have to know."

"Then we won't call her now, if you don't mind. I'd rather understand first."

"There's so much to explain that it's not easy to know where to begin. For one thing, I had to kill Feltham, and you know I shouldn't have done a thing like that if there'd been any way out."

Lady Crystal's eyes opened widely at this rather startling information, but her response was such as any husband might desire under similar circumstances, and many would fail to get. She showed neither revulsion, nor horror, nor did she make any foolish protests of terror on his behalf as to the possible consequences. She said: "Oh Stan! How did it happen? I always hated that man."

Stanley thought, with reason, that she took it well. He felt that he was over the first fence, and still riding easily.

Her imagination somewhat widely skirted the truth, thinking that Feltham had gone mad and endangered her husband's life. The right man had been killed. She had no thought of murder in its more sinister forms. Perhaps she knew Stanley too well to connect him with the idea of a vulgar homicide.

As a fact, she came of a class to whom the idea of the occasional killing of men is less revolting than in the strata that she would have considered beneath her, except the lowest of all, which is one of the many points on which those extremes meet. In the middle classes, murder is not respectable. It is also illegal, with a shameful penalty. It is therefore barred by the two strongest taboos by which that class is controlled. English law is reasonably dreaded and less reasonably respected by all classes of the community, but they are both competitions in which the middle class is an easy first. Such remnants either of freedom or insubordination, such habits of independent judgment or action, as still linger in England, must be looked for in the highest and lowest classes of the community. The killing of men, under sufficient provocation or obligation, had been a (relatively) frequent occurrence among the noble ancestors of Lady Crystal Norchester. That she would be loyal to her husband under such circumstances, and cool and practical in his support, should have been obvious to him from the first. She would have regarded it as an unworthy and undeserved disloyalty that he should have paused to doubt it. Perhaps he might not have done so, had not Feltham's death been an incident in a larger project to which her complacency was less certain. He said: "Perhaps I'd better tell you the whole tale from the start."

"Yes. Go ahead," she said, and looked at him with loving and confident eyes. "I shan't interrupt." She had a feeling of contrition that she had not acted in such a way as to win his earlier confidence. She remembered that Sunday evening. Had she acted below her own standard of how a loyal wife should? She prepared to listen with a mind directed only to the question of how Feltham's death had occurred, and whether it threatened any annoying publicity such as might be detrimental to his career. If so, they would have a good fight together to prevent that catastrophe. At such an issue Stanley would have an able and powerful ally.

She kept her promise not to interrupt. She leant forward, with her right elbow on the arm of the chair, and her chin cupped in her hand. Her eyes were on his face as he began, but as the narrative developed she moved them on to the red cavity of a fire which had been built to last, but was now approaching the moment when it would collapse upon its burnt-out centre. Otherwise, she gave no sign.

CHAPTER TWELVE

STANLEY finished at last. It had taken a long time. It wasn't only the bare facts that had to be told. There were his own thoughts, his dreams, his plans, his explanations, his—he didn't call them excuses to his own mind, but he went on, and she gave no sign he said something that had the sound of self-defence which she had not asked.

"Well," he ended at last, "that's about all. I don't know how it'll pan out, but it seems worth trying. You'll be able to help me a great deal. It's too big to be faced alone."

She did not seem to hear him at first, and when at length she spoke it was not to answer directly. She said: "I don't think anyone could blame you for that. But it doesn't seem to matter much either way. I don't see why anything need come out. You really managed it rather well."

"I'm not troubling about Feltham. I reckon after they've had a look at Kensington Gardens on Sunday, they won't do much thinking about themselves."

Crystal spoke with decision. "You couldn't possibly do that."

Her words, and perhaps her tone still more, waked the echo of a doubt in his own mind. Suppose he were defied by a nation that would not yield? Or derided by one that would not believe? Would he have the resolution—perhaps criminality would be a better word—to carry out the threat on which his power would depend?

He had debated this with himself, and the answer would seem to be that the question could not arise. Or it could only arise if he allowed an appearance of hesitation to give confidence to those against whom his threat would be levelled. He said: "It won't be necessary to do anything. You'll find the threat will be more than enough."

"I didn't mean that. Of course, nobody'd believe such nonsense. You'd be a public fool."

"We should have to do something that would make them believe."

"Stanley, have you gone mad? You know you couldn't do such a thing. You've no right." She was not a coward, but there was a note almost of terror in her voice. Her world's foundations shook.

Suppose Stanley really did something silly, and it reacted upon herself, as it so easily might? Suppose—well, suppose that she were no longer received at Court? Suppose that her entrance to the Royal Enclosure at Ascot should be politely barred?

"Don't you think," he said patiently, "that it might be worthwhile, when you think of all we could do?"

"Don't say we," she answered with an asperity which overcame the poise to which she had trained herself from her boarding-school days. "What you'd do would be three months hard labor, if not six. That is, if they could trace it to you. And I believe Goldstone thought that we knew something about that letter. He must have noticed how Jehane looked at it, and then it was passed over to me. You can't do it, after that."

"But I don't mind people knowing. I want them to. That's the whole object of the demonstration."

"Stanley," she said, "if you're gone mad, I'm still sane. If you think Sir Bardsley's going to lick your boots because you make a mess in Kensington Gardens, and say you're setting up in business as a wholesale murderer, you'll find your mistake when it's too late. They'll have you certified in less than forty-eight hours. You'll find yourself in a straitjacket, where you can't do any more mischief."

"I'm sorry you take it like this, but I can't change now. I've thought it all out, and I know I'm doing the right thing. I hoped you'd have helped me in many ways. I expect you will, when you see how it's working out."

She looked at him in a half-incredulous desperation, which found difficulty in framing any adequate protest. It was such incredible nonsense! It was a procedure which would make him detested ay her friends. Detested, if he were taken seriously, and derided if not—which was even worse. It was such incredible nonsense! Stupid, dangerous lunacy, even to talk of such conduct seriously. It was—*disloyal to the Conservative Party*. At this last thought she saw the impossibility of being associated with it in any way. Stanley had *got* to be stopped.

With a recovered quietness, but in a voice which he recognized as one of finality, she said: "Anyhow, it won't be done from this house."

Stanley understood the threat, and saw that she had spoken within her right. Norchester House was hers. It was a fact to which she had never alluded, of which she had not appeared to think, since they had entered it together. But the fact stood.

"Very well," he said, with an equal quietness, "I'll go now."

He rose at the word. She had not meant that. Neither had he meant the response. But words are so easily, so quickly said, so hard to recall. Stanley realised for the second time that night that he was still something less than omnipotent. He stood for a second at the door. Perhaps he looked to her to withdraw the word. He said: "Jehane can bring my papers to me tomorrow. You might tell her I'm borrowing her two-seater. I mightn't get a taxi at this hour."

Her thought was: "I can't give way, but I'll get Jehane to fetch him back. He'll be more sensible in the morning."

Without further words between them, he went out.

CHAPTER THIRTEEN

LEFT alone, Crystal stood for some time looking down at the dying fire, with a hand on the mantelshelf, and a foot that tapped the fender in a restless way. Perhaps for the first time in her life she felt that circumstances were beyond her control. She could not be sure what it would be best to do. The whole thing was an impossible nightmare dream.

The fire fell loudly together, and as though roused by the noise, she stood upright, and her face cleared to the resolution that she had formed. Recovering her usual outward serenity, she went to her sister's room.

"Jehane, can I come in?"

"Yes, of course. What's the row? Found Feltham under the bed?"

Jehane spoke lightly, but she had been having her own speculations, her own doubts, since she had seen that letter about five hours earlier. She switched on the light over her bed as she spoke, and her feet were already in her slippers, and her dressing-gown being pulled on, as her sister entered the room.

"You'd better turn on the heater, that fire's past praying for," she said hospitably, assuming that Crystal had come on an extended visit. She sat down beside the embers of a dying fire. Crystal pulled forward a low chair on the other side of the hearth. She saw that Jehane expected some interesting revelation based on the letter which they had inspected together, but it seemed a wild incredible tale that she had to tell. She felt that Jehane would throw it from her, would reduce it to its true proportions with a jesting word. It was more because the murder of William Feltham was a comparatively credible, a comparatively commonplace incident, rather than that it was chronologically at the basis of her narrative, that she commenced with that incident.

"You won't see Feltham again. Stanley's killed him."

The flippancy had died, for the moment at least, out of Jehane's voice as she answered: "So that was it. Well, I'm glad it wasn't the other way. What was it about?"

Crystal told the tale of Feltham's death over again, not quite as Stanley had told it to her, not quite perhaps as he would have chosen to hear it narrated, but it was accurate enough in its essential facts. Jehane listened carefully, and with only occasional interruptions. She was fitting it in as it proceeded with the facts she already knew.

Crystal paused as she completed the earlier portion of Stanley's narrative. She waited to observe her sister's attitude before disclosing his absurd intentions, and the quarrel which had followed.

Jehane appeared to have recovered from any momentary apprehension caused by the first news that her brother-in-law had indulged himself in a private homicide. "What a thrill!" she said lightly. "It seems to have been rather a neat job. I don't think you need lose very much sleep over that."

"It isn't that. Stanley wants to use Feltham's invention in the same way. Of course, I couldn't agree to that. So we quarrelled and he's gone off. Of course, he's got to be stopped."

"You mean you turned him out of the house? Crystal, you're being almost human! But what a silly thing to do, if you really wanted to get your own way."

"I didn't turn him out of the house. I only said that such things couldn't possibly be done here. He ought to have seen that."

"Only mentioned that it was yours? I see. And now I suppose you want me to bring him back to your longing arms?"

"I didn't say that. But I'm afraid I took him too seriously. He asked me to tell you that he was borrowing your two-seater, and he wants you to take his papers round to him in the morning."

"Then he shouldn't have taken the car. Still, they wouldn't go into it. I shall have to borrow the limousine."

"Then you know where he's gone?"

"I don't know, but I guess that it's Feltham's flat. Have I got to take his collars and ties?"

"He didn't say anything about clothes."

"Then it might be worse. Unless he was too angry to care. Shall I tell him you're sorry for what you said, and you want him back?"

"You can say anything you like, only he'll have to give up this nonsense about Feltham's invention. I don't want to have to talk that all over again."

"Then I shan't say anything. Not till you've learnt sense. It's no use wasting words. But I'd better telephone before we lose any more time."

She went to the telephone book, and after consulting it she gave a number which was strange to Crystal. "Is the Editor in? Tell him Lady Jehane Norchester wants to speak to him particularly. Yes. That Mr. Goldstone? You know that letter you showed us tonight? Well, you'd better print it on the front page. Yes, it's a straight tip. Straight from the horse's mouth. (Be quiet, Crystal. I know what I'm doing, if you don't.) Well, print it somewhere, anyhow. Put it in the sporting news, if you like. You'll be sorry all your life if you don't. Yes, of course. Should I be ringing you up like this if I didn't know? Yes, that's talking sense."

Crystal sat more or less silently while this conversation proceeded. She knew that it was useless to intervene. Would, indeed, have been too late to do so when she first realised her sister's intention.

To explain to Goldstone, to ask him not to print it, would only be to invest it with greater authenticity, and to make its appearance sure.

After all, whatever politeness might have led him to say to Jehane, he would probably think again, and hold it over, unless the *Morning Standard* had a comic page.

"Jehane," she said, "why on earth have you done that? It might ruin Stanley if it's ever found out who wrote that letter."

"I couldn't help it, Crystal. You ought to see that. You told me he wanted it in. Can't you see that the effect of the whole thing depends upon it being announced beforehand? Don't you see that I had no choice? I'm a secretary. It's different with you. You're only a wife."

"I should have thought you'd have given it up after what I'd told you. That is, unless you could make him see sense before it's too late."

"I don't know about that. I mean about giving it up. I don't mean about making him see sense. He's not short of that. I mean, I couldn't give it up without notice. I don't know how much secretaries have to give. I expect it's three months, if not more."

"Jehane, can't you be serious about anything? Can't you see that he's risking his whole career on this ghastly nonsense? You know you can give up the secretaryship any moment you like. You're not dependent on that."

"Oh, I'm quite serious, Crystal." She spoke without flippancy now, for her mind had gone back to that blackened acre in Ditching

Wood. She did not doubt the reality of the threat that Stanley's letter contained, or the incalculable and dubious, nature of the consequence which might follow its publication.

"I'm quite serious," she repeated. "It's only that I can't be a rat like you."

She looked contemptuously at the silent anger in her sister's eyes. She knew from other experiences that Crystal would never compete with her in the undignified exchanges of a verbal quarrel. "I don't think," she added, "I'll trouble you for the limousine. I shall need a van."

CHAPTER FOURTEEN

MR. GOLDSTONE did not print the letter on the front page, nor did he insert it as a tail-piece to the sporting news. He marked it for ten-point type in the correspondence, and hesitated a good deal as to the heading which it should receive. For some moments he inclined to "It's Well to Know," but "Too Bad for Kensington," was his final decision, and so it appeared, except only at a sub-editor altered it to eight-point on his own authority, because, whatever else may happen, advertisements must not be crowded.

Mr. Goldstone, rather puzzled by Lady Jehane's telephone conversation, decided to risk no possibility, however faint, that he might afterwards be blamed for lack of acumen, and sent the letter itself to Scotland Yard, with a personal note. "You will form your own opinion about this," after which business-like procedure he turned his attention to more important matters.

Scotland Yard sent a copy of the letter to the Curator of Kensington Gardens, and warned the constables on duty in that neighbourhood during the early hours of Sunday morning to keep a look out for any maniac who thought he could set fire to grass or trees on a wet day, for the B.B.C. had announced that a depression was approaching from Iceland, as it usually does, except on those occasions when it observes one to be hovering over the North Sea.

The letter must have aroused many isolated comments, but there was an absence of public excitement, such as may be symptomatic of the stolidity of the English character (unless stupidity be a better word).

The life of London proceeded normally until the end of the week and Sunday morning didn't exactly dawn, but the gloom of night lessened perceptibly as the time arrived for the opening of the public parks. A dull sky and a foggy atmosphere, occasionally improved in visibility by a drizzle of chilling rain, tended to keep the public parks comparatively empty, but would not have prevented the presence of the thin stream of people who utilise the passage of the Broad Walk to shorten transit from the main thoroughfares of Bayswater and Kensington Gore. Yet, except in one place, where police and keepers congregated in a condition of nervous excitement foreign to the reputation either of the nation or organizations to which they belonged, the Walk was bare and silent beneath the gloomy drizzle. The reason was that the hours passed and the gates remained closed. Around each of them a force of police was posted sufficiently strong to explain the puzzled curiosity of the little groups of civilians who surrounded and questioned. Once a gate swung open, and a covered ambulance entered. Twenty minutes later it emerged again, and went rapidly eastward. The exposure of its interior would have explained the measure if not the origin of the official excitement which had disturbed the gloomy quietude of the London Sabbath. It contained a man's leg.

Not that the removal of a detached or semi-detached leg is an unusual incident in the life of an English policeman. Had it been no more than the separated member of one of the 196,837 persons who had been killed or injured in the road accidents of a previous year, it would have been removed with the unemotional promptitude with which a leg of pork is handled in the Smithfield market. But this was a special leg.

It was the leg—the alleged leg, as Mr. Goldstone will be careful to have it described in tomorrow's *Morning Standard*—of Park-Inspector Kimpson, and the remainder of Mr. Kimpson had disappeared, leaving no trace. There was a singularity about this leg which puzzled Police-Surgeon Richards, who had been the first medical man to observe its condition, and would cause the Home Office expert, Sir Lionel Tipshift, to admit, at the inquest of the following day, that he was puzzled also, for the first time in his distinguished career. The mystery lay in the manner of its severing from the body to which it had belonged so recently. It had been found at the edge of a blackened acre of land, slightly to the east of the Broad Walk, and about a hundred yards from the southern boundary of the park. It had been severed, apparently, by a downward stroke, as it had been moving forward, the most part of the front of the thigh remaining, but having been shorn away at a slant, so that the back portion was missing, almost to the knee-joint. Cloth and muscle and bone had been cut as cleanly as by a steam-saw. Yet the operation did not appear to be one either of steel or fire. The smooth surface of the separated flesh had been cauterised, so that it had not bled. It was slightly darkened in colour, but not scorched. The severed clothing around it had no sign or smell of singeing. It was as though it had been shedded off by a gigantic knife which had come down from the sky.

And the patch of ground at the edge of which it lay was an equal though not so horrible a wonder. It had been of turf, with a thin scattering of well-grown trees, tall rather than broad, standing yesterday in a mist-soaked nakedness, and now—they were not there. Trees and grass had gone, and there was no more than a dark powder thinly spread over the land, with a tiny mound of ash or dust where the trees had been. It seemed that the tall boles must have collapsed so gently that they had descended straight downward, without scattering in their fall. There was a little mound of dust, rather darker in colour, opposite the position of Mr. Kimpson's leg.

CHAPTER FIFTEEN

AT three o'clock on Sunday afternoon, Mr. Israel Goldstone was in his editorial office, with the news, sporting, and society editors, and two or three other senior members of the staff grouped excitedly around him.

Miss Rimington, his personal secretary, was at the telephone. "It isn't Scotland Yard this time, sir," she said. "I rang them off just as I heard you coming up the stairs. I told them to try again at four P.M. if we didn't call them before that. It's the Home Office. I think it's Mr. Marshall himself "

"Tell him to go to—" Mr. Goldstone began, and then altered it to, "No, I'll speak." He picked up his desk instrument, and the next moment the silent audience around him had the benefit of the more interesting end of the conversation that followed.

"Yes, I've heard that. Yes, so it ought, but I haven't got it. I sent it to Scotland Yard. You'd better get on to them. Is it likely we should remember a thing like that? How can I tell when I've only just got in? I'm here to get information for the public. I'm just sending two of our best men up to Kensington. If they find anything out that you've missed, you can depend upon us to pass it on. Oh, you can't do that. You know it's impossible in a case like this. Not with us, anyway, after we've had the letter and passed it on. I can't tell you what I think yet. I haven't thought. You'll know that in tomorrow's leader. I might think that Scotland Yard's about ten years behind the times. They ought to have known I shouldn't publish a letter and send it on to them unless I thought it looked genuine. Well, perhaps they did; but it wasn't enough anyway. What I want to know now's whether you'll let my men into the park. Of course, there's no bargain. I know you wouldn't make one, and I wouldn't, if you would. But if the police act sensibly, and let them in, I shall know they are sensible men. If they're sensible men, I'm not going to call them fools on the front page tomorrow. That stands to sense. Yes, I'll send them on now." (He nodded to the news-editor, who left the room.) "You'd better call Scotland Yard off, so far as this offer is concerned, till you give the word. I can't have you both on me in turns. Phone me in an hour's time, and I'll let you know if I've got anything worth telling."

He put the receiver down. "Gentlemen," he said, "we've got to find out who wrote that letter before we go to press tonight. It'll be the biggest scoop of the century."

They looked dubiously at one another. They appreciated the ability with which their chief had obtained a possibly exclusive permission to enter the Gardens. It might mean interviews, photographs, such as no other paper could offer to a madly-excited public. But as to who wrote the letter—well, since Scotland Yard had the original, what had they to go on more than anyone else?

"We might ask Jackie if he can remember the postmark," the society editor suggested dubiously. "It seems a poor chance. Otherwise, I don't see—"

"Well," Mr. Goldstone interrupted, "perhaps I do. Miss Rimington, get me through to Lady Jehane Norchester."

Mr. Goldstone was not put through to Jehane, for the sufficient reason that she had left Norchester House, and had not left her address. She had told Miss Preston that she would probably look in on Monday morning for Mr. Maitland's and her own letters, but a very little knowledge of Molly Preston (with whom Mr. Goldstone found that he was unexpectedly conversing) might be sufficient to raise a doubt as to whether he would be likely to obtain much information from her.

Molly Preston was Lady Crystal's social secretary. That was the description under which she had been engaged, and it was a triumph of a somewhat unusual personality which had extended her duties and authority beyond the ordinary bounds of such a position. She had been engaged on excellent credentials, and with a reputed knowledge not merely of the official nobility but of all the upper strata of English citizenship of an almost incredible detail and exactness. She offered also the usual secretarial qualifications, including some commercial experience, and a sound knowledge of housekeeping accounts. The last qualification had led to her first auditing the domestic expenditure at Norchester House, and then offering to save a thousand a year if she were permitted to do so.

She had asked Lady Crystal whether she thought it possible that the consumption of flesh meat amounted to a daily portion of one-and-three-quarter pounds per head, including that part of the year when the house was closed.

Lady Crystal thought not, but was vague as to the extent of any possible error. She supposed that there was a good deal of loss of weight in the cooking. There must be bones. Did Miss Preston think that anything was seriously wrong? Miss Preston did. "Theft and waste," she said definitely.

Lady Crystal hated the idea of waste. It offended her fundamental love of order and efficiency. She also hated unpleasant and un-dignified episodes. She remembered her mother telling her that, in their position, there were things beneath them which must not be probed too deeply. They would be accounted mean. So long as the household service worked smoothly and with a surface efficiency, it was best to let sleeping dogs lie. Still, if matters were seriously wrong, it might become a duty to hold an inquisition which she would not shirk. Had Miss Preston any specific fact to allege?

Miss Preston had nothing to go on except figures and common sense. Something might be learnt from the dustbins. Suppose Lady Crystal should inspect them unexpectedly tomorrow? Lady Crystal thought not. But Miss Preston might do so, understanding that she would be responsible if the kitchen staff should leave.

Molly Preston inspected the dustbins and other things. She had a talk with the cook, who was surprised. Molly was small, with soft plump contours, rather fluffy, with china-blue eyes, and a rounded chin. She had been regarded as a very pleasant and harmless young lady. But opinions changed.

She went to her own room and made calculations. She went to Lady Crystal's and made a proposal. If she saved £1,000 a year without reducing the amenities of the establishment, was it worth an extra £100 to her own salary?

Lady Crystal was dubious. She had gained some confidence in Miss Preston's ability, but she didn't want the house upset. She had plenty of money. Accounts were paid by the easy method of writing figures upon a cheque, which, to most women and many men, means so much less than if a bucket of silver coins were handed across the table. She said she couldn't think of doing anything mean. She could not, for instance, consider reducing the servants' wages.

Miss Preston said she hadn't thought of proposing that. She thought some of them might be increased.

In the end she was given a conditional authority, with the implied warning that she staked her own position on her success.

That had been more than a year ago. The last year's accounts had shown a saving of £1,103 4s. 1d., though the servants' wages had been somewhat higher than before. It was not only that commissions and peculations had been checked in a dozen forms and directions. Molly had the sense to see that such things, though of a low morality, do little economic harm. They are of the inferior means by which wealth, when concentrated in few hands, is returned to the general use of the community. They are as natural as the down-flowing of water. But waste is a different and far more terrible thing. Her main attack had been directed against the senseless, almost systematic, waste which is the disgrace of so many English households, and is almost universal in those which have a large service. It had meant some trouble at first, some changes of staff, and a scene with an outraged housekeeper, who had appealed to Lady Crystal, during which episode Miss Preston's position had trembled for fifteen minutes, but remained unfallen. The idea that dishonesty might be reprimanded on its discovery, or even punished if of too flagrant a character, was familiar to the domestic mind. It was a risk that they always ran. And many of them were honest and unafraid. But the idea that they must not waste was a strange and fearful thing. Those who would have hesitated to give half a leg of mutton, which was an employer's property, to a starving cousin, would throw it into the dustbin without a qualm. To waste freely was a natural attribute of the wealth they served. The idea that it was wrong left them stunned and bewildered. But the wages were good; the work reasonably easy. Some of then left in indignation. Some made feeble attempts at a reasonable economy, and then abandoned it, as its unconventionality oppressed their minds. Others found that old habits were too strong. Others, after recovering from the first shock, found it possible to behave as though they were in their own homes, and had married men with not more than £2,000 a year. In the end, the wastage did not amount to more than two or three pounds a week, and part of that was in overcharges and short weights and other details such as are of no loss to the community.

Through this process of adjustment, Miss Preston had not raised her rather childish voice, nor accelerated her pulses. It was a question of account entirely.

Now she lay on the couch in her own room, which she usually occupied on Sunday afternoons, and quite often at other times. Her attention was divided between the polishing of her nails and the perusal of The White-Hot Flame, which was a novel of the sublimated passions which her imagination approved. She had a little table beside her, bearing her Egyptian cigarettes, her chocolates, her manicure set, her handbag, and a telephone instrument.

Her thoughts wandered from the book to consider the partial confidence which Lady Crystal had given her concerning the recent withdrawal of Mr. Maitland and Lady Jehane. That partial confidence had been partly voluntary, partly precautionary, and partly necessitated by a partial confidence previously given to her by Lady Jehane from another angle. One result of these communications had been to cause Miss Preston to give instructions that if anyone telephoned for Mr. Maitland, they were to be told that he was away for the weekend, and nothing further; but that if anyone asked for Lady Jehane, they weren't to be told she was out, but put through to her. She bit a chocolate thoughtfully, wondering how long it would be before Mr. Goldstone would come through, and as she did this, Mr. Goldstone came.

"I'm afraid you can't," she answered him, in a tone of casual and rather childish amiability, "she's not in just now. No, she's away over the weekend. If it's so urgent you might ring up on Monday afternoon. Yes, I'm sure she'll be back before then" (and away again, she thought, with an instant's flicker of amusement in the china-blue eyes). "No, I couldn't say that. She didn't leave word. She might be motoring about. She's with Mr. Maitland. She's his secretary, you know. I think he's doing a speech for the House tomorrow. No, I'm afraid I couldn't. Lady Crystal's lying down. She's got Mr. Noel Wallace's new book, and she said she wasn't to be disturbed for anything till she rings for tea. Yes, I'll ask her to, of course."

In his Fleet Street office, at the other end of the wire, Mr. Goldstone laid down his ear-piece with something not unlike a curse.

"Drawn a blank, so far," he said impatiently. "No chance anyway, till Lady Maitland stops yawning and rings for tea. No, we've got to go carefully."

He had no doubt of the frankness of the young lady to whom he had spoken. In her pleasant childish voice she had given him desired information before he asked it. He had not enquired whether Mr. Maitland were in. It had not been necessary. And Lady Crystal was reading Noel Wallace's latest and must not be disturbed! What a useful light that threw on the peaceful state of mind of Mr. Maitland's wife. He would never have thought of asking that.

As a fact, Molly Preston had not said that Lady Crystal was reading the book, which was of an extreme improbability. That she had "got" it when she retired for the afternoon was solely due the fact that Molly had placed it beside her, and it had been so placed solely in preparation for a conversation which she foresaw. At the age of ten she had suffered for a discovered lie, and had reflected that, apart from its ethical deficiencies, it is a clumsy weapon to use. It is so much better to supply people with selected truths with which to deceive themselves.

But, on this occasion, she did not flatter herself that her verbal tactics could be of any important value. At the most, she had thrown up a smoke-screen which the breath of enquiry must blow aside in a few hours.

Meanwhile Mr. Goldstone was saying: "Mr. Maitland's gone off with Lady Jehane, so she says, to prepare a speech for tomorrow night. What's on then? I didn't know that it was anything in connection with his department."

The news-editor, who had returned to the room, produced a list of the parliamentary business of the coming week.

"There's nothing on on Monday," he said, "that concerns him. There's the second reading of the *Fleas (Preservation and Restriction) Bill*. That's the most likely, but I don't see that it's got anything to do with the Colonial Office. Not specially, that is. It's important, of course."

Mr. Goldstone didn't see it either. It was a contemporary historical fact that, since the European War, the human flea has become unaccountably rare. German vivisectionists, who use these active creatures largely in their laboratories, have found it necessary to advance their prices, and, even so, have been ill supplied. The phenomenon is not confined to the countries of Western Europe, but in the East also, where the human flea has been firmly established from the dawn of history. As the nineteenth century will be mainly distinguished in the celestial records by the disappearance of the Great Auk, so may the twentieth be by the two inexplicable disasters that the musk has lost its scent, and that the human flea will have died out.

Concerning the latter catastrophe, no parliament worthy of its high mission could omit to legislate. The English Parliament knows its duty to the democracy to which it owes its existence. It is to make laws. And more laws. Never even to contemplate the possibility that legislation should pause, while there is a place or moment of liberty which has been overlooked, and may yet be taken away! Great as may be the genius displayed in finding new subjects for these unending laws, yet there must be times when it becomes difficult either to discover or invent them. The threatened disappearance of the human flea was an opportunity not likely to be ignored. A proper record of flea-bites, to be supplied under sufficient penalties by all over the age of five, and by the parents and guardians of those of more tender years; licences to keep fleas in areas where they are dying out, even a bounty to those who should protect and nourish them; licences to kill them in districts where they should become too numerous' the appointment of the necessary inspectors; the provision of suitable government offices in Tothill Street—what a vista of public service and of the service of summonses opened to the bureaucratic mind!

All this was known to the assembled journalists. It was too obvious for mention. But why the Colonial Office should be interested to intervene, so that its Under-Secretary should have retired to prepare his speech, was something which they could not see.

"I think," Mr. Goldstone said thoughtfully, "though it seems going rather a long way round, I'll try to get a word with Sir George Donnington."

Though it was Sunday afternoon, Sir George was at the Colonial Office. He had, in fact, gone there for a brief call on his way to the Cabinet Council which Sir Bardsley Clinton had hastily and informally summoned. He said impatiently that the Colonial Office was not interested in fleas. Not in the least. If it had been mosquitoes or tsetse flies.... No, Mr. Maitland wasn't either. Not in the least. He'd had something on his mind for the last few days, but it wasn't fleas. Sir George was quite sure. He added something about Sir Bardsley having got another kind of flea in his ear this afternoon, but it was indistinct, as though he recognised indiscretion while the words came, and it died down to a mutter which Mr. Goldstone could not catch.

But he had got something, as a wide-flung net often will. Mr. Maitland had had something on his mind for the last few days. His instinct for news—an instinct which had raised him to the place where he now sat—was on a scent which he felt that he could not miss.

"Miss Rimington," he said, "my own car. Gentlemen, I'll tell you who's at the bottom of this. It's that Feltham who cleared out a month ago. He was Maitland's friend. Maitland's in this somehow, though I can't see where. It was Lady Jehane who tipped me to publish that letter, though I haven't mentioned that to a soul till now. Not even to you. Find out if anything's going on at Feltham's flat now. Find out who has been there, and when. I'm seeing Lady Crystal if I have to go up the back stairs. I'll write the leader myself when I come back."

As he spoke, Miss Rimington was helping him into his great-coat with pleasant, capable hands. "Thanks, my dear," he said, with his easy Hebrew affability, as she smoothed the collar.

Next moment, with the clumsy haste of an obese elephant, he was plunging down to the lift.

CHAPTER SIXTEEN

WHEN Stanley walked out of his own room, and left his wife in possession, he did it on an impulse of unreflecting anger, and it was not many seconds before he realised the inconvenience he had to face, apart from any major consequences of that moment's folly.

The broad landing leading to the circular well by which the central staircase made its spiral descent was still alight, but the hall below was in darkness. He switched on the lights at the stairhead, and descended at the pace of one who goes steadily to a known objective, but he paused in the hall with the realisation that he had no resources but those that his pockets held, and that he could not obtain even the necessities of the dressing-room without returning through that which his wife might still occupy, which he was unwilling to do.

He might have waited in one of the lower rooms, and gone up at a later hour, when she would have almost certainly retired to her own apartment, packed a suitcase, and departed in a comparatively provided way. But he felt that this would be an undignified, almost furtive proceeding, and rejected it without hesitation.

Fortunately, he had money enough. Nor was that of any instant importance, for his inclination was to go to Feltham's flat, rather than face the explanations involved in entering an hotel at that hour without luggage. The consequences must be matter for later consideration.

Fortunately, also, he had the keys of the flat, including a latch-key of the street door, in his hip-pocket. During recent weeks he had carried these keys constantly in that way, transferring them as he changed his clothes.

Having resolved to go to the flat, he hesitated as to whether he should not walk rather than trouble to get Jehane's car. It was the simpler way, and the distance was not more than two miles. He was of a mood to welcome the exercise, and the opportunity of thinking quietly in the cool air of the winter night.

But he was not accustomed to walking the streets after one A.M., and he was uncertain how great an interest the patrolling police might take in such pedestrianism. Ignorance exaggerated the possibility that he might be stopped and questioned. Also, he had told Crystal that he would borrow Jehane's car. He would do as he said. He made his way to the garage.

It was a rule at Norchester House that a chauffeur should always be on duty, ready for any sudden call, and he did not anticipate any difficulty or delay in that direction. But it was customary to order cars by the medium of the house telephone. The man on duty would doubtless have roused himself at the sound of the telephone bell to which he was normally alert, but he was less so to the sound of the entering footsteps. Stanley found him asleep on the comfortable cushions of Lady Crystal's private car.

The man was startled and sullen at this amazing invasion of his own quarters at such an hour. He supposed that it was a deliberate attempt to trap him—and having been found as he was, that he would be dismissed in the morning was a very likely thing.

Stanley took no notice of his emergence from that sacrilegious retreat. He told him to get out Lady Jehane's car. The man looked a natural surprise, and stood in a sullen hesitation, before he went, without audible protest, to fulfil the order.

His hesitation was natural. Lady Jehane never allowed anyone to use or drive her car except herself. Everyone knew this to be a rule which must not be broken at any emergency. Jehane had a theory that no car will do its best for more than one driver. It should pass at once under the control of its ultimate owner, and remain in a condition of strict monogamy. When its owner discards it, it may descend to any prostitution, it becomes a mere thing of the streets, open to any outrage, and liable to commit any delinquency.

The man's momentary astonishment gave way at the thought that Lady Jehane would presently appear, to take Mr. Maitland out. It was her custom to come into the garage for it herself, rather than that it should be brought round to the front door by other hands. That Mr. Maitland might be intending to drive it did not enter his head. Mr. Maitland never drove.

In fact, Stanley had his own car, but it was away under repair. He had driven himself in previous years, but had abandoned the habit since his marriage, in an atmosphere of waiting chauffeurs. As he stood now, he remembered with vexation that his driving licence must be long out of date. Suppose he should be stopped for that?

The man moved another car out of the way, but made no motion to bring the two-seater out of its corner. Jehane would do that for herself. She was of a practised expertness in the nice handling which that operation required. Stanley stood waiting for it to be brought out. He knew that he was still regarded somewhat as an outsider by the older servants. Important as Lady Crystal's husband, but not otherwise. Yet it seemed impossible that the man should hesitate to obey his orders.

"Is Lady Jehane coming down, sir?" the man asked, after an awkward pause.

"No, I'm taking it out for her." He added: "Hurry up. Don't stand there all night," with a sharp irritation, at which the man went slowly to the car, and got into it. He steered it out to the open centre of the garage and sat waiting for Stanley to get in.

Stanley had no intention of letting the man drive him at that hour, and leave him at Feltham's flat. He said: "Get out, Tucker. I shan't need you."

The man plainly hesitated. He seemed about to make audible protest. Then he got out slowly. He said nothing more, but his looks were eloquent. He thought it was a queer business.

Stanley, turning into the road, and, handling the unfamiliar car with a moment's awkwardness, was conscious that he had no reason for satisfaction at the events of the last hour. It was his audacious project to manage his fellow-men. To interfere decisively for their own good. He had attributed to himself more wisdom than theirs. He essayed to show that he had the will to govern. He had found that he could not guide his own wife. He was not master in his own house. Worse than that, he had not the will, nor the wisdom, to control himself. He knew that he was not now in the open street by necessity, nor by his own judgment, but as the price of a foolish word which he need not have said.

Certainly, he was something less than omnipotent, even though the destruction of London was in his power.

CHAPTER SEVENTEEN

EXPERIENCING no difficulty nor interference, Stanley entered the flat, after leaving the car at an adjoining garage.

As he had been careful to avoid any action which would imply a knowledge of Feltham's death, he had left the personal effects in the living-room undisturbed, beyond the extent of Mrs. Harper's limited ministrations.

He had, however, given permission for the bed-clothes and various soiled linen and other articles to be sent to a laundry, and the bed had been remade and was kept aired by Mrs. Harper in anticipation of its owner's return; and here Stanley saw that he must spend the remainder of the night in such comfort as he could contrive, and decide with the coming morning on his course of action during the short time remaining before he would have thrown down his challenge.

As he looked round that unattractive living-room, with its tragic, sinister memories, and thought of the strange and terrible menace to the lives of his countrymen which the dead man's brain had contrived, and which lay behind the heavy door, was it wonderful if he had a moment of irresolution or doubt as to whether Crystal might not be right in her condemnation, might not be correct in thinking that he would end his career in the obloquy or derision of those among whom he might have held a position of high and merited honour?

He was abandoning all that he had won so far in the hard battle of life, even his wife and home, as the last hours had shown, for a wild and criminal effort to obtain tyrannic power with no assurance but that of his own mind that he would not use it to a tyrant's ignoble ends.

He had no assurance of success. He could not even regard it as likely that his letter of warning would appear in the *Morning Standard* of the coming day. He had no certainty that the demonstration he had announced for Sunday morning would be successful, doing neither more nor less than he had foretold. Suppose Feltham's instructions had been deliberately incomplete or inexact? Suppose he had forgotten some small-seeming yet essential detail?

Having written that letter, how could he retreat without ignominious, perhaps even criminal consequences, should he find it impossible to make his assertion good?

He saw that he was commencing a course from which there could be no retreat, except of a disastrous kind. Perhaps he had gone too far for safe retreat already. He was not sure of that. But the doubt brought to his mind a more nerving conviction. To go forward in any spirit, under any circumstance, might be to invite disaster. That was beyond knowing. But to hesitate, to show irresolution now, was to make disaster sure.

He must be resolute to carry out the plan he had formed, and he must be equally so to control it, and to control himself, to the end which he had endeavoured to keep clearly and constantly before his mind since he had decided upon it. He must do that, not only for the sake of the people that he sought to save, but for the infinitely smaller but more personal issue, that he should save his own soul alive.

Yet he had little pleasure in his thoughts during the night hours, and his resolution was of the will only, to which his spirit refused to rise with the buoyancy which he knew that the occasion required. He could justify himself in argument to his own mind. He had done so repeatedly already. He might do it again. Yet was it not a sign of its moral weakness that any argument should be needed?

He had destroyed Feltham without scruple to save the world from the menace which he was now himself proposing to direct against it. He told himself that he was of another kind, working for different ends; but in that room, using Feltham's razor, even considering the possibilities of Feltham's clothes, he seemed more closely identified with the man whose brittle dust he had shaken into the blazing grate.

He had had little rest when the morning came, and felt tired and despondent, as he seldom did in the early hours of the day. It seemed that though he had not reached the reality of power, he was already at that which will frustrate or betray it.

William Feltham had breakfasted rather piggishly in his own room, in a manner which Stanley Maitland would have been inexpert and reluctant to imitate, even had it been possible to do so. But there was no food there. Jehane had looked into a cupboard in which the bread was hard and the once-tinned salmon of a darkening before it got any worse.

Mrs. Harper had interpreted her instructions liberally. Even an unopened packet of tea had been removed from the danger of deterioration. Stanley, vaguely opening the cupboard door, had observed without acute disappointment that only the salt remained.

Yet he hesitated to leave the flat at an early hour, which might be noticed by those who would conclude that he must have spent the night within it. During the short interval between the appearance of the letter—if it should appear—and the demonstration which was to follow, he had planned that he would do nothing which might draw attention to his connection with the premises of the absent scientist. He could not foresee what amount of excitement or enquiry its publication might cause. The sudden quarrel with Crystal, the separation from his home and the routine of his daily life, were complications which he had not anticipated, and the consequences of which were difficult to foresee.

He hesitated, but after a few minutes, courage conquered. He would not be self-confined ignominiously by his own fears, like a criminal in a cell. He went out to make the discovery that the restaurants in that part of London were not of the kind with which he was most familiar, and that their customers usually appeared at a later hour. He withdrew from one in which a charwoman slopped the floor.

In the end, he found a tea-shop bearing a popular name which catered for those who find it convenient to breakfast abroad. He chose a seat near to a good fire, and felt the comfort of exchange from the chilly pavement and misty drizzle of the winter street. He ate food which was good enough, though ill-served, and he was aware, as he did it, of a foolish prejudice against a glass-topped table.

He went back to the flat with a new doubt in his mind. He had imagined in broad outline that it was desirable that men should return to more primitive conditions of life. Might they prove unattractive in greater detail at a closer view? How would he react to them himself? Was it that men could not congregate in these unnatural cities without life becoming either wastefully luxurious or repulsively sordid?

Such questions might not be beyond answer, such problems not beyond solution. He knew, also, that they were not the only, perhaps not the more radical, evils against which he essayed to fight. It was the loss of human liberty, with its consequent diminution of courage, enterprise, self-discipline and self-reliance, which must be restored, if the nation itself were not to sink into the lethargy which precedes and presages an ignominious end. He would break down a system which offered safety to those who would sink their individualities in its soft embraces—a safety which, in the end, it might be unable to give, which offered comfort at the expense of character, which substituted for the ideal of self-discipline that of discipline by the state, a state in which it was becoming equally difficult either to starve or soar.

Yes, the doubts might be resolved in his own mind. All other doubts but the one which he might cast out, but which would wait at the door, and force new entrance continually. Was Stanley Maitland equal to his self-appointed task of reforming the world?

CHAPTER EIGHTEEN

ON his way back to the flat, Stanley bought a *Morning Standard*. He did not open it till he got in. He did not wish to be seen searching its pages in the street. When he saw that the letter had been inserted, he felt some lifting of spirit, something of the elation which comes to those of a good courage when they know that the moment of strife is near.

In this mood his mind waked more actively to face the practical problems which now confronted him. What would Crystal do?

Above all, what, if anything, would she say? If she should make it known that he was the author of the letter, his position between now and Sunday might be very difficult, though he could not be sure what would be likely to happen. He might even be arrested. An attempt might be made to break into the flat and investigate its contents, with incalculably disastrous consequences. More probably, he would be mocked as a practical joker, or treated as a fool. Well, that wouldn't matter—unless the sequel should prove it true. He had always remembered that possibility, and had calculated on the anonymity of the letter. If nothing happened on Sunday morning in Kensington Gardens, the contents of Feltham's laboratories could be sold for scrap, and no one need ever know of the folly that had possessed his mind.

But there was another possibility now. Before Sunday came, he might find himself certified as a lunatic, behind the strength of asylum walls. To warn the world would be useless then. It would be additional proof of his own infirmity.

Might it not be better now, in view of Crystal's knowledge, and the uncertainty of her silence, to hide himself till Sunday should have gone, and the experiment have failed or the warning been given?

Without deciding the question, he saw that there was one thing that should now be done without delay. That was the setting of the machine for the demonstration, which he had hesitated to do until he knew that the letter was published.

He proceeded to do this, following slowly and with extreme care the directions which Feltham had given him, and which he had written down on the following morning. Remembering the warning which Feltham had given, he had chosen a spot in Kensington Gardens adjoining Hyde Park where an error of fifty or a hundred yards would be of little importance. On the map which he had sent to the *Morning Standard* (which was not published) he had purposely marked this spot in a blurred way, so that a slight error might not be easy to detect. He did not wish to be the means of destroying an acre of Kensington Palace, or of the barracks at Knightsbridge, with their human contents.

The wisdom of these precautions was to become evident when he learnt on Sunday afternoon that the destruction had taken place several hundred yards away from the spot which he had chosen, and to which he endeavoured to set the delicate instrument which he controlled, but of which he knew so little.

Having completed this operation, he considered his next action, and decided that if Jehane had received his message she would try to bring the papers for which he had asked, though he was aware of the vagueness of that instruction. She might also wish to recover her car. With the knowledge which she already had, and with the additional information, whether much or little, which Crystal would give her, she would almost certainly try to find him at the flat, having no other address. Should Crystal have changed her mind, of which he had no more than a faint hope; they might even come together.

Otherwise, Jehane might try to reach him at the House, later in the day. If nothing happened earlier, he must consider whether he should go there.

For the moment, he must stay where he was, with nothing better than Feltham's papers and books to occupy his mind.

Under the fiction that Feltham would return, his papers had necessarily been free from any radical disturbance. Even the mathematical calculations which had been lying on his desk were still there. Einstein's mystical pamphlets lay beside formulæ which seemed to carry them on into deeper obscurities. Stanley was a good mathematician. He had graduated with honours. But they meant nothing to him. Looking upon them, he realised how unfit he was to control the power which was but two rooms away. It was like a thunderbolt in an infant's hands.

It was afternoon when Jehane came. She had not left Norchester House with a van, as she had threatened her sister that she would do. A night's reflection had shown her the folly of an open quarrel, especially just as Stanley had left the house.

Apart from that, she had no wish to quarrel with Crystal in any serious way. She had a certain amount of sympathy with, or at least understanding of her sister's attitude, though she thought she had acted about as foolishly as a woman could. There was nothing unusual in that. She was used to criticising Crystal with a sister's frankness, and from a standpoint of different values. Possibly Crystal had been right in her wish to dissuade Stanley from the course he had chosen. As she had told it, it had sounded both wild and foolish. Indeed, almost too much so to be entirely credible, for Jehane felt some confidence that Stanley was not a fool. But, in any case, in her judgment, Crystal *was*—for she had not gone the right way to attain he end she desired.

Apart from that, Jehane felt that Crystal's duty was to stand by her husband, even though she might differ. Crystal (Jehane reflected) always had thought too much of herself.

She went off with no more than three suitcases, one containing her own requirements, one being filled with such of Stanley's papers as she supposed he would be most glad to have, and one having been contributed by Crystal, in response to a suggestion from Jehane that she should put up some of Stanley's clothes, unless she wished him to go to the House in last night's collar.

She told her maid that she should probably be away over the weekend, though she was not quite certain. She took a taxi, and delayed instructing the driver till the boy who had loaded up the suitcases had gone back to the house.

She had a few parting words with Crystal before she left. They were mainly hers, and an auditor might not have understood that any bargain had been completed between them, but Jehane knew that there was one which was clear to both, and which her sister could be trusted to keep.

The letter having been published that morning, the resulting position must depend upon whether the demonstration followed. Jehane had pointed out in forcible and picturesque words that if it should become known to anyone that Stanley had written the letter, he would be obliged to carry out the demonstration, even though he might otherwise be persuaded to drop it, because unless he did so he would look such a ghastly fool. Crystal was to refrain from doing anything sneakish, and she was to do what she could to persuade him to return, and to avoid being appreciably sillier than men naturally are.

With the articles of this limited treaty clear in both their minds, and after a few words to Molly Preston, Jehane drove off, and directed the taxi-driver to take her to Dawlish Mansions, and there to await her further requirements.

She arrived at the door of the flat in a somewhat breathless condition, having, in all probability, won the world's record for the speedy carrying of two heavy suitcases up five flights of stairs, which she had not planned to do.

With the offhand imperiousness which was begotten by her own character upon her youthful experiences, she had directed the taxi-driver to carry two of the suitcases to the foot of the lift, which is a task beyond the obligations of their licences, which those gentlemen cannot always be relied upon to perform with a cheerful speed. But there are few things which are denied to youth and beauty when it is suitably dressed, and the man had obeyed with alacrity. He went back to his cab, and Jehane decided that it was needless to ring as she gazed upon the portent of an ascending rope. Then, as the floor of the cage could be seen descending toward her at the sedate pace which is common to hydraulic lifts of the older generation, the thought came suddenly that it would look rather odd that she should be arriving in this manner—that it might be best that she should be unobserved, in view of possible developments which she could only surmise in a vague way. Picking up a case in each hand, she started to mount the stairs.

She had not gone ten steps before she realised her folly in changing what should have been an ordinary into a conspicuous thing. Her only justification would be to gain the fifth floor without observation, and an agitation of ropes in the well of the lift showed that it was still actively occupied. She sprinted upward, and caused Stanley some natural surprise, as he opened the door, by exclaiming: "Whatever else you're going to do in the pre-Adamite line, I hope you'll leave us a few lifts."

Stanley said: "Yes? You surely haven't carried those up the stairs? Any more to come?" And then, as he saw the implication of her remark: "I suppose Crystal's told you everything?"

"How can I tell that? She told me about enough for one night. She's sent you some collars in that case."

"As a hint that she doesn't want me to come back?"

"No. The boot's on the other leg. She knows she's been catty to let you go."

"Is she telling everyone else?"

"Not a word. She's not quite silly enough for that. She wants you to drop the whole thing, and she knows it won't be very good for it to get out that you've written such a letter as that."

"And if I won't drop it?"

"Well, we hope you will. It sounds—well, I don't know whether you really could, but it doesn't sound a—well, not quite a nice thing to do."

"You haven't forgotten Ditching Wood?"

"Then you know that it's a possible thing."

"I know Mr. Feltham said so. It might have been so to him. But Bill's dead."

"And you mean I might fail where he wouldn't?"

"Well, there is a difference. I didn't mean to be rude."

"You weren't rude, you were right. I'm relying blindly on instructions I had from him. But I think he told me the truth, and, if so, I believe it will prove that he could do all that he claimed."

"And he was—in the grate, when we came in together?"

"Yes."

"I'm not sure," she said thoughtfully, "that you couldn't pull it off if you really try. But I hope you won't, all the same."

"Won't succeed, or won't try? What do you suppose I'm intending to do?"

"Crystal says we've all got to wear woad, and if we kick up a fuss we shall disappear by the next night."

"Crystal didn't really say that?"

"Not verbatim. I've just squeezed out the juice."

"So I supposed. Don't you think it might be possible for anyone to govern England to rather better purpose than is being done now? Take the state of the public roads. Have you calculated that at the present rate of accidents half the population of England will have been killed or injured before this generation dies out?"

"No. I can't say I have. I suppose we like the sport, and don't mind taking the risk. I sometimes let out a bit myself. By the way, what have you done with the car?"

"It's not two streets away."

"Then I'd better give the taxi the sack. But I've got my own suitcase in it. I don't want to lug that upstairs for nothing. We'd better get the programme mapped out first, and start quarrelling afterwards."

"What's the point?" There were implications in Jehane's last remarks which could not be ignored, but from which it might be awkward to make a wrong assumption.

"You needn't look so alarmed. I'm not proposing to stay here. I thought of going to Muriel's for the weekend. She hasn't invited me, but she wouldn't know that, and Rigby'll just stand on his head with joy. I thought if you've got an important speech to get ready for Monday you might come along."

"I couldn't possibly do that. Lady Muriel wouldn't think that she'd forgotten inviting me."

"No, of course. But I'll fix that. You shall hear me phone, if you like. It'll be the most natural thing in the world. You can't stay here, with Mr. Feltham coming down the chimney every half-hour during the night. I shouldn't care to sleep here myself overmuch, innocent as I am. I don't mean you did anything wrong. I don't see what else you could have done, shut up with a criminal lunatic as you were. But he's sure to feel annoyed all the same. You can't blame him for that."

"I've slept here last night, as much as I slept anywhere. If I didn't fear Feltham alive, I'm not likely to fear him dead. I'm not that kind of fool."

"Good for you. Some of us would feel differently. Still, I should think one night might be enough. Suppose we take these suitcases down again, and drive round to the car, and I take you somewhere

where you can get a good meal, and see what we can do with Muriel on the phone. Of course, you can go to an hotel if you like, but it'll look a queer thing to do."

Stanley did not see that. He thought he might have gone quietly to any seaside resort for the weekend, and the fact that his wife was not with him would have excited no remark. To stay in a London hotel might seem a more singular proceeding, but even that was not beyond explanation, and to whom need it be given? Should he prolong his absence, there would, of course, be an unavoidable publicity. Nothing could alter that.

But at present he was concerned with an equally immediate and more urgent question. He said:

"I suppose you're absolutely sure that Crystal won't say anything, beyond what she's done already to you?"

"Yes. She promised that. Besides, it wouldn't be a sane thing."

Well, if that were so, it was of no great importance where he might spend the next forty-eight hours, nor could there be much danger in leaving the flat unoccupied. He saw that Jehane was trying to get him to go with her so that she might use the time to dissuade him from his intention, but he was not sure that it would be either courageous or wise to refuse her the opportunity.

Such a discussion might assist to clarify his own mind. Her alliance, could he win it, might be of the first importance. Should he fail to persuade her, who was both shrewd and friendly, would it not be an. indication of the extremity of opposition which he must be prepared to encounter from the general public whom he sought to serve?

"Very well," he said, "come along." He picked up the suitcases. "I suppose I've got all I shall need here. Anyhow, I've got nothing else to pack. But there's one thing I ought to do first."

He laid down the cases again, and proceeded to prepare a lurid red-ink label, HIGHLY DANGEROUS, which he fastened upon the inner door.

Twenty minutes later he was privileged to listen to one end of a telephone conversation between Jehane and Lady Muriel Stilton.

"I'm sorry I couldn't possibly get down yesterday. I hope you didn't expect me to wire—you know how careless I am. Yes, of course; but I'm not sure that I can today. Stanley's getting a speech up for Monday. I think he wants to get off somewhere quiet for the weekend, and he's sure to want me to go along. I've been getting out figures for him all the week. No, it's not that. He's not interested in fleas. Besides, I don't suppose you've got any, even if we came to you; and Rigby'd never leave us alone. We'd far better go to Margate, or somewhere quiet. Well, of course, I'll ask him. I should love it, of course. I'll see what I can do. I shan't trouble to wire. I expect you'll just see us roll in. No, you needn't think about meeting us; we'll come by car." She rang off.

"There, you see," she said, in a careless triumph, "she thinks she asked me for yesterday, and I didn't remember; or, if she doesn't believe that, she thinks I'm so fond of her brother's eyes that I can't keep away for more than three weeks, and that'll do about equally well. And she thinks I'm dragging you down if I can as the only means of getting there myself, which isn't entirely wrong. It isn't all truth of the simplest kind, but it's got enough in it to go round. And, anyway, she'll be a grateful girl. She doesn't get an Under-Secretary of State to weekend there more than once in six months, and probably not that—and now for lunch—and don't look over to the far table on the left, there's that little toad, Jepson, there, staring at us with both eyes. If I start the car in the wrong direction when we get out, you'll know why it is."

CHAPTER NINETEEN

LADY CRYSTAL was not reading Noel Wallace's latest, neither was she asleep. She was facing an unprecedented position with a troubled but resolute mind.

She had heard nothing from her husband or sister since Jehane had departed two days ago, and she recognised the importance of suspending both action and judgment until she should know the result of her mission of reclamation, as she considered it to be. And of this reclamation she had had good hope, though her disposition was resolute and serene rather than sanguine in anticipation. She recognised, in a mind too secure in itself for the degradation of jealousy, that Stanley liked Jehane, and that she was of a probable influence. She assumed, with a partial accuracy, that Jehane would feel as she did regarding this amazing folly. She knew that she had a gift of expression which, however deplorable in its more vulgar lapses, could be relied upon to make her meaning clear. She did not greatly resent Jehane's freedom of language toward herself, because she had been accustomed to it from their common childhood, and because she considered that it had been partly silly and partly true.

It had been absurd to call her a rat. Rats desert sinking ships, and she hadn't deserted anything. It was Stanley who had deserted her. But she recognised that she had been foolish, if not in her reaction to Stanley's insanity, in the frankness with which she had expressed it. She saw that she would have exercised a superior discretion, a stronger restraint, had she been dealing with anyone but him. That was the betrayal of self which marriage brought, even such a semi-detached one (the word was not hers, though the idea was vaguely present) as that to which she had committed herself.

Yet all she had said was that Norchester House would not become the headquarters of anarchic criminality, which should have been obvious without words. (That, she saw now, had been her mistake. Many things which are obvious without words must be left unsaid.) It was the instant way in which Stanley had taken it which had disconcerted the argument.

Until lunch-time she had not been very greatly perturbed. She had a natural doubt as to whether Stanley would be able to make a defacing blank in Kensington Gardens, even should he continue obstinate in his determination. Unlike Jehane, she had not seen that rectangle of desolation in Ditching Wood. Even so, she would have said that Stanley was not Feltham, and would be unlikely to have succeeded to his diabolical wizardry. Beyond that, there was her hope in Jehane. She had a good digestion, and a courageous, though not sanguine, temperament. There was nothing to be done, beyond the exhibition of an outward serenity which would prevent any idea arising within the household that there was confusion among its rulers. This she did without difficulty, and no one but Molly Preston guessed that there was any threat to its enduring peace.

But with the afternoon the news came. The reticence of the police, the closing of Kensington Gardens, the comparative quietude of Fleet Street on Sunday mornings, had not been sufficient to prevent a rumour spreading through the London streets, had not prevented one prompt and enterprising journal having a special edition on sale at one P.M. with a flaring front page recalling the letter in the *Morning Standard*, and announcing a catastrophe which did not seem the less because it could, as yet, be only vaguely indicated. Molly Preston, alert for the event, had quietly obtained a copy of this paper, and it now lay on the table in Lady Crystal's room.

Looking at the query which crossed its front page in two-inch letters, WHAT IS HAPPENING IN KENSINGTON? she knew that, in spite of herself, in spite of Jehane, Stanley had gone ahead, and that the battle was about to join. But she was like a general who looks into a surrounding mist, not knowing from what point the attack may come. How then shall he order his troops? How direct his artillery? If she knew what Stanley were doing now! If only Jehane would come!

And, most inopportunely, she wanted Stanley with a stronger physical longing than she often felt, and too often subdued. Perhaps the fact that he had been so constantly in her thoughts during the last three days had its responsibility for this condition. If only he were coming to her this Sunday evening, as he would naturally have done! Looking out into the misty January street, and contemplating the probability that their mutual future, their almost certain political and social triumphs, had been ruined by his incredible folly, she was conscious that she did not feel the bitterness that she had anticipated would result if he should persist in this insane demonstration. She felt lonely. She felt almost—afraid.

The musical tinkling of the telephone bell—it was a special instrument, tuned to her own liking—broke into the sombreness of her thoughts. Miss Preston said that Mr. Israel Goldstone was at the door. He was urgent to see her. Was she at home? He said he wished to see no one but her.

No, she said, tell him she was not at home. She would be at home to no one today. What, she thought, could she say, when she was irresolute in her own mind? The promise of reticence to Jehane was ended by this morning's outrage. Should she lie, denying that which she surely knew? Should she repudiate? Should she betray?

Five minutes later she had learnt that Mr. Goldstone would not go. Having been shown into the waiting-room with the courtesy usually extended to those who were known, he had settled down there, with no disposition to withdraw unless he were forcibly ejected. If Lady Crystal were not at home, his visit was on a matter of such urgency that he would await her return. He went to a writing-table that was provided for the use of callers, and wrote a short note to be given to Lady Crystal when she should come in.

Learning this, she asked Miss Preston to bring it to her. It read:

DEAR LADY CRYSTAL,

The matter on which I wish to see you is of the utmost urgency as affecting your sister's liberty. Will you please give me five minutes? I am sure you will regret it should you decline to do so.

Yours sincerely,

ISRAEL GOLDSTONE
28.1.34

She was on the couch when Molly Preston came in. She had just rung for tea. She looked rather sleepy, but quite serene. She had been obliged to give Miss Preston a partial confidence, which might have to be extended further, but that was no reason why she should expose her feelings to her.

"Mr. Goldstone seems to be rather troublesome," she said lazily "You'd better see what he says."

Molly read the note aloud.

"What do you make of that?" Lady Crystal asked in the toneless voice of one who seeks information in a routine way."

"I think he's a clever Jew. Shall I see him for you, and send him away?"

"He's not clever, he's insolent. No, I'll see him myself. Have him shown up here. Molly"—she called her back from the door—"see that my tea comes in first. Send another cup in for him, after he's here. Just after. I don't think he'll be here long."

Three minutes later Mr. Goldstone was shown in. Lady Crystal received him without rising. He thought her a lovely vision, as she would have expected him to do. He thought her to be undisturbed by any expectation of the object of his visit, which was first blood to her. He admired her with reservations, as he might admire a costly and beautiful museum specimen, which did not stir his emotions to a desire for possession. He liked women of a more softly opulent, a more subordinate kind.

Different though they were, they were alike in self-confident assurance of their own superiority, both individually and by right of sex, and alike in superficiality of understanding of their protagonist.

Lady Crystal said coldly: "I don't usually receive anyone at this hour on Sundays, but I thought you'd better come up to explain that note." The note lay carelessly open beyond the tea-tray, on the little table beside her couch. It was turned rather to him than to her. It seemed to have been cast aside as a casual thing. Her tone did not indicate any anxiety as to her sister's welfare. It seemed to ask explanation of an impertinence.

Mr. Goldstone would have preferred another opening. The question of Jehane's liberty had fulfilled its mission, which was to assist him upstairs. But he must follow the path he had chosen. He said:

"It's about that letter I showed you last Thursday evening. It's turned out to be a very serious thing. The police want to know what reason we had for regarding it as authentic, and why we didn't give them all the information we might have done when we sent it to them two days ago. As things are now, I can't refuse to give them any help in my power. But I thought I'd let Lady Jehane know first, and have any explanation she can give. Of course, she may be able to help very materially by putting us on the track of the murderer. But I don't want to have to give them the information that we published it on a tip from her, without having her explanation ready. It's a case of murder now, as well as a number of other things, and the police are in a mood to arrest anyone. They'd probably arrest on suspicion while their enquiries proceeded."

"Mr. Goldstone, are you suggesting that the police may arrest Lady Jehane on suspicion of murdering someone, and, if so, do you expect me to take it seriously? To begin with, would you mind telling me who's been murdered?"

"A park-keeper was killed in the outrage in Kensington Gardens this morning."

"Then you can tell the police that Lady Jehane wasn't occupied in murdering park-keepers in London. She's in the country for the weekend."

"I'm afraid that wouldn't be quite enough. Would you mind giving me her address, and I'll see what I can do?"

"Is it likely, after what you've just said? If you're serious, you can come and see her tomorrow. If you're suggesting that she had anything to do with that silly letter, I can tell you at once that you're quite wrong. It ought to be too absurd to discuss, but, if you want to know, I'll tell you that we talked it over after you'd gone, and I'm certain that she knew no more about it than I did myself "

"Then why did she telephone me during the night, advising me…to publish it?"

"Did she do that?"

"Yes, or it probably wouldn't have appeared at all."

"Have you any record of that conversation?"

"No, but I remember it clearly."

"And if she did, wasn't it good advice? Didn't it cause you to take it seriously and send it to the police, as you've just said? Do you really mean to tell me that you're going to inform the police that Lady Jehane's judgment was better than yours, and that they'll arrest her for taking that letter seriously? Mr. Goldstone, if I didn't think you were talking the most random nonsense that I ever heard, I should ring up Sir Bardsley, and ask him to speak to the Home Secretary. Do you know who we are?"

Mr. Goldstone did not answer that question. He felt that he was in acute danger of being ordered out of the room. The entrance of a butler with the additional tea-cup which had been ordered for him in advance gave him a moment's conversational respite.

As the door closed, he said: "You are doing me a great injustice, Lady Crystal. I came here as a friend. I have a theory as to the writer of that letter which I have not spoken of to anyone. It might exonerate Lady Jehane entirely, while explaining her knowledge of its authenticity. If I communicate her name to the police as having advised its publication—I might almost say guaranteed its contents—they may either proceed against her directly, or come to the conclusion that I have formed already.

"About three weeks ago one of the cleverest scientists of the age suddenly and mysteriously disappeared. Mr. Maitland was his closest friend, and his business agent. Since his disappearance, Mr. Maitland is known to have visited his flat and dealt with his affairs. My presumption is that William Feltham wrote that letter, and is in hiding while he watches what its effects will be.

"If I am right, he will be hanged within three months of this date. Whether Mr. Maitland and Lady Jehane will be merely giving evidence against him, or charged with him as accessories either before or after the event, I cannot say, but I suppose that it may largely depend upon their attitude now.

"Whatever they may know of that letter, much or little, it appears to me that it is of the first importance, in their own interests, that it should be promptly and voluntarily offered.

"You will appreciate that the scoundrel who wrote it, whoever he may be, has not only committed a murderous outrage, he has threatened a repetition of his crime on a larger scale. At the best, he is a dangerous lunatic, who cannot safely be left at large. Alternately, the police have the task of arresting one of the worst criminal pests that the world has seen. I suppose that, when the facts are known, there will be no one from end to end of the country who will harbour him for an hour. That he will be laid by the heels within the next few days is an almost certain thing.

"For Mr. Maitland or Lady Jehane to be associated with such a character in any way cannot be other than detrimental, unless the matter be handled very carefully, however innocent they may be.

"I have come to you in the first instance, while the police are waiting for information which, under the circumstances, they expect to be promptly given, and you will pardon me saying that you are hardly receiving me in the wisest way."

Lady Crystal listened to this somewhat lengthy statement with an expressionless face, and without interruption. She did not offer him the tea for which she had made provision, the cup remaining empty between them. As he finished she rose, saying: "You are mistaken in that, Mr. Goldstone, as in other things. I shall pardon nothing that you have said this afternoon, and you have entered my house for the last time.

"You make a random assumption that the letter was written by Mr. Feltham, and on that assumption you make a number of offensive suggestions, as though it were a proved thing. When I tell you that I am sure you are wrong about that, and that Mr. Feltham never wrote it at all, you can form your own opinions to what I think of the other suggestions that you have thought fit to make.

"If any member of my family should be annoyed by the police, they may find that we are quite able to defend ourselves. If we should be attacked in any other manner, I would remind you that there is a law of libel which we are not too weak to set in operation against you. Miss Preston, Mr. Goldstone is leaving now, and you will give instructions that he is not to be admitted again."

Molly Preston, who had entered in response to the bell which had rung in her own room, led Mr. Goldstone to the end of the corridor which was the entrance to Lady Crystal's private apartment, and handed him over to the care of a waiting footman.

Mr. Goldstone had risen when Lady Crystal rose, and had heard his dismissal with an impassive face. He could conceal his feelings as well as she.

Only when Miss Preston was parting from him did his face break into a smile. "*Au revoir*, my dear young lady, *au revoir*," he said pleasantly. She made no answer, nor did she repeat the remark to Lady Crystal, by whom she was right in supposing that it would not have been well received.

Left alone, Lady Crystal dropped the catch on the inside of the door which secured her from the improbability of unsummoned intrusion. For the moment, she was unsure of herself, unsure of her self-control.

What had she done? What had she meant? Where did she stand? Was Stanley already a hunted criminal whom no one, knowing him for what he was, would harbour in all the land? Had she stood by him, or cast him off? Was there still time, still a way, in which this monstrous evil could be pushed aside? If so, she knew that all her influence, all her wealth, would be employed on that service. If only she could have Stanley back and resume the sane prosperity to which she had mapped their lives! If only Jehane would come!

CHAPTER TWENTY

MR. GOLDSTONE'S car returned rapidly through the deserted Sunday streets, and his brain moved with an ever greater agility.

He had been repulsed, but he was not entirely dissatisfied. He did not guess the truth. Against that, Lady Crystal's attitude had screened her husband successfully. She had given him the impression that she was angry rather than agitated, and that that anger was occasioned by the enormity of his suggestion that this matter could invade her peace. Yet in the assumption of that attitude she had made certain statements which showed him that he was on the right track, even though he might be in greater doubt than before as to what its end would reveal. She had said two things which his trained instinct for news had retained for a later consideration. She had said that Jehane knew no more of the letter than she did herself. There was an ambiguity about that declaration which he had not appreciated at the time, owing to the way in which it had been spoken. He saw now that it had no more than a doubtful significance. But she had also said with assurance that William Feltham had not sent that letter. He had recognised a tone of conviction in that declaration, which disposed him to believe her, which he was yet reluctant to do. He had felt sure that it was Feltham's work. Everything had pointed in that direction. If it were not, he did not see whose it could be.

Yet, without more knowledge than she had disclosed, how should she be able to meet that suggestion with such a confident negative? Had she written it herself? It was too absurd to consider. Had Mr. Maitland? The absurdity was no less. Lady Jehane? He might, with difficulty, have considered the possibility that she had done it as an anonymous joke, but there was no joke in that blackened patch in Kensington Gardens. No joke in that severed leg. Such speculations were a waste of time. Respectable people in assured positions did not indulge in such criminal pranks, even if they had the diabolical knowledge that they required. And neither Maitland nor the Norchester women had any training in or special knowledge of applied science.

No, Feltham was the man. And if Lady Crystal knew that it was not he, she must know something—it was a probability, though not strictly a logical consequence—of who it was. Why should she seek to protect such a character? Might not the explanation lie in the wording of the note by which he had gained access to her? He decided that he had overreached himself by an unwarrantable suggestion which she would not forgive. Yet, even so, he was not disposed to condemn the course he had adopted. It was better than to have come away without seeing her. And now, what should he tell the Home Office, or the police?

As to that, his disposition was to tell them what he knew or surmised in a way that would make Lady Crystal regret her rudeness. He could easily put the case in a way that would give her further trouble before the evening would be over, that would oblige her to give Lady Jehane's address, lest it should be sought in more public ways. That would be what she deserved.

Yet he hesitated, with a doubt that he had not determined when he descended ponderously from his car, and ascended to his editorial office. It might be considered his duty to the State to inform the police of that midnight conversation with Lady Jehane, yet he saw that, if he were silent, it was a thing which no one would ever know. She was not likely to talk of it. Had he a record of it? Lady Crystal had asked. Of course, he had none.

And he saw that, if he kept silent about that incident, and about the interview that he had just had, there was nothing, even, that could connect the letter with the absent Feltham. That meant that he could use the resources of his paper for the further scoop of a private discovery. He need tell nothing to the police till he could say: "The murderer is there—and here is the evidence to convict him." Knowing what he did, was it not almost certain that he could outdistance the police in a chase at which all the world would be looking on?

It was a tempting, but somewhat dangerous course to prefer, and he was in sufficient doubt to be disposed to ask the opinions of his colleagues, as he rarely did. But when he entered the office he learnt something which quickly resolved his mind.

He found excitement and the anger of disappointment. The Home Office had let them down. Where they had anticipated exclusive copy, they had got no more, perhaps even less, than their rivals. It was not that Plumpton Marshall had acted with deliberate bad faith, or had endeavoured to dupe Mr. Goldstone into supplying the information which he so urgently needed. That would have been too dangerous a procedure, even had it not been alien from Mr. Marshall's habitual rectitude. A great newspaper can hit back in so many ways. It was the result of a decision of the Cabinet Council which Sir Bardsley Clinton had hastily summoned that afternoon. Whether to inform the public fully upon the character and circumstances of the outrage before there could be any announcement of the discovery of its perpetrator was a question on which Mr. Marshall had been vacillating for several hours, and to do so was against the judgment of Scotland Yard. He had given way in the hope of obtaining valuable assistance from Mr. Goldstone in return, seeing clearly enough that the vital issue was not whether the public should be momentarily alarmed, but that it should be protected effectually. If information could be obtained, it would be a high price that he would not pay.

But the Cabinet decision had swept these doubts aside. There had been a sharp division of opinion as to the gravity of the affair. Some held that the country was menaced with an impossible tyranny, or an outrage of the first magnitude. Others saw no more than an elaborate practical joke of a monstrous kind, which had resulted in an unexpected fatality. But there was a general agreement that nothing would be gained by official reticence. The press and the public had got to know.

Scotland Yard (there was an equal agreement) had shown extraordinary ineptitude. To have regarded the letter as a silly hoax, and to have done nothing, might have been no worse than an excusable error of judgment. To take inadequate precautions was of a less defensible folly. Was it not evident that the miscreants who had committed the outrage must have secreted themselves in the Gardens before the gates were closed on Saturday, or scaled the palings during the night? To be warned in advance, to regard that warning with sufficient seriousness to take certain precautions, and for these precautions to be so inadequate!

Mr. Plumpton Marshall, foreseeing resignations at Scotland Yard, and in some concealed trepidation as to whether the public might not think they should include that of its official head, however little responsibility he might really have, suggested weakly that no one could guard against an unsuspected treachery. Was it not highly probable that the outrage had been committed by Park-Inspector Kimpson himself, and that he had lost his life through withdrawing too tardily from the area which he had been hired to desolate?

This suggestion was somewhat coldly received by his fellow-ministers, but its possibility was hinted in several of the newspapers of the following morning, and was widely accepted by the public during the day.

Mr. Goldstone assembled his staff. He said that he had made a bargain with the Home Secretary a few hours ago which had not been kept. He would say no more about that. They would understand that, on this matter at least, the *Morning Standard* would give neither assistance nor information whatever, either to the Home Office or the police. But it was of the first consequence for the prestige of the paper that the discovery of the writer of the letter should be made by them. On this trail he could give them pointers which should enable them to outpace their competitors in the search. Mr. William Feltham, the missing scientist, was, in all probability, the inspiration of the letter, if not its actual author. Lady Jehane Norchester probably knew more about it than she would be ready to tell. With this information he could trust them to have something for him within twenty-four hours which it would be a pleasure to print.

He dismissed them to the chase, and turned to Miss Rimington to dictate his leader on "The Supineness of the Police." He considered that it would be about by next Thursday that the time would be ripe to follow it with another entitled "Plumpton Marshall Must Go." He could not know that by that time he would be thinking about quite different things.

He was condemning the supineness of the Metropolitan police in sonorous sentences when Mr. Marshall rang through again to know if he had any information to give him, and received a curt and final negative.

It was a first result of this reticence that the police ran on a cold scent, and that Stanley Maitland walked into the House of Commons on Monday afternoon having been unmolested during the day, and without exciting more notice than is usually given to Under-Secretaries whose departments are not concerned with the business which is before it.

CHAPTER TWENTY-ONE

IT was Monday afternoon when Jehane's car, of which she was the only occupant, arrived at Norchester House, and slackened speed as it turned into the wide passage-way which ran along the side of that imposing structure to reach the extensive stabling in the rear, part of which had now been converted into a glass-roofed garage.

As she turned slowly from the treacherous surface of a freezing road to that of the gravelled byway, a young lady stepped forward, and said in a pleasant manner, but with a nervous quickness, "May I speak to you for a moment, Lady Jehane?"

Jehane pulled up: "Yes, of course. What is it?"

The young lady presented a card which declared that she was Miss Vera Hastings, of the *Morning Standard*. She said, "I've been trying to see you since early this morning. It's very important that I shouldn't go back without—I mean important for me. It's my first week at the job."

"Well, you've done it now." The words might have been satirical, but for the smile with which they were said. The two girls looked at one another with a mutual liking. Jehane paused for a moment, debating the wisdom of such an interview, but she was in excellent spirits herself, and disposed to be kind to others. Miss Hastings' plea that it was important—for her—was irresistible. But she was not going to show that she guessed the object of this importunity. She asked: "You want an interview about something?"

"Yes, very particularly."

"Then if you'll ask for me at the front, I shan't be more than ten minutes. Tell them I'm expecting you, and you wish to wait till I return. You needn't say I'm here now. If you do, you'll probably have to wait for another hour."

Jehane thought that any publicity given to her arrival might mean the commencement of an interview with her sister of uncertain duration. She thought she would get this one over first. Also, she needed a wash.

She would have driven on but for the evident dissatisfaction in Vera Hastings's face at the instructions she had received. Vera hesitated whether to speak, but a risk was better than a certain failure. "I don't think," she said "they'd let me in." She looked at Jehane's face in some doubt as to whether this evidence of her unpopularity at Norchester House would result in a refusal of the promised interview. Jehane certainly looked more thoughtful than before. Then she said cryptically, "So the game's begun already? Hop in." She leaned over to swing the door wide. Vera got into the car, which was run quickly into the garage.

There was a side stairway designed for the use of the master of Norchester House at a time when one of its most famous features had been the horses its stables held. It led from the upper floors to a passage the door of which opened into the garage yard. Now it was little used except by Jehane, who held the key of its Yale lock, and with a brief instruction to the garage attendant to have her suitcase sent up at once, she led Miss Hastings to the privacy of her own rooms.

"Come in here," she said easily, with the lack of reticence which grows on those whose attendants are always round them, "while I get rid of some dirt. I can't give you more than a few minutes. What's the racket about?"

"I want to ask you a few questions about the Kensington Gardens outrage."

"So I supposed. Everyone seems to be asking everyone else questions about that today. But why me?"

"Because Mr. Goldstone says that it was through you that the letter was published."

"That rather reflects on himself, doesn't it? Couldn't he see it was genuine without help? Well, I gave him the straight tip. What of that?"

"Well, I hoped…"—Miss Hastings smiled appealingly—"…I felt sure you'd be able to tell us a bit more."

"What about?"

"We're naturally anxious, as we published the letter, to be the first to announce the author's name. Of course, we see that it can't be kept back many hours. It's too big a thing, with all the excitement it's caused."

"I'm sorry I can't tell you that."

"But you do know?"

"Yes, I know all right. I don't mind telling you this. Sir Bardsley Clinton will know it before midnight. I suppose all the world will know it tomorrow. But I think that will rest with him to decide."

Miss Hastings looked interested. Her pencil became busy. She I also looked puzzled. "I don't see how even Sir Bardsley could keep a thing like that to himself. You see, apart from any other considera-tion, it's a criminal offence. The inquest's being held this afternoon. Lady Jehane," she added, her voice changing to an appeal, "you can't really want to shelter a man like that?"

"Of course I don't want anything so silly. I'd as soon think of sheltering St. Paul's with a parasol."

Miss Hastings smiled at this unexpected reply. It was a different view of the matter from that prevailing in the offices of the *Morning Standard*. She smiled: "So that's how it appears to you?"

"Yes. That's just it. You can tell Mr. Goldstone from me that I gave him the straight tip before, and I'm giving it him again. He'd better write another leader for tomorrow telling people that that let-ter meant just what it said, and it's going to be a great game. Now I'm sorry, but I shall have to ask you to go…Clara," to the maid who had entered promptly, in reply to the sharp brevity of the ring which was known through the house as Lady Jehane's characteristic summons, "show Miss Hastings the way out; and tell whoever's been rude to her when she called before that they're not to insult my visitors again without orders from me direct. Not if they want to stay here."

Clara said: "Yes, my lady," with a discreet acquiescence. They both knew that whatever had occurred must have been at Lady Crys-tal's own order, and Norchester House was hers. But Jehane had never been one to settle down in a back seat. And this afternoon she felt in particularly good form. In the metaphor of her own vocabulary she had her tail in the air.

She delayed Clara for a moment to ask, "Is Lady Crystal in?" And then, "Let her know I'm coming along. I'll have some tea brought in there."

She occupied a few further moments in the completion of a careless toilet, and to give time for Crystal to be informed of her arrival, and then went to her sister's apartment.

CHAPTER TWENTY-TWO

LADY CRYSTAL showed neither surprise nor any other emotion on learning that Jehane had returned. "Oh, yes. Thank you, Clara. Yes, tea for both of us here." That had been her occupation since Mr. Goldstone's departure on the afternoon of the previous day—showing no emotion to anyone; and, though it is not an expression she would have been likely to use, she had found maintaining of that outward serenity to be a full-time job. She had not known, from moment to moment, when the bomb which Mr. Goldstone had threatened, and which he was certainly able to fling, might explode beneath or around her. She could not guess whether she had outfaced him successfully. She read his leader in the *Morning Standard*, and felt some hope that she had, for she was of a trained and perhaps inherited shrewdness of judgment on all questions of a political kind, and she did not think it to be written in the tone of one who had just assisted the police with vital information of an exclusive kind. Still, he was not a man who would be easily silenced. Nor were the police enquiries dependent entirely upon him. Knowing what she did, it seemed that Feltham's name, the mystery of his disappearance, the originality of his genius, the probability that he was in some way concerned in the outrage which had startled London, must be present to every mind. She did not sufficiently realise the extent or variety of the possibilities which the police must consider, or that she herself, however important, was only one among five million of Londoners, and Norchester House only one among a million homes.

She could only think that her husband, Stanley Maitland, till yesterday of unstained reputation and the expectation of a brilliant future, was today an absurd and monstrous criminal, of whose arrest she might hear at any moment that his identity should become known, that she might hear at any moment that her sister had been traced and ignominiously detained for complicity in what she could not regard as other than a hateful, useless, communistic crime. And she could do nothing more, nothing better, than to maintain this aspect of serene indifference, while she waited for some development, of whatever kind. To move, to speak, could have no effect but to draw the lightning upon her house, and while there yet remained the faintest chance that the storm might pass, leaving it still unwrecked—so she thought, looking for Jehane's return, for it was in her that her hope lay.

Jehane entered the room.

"Hullo, Crys," she greeted her with irreverent sisterly freedom, "been wondering whether I'd bring him back to your longing arms? Well, I did what I could. We had it out all the way to Merton-Ash in the car, and half Sunday morning, while Rigby sulked in the rear, and all the afternoon while I was supposed to be taking down a great speech for tonight, and the trouble was that at the end of it all I hadn't converted him; he'd nearly converted me. And then at tea-time someone had a call through from London, and we heard what had happened, and, of course, there's no going back after that. So we talked it over this morning, and Stanley's gone to the House, and I've come along here to let you know."

Crystal struggled for an outward calmness. She would have facts in a falling world, "What does Stanley propose to do at the House?"

"Nothing particular tonight, unless he stops that silly bill about the performing fleas."

"Can't you be serious, even now? You know there isn't...."

"Well, then, the conforming fleas. You can't deny they'll have to be that if the bill goes through. With all the officials they'll have to keep them in order, they'll have to be conforming to something or other all the time. They'll probably make them jump to a measured length; or say they're not to jump at all except between six and eight. You couldn't say Stanley'd be doing any harm if he stopped such nonsense as that."

"You seem to forget that Stanley's in the Colonial Office. The bill's no business of his. Besides, it's a government measure. He's bound to support it if he says anything at all."

"Well, I dare say he'll let it go through, though I don't see why he should. The fleas haven't done him any harm. At least, not that I know of. You ought to know best about that. But he'll probably have more important things on his mind. All I really know is that he's going to have a heart-to-heart talk with Sir Bardsley some time before morning, and after that he'll decide whether the government's to remain, or whether he'll carry on in his own way. But what I promised him was that I'd find out whether you're going to fit into the new scheme. He seems to think you're a size too small."

At another time, with smaller issues at stake, perhaps even at such an extremity had it been of a more precedented or conventional kind, Crystal would have declined to discuss her relations with Stanley, and would have resented the fact that he should have done so. She would have closed the conversation with the chilling silence with which Jehane was familiar from early days, but which she had never allowed to lower her own temperature to any discomfortable level. As it was, she answered with a literal seriousness.

"If he wishes to know that, you'll have to tell me more clearly what he proposes to do. If he's trying to find a way out of the trouble he's in, he's only got to come home and talk it over, and I'll help in every way that I can. I think you both know that. It seems to me that it was Feltham's doing rather than his. It was unfortunate about that park-keeper being killed, but I'm not sure we couldn't get over that. We might have Feltham's horrible things destroyed, and Stanley thanked for finding them out, and all the risks that he took. If I got Sir Bardsley here to dinner tomorrow, and Jimmy Shackston, and perhaps Sir George, and we talked it over frankly together.... I've been thinking about this all day, if things haven't gone too far before then. Of course, Sir Bardsley could stop the police, and if it were put to the press in the right way. And if they said that Stanley'd have to resign, we might go abroad for a time, and when the next election came they'd be glad for us to help again. I'd do that, and more. I'm married to Stanley, and when people are married I don't think any trouble ought to separate them. But if you mean that Stanley's trying to upset the government that he's pledged to support—well, I don't know whether I'm a size too small or too large, but I'm not the right size for that."

Jehane looked and listened. She knew by every sign that the fight was lost, and restrained a characteristic impulse to end the conversation with a scornful word. But she had pledged herself to Stanley to explain matters from his standpoint, and she saw that she must exercise her limited and unpractised stores of diplomacy and patience if she were to keep her promise. She said:

"He doesn't want to cut loose, and I suppose you think you're a cross between an angel and a good sport, or something a bit better than that. But the trouble is that you think too much of Jumping Jimmy and Sir Bardsley's beard. Not that he's so bad in himself. Sir Bardsley's a dear. But what Stanley wants to do is to stop them going on making laws that get sillier every year, like the one they've got on tonight."

"If you really think that Sir Bardsley and all the other members of the government are going to do just what he tells them because he threatens them with wholesale murder unless they do, it only shows how little either of you understand what politics are. I'm not discussing whether it would be right or wrong. If they agreed to his face, they'd find a hundred ways of getting round him till they could get this thing, whatever it is, out of his hands. And, besides, unless he could command a majority in the House…and it wouldn't make much difference if he did. If people knew he was forcing laws down their throats they wouldn't swallow them, any more than they swallow prohibition in the United States."

Jehane knew, though she might not welcome the knowledge, that there was much both of truth and common sense in her sister's first contention. But she had never thought that Stanley was taking on an easy thing. It was that that gave it the thrill! Yet as Crystal spoke, she admitted to herself that to control the fifteen men who formed the inner circle of the coalition government to any continuity of straightforward action which was against their own interests or desires would be an almost impossible thing, even under the impulse of an urgent fear. She knew them too well; she had seen them at close quarters, these men who had talked and schemed and wriggled themselves into the positions they held. And she knew, too, that there was force in Crystal's second argument. One man can lead a horse to the water, but—. She thought of Bismarck's "imponderables." Recognising its strength, she refused battle on the ground that Crystal had offered.

"You don't understand in the least," she answered, "because you don't try to understand Stanley's point of view. You begin by being sure that it's wrong. He doesn't want to make any laws, or scarcely any at all. It's the ghastly habit of making laws without ever stopping that he wants to knock on the head. Nobody really wants it done, and nobody really understands how it all began. But it's got to a pace now that can't stop itself unless someone interferes from outside. No one really wants all his money spent for him. He'd far rather spend it himself. What Stanley wants to do is to teach English people to walk without holding a nurse's hand. He says we did it once, and we can do it again unless we're all suffering from senile decay. It does sound the better way, even if we fall now and then, and get a bruise that we might have missed. Fancy being able to buy a match after midnight, without looking at the clock first."

"I don't know," Crystal answered coldly, "whether you've really got any idea what nonsense you're talking. All the progress of the last fifty years—the Shop Hours Restriction Act has been of immeasurable advantage to scores of thousands who...."

"Yes, I dare say it has. First we're given all the comfort and safety of slaves, and then there's nothing left for us but to die out, as slaves always do. Already we're being killed in scores of thousands on the roads, and we haven't the courage or wit to stop it, because there's a great vested interest and a lot of other people's pleasure at stake. No one seems to mind that happening, as long as we've got plenty of laws about it, and the slaughter's all regulated."

"You've had one or two accidents yourself."

"Yes. And you're having one now."

The two retorts indicated the bankruptcy of reasoned argument. Jehane became uncomfortably aware that she was echoing Stanley's opinions rather than expressing her own, and that it was even possible that she was not stating them quite as he would have approved. The fact was that she could have gone on very contentedly without being aware of the various slaveries she endured. She knew the joy of watching the speedometer's hand move downward to those figures which must be safe, because there is numerically overwhelming evidence that all accidents take place among cars that are running at lower speeds. She knew the joy of cutting in when the safety margin of seconds is scarcely plural, and had twice been landed in the ditch from the usual cause, which is the bad driving of other cars. She was joining in with Stanley because, in her own phrase, she thought it a great game.

Crystal withdrew into silence because she felt that such argument was a futile folly. If Stanley supposed that he could manage the British Empire, that he could stay "the wheels of progress," or alter the minds of men, he had got to learn sense, and her own sense told her that that learning might be a very painful thing. And what could she do, for him as for herself, but stand aside, and give any help which might still be in her power when the inevitable end should come?

She did not observe that it was those "wheels of progress" which she had been trained to respect, which had placed in Stanley's hands the fatal power which Feltham would otherwise have used to a more sinister purpose.

It was after a period of silence, pregnant with mutual understanding, that Jehane, asked: "Are you going to turn me out too?"

"I haven't turned anyone out. I couldn't have anything of that kind carried on from this house. You ought to see that."

"Well, I'll think it over. I shan't go unless I want. We'll see which way the cat jumps."

Jehane got up abruptly, and left the room.

Crystal touched the bell. She rose also, and walked to the windows, standing with her back to the room while the tea-things were cleared away. For the moment, she was not sure that she could show the outward serenity which she had maintained for the last two days. She looked down upon a darkening pavement, and into an air through which a thin sleet was falling. She remembered that the High Anglican Church which she supported did not approve of divorce under any circumstances. Even dishonour, even lunacy, was not sufficient to justify the breaking of marriage vows. And what lunacy could be worse than this? Had she failed on her side? She could not see that she had. She had not deserted Stanley, but he her. He had not merely contrived a physical desertion. He had deserted all their common interests, their common ambitions, the way in which they had planned their lives. She had given him all she had, and she had got less than nothing in return. Perhaps for the first time, she wished that she had had a child. She thought her church had a hard law. And she could do nothing but wait events.

Sir Bardsley Clinton sat rather sleepily in his place on the Front Government Bench. He was not a young man, and the long irregular parliamentary hours tired him more than they had done in earlier days. Long experience in that position, and on the opposite bench, had taught him to doze in an unobtrusive way. The House had filled an hour ago to hear Mr. Plumpton Marshall make a statement upon the Kensington Gardens outrage; but it was nearly empty now, while a back-bench member urged the necessity of controlling the undisciplined, uncultivated, unrestricted flea.

No one noticed particularly when Mr. Maitland changed his position. He moved to the seat immediately behind the Premier. He touched him lightly on the shoulder, and leant over whispering. Sir Bardsley Clinton roused himself to reply. "Certainly, Maitland," he said, "certainly. About the Kensington Gardens outrage? You might join me in my own room, say, in ten minutes from now." That would give him time for a whisky-and-soda, before Maitland would follow. The back-bench member sat down, and Sir Bardsley rose at once, and passed out behind the Speaker's chair. By going at that moment he avoided offending even the most obscure, the most tiresome of his too-large majority. No one would resent the Premier's withdrawing while his own eloquence was descending upon him. It was largely by such unobtrusive urbanities that Sir Bardsley had won the position which he now held.

CHAPTER TWENTY-THREE

SIR BARDSLEY CLINTON was a mild-mannered man with a courteous manner sometimes approaching the deferential, and a benign beard. No one had ever seen him seriously disconcerted, or his temper the worse for wear. When the Hon. James Shackston had threatened mutiny before the last election if Sir Bardsley allowed Sir George Donnington to have his way over the Australian difficulty, he had listened without interruption for about twenty minutes to Shackston's angry protests, and then said patiently: "And now, Jimmy, would you mind passing the nuts?"

Rightly or not, the country saw strength in that imperturbable attitude. It credited Sir Bardsley with a cool sanity on which it relied. It might throw him over in its more hysterical moods, but it would come back to him again. It had known all the time that it would be likely to do so, and so, doubtless, had he. It considered that he was a very safe man.

He showed no surprise when Stanley said that he could inform him fully concerning the anonymous letter and its following incident, though his eyes became more alert under their bushy brows. "I rather thought," he said quietly, "that we should soon know."

"If we could have an uninterrupted hour," Stanley replied, "I think it might be best to explain the whole matter, so that you will know just where I stand."

"You wish me to infer that you are personally concerned?"

"Yes."

"Then I think, Mr. Maitland, you have done well to come to me at once. There are aspects in which it is a matter of some gravity. If it will assist you, you may accept my assurance that, so far as my public duty will permit, I shall respect your confidence—so far, of course, as that will permit."

"It is a point which I am prepared to leave to your discretion," Stanley answered. The words were not impolite, but the tone, and perhaps the form of the sentence, had a shade of difference from that in which Under-Secretaries of State would usually address Sir Bardsley in such a conference. It is unlikely that he failed to observe it, but he gave no sign. He only said: "The division is not likely to be taken in less than fifty minutes from now. I can give you till then."

"Very well, then I'll take it from the start. You'll remember how Feltham disappeared a few weeks ago? Yes. And I dare say you know that I was his business agent, and practically his only friend. That's how the whole thing began. He didn't really disappear. At least, I mean he didn't go away. He disappeared a good deal more completely than most men do. He went up the chimney in a rather acrid brown smoke. He died of a poison which he had just tried on a cat with the same result, and then I tried it on him. If he were here, he'd say that I poisoned him in a very treacherous way."

"Are you sure you are wise to be so extremely frank?"

"Yes. I know where I'm ending up, and you'll understand better if you know how it began. I'll tell you how Feltham died, and why."

Sir Bardsley listened to the narrative that followed without further interruption, until Stanley came to where he shook those brittle ashes into the fire, and cleaned up the mess. Then he said mildly: "I think you acted with a courageous discretion. I think we owe you a debt."

"Well, I'm glad you look at it like that."

"Up to that point, yes. As to what may follow, I cannot judge till I hear. But I think you should have informed the police. Perhaps, if you had given me an earlier confidence—."

"Well, I thought about that. As it's turned out, it might have saved a park-keeper's life, which I should have been glad to do. But I don't know that you'd have taken it seriously. I think Feltham'd probably say that I haven't done enough now. But I'd better go on from that point, and make it all clear."

Sir Bardsley said, rather coldly: "Yes. I think you had."

He sat very still while the narrative proceeded, with an expressionless face, and then asked with a quiet seriousness: "Do you wish me to understand, Mr. Maitland, that this infernal apparatus is set so that, if anything should happen to you—if you should suddenly die—it would destroy a large part of the centre of London on the 31st of December next, and no one could prevent that result?"

"Yes, that's just how it is. If anyone should interfere, without understanding the controls, it's almost certain that they would set it off at once. Practically a certain thing."

"And you have allowed this appalling possibility—?"

"I am a young and healthy man, and I have been very careful of my life during recent weeks."

"But the dangers of the streets—the incessant dangers—I wonder that you could dare."

"On the contrary, I have thought of them as a reason why I must go ahead."

"Do you mean that you think that they can be sensibly diminished? I can assure you, Mr. Maitland, as you should already know, that we have done all that has been humanly possible to reduce the number of these distressing fatalities."

"They could be stopped in a week."

"You are speaking with some heat, Mr. Maitland. Perhaps with more heat than you are aware. I can assure you that if you have any feasible plan. But it is better to keep our minds cool. Perhaps if we regard abstract considerations in the first place and let the concrete remain to a later stage. No, Reynolds"—to an anxiously intruding secretary—"I know that's the division bell, but I'm not coming out to vote, nor is Mr. Maitland—you're quite safe without us? So I supposed. I shan't want to be disturbed tor another hour."

CHAPTER TWENTY-FOUR

STANLEY had found a good listener. Sir Bardsley interrupted little, and then rather with a view to informing himself more accurately than of intruding his own opinions.

Mr. Reynolds did not venture a further interruption, and it was more than an hour later that Sir Bardsley remarked, with his usual mildness: "There's a good deal in what you say, Mr. Maitland. You've interested me very much. We're always making new laws, as you say, and I dare say we've got into a habit of thinking—or of assuming without thought—that a country needs a supply of new laws every year, just as a man needs another meal every morning, or some new clothes every spring. And as we don't throw off the clothes we've already got, some overheating results. But, all the same, they may do less harm than you suppose, and sometimes they do actual good. And they keep the people quiet, Maitland. I wonder whether you've thought of that—and they're a great boon to the press.

"And you look round and see abuses, Maitland, and you feel indignant, as the young do—you'll pardon me for putting it in that way, but I'm a much older man—and you think that we might exert ourselves a bit more to stamp some of them out, and I don't say that you're wrong. But we haven't really much power, and I'll tell you how it's appeared to me for a good many years.

"You'll see that I'm paying you the compliment of taking you seriously. You're a much more dangerous man than Feltham could ever have been, because you're not thinking about yourself. We should soon have dealt with him, and if we hadn't, he'd have been no more than the nuisance of a few weeks, and then died out like a beast.

"I've been Premier of this country for a longer time than most of my predecessors, and I haven't mistaken myself for Mussolini, or thought that I was ever likely to rule the land. I've thought of myself as a doctor rather than a king. There may be abuses all round us—a wen here and a pimple there—but if the patient doesn't get feverish, I don't advise an operation. I don't think it's serious enough for that. The patient probably wouldn't consent, and if he did, I might do more harm than good.

"But if the temperature rises, then I know something ought to be done, and I give the best advice that I can; and if they don't like it, they call in someone else, and I cross the floor of the House till they feel they'd like to have me again."

"It's not a bad illustration," Stanley conceded. "Though it might be put in another way that wouldn't sound quite so well." He felt a greater difficulty in maintaining the attitude on which he had resolved against this considerate, almost deferential reception, than he would have done against a more hostile attitude, as a bullet may find less opposition in a tin plate than a feather bed.

"No doubt," Sir Bardsley agreed, without visible resentment. "Most things could...but I'll give you an illustration of what I mean. Take your own profession, which you haven't mentioned, though you've mentioned a good many things. It's got enough abuses to fill a book. It's so grossly overpaid that it has been customary for me to receive a smaller salary as Prime Minister than has been necessary to content my own Attorney or Solicitor-General. Had I thought that I could put the world right, that might have been a natural point at which to begin.

"But apart from that, there are the abuses of the law's costs, and the law's delays, of which everyone knows, and which a resolute effort by any government might sweep aside, for a time at least. Though I needn't tell you how fierce the opposition would be before we could dig out all the holes where your fraternity are entrenched—and the next generation would have things just as bad again in an altered form.

"But that isn't my point. What I want you to think over is that these tolerated abuses are seldom wholly bad, or they wouldn't be tolerated as they are. You said a little while ago that we share the profits of patent-medicine quacks instead of stamping them out, and so we're no better than poisoners and thieves. But even these things may do some good. I believe most of them are quite harmless, and they make a great many people happy, and some are cured by faith; and, for all I know, there may even be some preparation that does real good. You must see that it's a possible thing.

POWER, BY S. FOWLER WRIGHT * 103

"But I was talking about your own profession. You know even better than I how rank it is with systematised abuses and forms of cheating that the taxing-masters permit, and yet—quarrelling's always a bad thing. Are you sure we should make a happier world if we made it cheap and easy to do? And the law's delays, don't they give people time to cool down, and often come to terms?

"Mr. Maitland, I won't say more about things that you understand better than I, but I'll ask you to think of this"—and a persuasive earnestness came into his voice, such as he would often use on the public platform at the conclusion of one of his temperate, reasonable speeches which made the vehemence of the opposition seem such empty froth—"it's easier to break down than to build again. It's easier and more quickly done. But the thing that we would have in its place is a harder matter to contrive, and is often beyond our power."

He rose with the last words. He added in a lighter tone: "It's been a most interesting talk. It's a matter on which I must consult my colleagues. You won't expect me to say more than that tonight. I may say…." (with a slight disarming smile) "I don't think Feltham's invention could easily have fallen into worse hands. You'll take care of yourself, won't you, tonight? I'm rather fond of Westminster Abbey, and a few other things within the condemned area. I'm inclined to think I'd better ask Marshall to put a guard round Norchester House. I suppose you'll be there tonight?"

"No, I'm putting up at the Rafton."

Sir Bardsley looked puzzled for a brief moment, and then asked, with that acuteness which his opponents had learnt to dread: "Lady Crystal doesn't approve?"

"I haven't seen her since Thursday," Stanley fenced in reply.

"Women don't always see far ahead," Sir Bardsley answered. It was a generalisation beyond contradiction, and not requiring reply.

Stanley went, and Sir Bardsley was prompt to find Mr. Plumpton Marshall. He said: "Marshall, I wish you'd tell Scotland Yard at once that they're to watch Mr. Maitland wherever he goes. He'll be at the Rafton tonight. They must use their best men, whatever they have to call them off. They're to protect him from dangers of every kind, especially in the streets. And they're to watch the top flat in Dawlish Mansions in the same way. No one but Maitland's to be allowed in there in any circumstances. Let them know that the slightest failure will mean resignation all round. Yes, it's the Kensington affair. I'm telling Reynolds that I want a Cabinet meeting for tomorrow afternoon. I'll explain it all then."

CHAPTER TWENTY-FIVE

"I THINK, gentlemen," Sir Bardsley said to his assembled members, when Sampson Lynes broke in with an astonished query a second time, "I think I must ask you to hear me without interruption. When I have stated the position as I understand it to be, I shall be glad to have your views upon it."

The Minister of Education subsided into a difficult silence, and the Premier proceeded with a lucid unemotional statement of the power which Stanley Maitland claimed to possess, and of the use to which he designed to put it. "I have asked him," he concluded, "to meet us here in half an hour from this time."

The Hon. James Shackston opened a hard-set jaw to ask curtly: "What's the real game?"

"I am not aware," Sir Bardsley answered, "that I have failed to make the position clear. Mr. Maitland may be wise or foolish, but my impression is that he is an honest man."

"Of course, we're all that," Jumping Jimmy answered brusquely. "What does his honesty mean to do? Is he trying to kick us out and boss things his own way? And are we standing for that?"

"I'm not clear that he wishes to turn anyone out," Sir Bardsley answered mildly. "Not, at least, if we can come to an understanding today. He seemed to think we might work together to the same ends. Except," he added, "to be exact, except in the Ministry of Education." He turned to Mr. Sampson Lynes to explain. "He said that he considered it essential that your position should be occupied by an intelligent man."

Mr. Lynes responded to this incredible insolence in a way with which it is easy to sympathise. He said "I don't think it's a matter that needs much discussion. The man's a confessed murderer. We'd better have him arrested when he comes in."

Sir Bardsley looked at him thoughtfully. He said: "Yes, that is your view. Are there any others who regard it in the same way?"

The President of the Board of Trade, who was Mr. Lynes' closest political ally, interposed the question, "Did he let out why he attacked the Minister of Education particularly? What's his grudge against him?"

"There was no suggestion of any personal feeling. He said that if a carpenter thought he could use all kinds of wood in the same way...I'm afraid, Mr. Lynes, you would consider his ideas rather reactionary. I didn't go into the matter fully. It was only touched on in passing. He has ideas on so many things. He did suggest that a parent's views are entitled to consideration. If I understood him rightly, he would put them second only to those of the child. It is due to him to say that many of these ideas which seem disjointed are consistent with a common principle. He thinks that we are faced by a threat of national decadence. He regards it as a sinister fact that breeding has slackened, and emigration ceased. He appears hopeful that the virility of the race would revive in a freer, less governed atmosphere. He may be quite wrong about that, even if the nation would consent to walk on its own feet, after being wheeled about for a generation. Even if we accept all his hypotheses, we may still wonder whether he would do more than discover the difference between a perambulator and a Bath chair. Donnington, you know Maitland best of any of us here. How does this matter appear to you?"

Sir George answered with hesitation. He was a sound rather than a brilliant man, who had gained his present position by hard conscientious work, assisted by an inherited gift of bluff effective platform oratory, and the traditions and wealth of a great name. He said: "I've always liked Maitland. He's been the best Under-Secretary I've ever had. A bit uncertain in his ideas when we've been talking at large, but very practical when we a got an actual problem to face. I shouldn't think he'd be likely to play the fool. But it's a queer tale, all along. It isn't easy to take it seriously." He added inconsequently: "I wonder what Lady Crystal's thinking?"

"Mr. Maitland," Sir Bardsley explained, "has withdrawn from Norchester House. He's at the Rafton now."

"I'm sorry about that," Sir George answered, though he didn't say why. He added: "I shouldn't take this over-seriously. I don't think Maitland's a man to do anything really dreadful. Why not find him a place that would keep him busy among ourselves? But you've had the night to think this over, Clinton. I'd rather know what you think yourself."

"Gentlemen," the Premier said quietly, in response to this invitation, "so far as it rests with me so far as it's a possible thing—I'm inclined to give Mr. Maitland a chance."

The Hon. James Shackston stared at him with hard incredulous eyes. "And I say I'll be damned before I agree."

The abrupt defiance caused a sudden silence to fall on the room. If this were a signal of open war between the two strongest personalities in the Government, it might be one of those crises at which man may destroy or make his political future in a moment by the side he takes.

Sir Bardsley looked at the Hon. James in his unperturbed considering way. "Of course," he said, "you can resign. It might not be a bad thing. I'm not asking you to go, but a split in the Government over this might be just the thing to give Maitland the chance he needs."

There was subtlety here of a kind the results of which were familiar enough both to Sir Bardsley's friends and opponents, though it was seldom that he allowed it an open expression.

Jimmy Shackston stared at him harder than before. He half rose as though to withdraw from the room. As he did so, he looked across at Viscount Okehampton, on whose support in such differences he could rely with some confidence, but that gentleman kept his eyes on the table, and gave no sign. "Perhaps," he said, "it might be better to hear what he's got to say first."

"It does sound wiser," Sir Bardsley said tonelessly. The Hon. James looked at him with angry contemptuous eyes. He scribbled a note which he folded and passed along the table to Plumpton Marshall. That gentleman read: "*How about a couple of good alienists?*" and put the paper into his waistcoat pocket without any outward response.

The telephone instrument buzzed at Sir Bardsley's elbow. He took up the receiver. "Yes, Reynolds," he said, "show him in at once. Gentlemen, Mr. Maitland is here."

CHAPTER TWENTY-SIX

"I HOPE," Sir George Donnington remarked, in the brief pause which preceded Stanley's entrance, "I hope we're not going to wrangle before Maitland."

"I'm not going to be committed to anything," Shackston answered. "I'll speak out before that."

"I propose," Sir Bardsley explained, "to ask Mr. Maitland to state his own case, and it is open to anyone to ask him questions upon it. Such questions can be so framed that they do not disclose our own opinions. You may agree that it will be wiser to delay to do so, either individually or collectively. He may be asked to withdraw while we debate the position which has arisen."

Shackston said curtly: "That goes with me," and as he did so, Stanley entered.

He looked for the first time upon the Cabinet Room in which hundred momentous decisions have been taken, which has heard the altercations of a hundred government crises, and upon the dignified form of Sir Bardsley Clinton, sitting centrally at a long narrow table, with his back to the ample fireplace, as Disraeli and Gladstone and a score of English Premiers before and since had sat in that comfortable, plum-coloured, upholstered chair, with their ministers seated to right and left to the length of the plain, white-pillared, white-painted room, with its dull bookcases, and the bow-window facing Sir Bardsley which opened into a garden which was bleak enough now, but would be pleasantly cool and shaded in summer days.

"Mr. Maitland," Sir Bardsley said, as Stanley took the seat which was indicated, "I have already explained the nature of the power which you claim to hold, and the threat which I understood you to convey in the course of our conversation last evening. I may say that there is a more or less general feeling among us of doubt, or even of incredulity, as to whether that threat can be taken seriously. I am speaking for myself only, but I think I am expressing an opinion which would be generally shared when I say that though some things may have been done already which are, from one standpoint, of a somewhat serious complexion, such as the—the disposition of Mr. Feltham, and the obliteration in Kensington Gardens, with the unfortunate and doubtless unforeseen fatality which it entailed, yet we should not wish to be slow to recognise the exceptional—I may say the unprecedented—circumstances with which you were confronted, and I should myself be prepared to recommend to the House a short Bill of Indemnity, perhaps even with some substantial recognition of what might be regarded as a further service both in that which has been done already, and in refraining from that which it might still be, I will not say in your power, but in the power of a lesser man to do.

"Sir George Donnington, who has spoken of you in high, and doubtless well-deserved terms, alike as colleague and friend, appears to be clearly of opinion that you are as incapable as any among us of using this strange power which has come into your hands either for any selfish aggrandisement or to any arbitrary or unworthy end."

Sir Bardsley paused a moment as though inviting Stanley's assent to the certificate of character which he had bestowed upon him. The listening ministers realised, as they had done many times before, the Premier's high dialectic qualification for the position he held. More than one secretly complimented himself on the caution which had delayed a choice of sides at the recent issue. Would Sir Bardsley talk over this audacious Under-Secretary, and the threat of crisis die down as rapidly as it had flamed?

Sir George Donnington took advantage of that moment's pause to interpose in a manner which the reference to his opinion might be held to redeem from the category of the unmannerly: "What I thought, Maitland, was that you have done us a service which we ought to recognise. I put it that we ought to find room for you among us. I said that you were the best Under-Secretary that had ever had."

Stanley had entered the room in a mood which had been resolute to assert the position which he had declared already. He was prepared for opposition, ridicule, or threat, and thought that he should be equal to overcoming them. He found the spirit in which Sir Bardsley met him more difficult to resist, as he had found it the night before. He turned towards Sir George Donnington, with a note of apology in his voice: "It is kind of you to say so. I wish I could accept. But I am aiming at something different. Something less for myself, and something which in other ways is a good deal more."

Sir Bardsley Clinton concealed his annoyance at this diversion. He had hoped to say much more, and to raise several interesting side-issues before giving Stanley an opening for the declaration which he had now made. He had stated a few minutes before that he was disposed to give him a chance, but that disposition was contingent upon a previous failure to overbear or cajole. He was right in thinking that, of the fifteen men assembled in that room who had made a trade of persuasion, and had established themselves successfully in the business which they had chosen, he himself was the most adroit, the most ductile, the most patient and resourceful. Sir George should have left it to him.

So he felt rather than thought, his mind being active on the position as it developed rather than its lost possibilities. He abandoned his intended peroration to say in a reasonable persuasive way: "I wonder, Mr. Maitland, whether you have adequately assessed the strength of the opposition which will be aroused by your proposals—however wise, however salutary they may be of themselves—I am not contesting that—if there should be what can hardly be described otherwise than as a threat of wholesale criminal violence to enforce obedience to them. The English people are very hard to drive.

"I am inclined to wonder, also, whether you have adequately weighed the immense power for good which may come into your hands of itself, if it be publicly known that you have saved the country from an unprecedented calamity, and with the recognition that we are prepared to offer. A high seat among ourselves..."

Sir Bardsley avoided the eyes of his colleagues as he paused upon this attractive offer. A high seat could not be occupied by Stanley Maitland until it had been vacated by the gentleman now enjoying its comfort. The faintest hint of who might be the selected victim would be sufficient to complicate a position which was already sufficiently difficult, and should Stanley refuse the offer, as appeared most probable, Sir Bardsley might have made a lifelong enemy for no gain whatever.

As it was, the President of the Board of Trade, with whom there had been some friction a few weeks earlier, and whose resignation had been generally expected, had a difficulty in looking unconcerned. The position to be offered might be other than his, but it might well lead to a general reshuffling in which he would be asked to go. He watched Shackston's face. It was there that his hope might lie.

"I should like, in the first place," Stanley answered, "to make one thing quite clear. I am not threatening any wholesale violence, whether criminal or not. I am placed in a position in which I can prevent a great catastrophe which was designed by another mind. I am willing to do this, but I make a condition that you will allow me to do what I can to save the nation from an even greater catastrophe of another kind."

"Do I understand," Viscount Okehampton enquired, with a faint derisive inflection in his voice which interpreted the sarcasm of the smiling eyes, "that you consider that you could govern this country somewhat better than we are able to do?"

"Meaning," the Hon. James interjected harshly, "that we're no better than mugs?"

"Meaning," Stanley replied, "no more than that you cannot expect to succeed at something which you never attempt."

"And you reckon that you could?"

Sir George Donnington interposed again. He knew Stanley well enough to realise that, though he might keep his temper better than Jimmy Shackston, he was even less likely to be overborne by a bullying manner. He said:

"Suppose we ask Mr. Maitland to tell us shortly, in his own words, what he does propose, and what is the alternative which isn't a threat."

"It would, I think," Sir Bardsley agreed, "be the most orderly way.

Stanley saw that the moment of decision was upon them. He saw that he must either compromise now, or take up a position which might isolate him from his fellows, which might lead to tragic or even comic failure, to ignominy or death, which, even if it succeeded, might leave his name a permanently execrated memory for the follies which he had inflicted upon a reluctant world. There had been a tone of aloofness, if not of hostility, in the phrasing of Sir George's suggestion, which he was quick to feel, coming from one with whom he had been on terms of mutual respect and friendship up to a few hours ago. "The alternative which isn't a threat." How absurd, how disingenuous, it sounded, when it was put like that!

Yet this isolation roused him to a firmer attitude, as had Crystal's earlier defection. It was like the exhilaration of a cold wind.

"What I ask," he said firmly, "is that there be some cessation, some relaxation, of the incessant law-makings that are strangling England. I should like, also, to see some attempt to govern honestly, some attempt to stamp out the grosser social abuses which you have lacked either the will or the power to control. If you think that such action would be unpopular, except to the vested interests concerned, I think you may find yourselves to be wrong. But my main purpose is to restore some measure of freedom, to cultivate the old virtues of self-dependence and self-control. I don't want to govern. I want to release. I don't want to do this myself. If I thought you would do it, I would stand aside, and be more than glad. If you will co-operate with me to such ends, it is all I ask. Only if you decline, I ask you to stand aside.

"On this condition, I will continue the work of relieving the country from a great peril which I did not originate, and from the imminent risk of which I have saved it already, at the cost of a human life which I was obliged to take.

"There is only one other point which this position—the fact that anyone can be in such a position as I am today—must bring into prominence. Is there any way by which the civilised world can be saved from the menace of further scientific discovery, from the effects of which it is already acting as though feverishly aware of its approaching doom?" (Sir Bardsley, coolly and watchfully critical of a drama that he had decided to permit its own development, thought the construction of the last sentence to be deplorably poor. "Made that up beforehand, and didn't memorise accurately; he'll know better if he lives to my age, which doesn't seem very probable." So he thought, as he listened to Mr. Sampson Lynes's reaction to the same statement.)

"Do you really mean, Mr. Maitland, that you would stay the beneficent progress of science? That you are blind to all the countless blessings which it has conferred, and is still conferring, upon mankind?"

"They are such blessings that its disciples ask in thousands whether life has any hope or purpose, whether it is worth living at all. It destroys faith, and offers no substitute worth having. It tells men that they can live by bread alone, if it be baked by them, and it turns to stone in the mouth."

"I suggest, Mr. Maitland," Sir Bardsley answered, "that that picture is neither fair nor complete."

"I know that," Stanley conceded frankly. "But it seems to me to be vitally true. Perhaps *the* vital truth of the whole matter. Science gives richly; but are they not a devil's gifts at the best? Religion taught standards of conduct, and science offers standards of comfort instead. And when we have learned them, we look round and notice that we are a comparatively dying race. But we are not greatly concerned, because we have lost faith in everything, even ourselves. Religion taught that this world is a small thing compared with a following eternity, and men, like God, called it good. Science concentrates on improving this world, and its value lessens, until men are even prepared to accept complacently the futile nightmare which the spiritists offer us to succeed it. But"—he added impotently—"it's a difficult subject. Surely some effort could, at least, be made to check the development of destructive agencies. If men could only seek knowledge without attempting interference for which they are so plainly incompetent!"

Viscount Okehampton asked with the faintly-smiling sarcasm that he had shown previously: "Do I understand, Mr. Maitland, that your idea of saving a dying race is to discourage the genius of our own scientists, while those of other nations outstrip them in research, and devise weapons for our destruction?"

"I thought I told you that these are questions which seem to me to be almost insuperably difficult. I have not suggested any solution. I only say that there are dangers that ought to be recognised, and the proof that they are real is that I am sitting here now."

Viscount Okehampton answered with the same outward courtesy, too thinly veneered to conceal the texture of the thought beneath it. "You will forgive me saying, Mr. Maitland, that I am a little surprised that there should be a subject which you feel yourself unequal to resolving. But I admit the force of the illustration. Yet even that force may be reduced if the event should prove that we are equal to dealing with it, as, if you will allow me to say so, I think it may."

The Hon. James Shackston broke in, before Stanley could reply. He had been watching the temper of his colleagues. He judged that Sir Bardsley's effort to talk Maitland over had definitely failed. It was time to handle him in a firmer way, for which he felt that he was the man. Success would increase his prestige, perhaps to a decisive degree in the Cabinet struggle which he was plotting for the autumn months.

"I don't want to be rude, but the fact is, Maitland, I think we've listened to you about long enough. If you want to know what I think, you're not a politician at all; you're a B.B.C. lecturer. That's your job, and you'd talk the kind of claptrap that goes down with them about as well as anyone I've ever heard.

"You've had a big slice of luck, and I don't say you haven't used it well. You've staged this hold-up, and here we are. But you mustn't open your mouth too wide. I'm not against anything Sir Bardsley's offered. But if that isn't good enough, you may find that you'll get nothing at all—or even a bit less than that. We shall just call your bluff, and where will you be then? I don't know whether you could make the bust-up you've threatened or not. But I know you'd never dare to try. We all know that. And it wouldn't do you any good if you did. I don't know where London'd be, but I know where you would half an hour after it happened. You'd be strung up on the nearest tree.

"That was what Feltham said," Stanley answered quietly. "He said no one would believe in advance. That was why he wanted to destroy London first and talk afterwards. I wouldn't hear of that then, and I won't now. But we might try Seven Pines. Suppose I give you till Tuesday next to clear out, and if anyone's left in the place by that day—well, they'll have been warned?"

The Hon. James Shackston flinched visibly at this suggestion. Seven Pines was one of the most magnificent residences in England, built with the money of his American wife, whom he had married at a date when heiresses were still exported from that country. But he was of a good fighting spirit, and though his face paled, his jaw set truculently, and he would doubtless have given a defiant reply, had not Sir Bardsley interposed with a note of authority in his voice which was rarely heard.

"Mr. Maitland, I must remind you that you are here by my invitation, and with the object of laying your views and proposals before us, not as individuals, but as the assembled ministers of the Crown. Had I thought that you would be capable of making individual threats of such a nature as that.... If you please, Mr. Shackston, I will deal with this matter myself. I think, Mr. Maitland, that we understand the position sufficiently. If you would kindly retire for a short time, I think we shall be able to arrive at a decision."

Stanley restrained the desire to retort that the Chancellor of the Exchequer had got nothing more than he had asked for in a rather loud voice. He only said: "Very well. I will wait."

He was shown into a comfortable room containing a sufficient library to have occupied his mind in different circumstances, but he was too conscious of the magnitude of the forces which he had challenged, the momentous nature of the decision which he was waiting to hear, to give their titles more than a half-unconscious scrutiny.

He walked backwards and forwards across the length of the soft and silent carpet. Was he suffering from a madman's delirium, or on the threshold of a great career? If only Crystal were loyal! But had her defection hardened him to a resolution which he had been slow to make? Or was it a disregarded warning that none, not even those who had been closest, would support him now? Not exactly that. There was Jehane.

He waited there more than an hour, and when at last Mr. Reynolds came to say that the Premier was ready for him again, he was aware that the corridors were guarded as they had not been previously. He was not too ignorant to recognise that No. 10 Downing Street was in charge of plain clothes officers from the Yard. For his benefit, or detention, or for what else?

Mr. Reynolds's face (if he knew anything) gave no sign.

CHAPTER TWENTY-SEVEN

STANLEY came back to a room somewhat less occupied than it had been an hour earlier. There were empty chairs dividing the assembled statesmen.

Sir Bardsley Clinton commenced at once: "Mr. Maitland, I will be frank and brief because the time for decision has arrived, and instant action must follow.

"I must inform you first of certain events of the last hour—I wish you to share our confidence fully—and I must then ask you one or two further questions. I will tell you at once that we who are sitting here have resolved to give you a certain measure of support, subject only to what those replies may be.

"You will have observed that some of the places which were previously occupied are now vacant. They are the places of these who do not approve of the step which I am now taking. Should your answers to the questions which I have indicated be to our satisfaction, I shall accept the resignations of those gentlemen before midnight.

"So far, I have taken no overt action, beyond requesting the editors of the principal London dailies, and other representatives of important newspaper interests, to meet me tonight, when I have promised them a full statement of what has occurred, together with the intentions of His Majesty's Government in reference thereto. The only stipulations I have made, both on patriotic grounds, and as a condition of attending that meeting, is that there shall be no earlier publication of unauthorised rumours, and, from past experience, I have some confidence that they will be generally observed.

"I expect you will have noticed that the doors and corridors of this house are guarded by members of the Metropolitan Police Force, and you may have wondered whether they implied anything hostile to yourself. I would prefer to say nothing further on that point at the present stage, beyond assuring you that I did not authorise this action, and was not aware that it was being done."

Stanley thought, "If this is brevity—," and had no further time for abstract reflection. The questions were upon him.

"In the first place, Mr. Maitland, do you propose to interfere in any way with religious practice or belief?"

"Not in the least. I wish to increase freedom, not to further restrict it."

"That's well; because though the average Englishman wears his religion somewhat loosely, he is roused by any threat of interference to an almost reckless extremity of defence.

"In the second place, if we give you the measure of support which is implied in explaining to the country the position which has arisen in a sympathetic manner, have we your definite pledge that, if you be allowed to experiment with our customs and laws to the end of the present year, you will then do all that lies in your power to remove the menace of Feltham's invention, seeking no further authority for yourself than you may be able to retain, or receive from your fellow-citizens without its support?"

"Yes, I will promise that."

"Third, can you give us definite assurance, pledging your honour that this menace is real, and that, apart from your intervention, you believe that this calamity would actually occur—that London would be instantaneously destroyed at the end of the present year, or earlier if there should be any attempt to interfere with the apparatus which Feltham has set up? You will appreciate that every man here would have ruined his political future, if it should afterwards appear that we had been misled as to the gravity of this danger."

"You see, Maitland," Sir George Donnington added, "it's a rather stiff thing to believe. I mean that, because you've made a few trees go up in smoke or come down in ash, or whatever they do, it doesn't follow that hundreds of thousands of buildings will respond in the same way."

"No, I see that," Stanley answered. "I can't say more than that all that Feltham claimed has proved so far to be genuine, and that he seemed sure.

"As to it being instantaneous, the operation, as I understand it, is that of a disintegrating ray which can be electrically controlled so that it will operate from a centre at a selected distance and direction from its source of origin. Its speed is approximately that of light. It produces some chemical change by which all substances disintegrate into certain volatile gases, a residuum sinking to the ground. It sounded almost simple as Feltham explained it. Just what you might expect to happen. He said he was surprised that no one had thought of it before."

"I think, gentlemen," Sir Bardsley remarked, looking round upon his remaining colleagues, "that those answers are satisfactory."

There was no sound of dissent, though there were some whose yes were downcast. The room was very still, as the Premier continued: "What I propose, Mr. Maitland, is to introduce a short Bill immediately, and to give it such facilities that it should be on the Statute-book before the week closes. It will give Orders in Council countersigned by yourself an absolute authority in law-making, repeal, or administration, up to the end of the present year. I cannot, of course, control the voting of the House. I can do no more than make it a matter of confidence. If that should fail, you will be free to take your own course, whatever that may be. If it should become law, I think that I can arrange that such Orders in Council will be promptly made, as they are required by you.

"Up to the end of the year, His Majesty's Government will be reduced to little more than a committee whose trained abilities, such as they are, will be at the service of your own policy, and in that capacity I trust that you will avail yourself of such help as we are able to give."

"Thank you," Stanley answered. "I could not ask for more than that. I could not reasonably have expected so much."

He saw that the help of these men, if it were genuinely given, would be beyond valuation, and might reasonably have been refused. He saw, also, that the course which Sir Bardsley had taken was calculated to maintain contact, if not control. It was characteristic of the man who considered himself rather as physician than ruler of the nation which chose him to preside over its government. The patient, for the moment, might be beyond his direction, but he would still be near the bedside to influence, to persuade, perhaps to warn.

"To regularise the position," Sir Bardsley was saying, "as far as possible—to observe precedent as nearly as unprecedented circumstances will permit us to do—I shall be pleased to retire from the position which I now hold immediately that the proposed Act shall be passed, and to recommend to His Majesty that he shall call upon you to form a Ministry, in which I shall be prepared to serve. Or, otherwise, should you not wish to disturb the existing routine, it will be open to you to accept the position of Chancellor of the Exchequer which Mr. Shackston is vacating."

Stanley might have liked an interval for reflection upon these propositions, but he knew that he must cultivate the habit of prompt decision if he were to succeed m the strange adventure he had undertaken. He felt that he could not, even had he wished, displace Sir Bardsley from the position which he already occupied, after the courtesy and consideration which he had shown to himself. He had not learnt the ruthlessness of the suavely-worded warfare of the arena into which he had entered. On the other hand, he rather liked the idea of taking Jumping Jimmy's exalted office. He felt a personal antagonism which this succession would emphasise, while it gave him a feeling of having conquered in the first round. He may have had better reasons than these, but he was most conscious of them as he answered: "I certainly do not wish any change of office to take place on my account." (He looked, before he spoke, at Mr. Sampson Lynes's unoccupied seat.) "I shall be pleased to accept the office which Mr. Shackston has vacated."

Sir Bardsley showed no sign of any feeling, as he answered: "I think you may have decided wisely. It will avoid any change in the existing machinery of government, and will have the incidental advantage that it will enable you to address the House as a member of the existing Cabinet.

"What I propose, subject to your approval, will be this.

"I shall make a short statement in the House tonight to allay public anxiety, and to discredit any unauthorised rumours that may be circulating.

"After that I shall give the press interview I have already mentioned, and urge that it should adopt at least a friendly neutrality till the position which has arisen has been laid before the country by His Majesty's Government, as it will be tomorrow night.

"Tomorrow I shall introduce the agreed Bill, and you will have an opportunity of explaining your position and intentions before the House in your own way. I need not urge upon you the importance—

possibly the decisive importance—that that statement may have, both in securing the passing of the Bill and its effect on the country.

"If I may suggest, I think it would be inadvisable for you to attend the House tonight, or give opportunities for discussion with other members, or interviews to the press, prior to the formal statement which must necessarily be made tomorrow."

Stanley had a feeling of hesitation, and a shade of resentment, as these proposals developed. He felt that the position was being stage-managed by Sir Bardsley to a degree which might become dangerous unless he could rely both upon his good faith and his goodwill. It was like being in the hands of an overzealous, over-competent secretary, who may become the exacting master of the man he is supposed to serve. But the plans, in themselves, were sound. Of the capacity of Sir Bardsley in his self-appointed office, there could be no doubt. Stanley said: "Yes. I think that will be the best way."

As the meeting broke up, Sir Bardsley came over to him. "You are still staying at the Rafton?" he asked courteously.

"Yes."

"Then I am sure you will not misinterpret any precautions which we may take. They will be for your safety only. And in the same way, we shall have protection provided for Feltham's flat. I am sorry that you should be in any way separated from Lady Crystal at this time. If there is anything I could do or say, as an old friend of her father, as one I have known from child...."

"No. I think you must please leave that to me."

Sir Bardsley saw his mistake. He said: "Yes, of course. You must forgive an old man's proneness to interfere." He smiled with his disarming courtesy.

Stanley had a feeling that he might have been needlessly curt. The offer might have been made without any but the simplest and kindest motives. Probably it was. But he felt that he had had sufficient courtesies from Sir Bardsley Clinton. If a reconciliation with Crystal were to be added, it might make an embarrassing total.

Besides, the difference with Crystal was for themselves alone. It was not a matter on which he could authorise anyone to interfere.

"I expect," Sir Bardsley was saying, "you'll wish to concentrate on your speech to the House tomorrow. I know I should. No, of course, you can't take a taxi. I'll drop you at the Rafton myself. My car goes close by, whether or not."

A few hours later, Lady Crystal was gazing at the front page of an evening newspaper. There was a short paragraph in leaded type, headed '*The Kensington Outrage*.'

In reply to a question by the hon. member for Belbroughton, Sir Bardsley Clinton made the following statement in the House of Commons this afternoon. "There have been important developments during the last forty-eight hours, the nature of which will be explained fully tomorrow, when the Government will request the leave of the House to postpone the business of the day, and to bring in a short Bill, as a matter of urgency.

"Pending the full statement which will be made in this House tomorrow afternoon, I should like to take the opportunity of appealing both to private individuals and the press neither to assist in circulating nor to regard seriously certain idle rumours which I understand to be in circulation in some quarters. Nothing has occurred to occasion panic, and, speaking with a full sense of responsibility, I can assure you that there is no probability of such an eventuality. We—the present members of His Majesty's Government—are now fully informed of the nature and occasion of the disturbing incident to which the Hon. Member for Belbroughton has made allusion, and the Bill which I shall introduce will be adequate to deal with the emergency.

"It would be premature to say more than this at the present moment, but it may be convenient to add that, owing to some difference of opinion regarding the policy which I shall recommend, I have accepted the resignations of Viscount Okehampton, the Hon. James Shackston, Mr. Sampson Lynes, Mr. Ricardo Tomplin, and Mr. Goodwin-Pemberton."

Lady Crystal read this paragraph more than once, and was still unable to estimate its significance. A month ago, the resignations of so many prominent members of the Government, and of its Chief Whip, would have seemed an event of the first magnitude. It would have given her a more pleasurable and more stimulating excitement than if she had suddenly been informed from Heaven that she was shortly to become the mother of a pair of Divine Twins.

Now she gazed upon it with frowning eyes, and a mind that was disturbed and doubtful. The resignation of Mr. Ricardo Tomplin, the President of the Board of Trade, was of little moment. For some time past, it had been a half-expected thing. But the other names were those of some of the Government's more virile supporters. Men who would not lightly resign. Would, indeed, be very unlikely to do so concerning any earthly matter, unless they foresaw a possibility of overthrowing their opponents and ascending to more exalted office over their prostrate bodies. Or they might be leaving a sinking ship. Jumping Jimmy, she realised, would be very quick to do that.

She could not doubt that it was Stanley who had made this trouble. That it was his wildly criminal threats which had divided the Government, and so might have contrived its fall. Such was the evil that his madness had wrought already!

But her trouble was that she could not tell from Sir Bardsley's statement who were Stanley's supporters, or who had shown sufficient courage to stand out against him. Her first inclination would be to sympathise with Sir Bardsley's difficulties. He was not only the head of the political party her adherence to which had many of the attributes of a religious faith, he was a man she had known and revered from childhood. She noticed also that the men who, by the implication of silence, were with him still—Sir George Donnington and Mr. Plumpton-Marshall among them—were those who might not be individually the most brilliant, but were the more stable elements of the Coalition Government over which Sir Bardsley presided. Reasoning soundly enough, but from a mistaken premise, she concluded that Jumping Jimmy and his friends, being the more likely to engage in criminal adventure if they supposed their profit to lie that way, had withdrawn from the Government to give Stanley their support, he having convinced them that he was in a position to hold his country to ransom, with the morality of a highway thief. She saw Sir Bardsley withstanding him in a spirit of fearless patriotism. He would bring in a Bill at once to deal with this unprecedented emergency. Probably Stanley would be indicted for high treason before the Bar of the House. Perhaps he would be beheaded. Perhaps hanged. Perhaps he would be consigned to greater ignominy in the Old Bailey dock. She was not quite clear on these provisions and procedures of the criminal law. She had never supposed that they could be of more than an impersonal interest. And in any case a special Act—

Well, she knew where her sympathies lay. She had done with Stanley from now. She had married him, giving him all she had, and he had disgraced her name. She might be known for centuries merely as the wife of one of the worst criminals of history—or, perhaps, one of the most crazy.

Of course, if he were actually arrested, she would stand by him in ways that a wife should. She would find money for his defence. She might be able to get him certified as insane. Her money and influence should be sufficient for that. But would her influence last? That might depend upon how promptly, how absolutely, she should disassociate herself from him. In his own ultimate interest as much as her own, she could not do this too thoroughly, nor too soon. She wrote Sir Bardsley Clinton a note of sympathy and indignation. She worded it so that her own position should be quite clear. She sent it to the post at once. As she did so, Jehane entered the room, with a copy of the same newspaper in her hand.

"Oh," she said, "I see you've got it as well. It's a bit on the cryptic side. What a lot of words these politicians can use without saying anything! But I should say it's first blood for Stan. He seems to have started cracking the nut without losing much time. He's cracked the Government up anyway, in about ten minutes. That's the one thing that seems clear."

"It isn't the first blood," Crystal allowed coldly, "and I should be glad to think that it will be the last. The first blood, unless you count Mr. Feltham, was that poor man in Kensington Gardens."

"Oh, well, have it your own way. I told you you were a size too small. I thought you didn't know your luck when you married Stanley, and I'm quite sure now."

"Considering," Crystal answered, with something more than her usual patience, "that all we know yet is that he's broken up the best Government we've had since the war! I can't understand how even you can take it the way you do, when I think how you worked to keep Sir Mortimer's seat at the last election."

"Yes," Jehane agreed complacently. "Mortimer said he polled a couple of hundred of women's votes that he wouldn't have had but for me. I kissed more babies than we seem likely ever to have in our family. But I haven't taken to mentioning the Conservative party every night in my prayers. I've left that to you. And, anyway you don't know that Stanley's going to do it any particular harm. Why don't you wait a bit before you make up your mind. Sitting on the fence may be a poor game, but it's better than jumping down on the wrong side."

"I have just written to Sir Bardsley," Crystal answered firmly, "to assure him that I have neither part nor sympathy in the course which Stanley appears to be taking. I have told him that Norchester House is closed from this day to Stanley and those who may be politically associated with him, and that all the influence I have will be exerted on behalf of those who have had the courage to stand out against such threats as that dreadful letter contained." She added, as she saw incredulity struggling with amusement in Jehane's eyes—an amusement for which she could see no cause—"You may laugh now, if you like. You seem to be able to laugh at anything. But the day may come when even Stanley may be glad that I have made my own position clear from the first."

"And so you've written to Sir Bardsley that you won't let Stanley's political friends enter this house?" Jehane's laughter rang out unrestrained, startling the sober footman who had entered to stoke the fire. She had difficulty in waiting till the door closed upon him again before she added: "Oh, Crystal, what a holy joke! You'll be the fool of the piece."

"I don't see…," Crystal began in a very natural resentment at this raillery.

"No, because you didn't look. I can see what you did. You just read the first page, and thought that Stanley'd gone in with Jumping Jimmy and that crush. What a priceless joke! Why, oh why, didn't you turn it over and have a look at the stop-press column?"

Crystal turned the paper without answering. The stop-press column contained no information except the names of some winning horses and the news that Pellet had been scratched for the Grand National. "I don't know what you mean," she said irritably. "There's nothing here."

"Well, try mine." Jehane passed her a slightly later edition. In the stop-press column she read:

"We are informed on reliable authority that Mr. Stanley Maitland, Under-Secretary of State for the Colonies, has been offered the position of Chancellor of the Exchequer, and has accepted that office."

"The report," Lady Crystal said, but without conviction in her voice, "may be quite unfounded. You know what these papers are. He might even have had it put about himself to see how people would take it."

"Such things have been," Jehane agreed. "But it won't help you this time. Nobody'd spread that report if he'd gone in with Jimmy's lot. I should get that letter back if I were you; if it's not too late."

It was advice of an obvious wisdom, but Lady Crystal did not require it. She had rung already, hopeless as the proposal seemed, and as it proved to be. The letter had been posted ten minutes ago.

Jehane said: "I wonder no one's rung up to enquire about the report before now. You haven't made a public statement that Stanley's left here, have you?"

"I haven't made anything public. I told Molly whatever calls might come through for Stanley, they were to be told he was out. But I didn't want to hear anything about them myself."

"Well, if you *like* Miss Preston to know more about your affairs than you do yourself—"

"Isn't that what secretaries are for?"

"I dare say it is. I think I'll ring up the Rafton, and see whether I'm wanted there. If you don't want Stanley here, I suppose it means migration for me. I had a faint hope that you'd show more sense. The trouble is that you won't back a winner when it comes out of your own stable."

Crystal made no answer. She let Jehane have the last word. The injustice of the accusation did not merit reply.

CHAPTER TWENTY-EIGHT

SIR BARDSLEY CLINTON'S experienced glance passed over a well-filled room. He saw the editors of *The Times*, the *Daily Post*, the *Morning Telegraph*, and a dozen other of those upon whose presence he had counted confidently. But he was most conscious of those whom he did not see. He whispered to Reynolds: "Menzies not here?"

"No, sir. It's all right. Influenza. Tom Bellam's here for him."

"Goldstone?"

"I'm afraid not, sir."

"Then get me through to him as soon as I'm clear of these." He rose at once to address the assembled editors.

"Gentlemen," he said, "I have asked you to meet me because it has always been my rule to show confidence in the press, and because it is better that the public should know the facts of one of the most extraordinary events which have come within my experience than that they should be troubled and perhaps unduly alarmed by confused or contradictory rumours.

"You are all aware of the recent destruction which took place in Kensington Gardens, and of the letter which foretold it. I need not remind you that that letter contained a more formidable threat, to be put in operation, if at all, at a later date, and a condition—you may regard it as a monstrous or impossible condition, as I did myself when I read it—under which that threat would not be carried out.

"Now, gentlemen, I have to tell you that that was a genuine letter, and, to the best of my belief, the threat that London—the very area in which we now are—might be destroyed as instantly and utterly as was that limited space in Kensington had a solid foundation. The apparatus—the most devilish apparatus—designed for this purpose actually exists and has been twice tested successfully—once at Kensington, as you know, and earlier in a small wood in the neighbourhood of Ditching Common.

"Those are facts. The apparatus was designed by the well-known scientific inventor, William Feltham, whose recent disappearance was a matter of some publicity. His declared object was to hold the world to ransom under threats of wholesale devastations which there would be no means of combating, and which would enable him to demand what tribute he would. In his own phrase, he designed to be 'King of the World.'

"Gentlemen, William Feltham is dead. Nemesis overtook him at the hands of a member of His Majesty's Government, Mr. Stanley Maitland. It overtook him at a moment when he was contemplating not merely a threat, but the actual destruction without a moment's warning of the centre of London, in the cynical expectation that this appalling demonstration of his power would bring the world to his feet more abjectly than any threat would be likely to do.

"From this terrible catastrophe—a catastrophe which staggers the imagination to contemplate—I am satisfied to say that England—I may say that our civilisation—was saved by the coolness and courage of Mr. Maitland. For that service we owe him a debt of such magnitude that you may agree with me that it will never be possible to repay it.

"The sequel to this incident was that Mr. Maitland was left in possession and control of the deadly apparatus which William Feltham had constructed to overawe the world. The ingenuity—I might say the perverted genius—of its inventor had set this apparatus in such a way that, as it now stands (and on the supposition that his claim be genuine, which there is, I fear, little reason to doubt), it will effect the destruction of the Central London area on the 31st of December next. It is so set, so I am informed, that any interference, any attempt to put it out of action, may hasten the catastrophe. Mr. Maitland alone is in possession of the knowledge which can safely disconnect it (if that be the right word), and finally end the peril which overhangs us today—and, for doing this, Mr. Maitland, rightly or wrongly, has asked a price.

"It appears that he holds a belief that this country is suffering from various social and political evils which originate in the excessive legislation which has distinguished the last half-century. The belief is not singular to himself, and may have been held by an increasing number during the post-war years. He believes further that these evils can only be successfully combated, if at all, by someone with authority to control or repeal the existing laws, or even enact such further legislation as the situation requires.

"Holding this view, he has made what may appear to you, as I will own that it did to me, the audacious condition that he should be allowed such power, autocratic and absolute, up to the end of the present year, at the end of which period he will use his knowledge to remove the existing menace, and will leave himself absolutely in the hands of his fellow-citizens to repudiate or reward, as their disposition may incline them to do.

"Mr. Maitland has rendered us a great service already. He is prepared to render us another. For this second service he asks what may prove to be a disastrous price. On the other hand, it may not. It may not strictly be a price at all. It may be a blessing which will place us under a heavier weight of obligation than we already are. There is the doubt. Against that, there is this shadow of approaching destruction, about which there is no doubt at all. Having to weigh the certain against the doubtful evil, there should be no question as to where our choice should lie.

"That, at least, has been my own decision. After conferring with Mr. Maitland, and forming my own judgment of the character and abilities of the man who asks for a position of greater, though more temporary, authority than any man can claim to possess in Europe, even in Italy today, I decided that whatever influence I possess shall be used to secure that he shall have the opportunity for which he stipulates. I offered to resign my own position in his favour, subject, of course, to the constitutional procedure which such a change would require. This offer he declined. I then offered him one of the places left vacant by the fact—of which you will have learnt already—that certain members of the Government have resigned owing to a difference of opinion as to the wisdom or propriety of the course which I have taken. That position, I am glad to be able to announce, Mr. Maitland has consented to fill.

"Gentlemen, it is easy to criticise any course of action which is taken to meet an unprecedented emergency, and especially so before its results are known. Regarding those who have deserted (for so I regard it) at the moment of danger, I do not wish to say anything harsh. It is enough to observe that what might have been a decision of incalculable gravity, had it been taken by myself as representing His Majesty's Government, becomes in those who have resigned a mere irresponsible demonstration.

"Should the House of Commons decline to support me tomorrow night, or should the force of public opinion, on which all must ultimately depend, decline to accept the position which will result from the course of action which I shall recommend, I cannot say what the consequences may be. We shall be absolutely in Mr. Maitland's hands.

"Tomorrow night, he will make his own statement to the House.

"In the meantime, I do not feel that I can ask you to support the conclusion which I have reached in the newspapers which you edit or control. It would be asking too much. Apart from personal confidence in myself, I feel that you have not sufficient information on which to base such a decision. But I feel that I can ask, and that it is my duty to urge upon you, that you will bring this matter to public knowledge in such a way that opinion will not be exasperated nor alienated in advance, but that judgment will be suspended until the position shall have been fully explained and debated tomorrow night.

"I do not, of course, ask for any individual pledges. I have only to thank you for the courteous patience with which you have listened to the statement which I have made. I am—but I matter nothing in this comparison—I may say that the welfare of the country is in your hands."

Sir Bardsley Clinton knew the art of clothing his ideas in such ample garments of words that his dullest hearer had time to understand them as they were paraded before him, and he had exercised it tonight. He knew also when to stop, which is an even rarer accomplishment. He dismissed his audience at this point, with a few courteous parting words and a recognition of the fact that they were busy men. They lost no time in departing. Some of them, whose machinery was least adequate in proportion to the area which their early morning edition attempted to cover, should have been going to press almost immediately. Now there was instant decision to be taken as to the tone they should adopt, and the nature of the leader that must be written. They lost no time on the stairs.

Sir Bardsley felt that he had done well. If his experienced instinct were not at fault, he had gained breathing-space. Time in which to be heard. Time by which the first shock of the position would be absorbed in the public mind. Yes, he had done well so far. Now for Goldstone. But Mr. Goldstone would not be wooed. His assistant editor said, with apologetic finality, that he had given instructions that he was not to be disturbed. Probably he was meaning some mischief, but Sir Bardsley felt that there was a limit to the harm which could be done, even by the *Morning Standard*, if the rest of the press adopted a different tone.

Anyway, he had done all that he could. He was not a young man, and he had had a tiring and anxious time during the last two days. He went home to bed.

CHAPTER TWENTY-NINE

THE English character has many deficiencies. Among these is a sub- or supernatural slowness for which comparison is difficult. Even oxen can be stampeded. You can frighten a snail. The English had been engaged in the greatest war of which there is any historical record for several months before it occurred to them that the employment of vigorous men in trimming their hedges might not be exactly wise.

They read the various leaders in their morning papers, and the information by which it was supplemented in the news columns without as much visible excitement as they displayed on discovering that the coffee was cold.

Yet they were not unmoved. They knew by the size of the headlines that they were reading something of real importance. They looked with interest at pictures of William Feltham, of William Feltham's flat (indicated by a cross in the top left-hand corner), of Stanley Maitland, even of Lady Crystal Maitland and Norchester House. They read accounts of William Feltham's career, of Stanley Maitland's rapid advance in the political arena, and of the brilliant marriage which had assisted his progress. They took down the accustomed shutters, or caught the usual train with an underconsciousness of some pleasurable excitement. Something was hinting that it might happen to vary the routine of their harnessed lives, in which anything so rarely did. Something about which to read and talk, even to think. That it would make any personal approach of a threatening or disastrous kind was not easy to imagine. What are the police, what are the trade unions, what is the Government for? Quietly and confidently, and perhaps in slightly better temper than usual, they took up the daily duties of their docile blinkered lives.

No doubt the tone in which the news was conveyed helped toward this temperamental reaction. They were asked to wait, to suspend judgment, to hear what would be said in Parliament that night. Sir Bardsley Clinton had the matter in hand. He was a safe man. Even his political opponents felt that. Tricky, of course. Densely blind to the country's needs. But, all the same, a particularly safe man. Of Jumping Jimmy they would have been less sure. A brilliant man, it would be allowed. A good man to have on your own side. It was always a pleasure to read the speeches in which he showed up his opponents as the fools which they surely were. But a dangerously clever man. Not one that you could trust with a quiet mind.

Anyway, there was no immediate cause for alarm. Outside a three-mile area of Charing Cross, there was not even a remote threat of anything happening at the year-end. And within that area—well, the buildings had a reassuring solidity, and you were in no more peril than everyone else, which, to the average English mind, is a consideration of the first importance. Others were going quietly about their business. Obviously, you did the same.

Being in no present alarm, it was natural that there should be vague speculations in many minds as to the price which Mr. Maitland would ask for the rescue which only he could give. Vague fears or hopes as to individual burdens or benefits which it might entail. But as yet it was all too indefinite for any sharpness either of hope or fear. Later, if vested interests were damaged, if personal habits were threatened, there might be very different moods which would become slowly articulate, slowly formidable, to whatever end. But they were not yet.

Mr. Stanley Maitland, as he was slightly known already, and as he was represented in the morning papers, was not a dangerous man, and he was being made Chancellor of the Exchequer by Sir Bardsley Clinton. Surely that would satisfy him. The restraining effects of office! It has been seen so often before.

Fleet Street, busily preparing its afternoon issues, was well content. It was less interested in the end of the year than in the phenomenal sales which it anticipated for the coming week. The shares of the Universal Press were marked up two points on the Stock Exchange at midday.

Sir Bardsley Clinton (clad in a silk dressing-gown of a richly sombre pattern), commencing upon the egg-and-bacon which he negotiated every morning, as a Conservative leader should, looked first at *The Times*, and the *Morning Standard*, with a very lively interest. He had little doubt that Goldstone was plotting to queer the pitch, though he was puzzled as to the line which he would take. A message from a friendly and well-informed source, which had been given to him before he rose, informed him that Mr. Goldstone and the Hon. James Shackston had met at the residence of the latter gentleman and had a long conference during the early hours of the night. Well, the results would be here.

Sir Bardsley turned over the pages. He glanced at the leading article, raised his eyebrows slightly, and turned away. On one page he found a short paragraph, headed, "*Where is William Feltham?*" It stated that the missing scientist was reported to have been seen by two persons (by one of whom he was well-known) landing from a cross-Channel boat on Saturday evening last. "It remains to be seen," it added, "whether this event is a mere coincidence, or had any connection with the destruction in Kensington Gardens on the following morning. The police have the matter in hand, and early developments may be confidently anticipated."

On the opposite page there was another short but prominent paragraph headed, "*Why at the Rafton?*" It stated that Mr. Stanley Maitland, whose association with Mr. William Feltham and possibly with the recent outrage in Kensington Gardens was likely to bring him increasingly before the public during the coming months, was understood to have left Norchester House, and to be staying at the Rafton Hotel, where he had been joined by Lady Jehane Norchester late on the previous evening. It added that Mr. Maitland was understood to have been absent from Norchester House at the time that the Kensington outrage took place. He had been staying over the weekend at Merton-Ash, after which he had not returned home, but had gone straight to the hotel. Lady Crystal Maitland, it added without comment, was still in residence at Norchester House.

On another page, it had reproduced a picture of Mr. Maitland's wedding with Lady Crystal Norchester.

Beyond this, the *Morning Standard* had refrained from any attack either upon Mr. Maitland or Sir Bardsley himself. It announced the resignation of various members of the Ministry in its news columns. It printed the brief explanation which he had given to the House. But it was utterly silent upon the larger issue which he had laid before the assembled editors, and of which Mr. Goldstone must have known, not only because he had a score of channels by which the events of that meeting could be communicated to him, but because he would have had it, with greater picturesqueness of detail, from Jimmy Shackston also.

Neither—beyond those two short paragraphs—had any use been made of the information that Miss Vera Hastings, and half a dozen other members of the staff of the *Morning Standard*, had been collecting during the previous day.

Sir Bardsley considered these facts in a very thoughtful mind. He did not doubt that Feltham had been reported to have been seen landing at Folkestone. Such reports were reaching the police continually. Neither did he doubt that it was as baseless as such reports usually are. But he saw that it would tend to question in advance the truth of the tale that Stanley Maitland told. And he recognised that there was only Maitland's own word for the accuracy of a really remarkable narrative. Suppose it were false? Suppose Feltham still lived, and Stanley were no better than the tool of a lawless criminal? Perhaps an unwilling, frightened tool? Suppose Lady Crystal knew this, and with a finer courage had declined to be associated with a base conspiracy? He did not believe this, but he saw, if a doubt could be so easily raised in his own mind, that it might spring to more vigorous growth in the minds of others less conversant with the actual facts and the persons concerned. The information about Maitland having left Norchester House, which said nothing and implied so much, was also clearly intended to undermine a position which was not openly assaulted. He was not puzzled by these attacks, but by the absence of a more direct challenge. "I wonder," he said aloud, "what Jimmy's up to now?"

He turned back to the leading article. It was headed, "*Is it a decent thing?*" Its theme was a measured and reasoned protest against the public exhibition of the Pastograph screens. Its point was that no one could tell from hour to hour or at any moment what of horror, of unseemliness, even of obscenity, these screens might portray to the mixed audiences which gazed upon them. They spied upon the actions of men and women, who were unaware of the possibility of such ultimate publicity, and the fact that they were long since dead did not alter the nature of the exhibition from the angle with which the *Morning Standard* dealt.

It had an impressive text in an incident which had been shown on a screen in Dorking during the previous week. The scene was a well at the side of a field-track to which a number of villagers would come daily for water. It might be deserted for long hours, but was a place of occasional resort or gossip. Those who had patience might observe strange and intimate glimpses of peasant life in Elizabethan days. The well was surrounded with a low brick wall, which had broken down at one side, and not been repaired. A time came when those who watched saw a child of four or five years who wandered along the path and sat down to play by the well. She came to the side that was broken down. She pulled weeds from the brink. The audience watched in a somewhat anxious mood. Would no one come? But they were not over-concerned. Used to the unreal cinema world, they knew that someone would come soon enough. It was just a thrill. But a half-hour passed, and no one came. The tension of those who watched and could not interfere increased as the minutes passed. A woman fainted, and was carried out. Grave and deliberate in her play, the child gathered pebbles from the gravelled side of the well, arranging them in patterns upon the edge. From time to time she would push the hair from her eyes with her left hand, jerking her head as she did it in what was clearly an unconscious habitual action. As they watched, she became living, individual to the audience. She was a child they knew.

At last she stood up to go. She looked down into the depth of the well, and then, perhaps in a sudden fear, put out a hand to grasp the broken edge of the low wall where it ended beside her. The loose brick gave way to her hand, and in an instant she disappeared.

The screen gave no sound, but she must have cried as she fell, for the next moment a rather loutish youth came through a gap in the hedge, with a billhook in his hand. He looked round puzzled, and then, fearfully, over the edge of the well. His face changed into a vacuous horror at what he saw, but he stood still, irresolute and afraid. There was a bucket and rope by which he might have descended. With courage and promptitude, and perhaps with a preliminary cry for the help of others, he might have been able to save. But he just stood in irresolute shameful panic, and then his head moved round. He seemed to search the view which the audience could not see. He must have decided that he was unseen, for, visibly trembling, he scrambled back through the hedge, leaving the child to drown.

They were all dead long ago. The child, and the lout who would carry the memory of shameful cowardice to his grave, and the frantic mother who would see the child's body hauled up on the next day, all dead three hundred years ago, and what could it matter now? They would be dead just the same if they had ruled their lives to different or nobler ends. Just the same? We may doubt that, if we will. But it was rather late for tears over that ended life. There are enough of children who die under our lorry-wheels today, and we have few tears for them.

The management had closed the screen from the public on the following day, and when it reopened the auditorium had been filled with a morbidly excited crowd who had come to gaze at the well.

Mr. Goldstone's contention was one on which it is possible to differ, but he made his case well, stating it with moderation and skill. He touched lightly also on the mechanical and other difficulties, such as the impossibilities of obtaining interiors, which had resulted in Mr. Feltham's invention falling short of the first anticipation that had been aroused. Instead of Elizabeth at Tilbury, or Drake at bowls, or even a glimpse of the flashes of gunfire as the Armada battle straggled along the Channel, or a performance in the Globe Theatre, the best that had been obtained had been bucolic scenes of crops and cattle, a village green, a garden in Chester, and a side street in Southwark—in which the running gutter which adorned its centre often the only moving thing.

There was no suggestion that these pictures should not be taken, but only that they should not be open to the public as the first impressions were received. Afterwards selected views might be shown. It was a reasonable contention, on a matter of public importance, such as might be put forward without any personal intention. Sir Bardsley saw that. He saw also that it threatened to reduce the commercial value of the invention, perhaps even to a point at which it could not be exploited at all. People came to watch the slow changes upon the screen just became of the uncertainty of what, at any moment, might appear upon it. That they would come afterwards to watch that which was known was less sure. In any case, to close the public from the first filming was to stop the receipt of a huge income which accompanied and did much to pay for the heavy cost of these receptions.

Sir Bardsley saw the menace to William Feltham's, perhaps to Stanley Maitland's, income. He was confirmed in his opinion that Israel Goldstone was a very formidable antagonist. But he saw that, for the moment, he was preferring a guerrilla warfare to the risks of decisive battle. The real question was what would happen in the House tonight. Sir Bardsley, having finished breakfast, proceeded to dress in his usual leisurely manner, but his mind was active, and he was prepared for a busy day. Already a draft of the projected Bill was being prepared for his consideration. Already Reynolds was busy at the telephone, marshalling his forces, and making the preliminary dispositions made necessary by Goodwin Pemberton's desertion. Sir Bardsley might have the reputation of a slow man, but no one doubted the courage or ability with which he would handle his forces when the political battle joined. And all the time, even from when he had laid down the *Morning Standard*, he had guessed correctly what Jimmy Shackston would do, had guessed much of the conversation which he had had with Israel Goldstone during the previous night. But a guess is not a certainty. He went on with his preparations for a battle which his opponents would not accept.

CHAPTER THIRTY

IN a silent and very crowded House, Sir Bardsley Clinton, not without a shadow of inward doubt as to whether he might not be committing political suicide in a more picturesque, perhaps in a more grotesque, manner than had ever been previously attempted, introduced his Bill.

It was a short measure, in accordance with the promise he had made. Stanley, waiting his time to speak with a greater nervousness than he had known before, recognised that Sir Bardsley had kept his word. If the division lobbies affirmed the measure, if the House of Lords gave it the support which he had been assured was an arranged thing, he had the chance for which he had asked. The failure would be his own.

Whatever doubt he might feel, he was outwardly calm and confident enough as he sat listening to the Premier's skilfully moulded sentences, in a speech which we need not delay to hear. Adapted to his different audience, and to the wider publicity which it would have in the press tomorrow, it was on the same lines as that which he had addressed to the assembled editors the previous night. He urged that they were attempting a bold experiment, yet there were times, there were situations, in which boldness was the truest caution… but, as to his objects, his intentions, Mr. Maitland must speak for himself.

He sat down to face an unexpected silence. No one rose to oppose the Bill. For a long minute the Speaker waited. Then he looked directly at Stanley. Stanley had not expected to speak till after there had been a general debate upon the position which he had originated. He had expected to hear himself praised for what he had done, and execrated for what he had failed to do, or for the condition which he had made; to hear protests against an attempted tyranny, perhaps subtle constitutional objections to the validity of the projected legislation, perhaps scepticism or ridicule of the power he claimed, perhaps personal appeals to be content with the high office which was to be conferred upon him; and to end at once and without further condition the peril in which the heart of London lay.

He would have welcomed such words as these. They would have provided substance for his reply. It is always harder to speak in assertion than contradiction. It was particularly so to his temperament. But he saw that it was not unreasonable that the House should wish to hear him first. He read nothing but that in the surrounding silence. He could not shirk the issue which he had raised. He rose to the sound of a murmur which was scarcely a cheer.

He spoke slowly at first, coldly, even haltingly, without the self-confidence that he had always shown when he had answered questions or joined in debates pertaining to his department. But he had been conscious then of his own efficiency; he had felt adequate to the occasion. He had no such feeling now. As he paused for an evading word, he had a disconcerting memory that Jehane would be watching and listening overhead.

Yet, even then, he was speaking better than he was aware. His mind had been dwelling incessantly during the past days upon social abuses and bondages, which are rendered tolerable only by their familiarity, and which, if he were equal to his opportunity, he might do something, however partial, however temporary, to break. The intensity of these feelings gave a tone of sincerity to dispassionate and disconfident phrases, of which those were sympathetically conscious who were willing to respond to the speaker's mood. But the general feeling of the House had been critical, if not actively hostile or derisive, with an undercurrent of fear, the existence of which it was unwilling to recognise. (A letter from Professor E. Crozier was being passed from hand to hand in which he expressed his view that Maitland claimed an impossible thing. You could have no higher authority than that.) Against an overbearing manner it might have cowered in silence, or become defiantly vocal. But this hesitant, almost diffident manner—there was no Mussolini here! Interruptions came in the tone of a relieved tension, of a jeering or jocular kind. And in reaction to these Stanley stirred as from an unexpected blow—he stirred and struck back.

It was a word from Peter Quinnick, the member for Hoblin Burghs, that first roused the fighting spirit which the occasion needed. Quinnick had been, like himself, an Under-Secretary in Sir Bardsley's government. He sat now on the cross-benches behind the Hon. James Shackston. He was largely responsible for the framing of the rules by which the department to which he had belonged enforced the Traffic Act of 1931. It was notorious in the House that his sympathies were with those whose conduct has stained the English roads with the bloodshed of a continual war. He had publicly expressed the opinion that a pedestrian ought to carry a light after dark. Now he interjected a remark that Stanley could only partly hear, but the words "Kimpson's murderer" sounded plainly across the floor.

He turned quickly upon the speaker. "You call me murderer! You are shocked at the death of one unfortunate man! I tell you I will not loose the power I hold, not if my own life remain, till I have saved a score of thousand lives which are doomed today. Men and women and children who are walking about unconscious that they must die before the year is dead, in the callous causeless slaughter of the public streets that such as you are content to regulate and permit."

The sudden outburst took the House by surprise, and the words were said before the Speaker's interposition could stay them. Now the Hon. James Shackston was on his feet on a point of order. The personal address to an individual member, and the attack upon him, were breaches of the etiquette of the House. There could be no doubt about that. Mr. Shackston made his protest against "this unbalanced outburst" in a tone that conveyed a half-amused contempt of the speaker, which might have disconcerted a weaker man, but roused Stanley with the impulse of the personal antagonism that lay between them.

The Speaker was diplomatic and conciliatory. The accusation which had been made against the Hon. Member for Hoblin Burghs was unparliamentary both in itself and in the form in which it had been addressed to him. He was sure that it would be withdrawn. But, if he had heard aright, there had been exceptional provocation in the equally improper expression which had prompted the reply. He thought that both the Hon. Members concerned should withdraw and express their regret.

As the incident was closing in this routine ceremony, the member for Lower Prestwick, whose income was derived from the manufacture of the metal furniture that motor bodies require, rose to ask: "Whether the intention was really to attempt to arrest the wheels of progress in the modern world? Because, if so, they'd better be told so plainly, and know where they stood." He sat down, muttering something about ruin, madness, and Mrs. Partington's broom.

Stanley was quick to reply. "I wonder," he said, "to how many people it has occurred that we have come to describe the changes of which we may be too ready to boast by a word which implies the expenditure of energy in its least productive direction? Is there any other period which has required the word progress to describe the changes of custom or habits of life which it has contributed to the history of the race? We substitute motion for production, as though it were an end in itself, oblivious of the facts that we can never be in two places at once, and that we mostly end up where we begin. Progress! Could not the Gadarene swine have made an equal boast, and would they not have been as quick to trample anyone who should have attempted to arrest their course?

"We find that perpetual motion is not prosperity, and look around with bewildered eyes, feeling that we have been betrayed by our own gods. Should we desire a visible deity, should we rediscover a capacity to worship anything but ourselves, it would not be a golden calf that we should set up, but the absurdity of a rotating wheel. I am asked whether I can stop this wheel of progress. It is a question which I cannot even attempt to answer, but it is a wheel which, so far as I can control it, shall not be red with innocent blood."

"Now I wonder," Mr. Simpson Lynes remarked, in a clear-sounding whisper, and a tone that was as lightly derisive as his lifted brows, "I wonder how he means to do that."

"He means to do it," Stanley answered, "in very simple ways." But he recognised as he spoke that he was being drawn aside from the mid-current of the speech which he had intended to make. To check the once lawless and now legalised bloodshed on the public roads might be a simple and obvious duty of anyone who should find himself in a position of sufficient authority, but it was in larger ways, in deeper, more fundamental issues, that he must justify the opportunity which he claimed. He went on in recovered confidence to outline no actual measures, but the policy of increased freedom and self-reliance by which, even though it might entail some of the disadvantages and perils that freedom brings, he dreamed that he might restore virility to a faltering race.

When he sat down, Mr. Shackston rose. He said briefly that they were faced with a position which was without precedent. The Premier, in the opinion of himself and many other members of the House, had succumbed to what he hesitated to describe as political blackmail of the most criminal kind, but which he found it difficult to define in more parliamentary language. He regarded the Bill which was now before them as fundamentally unconstitutional, and so it would remain, by whatever majority it might be adopted, either there or in another place.

Holding this view as he did, he was unable to countenance further debate, or to take part in a vote which ought not to be put to the House. He could do nothing but withdraw. He walked out, followed by about two hundred members who were content to accept his guidance. Sir Bardsley watched the procession with an expressionless face. He saw that Shackston had hesitated to produce the position which would have followed should he have succeeded in defeating the Bill. Or it might be as though he said: "You must go forward now in the path you have chosen. I will not interpose to save you from your own destruction." Well, the end was not yet.

Sir George Donnington judged the manœuvre in the same way. "Rope to hang ourselves," he said in a smiling laconic aside to Mr. Plumpton-Marshall, who sat next to him. That gentleman answered phlegmatically: "He hasn't hanged us yet." He reflected comfortably that Jumping Jimmy had been a bit too clever once or twice before. So far, his cleverness had led him on to the Opposition benches, while he, Mr. Plumpton-Marshall, was still drawing the salary which is attached to the control of the Home Office. If you trust Sir Bardsley Clinton to lead you—well, you should trust him. That was his motto. For many years it had served him well, and it saved thought, which was not his strongest suit. But he was vaguely troubled as to what Mr. Maitland might be proposing to do. He hoped that it wouldn't be anything to damage the banks, for most of his income was derived from a large holding of London-Northern shares. It wasn't likely that he would try anything like that. And while the banks stand firmly—well, there you are!

He got up to join the procession that was parading towards the aye lobby. The broken and dispirited opposition to Sir Bardsley's government, which did not accept Mr. Shackston's leadership, straggled into the other lobby, and were supported by a few members of independent minds, but the result was never in doubt. The first reading was carried by a majority of 247 votes.

CHAPTER THIRTY-ONE

WITHOUT waiting for the result to be declared, Stanley had left the House. Jehane's car was waiting for him, as had been arranged, and, as it turned into Parliament Street, a police car slid smoothly before and another took its place behind it.

"It certainly saves time," Jehane remarked, as the car that led them held up the traffic with the precedence which the police claim. She added: "I wish you'd tell me how you think you can stop people getting killed on the roads. I'm really curious about that."

Stanley smiled. "If everything were as simple as that! For one thing, I'd stop the endless, useless fining that goes on now, and most of the equally useless and more objectionable imprisonment."

"It sounds rather an Irish way."

"So it would be, if it stopped there. But it won't. A man who drives dangerously once won't get a second chance. His licence will be cancelled for life. If every man knows the penalty, he'll be a lot more careful than most of them are now. Besides, it's the only sane way. You wouldn't expect a locomotive-driver to be put back six months after he'd run his train off the lines. You wouldn't expect him to be put back six months after he'd been lifted off the footplate dead drunk. And running a car's a much more difficult thing than running a locomotive. It has to be done without the guidance or separation of rails, and with more complicated signals to control you."

"Is that the whole recipe?"

"No, of course not. Something could be done by controlling, if not prohibiting, third party insurance. At the most, it should only be supplementary. It should insure that the victim would get compensation, not that the aggressor should escape liability. Every man should know that if he injures another in so-called accidental ways, he himself, not an insurance company, will be made to pay."

"But you couldn't make a poor man pay?"

"Oh, yes, you could. Say up to half his wages for five or ten years, provided always that his children didn't suffer. Nothing on earth should be allowed to occasion that. That's why I say that insurance may be permissible in a supplementary way."

"Anything else?"

"Yes. It would have an excellent effect if, in all cases of highway fatality, no one were allowed to touch the body for two days. Let it lie where it fell, and the traffic move round it."

"What a ghastly idea!"

"Not so ghastly as the killings themselves, and the psychological effect might be excellent. But those are only two or three almost random ideas. There are fifty ways of stopping the present slaughter of which any intelligent man might think if he were in earnest about it."

"Well, don't think of them now. Here we are, and I expect Rigby's waiting upstairs!"

"Rigby?"

"Yes. I phoned him this morning to come along, and bring some of his own set." She added mischievously: "I expect he did about eighty an hour, if not more. You'd better see if there's any blood on the wheels. And I told Muriel to rake up a second line of defence."

"Against what, may I ask?"

"Against the rest of the world, of course. I don't mean to have anyone in the Rafton by this time tomorrow that I don't know."

"But there must be two or three hundred people here at the present moment." (They were in the lift by now.) "You don't think you're going to pay calls on the lot?"

"No. They're going to clear. There won't be one who hasn't checked out by this time tomorrow. The manager's seeing to that."

"Do you mean that you've taken the hotel?"

"That's the idea. I fixed up twenty-eight rooms for tonight, and the rest are to be ready tomorrow at six P.M."

"You must forgive me if I'm a bit slow. I've had a rather busy day. Will you tell me how many friends we're supposed to be entertaining here, and, perhaps, why?"

"Yes. But come in here. I shan't see Rigby or anyone till you've had something to eat. All the twenty-eight rooms I wanted clear for tonight aren't exactly for friends. I rang up the Secretaries' League this morning to send me twenty of the fastest young swine—"

"Fastest *what?*"

"Fastest swine. It's your word. I never use such language myself. I rang up for twenty of the fastest, most progressive young Gadarene swine that they could find in the city of doom, to be installed here tonight, ready to start work at nine A.M. tomorrow."

"Again, may I ask why? And why I wasn't allowed to know?"

"Because you'll need them. Have you any idea what the post's likely to be, now the *Morning Standard's* let out where you are? I suppose you don't know that Molly sent two sacks over from Norchester House this morning? I didn't tell you before you went to the House because you might have said it was too soon till you saw how the cat jumped, and I knew you'd need them more than ever if there was a row there. And I thought I'd have people I knew round us rather than not. These detectives all look as though they might be one of the wrong sort, and you couldn't tell."

"Have you thought of the expense?"

"Yes, first thing. The manager thought of that too."

"I couldn't possibly afford...."

"Considering that you're to be Chancellor of the Exchequer.... But I'm quite able to manage that. I suppose you know that I can shake out a few pence when I really try."

Stanley knew that. He knew that the Duke of Norchester had left his estates and his huge fortune to Crystal. They must go together, and remain intact so far as taxation permitted. To Jehane he had left an annuity of £500, and a free sum of £30,000 under her own control. That, he had said in his will, was as much as a woman without the responsibilities of property should ever need. But its adequacy would be quickly ended if it should be charged with running the Rafton Hotel.

"You know I couldn't possibly let you do that."

"I don't see why you need. For a man who's setting up in business as a world-dictator, I think you're a bit slow."

"I never thought of using the opportunity to make myself a rich man."

"No, I suppose not. We'll call this the petty cash. Anyway, there's no reason for dallying with the Dover sole. It's quite good. I told the manager to cook it himself, to see that no one slipped anything in. But if you're really worried about the young Gadarenes' wages, I'll have a few words with Sir Bardsley myself tomorrow.

Considering the way he's queered the pitch for you already, the least he can do is to tell the Treasury to shell out anything that you happen to need till you take charge."

"Has he queered the pitch?"

"I should think anybody could see that. You ought to have told him to take a back-seat from the first. To go home and forget."

Stanley made no answer to that. Jehane had voiced a doubt that was in his own mind. Sir Bardsley's considerate attitude had been a restraining influence from the first. The power which he was proposing to put into his hands might appear, for the few months that it would last, to be far more absolute than any man had held in a modern state; but there would still be a machine to function, possibilities of debate, delay, of a hundred difficulties ingeniously raised to promote doubt in his own mind, to reduce him to the impotency of indecision while the unreturning days would go by. He could see that already, even if there were no trap concealed, no subtlety beyond this view.

And the high office which he had been induced to accept already was diverting his mind to prospective details of a budget which he would have to frame during the next few weeks. He saw now that he should have refused it. Yet there was no way left but to go on. He must not show irresolution, nor admit mistake. What was done was done, and he must mould it now to the best end he could.

He saw already the human limitations which make absolute tyranny such an impossible thing. He saw for an instant the wild futility of his audacious dream. But he saw also, by the same reasoning, the reality of the tyranny that he sought to break. A single monarch, however absolute, must sleep, must play, must have times when he feels unwell. He may waste some wealth, he may do occasional arbitrary and oppressive things, but he can only think of one at a time. Also, he is likely to prefer popularity to the assassin's knife. Beyond that, he is temporary. He will age and die.

But the ballot-box does not sleep. It does not age. It does not fear the assassin's knife. It does not care though it may cause fifty thousand people to be wild with rage, if sixty thousand are on its side. It creates a myriad official tyrants who will leave no freedom for any in the remotest acre of English land.

"I'm sorry," he said, "I didn't hear. No, I shan't do anything more now. I'm going to bed."

An hour later, Jehane (having fenced lightly for a few minutes with Lord Rigby Stilton, congratulated him on the two sporting guns and the army revolver which he had brought in a literal interpretation of the instruction he had received, interviewed the manager of the hotel with a businesslike brevity, and the young lady who had been recommended by the Secretaries' League as suitable to control the remainder of her hastily recruited staff in a more human way) went to bed also, or, at least, to the privacy of her own room.

She was in no mood to sleep, though she yawned without restraint, as she stood before the mirror, raising smooth bare arms over her head. How she wanted Stanley! Longing for him with all the unexhausted strength of her fastidious virginity. If Crystal didn't want him herself, why hadn't she left him for her? And what a fool Crystal was! Not the only fool. It seemed that there were two in her family. What had Muriel told her more than once before now? Safety in numbers. If you didn't have a lark now and then when the chance offered, you always went mad at last for a man that you couldn't get. That was Muriel's creed, and she certainly practised the thing she preached. Jehane liked Muriel, but her discreet amours did not attract her to imitation. And this was the price she paid. She became aware, with a frowning anger, that her teeth had torn the lace handkerchief in her hand. What a pig Crystal was! And what a fool also. Which made two. She had worked out that sum once before.

CHAPTER THIRTY-TWO

THE next morning Lady Crystal, breakfasting in bed, as her habit was, laid down the *Morning Standard* in which she had been reading the report of the last night's parliamentary proceedings with more interest than satisfaction, to open a letter from Sir Bardsley Clinton. She had selected it from the little pile on her tray, which Molly Preston's unfailing discretion had sent in to her unopened. She did not expect it to be a pleasant letter. It was one which many people would have left till last, but she had never been one who shirked her fences. She knew that there would be something from Sir Bardsley, and she turned over the little pile in search of a well-known crest.

DEAR LADY CRYSTAL,

I have just had your note, which seems to have been written under some misapprehension of the existing position.

May I say how much I regret that you appear to have separated yourself from your husband at a time when your practical limitations (if you will excuse this definition from so old a friend) might have been particularly valuable to him, at a crisis in his career to which you may be inclined to regard with some natural anxiety.

Your sincere friend,

BARDSLEY CLINTON

Crystal read this letter with frowning eyes. She read it again, and her frown deepened. In his careful diplomatic language, she saw that Sir Bardsley had called her a fool. She remembered that Jehane had done the same with a more forceful brevity in the course of a stormy interview which had preceded her final departure.

And the worst of it was, she was not sure that they were wrong.

A majority of 247! You couldn't get over that. Her political training had taught her that almost everything is condoned by victory: nothing compensates for defeat.

Stanley had not upset the Coalition Government, neither had he destroyed himself. He had become one of its most important members. He had blackmailed it into introducing this amazing Bill, *and the Bill had passed*. Passed its first reading, at least.

She did not think that his methods had been defensible, or that her own opposition had been wrong. But facts are facts, all the same. There were 247 justifications for the course he had taken. It transformed a wild criminality into a political coup of the first magnitude. It still seemed to her to be fraught with peril, and to have disaster for its probable end. She would quickly have given half her wealth to have had things back upon the solid foundations of a month ago.

But that could not be. Stanley had to stand or fall now by the audacious choice he had made, and she supposed that his chance of victory, whether large or slender, must be lessened by her defection. So far, it was not Stanley, it was Jimmy Shackston who licked his wounds. She felt some satisfaction about that. She did not like Jimmy, and his American wife was worse than he. She had Jehane's freedom of speech, without the right to such freedoms which a ducal parent can give. It would do her good.

Her mind reverted to that last quarrelsome parting with Jehane. She had talked, in her unbridled way, as though Stanley might be in some personal peril, from which he would have been free in these friendly walls. "If he gets a knife in the back, I shall feel like putting one in you at the same spot."

Silly talk, of course. In any case, what was it to do with her? Resentment rather than jealousy stirred at the recollection. Why should Jehane interfere in the way she did?

Well, she was his secretary. That had been Crystal's own doing. She tried to draw Jehane, by every device she knew, into the political arena which was so central to her own life. If she withdrew from her husband's side, she was fair-minded enough to see that she could not complain because he accepted the help of those of a more obstinate loyalty.

Yet she saw her action now as of a doubtful morality, and a doubtful wisdom. She could not blame herself greatly, for her memory was clear that she had never asked Stanley to leave the house. She had only said that it should not be used as the headquarters of criminality., and he had taken up the challenge so quickly that there had been no opportunity to modify, to explain.

Still, she was honest and acute enough to see that the mental repulsion had been hers, that the resentment had been hers which had led him to that decision to leave the house. If that were so, the first advance to reconciliation should be hers also.

Bending a difficult pride, she rose and went to her bureau. "Dear Stanley," she began, and tore through the sheet. She destroyed two further efforts before she finished the note to her satisfaction.

DEAR STAN,

> I may have been wrong, and should like to talk it over again. Could you come about three o'clock tomorrow afternoon—or, of course, earlier if you like?

> Yours,

> CRYSTAL

She looked at the note with some hesitation. She had not meant to put that last letter of "yours." It would have read very differently without that final "s." It had been a slip of the pen. But he would understand the significance of the commencing abbreviation. Anyhow, she could make it right when he came. She knew her power over him. There was the power of surrender always. The ace of hearts which a woman always holds in a game in which hearts are trumps. It didn't matter much how she worded the note. It was writing it at all that was the significant thing.

So she sent it to the post, and picked up the *Morning Standard* again, to read the long verbatim report of the debate of the previous night. She felt happier now. After all, there couldn't be very much wrong in a course to which Sir Bardsley gave his support. Unconsciously, as she read, she was already identifying herself with her husband's cause. She pondered the tactics which had withdrawn Jimmy Shackston's followers from the division lobby. Could they have defeated the Bill, had they had the courage to try? She saw that it would have been a close thing. Not all of those who were willing to walk out could have been persuaded into the Opposition lobby. There was a full list of those who had voted, both for and against, which she studied carefully. She knew the political record of almost every name. By implication, she knew, with approximate exactness, who Jimmy's followers were. There were a few surprises on both sides, as there always are. But she saw that Sir Bardsley had more than his numerical superiority in the ability and positions of those whose support he had retained.

So far, good. But what, to so unprecedented a position, would the public reaction be during the next few days? She understood the game well enough to know that everything would depend upon that.

What line did the *Morning Standard* take? She turned eagerly to the leading article, and found it to be little more than a restatement of the facts which were known to all. That was the tone of all the leading newspapers that morning. It was as though they were stunned. They waited each for the other to lead. Their editors tried in a hundred ways to find out what the public thought. The impression they got was that the public were as confused as themselves. On the whole (as long as no vested interest or social security of their own should be threatened) there were an increasing number of people during the next few days who were disposed to think that it might be well to let Mr. Maitland have his chance. You couldn't say that matters mightn't easily be improved from what they were now! Besides, he seemed to have the whip-hand. Articles appeared estimating the wealth that lay, much of it in unremovable treasures, within three miles of Charing Cross. And the swarming human life! Reading the speeches which Stanley made during those days when the later stages of the Bill were being hurried through, there was a general feeling that this sinister power might have fallen into worse hands.

He had shown at times a blunt and epigrammatic way of expressing those things that may be known in political circles but are never publicly mentioned in such naked ways, and this did not decrease his popularity. Once he had alluded to the ghastly burden of taxation which is ruining England, as though it were a preventable thing, and had met with interruption, calling his attention to the war-origin of so large a proportion of this total. Was England responsible for the war?

"No," he retorted swiftly, "but when the war was over, the French Government resolved that its share should be paid by its enemies, and the American Government resolved that its share should be paid by its friends, but the English Government resolved that its share should be wrung from its own taxpayers, with a few hundred millions added. Who was responsible for that?"

Even Sir Bardsley stirred in his seat a little at that remark. He had his own share of responsibility for those settlements. And the only reply, bad or good, which could be made was even more impossible than that blunt allusion to American business methods, for which he must apologise to the Ambassador tomorrow. Could he rise and explain: "From the day the Armistice was signed, we cared more for the Balance of Power than for the friendship of France, or the prosperity of our own citizens; and we therefore bamboozled the people with silly talk about hanging the Kaiser, and homes for heroes, and making Germany pay, while we fastened the financial fetters upon them with a practised skill that even Mr. Maitland will find beyond his capacity to undo?" No. He really couldn't say that.

Yet Sir Bardsley still believed that it had been the right course to take. He knew that he had acted for the best all along. Prosperity such as the country had never known before was to have come by increasing each other's wages and shortening each other's hours of work. He was a little doubtful of the soundness of that policy now, but at the time there was no trade union leader who had believed in it more simply than he. And yet he was an intelligent man. Even a novelist cannot explain that.

Lady Crystal waited in all the next afternoon, but Stanley did not come. She waited all the next day. At this time she had cancelled all her engagements. She was not at home to her closest friends. Only Stanley (she had told Miss Preston) was to be put through to her at once if he should ring up. Stanley or Jehane.

But there was no call from either. Did Stanley think that her conduct was beyond forgiveness? Did he think that she should have gone to him? Did he (hateful thought) suppose that she had only approached him because she thought that he was succeeding without her aid? If so, he might find that he was doubly wrong. The next time he should come to her—come to her when he had failed, as she still thought that he would be most likely to do. Anyway, he must come to her. From her side the last advance had been made.

On the third day of silence she decided that she could not stay longer in London, denying herself to all her friends. Neither could she go out, to be questioned about her relations with Stanley, as she surely would be. She would not know what reply to give. She said that she was going into the country for an indefinite period, and gave Miss Preston instructions to take the steps for reducing staff and closing rooms which were part of the routine of such migrations. Molly came to her later in the day, and asked if she might leave.

Lady Crystal would not show her astonishment, but it was not easily controlled. Molly was paid more than well. She had an exceptional position, which she would not easily get again.

Lady Crystal only asked: "When?"

"As soon as possible, please."

"Is anything wrong?"

"No, nothing. I thought I should like a change."

"That's what servants say. Molly, won't you tell me the truth?"

"I have been offered a very good position."

"Where?"

"At the Rafton Hotel."

"I suppose that's through Lady Jehane?"

"Yes."

"I thought she hadn't rung up since Tuesday."

"It was before that."

"Then why didn't you mention it earlier?"

"I hadn't decided what to do."

"You'd like to leave as soon as possible?"

"Yes."

"Then you can go now."

Lady Crystal wrote a cheque. It was for a full quarter's salary, much more than was due. Molly took it doubtfully. She was conscious that this abrupt exit would discommode her employer in many ways. She had not meant it to be quite like this.

The two women looked at one another in a pregnant silence. Both were on the verge of speech which did not come. Pride urged the one to silence, and diffidence withheld the other. Lady Crystal said: "I think that will be all?" as though she were dismissing a maid from the room. Molly Preston went.

She went feeling that she had done rather a mean thing. She had understood Lady Crystal during those silent moments better than she had done previously. But it did not alter the fact that her sympathies were entirely on Mr. Maitland's side. Besides, she always hated the country. She particularly hated going down to Norchester Towers, where a housekeeper ruled, and she was no more than Lady Crystal's secretary, treated no better than if she were a lady's maid, or perhaps rather worse than that. Her position and authority were here, and the offer to reorganise the staff and economy of the Rafton was an attractive one. Still, she felt mean.

Lady Crystal wondered, if she knew of that unanswered letter, would she be going like this? But it was not a question which could be asked.

CHAPTER THIRTY-THREE

IT was the morning of Sunday, the 11th of February. For three days Stanley Maitland had been dictator of England.

He stood now at the high window of the room he had made his own, and which even Jehane was not allowed to enter, looking down upon the smooth-running traffic of the half-deserted Haymarket. He had made that condition because some peace, some solitude, some period when he could be free from the necessity of controlling speech and expression, had become a vital necessity.

Three days! Days in which he had done nothing—perhaps less than that. But he was already experiencing the lack alike of personal privacy and intellectual intimacy which are the hard lot of all who would be leaders of men.

He was discouraged, dispirited this morning, perhaps responding to the drabness of the outer day. And it was a mood which must not be shown to any. He had breakfasted with Rigby and Jehane and Molly Preston, and had been no worse than quiet amid the light-spirited inconsequent chatter of his companions, who had developed another mood. "I suppose," Jehane had said, "we can call Sunday a day off? Anyway, there'll be no post today." He had agreed, of course; and, more or less, it would be a day off for them. They were caught, but in a looser net.

Molly had said that there were some things that she must oversee. She was attempting to reduce the almost incredible waste of the hotel kitchens to the economy of a well-ordered household.

Rigby would be playing bridge in the lounge on the ground-floor with some of his sporting friends, their weapons near to their hands, and ready to change places at intervals with those who guarded the outer doors. Whimsically, the presence of this friendly guard, that Jehane had gathered, reminded Stanley of the Alsatian bravos who had lounged and diced at Whitehall for the protection of the first Charles, before he fled from London to appeal to the arbitrament of disastrous war. The parallel might be inexact in important features, but it was of an ominous colour. He had not asked, would not have thought of asking, to be guarded in such ways, but the necessity seemed clear to others. Even the opposite building, lately occupied by the Mid-Atlantic, had been cleared by the police, and was now in charge of a half-company of the West Kents. His habit of standing at the window had been observed, and a bullet can easily cross the street.

Jehane had said that she must have a talk with the head of the Gadarenes, as she persisted in calling the twenty efficient young ladies who had been supplied to her requisition. Miss Trentham wished to consult her about various details, including the doubtful quality of Clara Hopkins (No. 17). Clara was one of those who had been employed in the preliminary sorting of correspondence under various headings. She had been trusted to put aside certain specified types of letter of obviously trivial or impertinent kinds. She was not unintelligent, but inclined to a careless, what-is-one-among-so-many attitude which disquieted Miss Trentham's mind. Miss Hopkins would go. But her departure would not resurrect Lady Crystal's letter, which was now in a sack in the basement, waiting its turn to assist in lighting the furnace fire.

Occupations each might have, but still, it would be "a day off" for them. There could be no day off for him.

He had been dictator of England for three days. Yesterday the *Morning Standard*, which had ignored him for the previous week, had published on its front page:

THE PRICE OF LONDON

1. The London Stock Exchange closes this morning
   until further notice.

That was all. Just the announcement of the bare fact, with the number which suggested a serial of which this was the sinister beginning.

And there had been a leading article in *The Times*, appealing to him in moderate dignified words to say what he meant to do. He saw that it was a reasonable request, which was emphasised by the financial crisis of the previous day. "Mr. Maitland, who has said nothing so successfully during the past week." That had been its description. And he knew that it was correct. After those first days of debate, his mind had become obsessed with the gravity of any spoken word, and he had concentrated his resolution upon the avoidance of definite statement of any kind. But now the time for action had come.

Up to Thursday evening, the Stock Exchange, in spite of some nervous flurries, and an amount of selling pressure from foreign centres, had been fairly steady. Speculation had been severely discouraged both by banks and brokers. Legitimate business had been restricted. Everyone had been inclined to wait and watch. The uncertainty of who might suffer or benefit had been too great.

But on Thursday night, he had made his first exception to the rule that he would give no interviews and receive no deputations. He had had good excuse for this attitude in the fact that every propagandist society in England, every anti-everything in the land, was clamouring round his door.

But a deputation representing the leading branches of the motor industry had succeeded in breaking through. They had had an exceptional claim, owing to the incautious, disturbing words that he had spoken on the night when Sir Bardsley had introduced is Bill.

Sir Bardsley himself had pressed him to receive this deputation. "A few reassuring words," he had suggested—"at any rate, they should know. I understand that some great personal sacrifices have been made to keep the market steady during the past week…financial disaster of the first magnitude. I am sure you would wish to avoid such a commencement." Stanley had said that he would hear what they had to say.

The deputation was introduced by Mr. Bigland, the Chairman of the Cranmer Motor Company. He had the good-humoured urbanity of one to whom success had come easily, and whose digestion was as good as the dinners which that success had provided. He spoke with a persuasive lucidity, and a practised trick of implication, by which he dwelt most upon the points upon which he anticipated unity of opinion.

The cause of this deputation was, he explained briefly, a certain amount of unrest and a degree of apprehension (which he did not share) existing within the industry owing to some remarks which Mr. Maitland had been reported as having made in the House of Commons on the 29th *ultimo*.

He observed that these remarks had dealt primarily with the accidents which had been, and still were, too frequent upon the public and which, he feared, were to a large extent inevitable, at least until a better road-sense had been developed, particularly among the pedestrian elements of the population.

He supposed he need scarcely say how keenly these fatalities were regretted by all who were in any way connected with the great industry which he had the honour to represent. Even as a matter of business, it must be evident that it was not to their interest that the railways should be regarded as the safer method of travel. For this reason alone, Mr. Maitland could rely upon the sympathetic co-operation of the allied trades in any effort which might be made to increase the safety of the new method of transit which, he might claim without undue boasting, had revolutionised the modern world.

He paused a moment to give full value to his last sentence, and Stanley interposed with: "Have you anything to propose?"

Mr. Bigland had intended to arrive at his proposals by a longer route, but he answered, as he could hardly fail to do: "We suggest that a select committee might be appointed to consider the whole matter, on which representatives of the manufacturing and distributing branches of the trade might be included, to give the committee the benefit of their expert knowledge and practical experience."

"Rather like asking the prisoner to consult with the judge as to whether any sentence shall be passed upon him! And, while these deliberations continue, is the present slaughter to go on?"

Mr. Bigland's face flushed somewhat at the brusque rejoinder, "I am sorry," he said, making a difficult effort for suavity, "that I cannot accept the metaphor. We are not criminals, and—!"

"I'm sorry to interrupt you, Mr. Bigland, but let us have that point dear. You were criminals, and inciting others to crime, until three years ago, when you obtained an act to legalise what was going on. Since then, you are not criminals, if it be possible to legalise manslaughter—a matter of dialectics which I'm sure you don't want to argue now."

Mr. Bigland did not reply directly. He was delayed by an urgent whispering from a colleague on his right hand. Then he said:

"We have had certain statistics prepared which I feel it to be my duty to lay before you. They represent the number of those who are employed directly or indirectly in connection with the motor-industry. They include not only those directly occupied in the manufacture of cars, and all the accessory and ancillary trades, but also the shop-keepers, garage proprietors, chauffeurs, road makers, and repairers, insurance workers, and countless others whose livelihoods are dependent upon this most important industry."

With an aspect of returning confidence, he passed some neatly tabulated columns of figures across the table. Even to himself, they showed an almost fantastic total. Anyone must be impressed by them.

Unfortunately, Stanley was impressed in a way which he had not anticipated.

"You mean," he asked, "that this incredible number of people are employed in an industry which produces nothing? Which only moves things about?"

Mr. Bigland was so momentarily confused by this unexpected—this most unbusinesslike view, that he could only reply feebly: "You must not overlook the importance of the export trade." With more time he might have made a better reply. As it was, he heard the obvious retort: "Which is more than offset by importations of petrol, rubber, and other materials that the trade requires."

Mr. Bigland felt that matters were not going as he would like them to do. He abandoned the export argument to say earnestly: "Mr. Maitland, I do not know what you may propose, but I urge upon your consideration that, if you should do anything to obstruct the great industry which I represent, you will produce widespread misery and a social upheaval the extent of which would be difficult to foresee. It is not too much to say that all England would be out of work tomorrow."

Stanley said: "There would still be spades," and regretted the words as they passed his lips. He was learning that he could say nothing, however casual, however obvious, which did not bear unexpected and sometimes unwelcome fruit. Probably there would be trunk calls to Birmingham and Sheffield and Wolverhampton during the next hour, urging that spade manufacturers should prepare for the coming boom. He answered the deputation in more careful words.

"Gentlemen, your case has been put by Mr. Bigland in a very able way. On some points, I am in sympathy with it, but, however skilfully it may be worded, it amounts to no more than a plea that your trade should be carried on, at whatever cost of human life and suffering, which have now risen to a worldwide total which is greater than that of a major war. I can only tell you that, so far as this country is concerned, if I can stop that slaughter, by whatever means, it is going to stop.

"Your idea that the prosperity of a country can be secured by the majority of its inhabitants being made busy in useless or detrimental ways becomes an absurdity when closely examined. England would be more prosperous today if one-tenth of these people whom you have tabulated so neatly had been occupied in the motor industry, and the rest had been paid to stand on their heads.

"I suggest to you, as intelligent businessmen, that this worldwide direction of energy into the cultivation of motion rather than production may be one of the major causes—though not, perhaps, the first or the greatest—of the economic crisis which has convulsed the world.

"Quite apart from the humanitarian aspects, consider the position which your business abilities have created in England today. The country is covered with hundreds of thousands of these road vehicles, many of which have cost the price of a house. Almost all of them have been produced within the last few years, and it is either true, or you would persuade the public that it is true, that within a few years they will all be worn out, and therefore require to be replaced continually.

"You offer to supply this increasing replacement, and you suggest that the country's prosperity is bound up in the transfer of wealth to those of you that this service requires.

"Have you considered that you cannot receive a single penny from the section of the public which does not profit from the industry which is not diverted from other forms of expenditure? That it has to work to support you as well as itself? Or that the time is upon us when the burden of supporting these millions that your tables show has become an almost impossible thing? I will tell you this: there are other matters with which I am more concerned than the prosperity of the motor industry or even the slaughter which it entails. In the debate you mention, I had no intention of alluding to it at all. It was thrown to the surface by the wave of chance. But since you are here, I will tell you plainly that I do intend to discourage the congestion of the roads, and the infatuation of people who spend money upon you which is needed in other ways. A man applying for a licence for a new car—I am not pledging myself to this method—may, for instance, be required to produce his income-tax receipts in evidence that he, or his family, will not suffer from the effects of the liability he is proposing to contract. There may also be an enquiry into the number of good cars in existence, and the number of new ones which you can throw on the market may be restricted accordingly. You cannot deny that the overproduction of new vehicles in recent years has been such as to depress the price of second-hand ones below the fair value of their unexhausted capacity."

"We have submitted to the Treasury several times," Mr. Bigland, interjected, "that the licence duties on old cars should be lowered."

"The question will not arise in future, because licences will not be taxed. You look surprised. The reason is no more than that while I am Chancellor of the Exchequer, common honesty will be practised at the Treasury as a matter of course. A tax on vehicles which has no relation to how much they are used is inequitable. That objection is final. So far as is humanly possible, honesty will replace expediency in the financial relations of the State and its citizens. You will understand that the tax on petrol, which has a more direct relation with the use of the car and the road, may be retained or increased. Beyond that, I can only assure you that I have no hostility to you, or to any industry whatever. It is for you to consider, as businessmen, if you have not carried your success beyond what the national requirements are likely to continue to be, and how far and in what directions you can utilise your machinery in other ways."

After that, the deputation had withdrawn with a minimum of courtesy, and with no satisfaction at all.

The next morning the pressure of selling orders at the opening of the London Exchange was so great that the shares of the great tyre and motor manufacturing companies fell during the first half-hour to unprecedented depths. For a time it seemed that it was a pit without bottom, that there were no buyers at all. Then there was a momentary rally. A rumour that the great banks were combining to support the market caused a spurt of covering by bears who had oversold. But the panic was too general, its cause too real, for any artificial support to subdue it. At the news that prices had steadied, new selling orders poured in. If the banks or anyone else wanted motor shares on Friday, February 9th, 1934, they could have them at their own price—they could go on buying till the whole industry would be theirs.

Later in the day, the financial difficulties that these losses brought threw other shares in huge blocks upon a market that was in no mood to absorb them.

At 3:30 P.M., the Chairman of the Stock Exchange Committee was on the telephone, not for the first time, appealing frantically for some reassuring message which might be sufficient to check the descending avalanche.

The call came from Secretary No. 3 to Miss Trentham, and from her to Jehane, where it got no further.

"This is Mr. Maitland's secretary."

"Another of them?" a voice answered, that was too troubled and excited to make politeness easy. "I want to be put through to Mr. Maitland himself."

"I'm sorry I can't do that."

"Then please put me through to the lady who can. It is a matter of the utmost urgency."

"I'm sorry there's nowhere further to go. Yes, this is Lady Jehane Norchester, Mr. Maitland's personal secretary. He says he knows all about that, but it won't really matter. He doesn't believe half the transactions are genuine."

A sound came from the other end of the wire like the groan of a maddened man. It became vocal for a moment, and ended in a cough. What is the use of talking to a lady about the benefits of a free market and the blessings of selling short? He said: "They're genuine enough to be ruining hundreds while we're talking now."

"Mr. Maitland says that's a mistake. No one's being ruined to-day. You can tell them that all the transactions which have taken place since the Exchange opened this morning will be struck out, or called off, or whatever's the right word. Mr. Maitland says it'll cool them off wonderfully if they know they're just wasting their time."

"I'm afraid that's impossible. We can't cancel transactions that have once been put through. It's no use talking about that. If you could get something from Mr. Maitland to steady the market, even at present levels."

"He says he's going to steady it where it was yesterday. There'll be an Order in Council to cancel all today's transactions. That is, if it's necessary. Mr. Maitland says you'll get that free of charge, and no stamp duty."

Mr. Shirebolt's reply paused. He was not without a personal stake in the matter. His own firm of Maltby-Johnson and Stokes, of which he was the senior partner, might have lost anything up to fifty thousand in the last two hours, but he was not thinking first of that. The prestige of the Exchange, its traditions, the possible sequel to such a cancellation, passed rapidly through his mind. He said: "If we're going to do that, we might as well close altogether."

"Mr. Maitland says if you can't keep your heads, it's quite the best thing to do."

So it had been. He had met the situation with an outward bold-ness, but the event had one significance which would not leave his mind. It had not been intended. It had not been foreseen. Everything he said or did might have incalculable consequences, apart from those which he might aim successfully to produce. A human civili-sation is a very complex organisation of interdependent parts. You cannot alter or withdraw one, you cannot even improve its effi-ciency, without the risk that another will break from the resulting strain, and that that breakage may have further consequences. Even God works His changes in gradual, age-long, often imperceptible ways, as though fearing to jerk the mechanism of the world He made. That is true—always true—when He constructs. Flood and thunder, avalanche and fire, may act with decisive speed, but they are for destruction only.

But men have no time for action with the deliberation of the Divine. Their lives are too short. Stanley Maitland's time was shorter still. A matter of eleven months. And in the first three days he was doing things which he had not thought to do, saying things which he had not thought to say, and being driven or drawn by the pressure of surrounding circumstance. Now, in the brief, snatched solitude of this Sunday morning, he must resolve once for all upon the limitations of that which he would attempt. He had arranged to dine with Sir Bardsley Clinton this evening. He would probably seek to draw him into discussion of budgetary problems. To assume and contrive that he would be sufficiently absorbed in preparations for the next budget to let other matters alone. And suppose that would be the wisest way? Considered separately, what a chance it was! When before had any Chancellor had the opportunity of framing a budget which was not limited by his party's policy, subject to the approval of the Cabinet, and liable to have any of its provisions thrown out by the House, with the consequence of his own eclipse, should he attempt any startling originality? Suppose that he could take such advantage of this opportunity that he should improve the whole basis of taxation and gain a reputation, an authority, which would leave him with his power established at the end of the year, not by a criminal threat, but by a popularity which he would have fairly won? And suppose that, should he attempt more, he would fail in all?

Thinking of his appointment with Sir Bardsley, his mind diverted to the recollection that, in other circumstances, he might have been spending the evening with Crystal, in the way which had been so dear to both. However much their marriage might have fallen short of ideal union—and no marriage with such reservations as theirs can be better than a maimed and hindered thing—they had, at least, not crossed too rashly "the space that makes attraction felt". From a normally consummated and fruitful marriage, they would either not have broken apart at all, or the break would have been evidence of probably irreparable disaster. As it was, they were both left with the bitter unrest and longing and injured pride that a lover's quarrel will produce. The instincts of both rejected the idea of finality in separation. But the pride of both withheld them from any further effort at reconciliation. Crystal could not know that the letter she had already written had never reached him, and he regarded her as having deserted him at a crisis that she would not share, an opportunity that she would not realise. He saw the dangers of his position. He would not ask her again to share them. Let her come back to him when he had proved himself equal to the opportunity he had seized! It was on the crest of such a victory that he could indeed possess and subdue her…and how he wanted her now! And she had gone down, as the *Morning Standard* had informed its readers—with a prominence and a lack of context or comment which had their own significance—she had gone down to Norchester Towers.

Thinking of the laconic prominence of that announcement, he realised how much her co-operation could have helped him now. Not in imagination perhaps, not perhaps in active sympathy with his aims or methods, but if she had done no more than accept them, as she would have accepted the official programme of her party whatever it might contain, her social influence, the prestige of her name, her resolute and clear-sighted tenacity, the practical sagacity that, because its vision was limited, judged so clearly within its boundaries—how they would have helped him now!

And now—his mind wandered toward her, letting the precious moments of solitude slip away. What should he substitute for the strength and happiness that would have come from their union now? What but the resolution that he would win her again by victory on the high and lonely adventure that he had made his own?

CHAPTER THIRTY-FOUR

STANLEY looked down into the Haymarket, and saw a car that he thought he knew. It was an open car, driven by a woman, who was its only occupant. It came rapidly down the centre of the deserted Sunday thoroughfare, and turned inward beneath him, passing out of his range of sight, as though it were stopping at the main entrance of the hotel.

He had a foolish momentary thought that it might be Crystal herself. Suppose she had felt as he, recalling the way in which their Sunday evenings had been spent before this sudden division. But, though his blood quickened at the thought, his reason rejected it as it came. The woman, vaguely familiar as she had been, was not Crystal, the car was not one of hers. Neither would she have come in such a manner. She had a driving licence. She had learned to drive. But she considered that her dignity required that she should be driven on the London streets, a vision of carefully-constructed-loveliness, leaning back in a cushioned ease. He could not imagine her jumping impulsively into an open car at Norchester Towers and driving herself here. Jehane might, but not she. Would he have liked her better had she been more capable of a reckless thing?

Yet, in a way, the reflection did her less than justice. He knew that Crystal did not lack courage, or the capacity for quick and decisive action. She might have come, but it would have been in a more stately way. Anyhow, it was not she.

Yet the idea gave him a momentary excitement, and when the telephone bell rang sharply, it seemed an expected thing.

He stepped to it quickly, and heard Jehane's voice. "There's Mrs. Shackston here, and Rigby says she won't go. Not without seeing you."

"Tell her I don't see anyone on Sunday mornings."

"I think she'll need something stronger than that."

"Tell her she won't see me if she waits all day. If I once begin seeing callers...."

"Yes, I know. But if you think Rigby could keep out a woman like that.... I'd better get to work on her myself."

"Tell her if she doesn't clear—. No, tell her to leave a note, and you'll see that I get it within half an hour, if she goes quickly."

"Very well. That ought to move the works. Wish me luck."

He put down the receiver and went back to the window. Damn the woman, he thought irritably, what can she want here? He must stop these continual interruptions somehow. Why didn't Rigby wring her neck? Anything would be justifiable with a woman like that. This was unfair to one of the best of America's exports from the Oklahoma oilfields, but Mrs. Shackston had the reputation of a very resolute character, and she appeared to typify all the thousands who pressed and clamoured continually by letter, telegram, phone, and personal waylaying, to distract him from his own thoughts. He would tell Rigby to put up a notice, "Women's necks wrung," across the door. Rigby would do that with a cheerful speed. Especially if Jehane had been treating him as badly as she mostly did. The thought restored him to better humour. He felt that he had done rightly to tell her to leave a note. After all, it was of some interest— possibly of importance—to know why Jimmy Shackston's wife should be so anxious to see him. She appeared to be writing it now. Anyway, she wasn't going. He wondered what sort of trouble Jehane might be having on the ground-floor. A duel of words between those two would be worth something for a front-seat ticket. But he was denied that pleasure (as so many others) by the power which he had reached to seize. He could only observe that it was a battle that Jehane had won, for now the car came into sight again. It swung out into the centre of the road in an abrupt contempt of the claims of others or its own risk, missed another by a bare three inches, and passed rapidly out of sight.

There was a tap on the door. "Am I allowed?" Jehane said, as she entered, "I know the rule, but you haven't made an Order in Council yet about letters coming up by themselves."

"Perhaps a slit in the door."

"Yes. What a brain you have. Here's the letter. I shan't stay."

"You can wait till you're turned out. You seem to have ruffled that woman's temper by the way she drove."

"No, it was you who did that. I just sympathised. I quoted Kipling: 'Nay, we be women together.' Isn't that right? She was like a lamb."

"Like a lamb and a butcher?"

"I can't answer that, never having seen them together. Anyway, she went. Here's the note."

Stanley opened it in some curiosity. He said: "Good for her," and passed it to Jehane.

DEAR MR. MAITLAND,

Jimmy tells me that you threatened to destroy Seven Pines, and wants me to take the children abroad before he gets really busy.

I've sent the boys where they'll be safe, and I've told the staff they can go or stay, but I'm not going to budge for you. So don't say afterwards that you didn't know.

Yours suitably,

LYDIA SHACKSTON

P.S. How long do you suppose it will be before someone else finds it out, and begins with you?

"An emphatic woman," he said, smiling. "I wonder where we should be if everyone took the same line? You'd better send her a few words just to say that Seven Pines is quite safe from me, and let the incident go to the press. Jimmy's going to get really busy, is he? I wonder how. Well, so am I. You know Sir Bardsley's coming to dinner with me tonight. I want you and Rigby to join us, if you will."

"Yes, if you wish. But Sir Bardsley won't like that. He wants to talk to you alone. He made that clear yesterday."

"Yes, I know; but I don't. I'm going to give old Bardsley the shock of his life. Shocks, rather. I want you to bring a notebook here, if you will. We've got a good hour before lunch. I'll dictate a few little crackers that I mean to fire off tomorrow, and I want you to tell them at dinner tonight in your own way."

He had felt different since Jehane had entered. The earlier hours of gloomy irresolute thought; the longing for Crystal which had hardened into a resolve to have her back on the crest of the victory which was yet to win, the import of that challenging note, each had its part in producing the buoyant fighting spirit which he felt at that moment. Jimmy getting really busy? He must be busy a day sooner than he. Others making the same discovery? He had always seen that that was a possible thing. It was only another reason to avoid delay.

All the weeks of brooding upon the legal abuses and social evils which chained and enervated the English people came to easy flower as he dictated rapidly for the next fifty minutes.

"Well," he said at last, as Jehane closed her book, and slipped the pencil back into the elastic, "what do you think of that?"

"I think," she said dubiously, "I think—it's rather a mouthful."

He understood the implied criticism, but declined discouragement.

"Yes," he said. "You've got the right word. It's the mouthful that starts a meal."

"I'm to tell Sir Bardsley all that tonight?"

"Yes, in your own way. But not just at first. Let him do the talking till we know what his cards are. He isn't coming here for something to eat."

"You really want Rigby?"

"Yes, we need four."

"Wouldn't one of the others do?"

"Not so well. I like Rigby. So do you. Why shouldn't it be he?"

Jehane looked mutinous for a moment, and then agreed. "Yes, he'll do as well as anyone else. I suppose it ought to be he. But we might have had Clifton Gales, and Molly's got more brains than the two. Two girls.... But I'll tell Rigby to let Sir Bardsley talk till you give me the signal to sail in."

She could trust Rigby to do as he was told. He was as good as a dog. The trouble was that she didn't want dogs.

"Well," she said, "I suppose lunch is the word."

CHAPTER THIRTY-FIVE

SIR BARDSLEY looked some surprise, and felt more. He thought it had been understood clearly enough that this meeting was to have been of a confidential character, and he had supposed that Mr. Maitland would have had an equal inclination for privacy.

He felt that he had done much for this surprisingly lawless young politician, and that, wherever the power might lie, there was an obligation to treat him with consideration, and his opinions with respect. To Mr. Maitland's inexperience, his advice and guidance must be of almost incalculable value. Friday's trouble on the Exchange should have been a lesson to him, which he had sufficient sense to learn. It was true that the drastic manner in which he had dealt with the emergency had averted its more tragic possibilities. But it ought not to have occurred. Surely Mr. Maitland would see that. In the result, the Stock Exchange was closed, and no one could say how or when it would reopen. It was a bad day's work at the best.

But if Mr. Maitland would concentrate upon the preparation of a really possible budget, and perhaps a few popular reforms of a minor kind, which most people would agree were overdue, but for which there had been no sufficient popular agitation to justify parliamentary action hitherto, all might yet be well. To these ends Sir Bardsley would give all the help that his long parliamentary and executive experience suggested. He would give it in good faith and without reservation. His policy was to guide events so that no disaster should follow from the power which had been placed in this young man's hands. If people should afterwards give him the praise, as one whose courage in crisis, and subsequent diplomacy, had saved the land, there could be no objection to that.

It was certainly an exceptional opportunity for introducing a popular budget, the difficulties of which he knew from a personal experience when he had occupied that office. There had not only been his own fears that any innovation might prove unpopular and wreck his career, there had been the difficulty of reconciling the other members of the Cabinet to a proposal of any novelty. Why not play for safety in the old familiar ways? Why not let sleeping dogs lie? Why risk defeats in the House—in Committee—upon the Bill? Then there had been the permanent officials, suave, even obsequious in manner, but steel in their determination to obstruct any form or reform of taxation which they did not approve. And what a power they had!

But Maitland had an exceptional opportunity, and with good counsel much might be done. Sir Bardsley even had one or two minor adjustments of taxation to suggest of what he considered to be very adventurous kinds, for which he was willing that Mr. Maitland should take the credit. The great thing was to get him occupied in some harmless manner, so that the time might pass in forgetfulness of his wilder dreams.

There were words of advice and admonition, cautious, which he felt that he might have spoken without offence, as the meal progressed (basing them on the Stock Exchange catastrophe), had they been alone, but in the presence of others they would require a greater circumspection. Perhaps it would be best to defer some of these points entirely, and ask for a talk in private after the meal. This idea partly, but only partly, consoled him. It would tend to make his advice appear more deliberate, more formal, and therefore more liable to cause resentment.

These feelings, clear, though too swift for mental articulation, moved in the rear of his mind, as he greeted Jehane with a fine, rather old-fashioned courtesy, and expressed his pleasure at meeting Lord Rigby Stilton since—in fact, since the last time he had done so. (But he put it much better than that.) His manners were indeed perfect under what he felt to be some provocation. Neither Lady Jehane nor Lord Rigby was beneath him in birth or rank, but they were—well, you might almost say they were Maitland's staff! There is an aristocracy of politics which is distinct from that of rank or wealth. There are occasions also. To bring these young people on to the scene on what had been understood vaguely, but sufficiently, to be one of those informal councils of war which are events of the first magnitude—well, Maitland's inexperience must be his excuse. He could not have meant to be rude.

The conversation opened lightly, hesitating toward the subjects that were in all their minds, and approached them nearly when Jehane mentioned the visitor of the earlier day. Rigby gave his account of the first skirmish. Jehane added the later episode when her superior feminine efficiency came to the rescue of the hard-pressed guard. Stanley told of the contents of the letter, and his reply.

"I was glad," he added frankly, "to have a good excuse for withdrawing a threat which I made on an impulse which was soon regretted. Though I'm not saying that a lesson may not be needed somewhat nearer than Seven Pines." In the privacy of his own mind, he knew that the threat should not have been made, if only because Seven Pines was far beyond the radius of Feltham's machine.

"I hope," Sir Bardsley said, with a mild seriousness, "I sincerely hope that there will be no such necess—occasion. Its consequences are rather difficult to foresee, and might be—disappointing. If you consider that the country has, from a point of view that I think we are bound to recognise, given what I may not unfairly call a blank cheque as an insurance against such possibilities."

"I feel as you do," Stanley answered. "I should be equally reluctant to entertain such a possibility. But an occasion might arise in which individuals might be endeavouring, shall I say, to dishonour the cheque which the country has issued, and it might be a necessity to take steps, not against the country, but against them."

Lack of intelligence was not one of Sir Bardsley's faults. There was a fighting metallic tone in Stanley's voice as he said this, which he was quick to recognise. Was it possible that he had failed to understand Maitland's character accurately? Or was the sense of power already intoxicating him, as it had done so many others before, so that he would rush to his own destruction? He avoided the direct line of argument to say: "I suppose it's the phrase in Mrs. Shackston's letter about Jimmy getting busy that makes you feel like that? But I don't know that I should take it too seriously.

"As a matter of fact, I had the same thing on my mind as I came here this evening. I don't mean that I knew anything of the letter, or about Shackston saying he's going to get busy. (It's only a word to a woman, after all. They don't always mean much, even if they're repeated accurately.) What I mean is that I was thinking what harm, if any, Shackston could do, and I can't see that that's much unless you play into his hands.

"I can't help inclining to the opinion that he thinks the same. He hasn't dared to oppose you openly from the start. He's waiting for your mistakes, and if you don't make them, he's no better than a damp squib. But he'll reckon Friday's was the first, and he's bound to have his tail a bit in the air."

"I don't call Friday a mistake," Stanley answered. "Or, if so, it wasn't mine."

"You certainly took the right line. You must have saved scores from ruin, and hundreds from losses they couldn't afford, but you'll allow that it's a bad day for England when the Stock Exchange closes its doors."

"I don't say you're wrong. Frankly, I haven't given it enough thought to have an opinion that's worth having on that point. But I suppose the sale of shares can still be privately negotiated. It prevents an easy market being available, speculation by people who haven't got any shares who ought to be doing honest work, and the public knowledge of a price at which business is being done. Bad and good seem a bit mixed. But perhaps it will be best to leave it as it is, at any rate till they know what the new budget will be in a few weeks' time."

"I think," Sir Bardsley answered, with something slightly less than the usual cordiality in his voice, "it would be a quite needless disaster to have the Exchange closed for so long a period. It isn't usual to give any hint of the contents of the budget beforehand, but, in this instance, perhaps a short statement, at least of some things which it will not include."

"I don't know about that," Stanley said doubtfully, "I want to give them one or two other things to think about before then. The budget's a good way ahead. Still, you may be right."

He had no wish to quarrel with Sir Bardsley. He was a man he liked. A man to whom some would say that he owed much. But he was determined to break loose from the firm though gentle pressure which was being exerted upon him, and the object of which, however friendly, might not be simply and entirely to assist his plans. He answered in a cordial tone. Sir Bardsley should not think that he was prepared to quarrel. In fact, he had no wish to do so. If his demonstration of independence should be peacefully taken it would be an immense gain.

Sir Bardsley said in his doubtful judicial tone, less as argument than as one thinking aloud: "I don't know that you'll find it easy to get people to think of other things, if finance is in any serious difficulty. It has so many reactions. But if that could be handled in the right way, and a few popular reforms—I mean such that only small minorities would suffer seriously. There is your own profession, Mr. Maitland. I think you said something about starting on that."

"I don't know that I said anything about starting. There seem to me to be so many more important things, but I've jotted down a few notes—." He caught Jehane's eye as he said this, and shook his head slightly in return. The time was not yet. Jehane had been silent so far, and had told Rigby beforehand that he was not to butt in. So they had been able to concentrate upon a really good dinner, only interrupted by a moment of low-voiced sparring. But talking and eating delay each other, though they go well together; each gallops the fastest that gallops alone, as Rudyard Kipling said about them—or about something similar. Rigby had laid down his implements upon an empty plate, while Sir Bardsley's partridge had only suffered one or two initial indignities. Idleness and Jehane's averted eyes induced him to contribute to the conversation. He said: "You might call the dogs off old Seeley at Beckett's Brook."

Old Seeley was a small farmer near Merton-Ash, who had had a dispute with a neighbour over a boundary fence. It was a matter which a competent impartial lawyer should have settled in half a day, and which, in any case, was not worth the expenditure of a longer period. But litigation had commenced, and had gone on from court to court long after both parties had ceased to care anything about it, but because by then they each knew that it would be ruin to give way. The fence had ceased to matter. The costs were a nightmare from which they feared to awake.

In the end, the case had gone against John Seeley, and he had been ordered to surrender a strip of ground worth thirty shillings, and pay five pounds damages. That had been seven years ago. Seeing that the sale of his small holding would not pay the amount they required, the lawyers had been lenient about the costs. He had handed over the slowly accumulated savings of two generations, and was paying the balance by yearly instalments still.

"I'm afraid we can't be retrospective," Stanley answered. "The consequences would be too complicated. The ideal reform might be to abolish advocacy entirely. One litigant would give notice to the other, and they would go to the lawyer's office together. He would investigate the dispute, and decide it, and be allowed to charge anything up to ten percent of the amount in dispute. If you think it out, you'll see how much better than the present system it would be. Of course, there could be a right of appeal, which might carry a heavy penalty if it were frivolously exercised, and the number of actions that a man might bring might be limited. Litigation should be discouraged as waste of time. But I'm not proposing anything of that kind. There are other things of so much greater importance to deal with.

"All I propose is an Order in Council limiting all costs to ten percent of the disputed amount in all civil actions, allowing both barristers and solicitors to do all classes of legal business for which they are competent and required, and making the Crown liable for costs, especially in all unsuccessful criminal prosecutions.

"Even to cover that ground won't be as simple as it sounds."

"No," Sir Bardsley said drily. "I shouldn't say that it will. Have you thought of how many thousands of legal practitioners it would ruin?"

"Yes. And that shows how needed it is. But a large number are wealthy enough to retire. There are certain accumulated funds from which others can be pensioned off, and entrance to the profession can be restricted in future, which will soon relieve the congestion. We must try to look beyond the pain of the operation to the result which follows. It would lift the cruellest and most dishonourable profession on earth, with the disputable exception of procuration, on to a different plane."

"Well," Sir Bardsley said doubtfully, "you're speaking of your own profession. You ought to know something about it, but I think you exaggerate. I've known lawyers that...."

"So have I. Most of them are. I said profession, not professors."

"I don't see," Sir Bardsley continued with a mild persistence, "how a ten percent limit would be a possible thing. The best services can never be bought at a low cost, and a man against whom an action is brought has a right to the services of the best brains he can get."

"So he has, but they should be in the judge's head. Do you know that there are men at the Bar today who win from sixty to seventy percent of the cases they take on?—and they're not easy cases to win. Men go to them when they're afraid, and are willing to pay a high fee, because it seems the only chance that they've got."

"It sounds as though they earn what they make."

"*Which the other side pays.* And if you think it out you'll see that a large number of those who lose must have been in the right. It's an arithmetical certainty. Men pay these outrageous fees to those who they expect to bamboozle a jury or out-argue a judge. If it isn't to divert the course of justice, what is it for? I've thought sometimes that it might be a good thing if there were an authority like the stewards of the Jockey Club to enquire into the running of any barrister who wins more than sixty percent of the cases that he takes on. It's evident that something's wrong with the administration of justice in such a case, though it may reflect on the judges more than on the man himself."

Sir Bardsley had a moment of silence. His face was mildly inscrutable. When he spoke it was in praise of mutton and caper sauce. After that, he resumed the subject, having seen a way to lead up to a point which he had wished to make.

"I doubt," he said, "whether an Order in Council could be sufficiently comprehensive, sufficiently detailed, to cover the somewhat far-reaching reforms which you have in view. I think you might find that an Act of Parliament would be a more satisfactory instrument."

"And how could I be assured that it would be passed in that way?"

"I think my influence, joined to the fact that the final power is always in your own hand, would be sufficient. I know that the legal element in the House is rather strong. It has always been strong enough to prevent any radical reform of legal procedure in the past, but in present circumstances even the lawyers might prefer that the matter should be dealt with in the form of a Bill which could be considered in committee clause by clause, and you could hear what they had to say. Yes, I think I could promise you that."

Stanley knew the Premier to be a man of his word. If he agreed, he would be the author of a far-reaching experiment in legal reform. That, and a budget after his own ideas. And the two things would keep him busy for the best part of the year. Yes, from his own point of view, Sir Bardsley offered much. Would it not be best to accept an honourable peace on such terms? So his mind hesitated, even while he was giving words to the more resolute thought of the earlier day.

"I think there is one insuperable objection to that in the time it would occupy. To get such a Bill through the House, and mould it, clause by clause, to an agreed shape, would take so much time that there would be none left for more important things."

"That," Sir Bardsley answered with a slight increase in animation, a more combative though still friendly tone, "brings me to the point which I wished to lay before you tonight. It appears to me to be of the very greatest importance that you should keep the House sufficiently occupied. I don't know whether you have given much consideration to that. My experience suggests that it is of the utmost importance in your own interests.

"I can remember once," he added reminiscently, "at a Cabinet meeting when I was no more than—well, a long time ago. I said that the programme had got only one defect. It would go through too smoothly. No one thought much of that. They didn't listen to me then, as, perhaps, they have done since. But we were out of office in three months.

"It isn't that most of the Bills matter much one way or other. You bring in half a dozen, and you know there won't be time to pass them all, and you don't really care. Perhaps you find an excuse to drop the one you really meant seriously before the session ends. You might say that there's just been floods of talk, and it's all waste of time, but it's kept people quiet, and—you're younger than I, and you won't agree—but I'm not sure that that isn't often the main thing. A Bill's very like a bottle of medicine. It mayn't have much in it but H_2O, but it keeps the patient content, even if he doesn't like the taste, and throws the bottle away. You must give them something at least mildly contentious to occupy their minds while Parliament's sitting."

"I hope to give them enough to think of before the week's over. But why should Parliament always be sitting? Why shouldn't it pass the budget and go home as it once used to do?"

"Because people wouldn't be satisfied. They like to feel that the men they've elected are working to improve their positions."

"Yes, I don't say you're wrong. The fact is we've roused a devil we can't lay. Though I'm not sure that it's the general public that would turn grey if every member of Parliament played golf for a month. It's the members themselves who'd think the country couldn't go on if they didn't give it the usual dose of new laws every year. And I suppose since they each get the salary of a second-rate clerk, they've got a right to think that they're of that value to the State, and ought to churn out something of the expected kind."

"Yes," Sir Bardsley repeated. "It keeps people quiet." His thought went on to add, "and the years pass." But he was too wise to say it. Stanley was too young to see the value of that. He wanted to make things happen. Sir Bardsley thought that if nothing happened as the year passed he had done well.

There was a pause of silence. Stanley had not altered his mind, but he found it harder to sustain the tone which he had meant to take. Sir Bardsley Clinton always had that effect upon him. Gentle, flexible, he yet had an unbreakable quality. Gradually he induced a feeling that he saw further than others. And he was so moderate, so reasonable, in all he said.

And yet—to have such a chance, and to have done no more than reform taxation, and clip the wings of his own profession! No, to success or failure, for life or death, he would go on. He said: "I'm not really as much interested in this lawyer business as I may have led you to think. I don't mind giving it half a day, and I suppose, like a hundred others, it's a thing I ought not to overlook now I've got the chance to strike a blow for freedom such as no Englishman ever had before.

"As a matter of fact, Jehane was good enough to jot down for me a few details this morning. Little things I meant to get out of the way before we come to more vital matters. For instance, we'll have an Order clearing Brixton Prison and debtors' gaols generally. That'll make the country a bit cleaner than it is now, and bring some joy into thousands of the most wretched homes in the land. And—but I'm not sure that I remember them all myself now. They were all obvious things, and all in the cause of freedom. No further tyranny, no added restrictions.

"I'll own that I find it hard to remember that. I think in these days we've all got bullying in the blood. I keep thinking of things I should like to do to coerce my fellows—of course, they're all for their own good. But I'm trying to keep to that rule, and to avoid anything punitive. You see I'm releasing the poor wretches who are imprisoned because they can't pay their rates, but I'm not doing anything to punish the officials and magistrates who showed no mercy themselves."

"Have you considered the added difficulty in rate collection that?"

"I don't think it will make any serious difference. Getting blood out of stones never has been a really flourishing trade. But I won't pretend I've thought much about that. I thought more about the misery that such methods of collection cause, and the importance of reducing the impositions themselves. The site of Brixton Prison ought to fetch a fair sum. But I don't know that I could recall all the little matters that I tried to deal with this morning. Perhaps Jehane might remember better, as she's got them down."

"I don't know that I could recall them all," Jehane answered. "There were about two dozen. I remember that trials are not to be reported publicly before their conclusion, unless at the request of the accused."

"The question of the effects of publicity—," Sir Bardsley began doubtfully, "doesn't it seem a pity to interfere, when there's no popular demand? You'll make so many enemies in the press—"

"I don't object to publicity. I think Jehane will tell you that one of my minor reforms will be the abolition of private executions. If we hang men, let us face what we do. But there isn't likely to be a popular demand for a thing like that. Only the accused and their friends and interests are at stake, and who is there to speak for them?"

Sir Bardsley sighed, and let the point go. He had been taught from his first entrance into politics that you must never say nor do anything which would alienate the press. Perhaps as they would still be able to report fully at the conclusion of a case—. But it seemed such a needless thing! He wondered whether there might be any of the two-dozen reformations which were to be ordered tomorrow morning which would be worse than that. "Perhaps," he said to Jehane, in the charming manner which he had for the women he liked, with a smile that was deferential, and yet as one who smiled from a height, "you might tell us any others that impressed your mind."

"Oh, I can remember some of them well enough. There's the one about married teachers, and another about a man selling his goods when he likes."

Sir Bardsley Clinton's face settled into a deeper gravity. "I wonder, Maitland," he said earnestly, "whether you have given all these matters quite the consideration that they require.

"I quite understand your feelings that a married woman should attend to her home, but the restrictions on their continuing in the teaching profession are already fairly general, and your own principle of freedom might have inclined you to allow some local right of decision in such matters.

"As to the restrictions on the sale of goods, have you thought of all the oppression and sweated labour that you may be introducing again?"

He might have said more, but he caught a gleam of amusement in Jehane's eyes, and he was quick to see the possibility of misunderstanding. Suppose it were all a joke, and these things were not meant seriously at all? Just to see what he would say? It would be in bad taste, of course, but he was wary in any skirmish of words. He turned to Jehane without any outward evidence of disconcertment, to ask: "Have I been a little denser than I usually am?"

"I don't think you've been dense at all. It was my—my condensing that wasn't clear."

Stanley said: "It was about the married teachers that Jehane ran you a bit off the rails. But as to local freedom, you can be sure that I shan't do anything willingly to restrict that. It's one of my dreams to re-establish local government, if it isn't too difficult now.

"There are endless local officials to carry out endless Acts of Parliament, and of course the endless taxation which such things entail, but local freedom, and consequently real local government, is almost extinct."

"It is an arguable point of view," Sir Bardsley conceded readily. "But what I feel is that you will alienate and disturb a hundred interests and established customs and prejudices by innovations of such kinds. It's like stirring a lot of hives that are lying quiet."

"Yes, I know that. I don't see that it can be helped, if I'm to do any good with the power I have. It's like the pain that comes when the blood flows back through a numbed limb. But the question of sweated labour and hours of employment doesn't arise in anything I'm proposing to deal with now. Those are some of the real problems in which it might be argued that the price of recovered freedom would be too high. I'm merely proposing a short Order that a man can sell his own goods, or serve in his own shop, at his own times."

"You'll have all the large stores, with all their supporting interests, in opposition to that. I suppose you know that it was mainly in their interests and by the agitation that they engineered that such legislation was passed?

"No, I didn't know that, but it hardly needs saying. No man who wanted to sell a turnip or a lawn-mower would make a law that he wasn't to do it after nine-thirty, or whatever the time may be—anyway, I mean that nonsense to end by tomorrow night.

"But about the married teachers, I think I ought to explain. The idea isn't to stop them teaching. It's just the other way. I think the forbidding of the marriage of women teachers is about the wickedest interference with human liberty that has occurred even in our own day. Our women teachers ought to be the very pick of the race, as they often are. To say that they shall live barren lives is a crime against the nation, as well as themselves. Are they expected to live celibately, or is some species of childless fornication to be condoned among them? And, are unmarried people the most fitted to guide the young? Besides, if a woman undertakes a certain duty and does it efficiently, what right is there to interfere with her private life? It is all part of the bullying servitude to which the endless law-making of the last century has reduced the race. But, of course, a mere tolerance of marriage would be a poor attitude. The real point to watch would be that motherhood should not be discouraged nor handicapped. As a matter of fact, the little Order of which I dictated a draft this morning doesn't deal with the subject except in a very indirect way. It simply removes forthwith from any public office any man who has voted in favour of any resolution differentiating against married women teachers during the last five years. Beyond that, there's no penalty for all the cruel harm they've done. I'm not a great believer in punishments, and the question would arise of whether such men are fit for a penitentiary. A home for the feeble-minded might be more suitable. And you'll notice that I've limited it to five years. That's because there's just a chance that a man who was such a fool six years ago may have learnt sense since. It's not sound policy, and it means that a lot of unfit men will remain in office, but the fact is that I can't do anything drastically. I can't help seeing all sides. Moderation is second nature. I've got Conservatism in the blood."

"I don't know," Sir Bardsley answered, "that I should have noticed that without being told. Have you thought of the confusion which may follow from the removal of so many men without notice from the public offices that they hold?"

"Not enough to worry. And the thing itself seemed such a common-sense way of clearing the ground of the more unfit of those who are controlling education now. I mean in anticipation of the real reform of education which lies at the root of any emancipation or recovered prosperity for the English race."

Mildly and tentatively, Sir Bardsley answered: "Yes?"

Stanley understood that he was invited to go on, but that an equal frankness from Sir Bardsley might not be easy to get. This was not quite the position which he had intended to reach. His aim had been to test the Premier with a disclosure of some of his more audacious prospects, and so discover to what extent he could rely upon his continued aid, or must be prepared for obstruction or even hostility from this formidable ally, whose support had been almost thrust upon him.

Sir Bardsley may not have read all that was in his mind, but his habitual caution was sufficient to avoid the pitfall which had been dug to trap him. His thought was that it had become a vital necessity to get to the bottom of Maitland's intentions. He no longer wanted to criticise, to argue. That could come later, if at all. Now he wanted to learn. He thought that the less he opposed or doubted, the more Maitland's cards would be exposed on the table.

Lord Rigby Stilton, watching in silence, and enjoying himself much better than he usually did when he wasn't allowed to talk, understood the situation exactly. He thought: "The old bird won't rise." He badly wanted to whisper this to Jehane, but the risk of being overheard was too great. That is why a large dinner is so preferable, where you can say what you will to your next-hand neighbour, and no one else will be either worse or wiser.

Sir Bardsley said, "Yes?" in his tentatively enquiring way, and Stanley saw that he must advance through the smoke-screen which his protagonist had developed, or let the moment go.

"I have thought," he said, with the frankness which was natural to him and is so often the most effectual weapon, both to defend and disarm—"I have thought that the abolition of compulsory education might cut at the very root of the present servitude, as nothing else would be likely to do. The fallacy that all men are equal has bound them in an equal slavery. Might not the truth that no two men are equal, or ever will be, release them to an equal freedom?"

"I am not sure," Sir Bardsley answered cautiously, "that I know what you mean. Might not a reduction in the standard of education place us at a somewhat serious disadvantage against other nations who are spending increasingly in such directions?"

"Perhaps the simplest answer would be, not if we expend our energy in better ways. But I had not thought of reducing the standard of education. I only thought we might apply it more intelligently, and incidentally reduce expenditure to about one-tenth what it is now."

"It sounds financially attractive," Sir Bardsley conceded. (Did he mock? Even Rigby was not sure this time.) "I wonder how you would proceed to that end?"

"I would make education free, but not compulsory. I would offer it as a boon, not in the form of a bludgeon. The schools should be always open to child or adult who would conduct himself within them in an orderly way. Equality of opportunity should be as absolute as it is possible to make it. At ten years a child should choose, as far as possible, the classes that it should attend. Before that age, it would not be found that many parents would keep their children at home, and, if they should, the child might be learning the lessons of life in ways equally valuable to anything that a school could teach. But if we imagine a mother so placed that the help of a child of eight in the home has become an important thing, then I don't think other people have the right to fetch it out unless they compensate the parent adequately, so that it is done by consent. A parent who provides for a child has a better claim to authority over it than the State can have, and a child's first duty is to the parents who gave it life.

"After the age of ten, children who should desire to continue as full-time students might be paid a subsistence allowance, so that they should not be dependent upon their parents, for which I suppose that ample funds would be released owing to the fact that the large majority would only remain as part-time students, if at all. Every educationalist knows in his heart that the majority of children don't respond adequately to a prolonged general education of the present kind. They know also that it holds them back from acquiring the large areas of knowledge that the schools don't attempt to teach. A boy might spend ten years at school and come away without knowing the difference between a larch and a poplar. He mightn't even know how to feed a pig.

"But the question of subsistence—the financial side generally— is beyond the scope of anything I propose to attempt. It will adjust itself; and when it does, it will depend upon many other adjustments which will follow when the nation has recovered its virility, and forgotten what a dole means."

"You are abolishing the dole?" Sir Bardsley enquired casually. His tone was as one who asks another if he takes cheese.

"Not immediately and entirely. The better method is to abolish unemployment, and the dole will abolish itself. The idleness of an able-bodied man is an absurdity while the nation has a need unsupplied. I have drafted a short Order which will have the effect of removing most able-bodied women from the dole within fourteen days."

"May I ask how?"

"Any woman with more than one child, who is without domestic help, may apply at a Labour Bureau for such help to be allotted to her. The woman so allotted to her will work for her free of charge, and will draw the dole so long as she is entitled to it, providing she puts in eight hours a day to the satisfaction of her employer."

"Isn't that a little unfair? The mother might sit back and do nothing while she was waited on by a—you might say a slave—to whom she paid no wages."

"Of course she wouldn't. But if so, why not? Isn't it more reasonable that a woman who is producing children for the State and is drawing nothing from it, should sit back than that she should work all the time, while another does nothing, and draws a dole?"

Sir Bardsley did not attempt to answer this question. He said: "It's been a most interesting talk, but I think it's time for me to be getting back."

He paused a moment, and then added: "I understand that the subjects we've been discussing are the trifles that we put right, so to speak, before we begin. Could you tell me in a few words—just to clear my own mind—I expect I've heard them before—what the more important ones are?"

"I think any matter is of major importance so far as it will enable us to win back individual freedom, and with it the self-reliance and self-respect that only freedom gives. And we have to use that freedom, if we can, to break away from the sinister domination of science—it isn't the right word to use, but that's what it calls itself, and you know what I mean—we must control or destroy it, or it will destroy us. It is the real master now. The law-making of the last fifty years has reduced us to the level of sheep. Science would take advantage of that docility to bring us into further and more abject bondage. It may mean well or ill, but in practice it may offer us nothing better than a slaughter-house to follow the fenced fields of the law. What I am doing, as I see it, is no more than seizing one of the butcher's own weapons with which to break through the fence with which the shepherd has closed us in. The escape must be to the freedom—the unprotected freedom—from which we came."

"It is an interesting imagination," Sir Bardsley conceded. "Are you sure that it is anything more? And, apart from that, are you attempting a possible thing? You cannot stay the progress of knowledge."

"I think men have done it before now."

"And their civilisations have perished."

"That is the price they have paid. They may not have thought it—it may not have been—too high."

"Suppose, on the other hand, that it is the cowardice of mankind that abandons the pursuit of knowledge, being afraid of its own power, just as it is on the threshold of discoveries which would transform the world? It may be the trial and tragedy of mankind that it approaches time after time a gate which it lacks the courage and persistence to open, and denies itself the Eden within its reach."

It was a tribute to the sincerity with which Stanley had spoken that Sir Bardsley had forgotten the trickeries of diplomacy and was answering him in the same way. Stanley knew that it was possibly true, and, if it were so, his efforts to frustrate it made him the arch-foe of his race. But he did not believe it. There was too much evidence, too much probability, in the other scale. He said: "Science loads us with gifts, which have a good look and a pleasant taste. And in the end she tells us that our children are in the way. She makes life so comfortable, so safe, that we ask whether it is worthwhile at all. In the darkest days of precarious living or plague or war, I doubt whether men asked that as they are asking it now."

Sir Bardsley said nothing. He looked at Stanley in a mildly speculative way, giving no sign of his thoughts.

Rigby listened also. He was interested but not impressed. He had never asked whether life was worth living. It had treated him kindly, giving him a good character, a good income, and a good digestion. He had no desire to revert to the wilderness, which is the hard destiny of the younger son. He remembered that Muriel would sometimes talk in that way, as though life were a doubtful good. But Muriel would go the pace. Even an only brother, who was fond of her, couldn't help wishing she'd drive herself on a tighter rein now and then. As to himself—if only Jehane would be reasonable! And, after all, it was she who had asked him here. You couldn't say that life was so bad.

Jehane was nearer to Stanley's mood, but even she—well, she didn't know! In a more primitive world, he might be as pleasantly unapproachable as he was now. It might be as impossible for her to attempt the seduction of her sister's husband. For that disability was of her own character. It was personal to herself. Probably it was attempted more safely, more frequently, and with greater success, in civilised than in any primitive conditions of life, and—well, she liked her car!

But Stanley thought of that little phial which he had carried in his pocket ever since a drop of its contents on the end of a spent match had been sufficient to reduce its inventor to a brittle heap. He considered that while the means of life are around us at the cost of a bent back and a driven spade, God having given them without asking our help in their discovery, yet beyond that, conduct and character are decisive for the happiness or misery of mankind. Man cannot live by bread alone. It is an eternal truth which remains unshaken, however cleverly science improves the bread. And even the improvement is a doubtful thing.

It is very clever to find out that what makes you feel unwell is a lack of Vitamin D, and to be able to cut out tonsils that grow too large, but might it not be even better to have plenty of the vitamin without knowing what it is? Is it not better to have strong legs than to have rickets very cleverly cured? Health or death is the natural law. Is it better to avoid both in a nursing home? A man may cling to his life, but is it so sure a gain to increase the old age and diminish the youth of the world?

Suppose he should use the power he held? The tiniest drop in the *café noir* with which Sir Bardsley always liked to complete his meal?

If he mentioned the possibility, he felt sure that the Premier would see that science can go too far. But he couldn't mention that He knew not to what end, with what vague purpose, he felt the inclination to carry that deadly phial. He, at least, was no natural murderer. But such powers were not fit for the hands of men.

What he could mention was the wider menace which was in his hands and through the power of which Sir Bardsley Clinton was sitting beside him now. Surely that was enough to make any man think. It was that of which the whole world was thinking, that which the whole world was watching today.

So he said; and Sir Bardsley answered quietly. "I don't think I should say all. A small fraction of one percent might be nearer than that. If all London should disappear tomorrow, half the world wouldn't hear, and most of those who did wouldn't care as much as they would if they missed a meal. But it's an interesting speculation. 'Not great enough for our own destiny.' That's the proposition you set up, and then you want to prevent us ever finding out whether you're right or wrong. It's been a most interesting talk."

Courteously, ceremoniously, Sir Bardsley Clinton went.

He left Stanley in doubt as to what his thoughts or intentions were, but feeling that he had made himself understood more fully than he had done before. He was forcing the pace of the fight, and with Jumping Jimmy getting busy in unknown ways it seemed the right thing to do. Tomorrow morning he would go to Dawlish Mansions and make sure that nothing was threatened there. He did not see how anything could be. Everyone had been turned out of the lower floors and the adjoining houses. Fusiliers and a machine-gun section occupied them now. No one but himself would be admitted on any pretext.

He did not think that anyone would venture interference there, and there was no immediate danger to fear. The public were taking that aspect of the matter with a splendid calm, as, perhaps, only the English would. Yet there had begun a slow steady exodus from the threatened area. Leases would be very difficult to renew. New tenants might be hard to find. The fact that the Rafton was within the area, and that he had taken up his own abode there, may have done much to quieten and reassure. He had done that deliberately. A quixotic, perhaps characteristic, action.

He went to bed tired, but not dissatisfied with the results of a fighting day, and his mind, relaxing, turned to the thought of Crystal, and the different evening that he might have had. When and how—if ever—would they meet again?

CHAPTER THIRTY-SIX

SIR BARDSLEY CLINTON declined the comfort of the waiting car. He said he would walk home. He wanted to clear his own mind, which he found to be an unusually difficult thing to do. So far, he had gone through life without rushing his fences, and without losing his head. Successes had come to him so quietly, so naturally, that he had become Premier of England without much internal exultation, scarcely feeling it to be a triumph of any exceptional magnitude. He had fought a score of bitter political battles in so unhurried a way that he had felt to be in a continual peace, as though, god-like, he watched—and perhaps profited by—a strife which he did not share.

And always his instinct had been to soothe, to compromise, to defer. Only once or twice, when decisive battle had been forced upon him had he shown that he had the strength to stand, as well as the flexibility which knows how to withdraw.

And always his own mind had been cool and assured, perhaps because he did not overvalue the laurels of victory, nor the issues on which the strife was waged.

When this trouble had arisen, he had acted after his usual manner, cautious, cool, resourceful, conciliatory, deferring action if no victory were assured. So far, he had not doubted that he had the situation in hand. When the immediate danger should be over, there might be questions to face in a quiet way. Questions of how the repetition of such incidents could be averted in future. He knew that they were being debated freely already in other lands, and a Dresden scientist, who had made some incautious boast, had died in the hands of a maddened mob.

But such considerations were for the future. His immediate duty had been to keep Maitland from doing anything foolish, till Feltham's diabolical invention should be frustrated and destroyed. Destroyed, he hoped, without the examination which he knew that more than one prominent scientist was anxious to make.

He had never worried hitherto, never worried unduly, even at the most critical issues either of party or national fortune, or at the declaration of a poll which might throw him out of office or confirm his power. Perhaps he had felt too confident in himself, perhaps he had realised that the game itself was not of the most serious kind.

But now—he was not sure. He was not even very sure of himself. Had he done wrong to make terms with Maitland at all? Would he have collapsed before such an attitude as Shackston would have adopted toward him?

He did not think that. It was the feeling that Maitland might be more formidable than he had realised previously which had disturbed his mind. He had thought that there would be more talk than action, that he could counsel, persuade, delay. He had intended to urge tonight the importance of preserving at least the form of parliamentary procedure for any innovation which he might desire to make. Once commence in that way, and Maitland would soon be involved in a bog of detail, his mind distracted and hesitating in a sea of conflicting argument. The year would soon pass. And with the budget as well—he'd need a good holiday, when the hot weather came. Probably by then he'd be glad to finish with that infernal apparatus, and end the strain.

And, in his own way, Sir Bardsley had meant to give a square deal. It was to end for Maitland in a blaze, or, at least something more than flicker, of popularity. That would be the reward of accepting his guidance, and would be to his own advantage also.

To some extent, Sir Bardsley considered that they were in the same boat.

But now he felt that Maitland would not be rowed at his pace. It looked rather doubtful whether he would be guided at all. Should he refuse to support him further, at whatever consequence? Should he offer undignified futile resistance? Should he accept his theories, support him boldly, and take what might be the only chance of emerging successfully from the political plunge he had taken?

He felt it hard to decide. He felt a sense of approaching calamity which he lacked the ability to avert, or the courage to meet. Was he getting old?

He remembered that he had pledged himself to Maitland. He might have thought when he did it that he could control the situation, but still the pledge stood. He should have his Orders in Council, let the consequences be what they would. Perhaps it would all end in a good way. But he went home a troubled man.

CHAPTER THIRTY-SEVEN

"I DON'T precisely desire," Professor Candleton said petulantly, "to be wiped out with my wife and family."

"Not to mention the Pekinese."—Mr. Sampson Lynes's attempt at pleasantry awoke no answering smile from the Professor's irritated features. His jests might be good enough on occasions, but had the reputation of being ill-timed.

Mr. Shackston said, "Shut up, Lyncs," with a rudeness to which an ex-Minister of Education is not commonly subjected. But Mr. Shackston did not mind that. He knew that Professor Candleton lacked humour. He considered that he and his—even his wife's Pekinese—should be taken seriously, and it was the Professor who had to be talked over now.

Mr. Goldstone was also somewhat recalcitrant. "The offices of the *Morning Standard*," he remarked, with a jocularity which might signify an even more difficult opposition than the Professor's irritation, "are the ornament of the Western World."

"You take this power seriously?" Mr. Shackston asked. It was a curious question considering the nature of the announcement that he wished Mr. Goldstone to make in the Professor's name, but none of them seemed to notice that.

The Professor, to whom it was addressed, answered with a grave deliberation. "I am unable to express any opinion as to the possibility of utilising it for the demolition of an extensive area. For a small space, its capacity has been sufficiently demonstrated on two occasions. I am satisfied that the destructions at Kensington and Ditching could not have been effected by any known agency."

"Well," Mr. Shackston said combatively, "you may be satisfied that it's been sufficiently demonstrated, but I'm not; and I'll tell you why.

"To begin with, there was that threat to me, which you heard, Lynes, and you know how it was said. Maitland had got his coat off, and he'd have said about anything just then which would have helped him to get his own way. But what happened after that? He didn't hold off because he thought I'd become his best friend, and it wasn't because Mrs. Shackston said she wouldn't budge half an inch for the likes of him. He mightn't have cared to wipe out Seven Pines with her in it, but if he'd been what she calls a wise guy, he'd have cleaned up a few trees, or maybe half the park, just to show what he could do if he got riled.

"Now I'm not saying the thing isn't genuine. Professor Candleton's opinion's worth more than mine about that. If he says that dust he analysed isn't like anything else on earth, I expect he's right. I expect Feltham destroyed that patch in Ditching Wood, and Maitland cleared the other at Kensington, and whether Feltham set up anything that could destroy thirty-six square miles of buildings—that's about; what a three-mile radius means, or would if you called it square—is a thing I don't know, and I don't see how Maitland can tell till he pulls the switch, or does whatever it is that sets the damned thing off. He may know that he can't, but he can't know that he can. All we can say is that it's a very unlikely thing.

"But what I do say is this. We've no proof that this thing can be handled so that you can be sure where it will strike, and when you think of the measurements and calculations that it would need—well, to set it off in Dawlish Mansions so that it would settle a block of buildings in Fleet Street, or a semi-detached house in St. John's Road, Lewisham, is it a sane thing to suppose?

"You'll notice the two places they've dropped on so far leave a wide margin for going wrong, and if there's any proof that they scored a bull's-eye either time, it hasn't come my way."

"You may be right," Mr. Goldstone conceded, "but it's the sort of risk I'd rather someone else took first."

"The question," the Professor added, speaking with more deliberation, "depends largely upon the nature of the agency employed. I am disposed to postulate the deposit of some substance of a magnetic-electrical character upon the site selected for destruction, which will attract the destroying factor on its release from the apparatus in Mr. Feltham's laboratory. In that event—"

"I don't know about that," Mr. Shackston interrupted. As might be expected from one whose trade was talk, he found it difficult to remain silent for more than one of the Professor's deliberate periods. "I don't know about that, but I reckon," he argued shrewdly, "Maitland's doing too well just now to want to queer his own pitch with any more murders. They'd leave a bad taste in the mouth, even of those who think he's a new Mahomet. We should have to poke him up a good deal more than we've done yet before he'd try those games, even if he knows how, which I don't believe. I reckon the time's come when we can call his bluff, and I'm arranging the third act without any help from you."

"I'll have nothing to do with that," Mr. Goldstone said firmly. "I don't even want to know what it is."

"Well, you're not asked, and you're not told. All I want you to do is to prepare the ground. Just rattle him a bit, and make other people more upset or uncertain than they are now. You can say 'we publish this report with…all reserve,' or something of that sort. You know the tricks of your own trade, better than you'll learn them from me."

Mr. Goldstone recognised the importance of the concession which was now offered. He was not lacking in courage of his own kind. He said: "Yes, I'll do that."

"You can't funk it, Professor, if Mr. Goldstone says that. You know he's in the first line. You can always come and sit in the Club here as my guest, if you feel your nerves want a few hours off. Maitland won't biff this Club. He's got too many of his own party using the premises."

With a visible and bad-tempered reluctance, Professor Candleton gave way. Having agreed, he got up abruptly, and walked out. He was irritated by the use that was to be made of his name and worldwide reputation, and even more so by the fact that he was completely baffled as to the nature of Feltham's invention, and that his reluctance to admit defeat had drawn him into this position. Feltham had been his pupil. How should he have discovered secrets of Nature which were unsuspected even by him? He was irritated by all these circumstances, but most of all by the eccentric idioms and constructions of Mr. Shackston's conversational style. And he could speak differently, if he would, as his public utterances showed. An insufferable man. Still, if he could upset Maitland, it would be a work worth doing. Stanley Maitland might cajole the mob, but the scientific world was united against him, however cautiously that feeling might be displayed by its individual members; for to the marvels of physical science he had shown himself as an open and very dangerous foe.

The next day the *Morning Standard* contained this paragraph:

FELTHAM'S SECRET DISCOVERED?

A circumstantial report which is freely circulated in scientific circles, but which we publish with all reserve, attributes to Dr. C. A. Candleton the honour of having penetrated the secret of William Feltham's sinister invention. It is anticipated that he will be able to neutralise (if he has not done so already) the apparatus which Feltham had set up at the time when Mr. Maitland's timely and courageous action deferred its operation, though he has not yet seen his way to remove the menace.

It will be remembered that William Feltham received his instruction in physical science from Dr. Candleton, whose lectures and demonstrations he attended for two years at the Rotherham Institute, and there is therefore something particularly suitable in the fact that it is he who has been able to discover and frustrate the unholy use to which that teaching had been applied.

Interviewed this afternoon, Dr. Candleton declined either to confirm or deny the truth of the reported discovery. Similar reticence is observed by Mr. T. P. Sturgeon, and Dr. Laketon, who have been associated with him in the investigation of the Kensington Gardens catastrophe, and the analysis of its ashes.

A short paragraph followed, setting out Dr. Candleton's qualifications, and asserting his international eminence.

The announcement naturally excited a general interest. It diverted popular attention from the bewilderingly rapid changes which Mr. Maitland's experiments were producing in the national life, some of which were of a general popularity, back to the dubious source of the power he held, as it was intended to do.

It suggested also that that power might not last much longer. Perhaps not for a single week. And so it raised a hundred doubts and confusions in the minds of those who were inclined to favour and assist Mr. Maitland's experimental changes, and brought hope and courage to their political and social foes.

Conflicting with these influences, the thought must have come to a million minds—already quickened by the experience of what

Feltham's invention had accomplished under what was, by intention at least, no worse than a beneficent tyranny—that if this power should be in the hands of others also, to what end might it not be used with the example of Maitland's success before them?

What was known of Professor Candleton? Of Dr. Laketon? Of Mr. T. P. Sturgeon? Were we to read tomorrow that the Rafton as a level ash-field, and that a new triumvirate were in control of England, perhaps to impose a scientific tyranny, in sombre contrast to the confused efforts toward releasing freedom which Mr. Maitland had instituted? Suppose it were discovered also by—suppose it should be sold to—a foreign power?

These doubts and fears were voiced in a considerable proportion of the leading articles which were a general feature of the newspapers of the following day. There was even a minority of them which went so far as to express a hope that the report might be without foundation, arguing that it was better to endure, even though it might be with some reluctance, the existing condition, than to "fly to evils that they knew not of." One Liverpool daily said bluntly that, rather than such knowledge should be allowed to spread, it would be better that Mr. Maitland should continue in the authority he held. "If these secrets of Nature," it concluded, "which the mass of mankind are unfit, both in character and intelligence, to control, should be in human hands at all, is it not better that they should be confined to one who is, at least, averse to the tyrannies which the professors of biological and chemical science might be only too ready to impose upon us? Who knows what sterilisations, what segregations, what innoculations, what managements and manipulations, might not be inflicted upon us and upon our children, at the hands of those who are unable to acquire any knowledge without the confident assumption that they can put it to better use than the Creator has been able to do? Who knows into what different hands than theirs, selfish, brutal, or criminal, such knowledge might pass at last? Should not our aim and anticipation be that Mr. Maitland will consent in his own time to destroy this knowledge forever, rather than that it should spread in other directions? We are inclined to hope that the rumour is without foundation, or that the situation is one which Mr. Maitland will know how to control."

In its special afternoon edition, the same paper was able to announce that Mr. Maitland had proved equal to the emergency. But it may not have been fully informed as to what that emergency really was.

CHAPTER THIRTY-EIGHT

IT was on the morning on which the article mentioned in the previous chapter appeared in the *Morning Standard* that Molly Preston expressed herself to Mr. Maitland with some freedom respecting the iniquity of the waste to which she had given battle, first at Norchester House, and subsequently in the still more difficult atmosphere of the kitchens of the Rafton Hotel. She was not exhausting herself in pointless comment, but with a definite purpose that one of the next Orders in Council, which were now published every few days, striking right and left at the abuses and follies of the time, so that no one could tell what might be prohibited or allowed tomorrow, should be directed to enforce a reasonable economy, even in the West End of London, where the senseless waste of food is probably greater than anywhere on earth, with the exception of some parts of the United States of America.

But she found that, though Stanley listened with sympathy, he was unwilling to use his power to check the evil.

"It is difficult to regard any waste, and particularly the waste of food," he agreed, "with sufficient patience even to analyse the causes from which it springs. The English are probably the most wasteful nation on earth, and to observe that it is a criminal stupidity may be true, but does nothing to explain its causes, because the English are not fundamentally a stupid people. Some great, some useful, even some noble qualities, such as generosity, may have their place in its explanation, but the doubt as to whether anything should be done to repress it by penal means does not arise from any tenderness toward its origins. It is rather because its repression, even its discouragement, would involve inspections restrictions, processes, penalties—new shackles when all my efforts have been to knock the existing shackles from English limbs—and these things are themselves a form of waste, which has meant nothing in the past, because it has not been regarded as an intolerable evil that men and women should stand idle, or be worthlessly employed, in a land where there is obviously so much to do, any more than that they should suffer privations in a land of potential if not of actual plenty. But those days should be over now. It is a daily effort to avoid using the power I have to attempt the coercion of others."

Molly's blue eyes opened widely with their usual expression of an enquiring simplicity. Her conversation was always on a simple plane; her peculiarity was that some of the things that she reduced to her own simplicity were of very difficult kinds.

"I shouldn't have thought that," she said, with a disarming audacity. "What about the patent-medicine people?"

"I didn't claim success," Stanley answered. "I only mentioned a daily effort. But the patent-medicine swindling was no ordinary matter, and you must recognise that I did no more, after separating the Treasury from a disgraceful partnership, than to make those who printed or accepted their advertisements equally responsible with the vendors for the accuracy of the representations they made."

"I didn't think that was quite all."

"It was everything of a permanent penal character. Beyond that, I took no more than the mildest steps to mitigate the evil, when the desire to hang the scoundrels was an almost irresistible impulse, as it would be to any decent man who had the power that is in my hands today."

Molly laughed. "I don't think mild's the word most people used about that."

Probably she was right. The Order which had dealt with this peculiarly pestilent part of the population had confiscated their accumulations of wealth for the reduction of the National Debt, burnt their stocks, closed their pill and drug-manufacturing dens, including some of an almost incredible output, subjected them to a medical examination, and removed all who showed any internal infirmity to nursing homes where they were to be dosed with the preparations that they themselves or their rivals made.

Probably few of Mr. Maitland's interferences with domestic commerce had been more popular with the intelligent members of the community, but it is doubtful if any of them would have recognised the mildness of these measures as certainly as it appeared to his own mind. Yet it was true that he had not set up any system of inspections and fines, he had instituted no penal processes. The culprits had escaped the jail or the rope, which is the lot of the mere retail murderer, and had been subjected to no substantial penalty-beyond the removal of wealth which had been won by the basest of human frauds There was nothing to prevent them commencing in business again tomorrow, beyond the fact that printers and newspaper proprietors might be less obsequiously at their service, and that they had had a lesson which might be repeated at any time.

"It was mild," Stanley contended, with an answering smile, "to what they deserved, and the retail vendors escaped with nothing worse than some empty shelves."

"Why didn't you outlaw them? You've done that to others for a good deal less."

"Because of the Government labels that their bottles bore. I could not refuse them the benefit of a law which had partnered them in what they did."

"I don't think I should have troubled about that."—Molly thought how impractical, how queerly ruled by abstractions even the best men are—"Why not outlaw people who waste food?"

"Because I want to keep that penalty for those of even more seriously anti-social conduct. It might be worthwhile to disqualify wasters from prosecuting others for the theft of their goods. If they don't value them themselves sufficiently to…"

"I'm sorry to interrupt you, Molly." Jehane said, as she entered the room, "but you've monopolised Mr. Maitland for the best part of an hour, and I think" she turned to Stanley to say—"you ought to see this." She laid the *Morning Standard* before him, with the heading *Feltham's Secret Discovered?* prominently exhibited

Miss Preston said easily: "I haven't been wasting time, Lady Jehane." She got up and went.

Stanley read the paragraph twice. He considered its wording carefully, and the direction from which it came. He said: "Bunkum more likely than not. It would be interesting if it were true."

"Yes, if you think that's the word."

"It's one among several that might apply. I'll have Dr. Laketon on the phone. He'd be the most likely to talk."

"I'll tell Miss Trentham to have him called up, if you're sure that's the best thing to do."

"It's the first, anyway."

Jehane took up the receiver, but found that Miss Trentham had already something to say to her. She announced a moment later: "Jumping Jimmy's on the phone waiting to speak to you. He won't say what it's about. He hasn't lost much time. Shall I say he can ring up in an hour?"

"Why the delay?"

"Do him good to wait."

"It might be no good to us. No, have him put through."

"Private line?"

"No, tell Miss Trentham I want a full record of all that's said. I rather think 'interesting' is going to be the right word."

Mr. Shackston might attempt to reach his goal by devious and unlighted paths, but his methods on the field of battle were free from the amiable weaknesses of Uriah Heep.

"Mr. Maitland," he said curtly, when, after five impatient minutes of waiting, he heard the right voice at the other end of the wire, "the game's up."

Stanley felt that he could see the cigar in the corner of the sneering mouth, the hard truculence of the eyes. It was to alter that expression as much as with any more intelligent purpose that he replied pleasantly: "I was just saying that it seemed likely to be an interesting day."

There was a second's silence on this retort, and then Mr. Shackston regained his wind, and came on again.

"Look here, Maitland, it's no good taking that tone. It's a day too late. Candleton's got on to it, as you might have guessed that he would. He's either got that, or something a lot worse, and I'm giving you a chance to come here and talk it over before it's too late. We don't want that Kensington Gardens business to start again if you'll see sense."

"I've no intention of starting anything of the kind."

"I didn't mean you."

"No? I'll tell you what, Shackston, you might ask Dr. Candleton to ring me up. I'm rather interested in his experience of the precipitations."

"His exper—I don't know what you mean, and I don't care. What you've got to realise is that your bluff's called, and you can't understand it too quickly for your own good."

Stanley thought that, whatever might be the truth about Dr. Candleton's activities, he would lose nothing by letting Shackston show his hand a bit further. He said: "Well, go on."

Mr. Shackston thought he heard the note of compromise, if not of surrender. He continued in a more moderate tone.

"What I feel is, Maitland, that you've done a lot of good, as well as upsetting a few apple-carts that need to be set going again. If you'd come and talk it over, we might fix up the whole thing without any more trouble, and without the country knowing much more than it does now. I don't say but that you and I could get on together a bit better than you and Clinton are ever likely to do. Anyway, we can have a talk, and if we don't agree, you're no worse off than you are now. And if you like to come, I'll promise you a few hours' notice before the fireworks begin, if you'll do the same for us. We can't go on talking like this over the wire. I've said too much as it is."

Stanley said: "So you have." The impulse to close the conversation on the neatness of that retort was irresistible. He cut off.

He looked at Jehane with a smile. "There's a very angry man at the National Club. I won't have Laketon now. I'll have a word with Sir Bardsley. No, not at once. You'd better get some typescripts of this conversation from Miss Trentham. Send one up to me. I want to read it carefully, and I want to be left alone. You can get on to Sir Bardsley yourself. See if he's heard of the article in the *Morning Standard*. Read it to him, if he hasn't. Read him my conversation with the Honourable James. When you're sure he understands how things are, put him through to me. Any real danger? Not the least. Not yet, anyway." Jehane went.

Left alone, Stanley considered the position. He had good reason for discrediting the report that the secret of Feltham's invention was available as a hostile weapon to be used against him.

He recognised that Dr. Candleton might have discovered the physical facts on which it was based, and that the same power might be in his hands. Sooner or later, someone would be sure to discover it, as they would doubtless discover many other sinister secrets of Nature which could be used for the scourging of their fellows, if God and man should allow the present developments of such knowledge to go forward to their inevitable and sombre end.

But to discover was not to be able to apply immediately. That had been Jimmy Shackston's oversight. It is hard for the most imaginative mind to simulate verity. Jimmy (so he thought) had been too impatient, and had overreached himself. He should have delayed a few months, to give time for the possibility of a rival apparatus being set up.

These reflections were logical enough, but did something less than justice to his opponent, whose purpose he did not entirely read. The scare of a competing discovery had been partly for popular consumption. It had been to create an atmosphere. It may be compared to the lion's roar in the night, which is said to alarm its neighbours so that they run about in a blind way, and deliver the meal on its own legs. If Mr. Maitland had been scared with the rest, and had gone over to the National Club, it might have ended the trouble in a manner satisfactory to Mr. Shackston's mind. He had rather expected this to occur, but when the conversation terminated abruptly, he did not feel that he had failed. He had other plans.

CHAPTER THIRTY-NINE

STANLEY MAITLAND had good reason for deciding that Dr. Candleton, even if he had the will, could have no present power to harm him.

Though his knowledge of chemistry was slight, and he could not follow the intricacies of William Feltham's apparatus, either in theory or application, he had had the advantage of studying the formulæ and notes which he had left, and examining the invoices for the various chemical substances, and the mechanical apparatus which he had assembled. He had taken sufficient steps to feel sure that similar purchases could not be made without his knowledge, in any dangerous quantities, though the possibilities of laboratory experiment were beyond his probing. But he knew that the basis of the preparation of one of the required chemical properties was a precipitation which had been regarded as impossible, but which Feltham had discovered could be obtained after certain treatment had been continued for a period of twenty days. His notes on this point were quite clear.

That implied twenty days for the successful laboratory experiment, and another similar period for the charging of the apparatus itself after the procuring in wholesale quantity of a very rare drug which was on the prohibited list. Those times were minimal, and, of course, in practice, they must be substantially exceeded.

It followed from this knowledge that he was disposed to discredit the tale completely. Had Dr. Candleton really been on the right track, the last thing he would have desired would be a premature disclosure of his success. It was to expose him to a useless danger, while his own artillery was unloaded. It was more likely that a chagrined and defeated man was allowing his name to be used in a way that "he would not confirm or deny." On this point, Stanley got very near the truth. His danger lay in the confidence which that assurance gave.

Immersed in these thoughts, and in the plans of action which they suggested, it seemed to him but a moment before Sir Bardsley Clinton was speaking to him.

Sir Bardsley had had his attention directed to the article before Lady Jehane had rung him up. He had not thought it to be of sufficient importance to trouble Mr. Maitland concerning it.

He had now had the benefit of hearing Mr. Maitland's conversation with the Hon. James Shackston. He was amused, but still unperturbed. He thought it was no more than an empty threat.

Stanley agreed, but wondered how his conclusion had been reached. Sir Bardsley replied that the procedure did not impress his mind as genuine. Incidentally, did Mr. Maitland know anything of Professor Sturgeon? No? Well, Sir Bardsley did. He said that if he were one of a group who had discovered such a power, particularly after the demonstration that Stanley had made of its possibilities, there would have been no easy unconditional placing of it in Mr. Shackston's, or anyone else's hands. He would be worse than Feltham. An equally unscrupulous and far abler man.

"Then you would do nothing?" Stanley queried. Sir Bardsley agreed. It was a case for contempt. "The noblest answer unto such," he quoted. Yes, Tennyson. Not enough read in these days. Sir Bardsley would have rung off.

But Stanley had other plans. Did not Sir Bardsley see the danger of letting these men's experiments go on? His own reference to Professor Sturgeon was a text for the argument.

Sir Bardsley agreed, though without excitement. What could be done? The progress of scientific discovery cannot be arrested. He had never been of the temperament which meets trouble halfway.

Didn't he see that this announcement had put the opportunity into their hands? Sir Bardsley evidently didn't want to see that. But he was not prepared to deny it. Of course, if Mr. Maitland felt that any steps were necessary for his own security, within the limits of moderation, and remembering the scientific eminence of the men concerned. Mr. Maitland replied that he was not concerned for himself—he did not think that he was in any immediate danger. He was concerned for larger issues.

Sir Bardsley was clearly not convinced. He had always found it a good policy to let sleeping dogs lie. Here the proverb might not be entirely applicable, but it was not a very dangerous barking. He was fond of proverbs. It had been frequently in his mind of recent weeks that the pitcher which goes often to the well will get broken at last. But he did not quote it. Courtesy forbade.

Now he gave way reluctantly, as he often did in these days. The measures which came into operation next day had nothing to do with the partial encouragement which they were to receive (as we have seen already) in the next morning's press, nor with the events of the coming night, to which we have not yet come.

But the next morning ninety-eight professors, engaged in various fields of scientific investigation, including most of those who were conspicuous in the regions of biochemistry, were collected in Brixton Prison, which was empty of debtors, and had not yet found a purchaser. They were not subjected to the senseless cruelties which had prevailed in that establishment previously. They were allowed to rise at what hour they pleased, and took exercise in the prison-yard when they preferred to do so, or not at all. They were in a world in which there was more freedom in prison-walls than there had been outside them three months before. But it may be doubted whether they appreciated the advantages that they enjoyed.

A week later twenty-seven of them were unconditionally released; sixty-eight were transported to a land where they must sustain life, if at all, somewhat differently than by their familiar methods; and three were publicly hanged, their laboratories having been opened four days earlier to public inspection, and photographed by the press.

Two vivisection inspectors were hanged on the same spot on the following day, and one had the fingers of his left hand removed with the assistance of a mallet and chisel, he having preferred this punishment to any of seven tortures which had been allowed under his inspections, and among which he would have been permitted to choose.

Vivisection was not yet prohibited in England, but dog-stealing subsequently became an unprofitable occupation, and the prices of guinea-pigs and monkeys fell.

Having arranged with Sir Bardsley Clinton the terms of the Order from which these consequences would promptly follow, Stanley concluded, somewhat too readily, that he had done sufficient to frustrate any hostilities which Mr. Shackston might be contriving against him, and his attention turned to the work of formulating the somewhat revolutionary budget which he proposed to introduce during the following week.

At this time he may have had the greatest personal authority that the world contained, and his life was one that a Dartmoor convict need not greatly envy. Feltham would have said that he lacked the resolution and audacity that the situation required, or imagination enough to understand the possibilities which it presented.

The protection of his life had become a matter of national importance. The possibility that some madman, enraged by the severity with which one of the new regulations had fallen upon himself, and blind to the broader issues at stake, might attempt his assassination, was a nightmare possibility against which Scotland Yard had professed its unwillingness to provide without military assistance.

If he were to die before the removal of the menace which he controlled, and while its secret remained in his own mind, what might not the consequences be? At the best, the evacuation by its human inhabitants of thirty square miles of the crowded heart of London, with the more portable of its countless treasures, while the resources of science would be exhausted in the effort to control and neutralise the infernal apparatus, without promoting catastrophe by an interference which could not be indefinitely deferred.

The ground-floor of the Rafton was now in military occupation, as were the opposite and adjoining buildings. Machine-guns guarded the roof. To avert the possibility of corruption, these military guards were changed completely without notice, and at uncertain intervals.

Callers who satisfied the scrutiny of the bayonets at the door were met by the amateur bodyguard which Jehane's prompt recognition of the dangers of the position had collected from among her friends. The staff of secretaries had been recruited too early for any of them to have been other than they appeared, but though some were allowed to disperse to their suburban homes when the day's work was over, they would have found it difficult to speak to a stranger without interruption from a detective officer, and the stranger would have been fortunate if the supervision to which he would be subjected had ceased in a week's time.

Stanley went out seldom, except periodically to inspect the top story of Dawlish Mansions, which was guarded with a vigilance equal to that of his own life, or on one or two necessary occasions to the House of Commons He moved through streets which were cleared before him, and with armoured cars before and behind his own. It was no pleasure to go out under such conditions, and he spent almost all his time in that upper-room overlooking the Haymarket, which he had made his own. He had arranged with Sir Bardsley that he should take his budget through the House, not as an arbitrary action, but as a measure to be attacked and defended on its own merits, and any feeling of pleasure which he now had was centred in the anticipation of that coming struggle.

A few words from Lady Jehane to Sir Bardsley had resulted in the expenses of the Rafton being assumed by the Government, and a supplementary estimate had provided adequately for that considerable outlay. Beyond that, it was public knowledge that Stanley had asked nothing for himself, and did not propose to do so. He would have his salary as Chancellor of the Exchequer, and that he proposed to earn in the ordinary way.

How different things might have been had he remained at Norchester House. How different for himself had Crystal remained beside him. These were thoughts which would come with an increasing bitterness, a keener regret, as the weeks of isolation passed. And yet, as he looked back, he saw that this separation was no unnatural fruit of a marriage which had never reached to that closeness of confidence, of intimacy, of physical union, which the most plebeian one may succeed to do. Had—or how far had—the fault of failure been his? How far was it in the circumstances and traditions of an artificial life? How far did it indicate a weakness of love, of passion, which could not burn these artificial barriers down? How far was it in the bargain of barrenness with which their married lives had commenced?

So he wondered, sombrely enough, as the solitary hours went by, and with the curious issue that he left the whole sphere of the relations of men and women untouched in the revolutionary edicts of freedom which he was imposing upon the English world.

Except for that one blow which he had struck for the lives of the children of English land, he did nothing to break down the bondages of the marriage laws, nothing to place the fact of parenthood in its moral place as a conclusive evidence of existing marriage, nothing even to cut out the cancer of prostitution, which, though it be a thousand times crueller and baser than any system of polygamy, aristocratic governments have lacked the will, and democratic governments the courage to clean away. He knew that he was even supposed by some foolish persons to have encouraged such practices, because he had ended the system by which prostitution contributes part of its earnings to public funds.

But, apart from the steady purpose that all he did should be of a releasing rather than a controlling character, he felt that while his own marriage lay in ignoble ruin he was not competent to interfere in such directions in the lives of others. If Crystal were beside him now—not in her aloofer moods, but as, at rare intervals, she had shown that she had the womanhood to be—it might be different then.

He turned resolutely from such thoughts to the consideration of an Order which would in a single sentence sweep away a thousand by-laws, reduce a thousand county and municipal staffs, by giving a man the right to build a house to his own liking on his own land.

Of course, with his natural and now cultivated habit of looking at things as they are, rather than as they are dressed to appear, he knew that the time when land or house had been privately owned in England had gone, beyond any method of adjustment that he could hope to provide, and perhaps never to return till our civilisation falls.

The growth of the custom by which county and municipal levies are made upon building values, without relation to the number of occupants, the services required or rendered, or the incomes of those upon whom the impositions are made, has produced a position in which the private ownership of any property is little more than a pleasant delusion, giving a conditional security of peaceful tenure so long as the rates are paid—and those rates have risen in recent years to a height which approximates toward the full annual value of the properties which attract this form of financial lightning upon them. The fact that most municipalities have incurred gigantic debts on the security of these rates—debts which are enormously greater than the value of any municipally owned property which exists to secure them—increases the alienation of private property, for these debts constitute a first mortgage upon the property of the citizens in whose names the debts are incurred. Even the people themselves could not by any common action return their property to their own possessions. It would be a matter for their creditors to say.

Stanley was considering this characteristically English position, by which the individual is allowed the appearance and some of the pleasures of private ownership, while its reality has been filched away and was in a momentary hesitation as to whether the freedom which he proposed to restore was not an illogical thing—for if a man may not really own any land, however much he may be willing to pay for it, is it not reasonable that a municipal surveyor should intervene, as representing the actual owners, to dictate the shape and size and other details of any building that he shall erect upon it?—and found such consolation as he could in the thought that if men would continue upon the path which he was attempting to reopen to them, the gigantic public debts would decline toward a point at which private ownership would again become something more than a sham, even if the whole grotesquely inequitable basis of such levies could not be swept away, when Jehane entered the room.

"I didn't know," she said, "whether you'd rather have dinner with us, or alone here. You seemed tired at lunch, and it's been rather an eventful day."

"Yes?" he answered. "Has it? Oh, I'd almost forgotten that. It isn't dinner-time yet, is it?"

"It's about that time—or a bit later."

"No, I'll come. I won't have it alone."

"You won't stop to change anything?"

"No, I'll come now."

"I thought you wouldn't. I told Rigby not to."

He rose rather wearily, and followed her to the private dining-room which was on the same floor.

It had become customary for him to share meals with Jehane and Rigby and Molly Preston. Jehane alone had his confidence. The others were the heads of his palace staff. It was a relief to talk for a time at random, or of trivial things. To hear the gossip of the place. To be kept in touch with what was happening immediately around him. And it did not require the effort that must be made if he had guests, of whatever kind.

There were other reasons that brought the four together at the evening meal. Jehane had found it an increasingly difficult thing to hold together the private bodyguard which she had first enlisted for

Stanley's protection. It had been regarded at first as no more than an exciting lark. To be told to come along at a good pace with shotguns and old army revolvers under the seat, to guard against the chance that Stanley Maitland would be attacked by evil-doers at the Rafton Hotel—what better could you ask of life, especially in a season when the shooting was so infernally bad? But to stay on, week by week when nothing happened at all, and when the military had taken over, so that it seemed abundantly certain that nothing ever would, was a quite different matter. There had been inevitable defections. There had been one or two very privately negotiated financial bargains. Jehane had found that she had got to be rather nicer to Rigby…but she wanted Molly to make a fourth.

Molly came, as she could scarcely refuse to do. She would much rather have been elsewhere. Idleness and propinquity had worked to their usual ends. Selby Ditchfield's interest in Miss Preston was in process of being encouraged with a demure serenity. William Feltham, dreaming obscenely of the way in which his invention was to add to the amatory experiences of the Countess of Blaire, would have been disconcerted to know that he was actually providing a mother for Selby Ditchfield's children.

The conversation dragged at the first. Jehane, feeling an atmosphere of dullness, if not of apprehension, for which there seemed no sufficient cause, attempted to stimulate it by saying she wondered whether Sir Bardsley had made up his mind yet about the M's.

Rigby asked if there were any reason why she didn't mention their full name.

"I can't do that," she said, "they've got too many…about nineteen, isn't it?"

The question was addressed to Stanley, who said he believed that was about it.

Explanation followed. Stanley, discussing his budget proposals with Sir Bardsley yesterday, had startled that moral-minded and practical politician by remarking casually that a citizen was morally justified in evading taxes if he were able to do so, unless they were justly levied.

Sir Bardsley differed. There was an obligation on every citizen to obey the law of the land. When once the legislation was passed, everyone was morally bound to fulfil its requirements. If they felt injured, they must proceed to obtain their remedy by constitutional means. Otherwise, if private judgment were allowed in such matters, there could be no order within the State.

"Yes, I know we're bound to talk in that way, but between ourselves we both know that it isn't true."

"I cannot admit that," Sir Bardsley had answered with unusual firmness. "The duty of every citizen to the State...." He had paused, as though the sentence finished itself.

Stanley had replied by putting a concrete problem. He had happened to notice, from an alphabetical list of the members of the present House, that there were singularly few whose names commenced with M. Suppose that, taking advantage of the fact that the protest of nineteen members must be such a feeble thing, the House were to inflict the bulk of the national taxation upon people whose names commenced with that initial? Or upon trades which shared in that fortuitous distinction? Would it be the duty of millers, and motor and mowing-machine manufacturers to grumble and pay, or would they be justified in resisting so arbitrary an imposition by every possible means? If we say that they would be justified in resistance, do we not admit that every minority is justified in resisting restrictive legislation the justice of which it denies? Does it not follow that the whole theory of the basis of democratic governments—the sacred rights of majorities—is no more than a very impudent fiction? Is it not a contention that might is right as shameless as that of any tyrant who rules by an army's strength?

Sir Bardsley, after a display of dialectical skill which gave him a drawn battle at the worst, and perhaps something rather better than that, had said that it was a point on which he seriously desired to convince rather than to out-argue. He would give it the best thought he could, and return to it at a later time.

Miss Preston and Lord Rigby Stilton listened to this problem with a satisfactory interest, but neither of them offered any contributory wisdom to its elucidation.

Rigby changed the subject by remarking that everyone seemed a bit rattled today. He had heard, just before dinner, that the Banffshire Highlanders were to be withdrawn at nine P.M., and be replaced by a detachment of Fusiliers. As the kilted gentlemen only arrived yesterday—.

Molly said she'd heard that two hours ago. Captain Callover, who would be in command, had called to notify the impending change.

Rigby wondered he hadn't seen him.

"It was while you were out," Molly explained.

"Well, I'm glad Callover's coming," he remarked. "Met him at polo last season. On the staff at Gibraltar then. Home on leave." He commented on his length. Arms like windmills.

Molly said he must have got him mixed up with someone else. Captain Callover was short, and rather tight at the belt.

Rigby said it couldn't have been Callover. No doubt his lieuten-ant—or else his orderly.

They looked at one another with the kindly tolerance with which we regard the infirmities of our friends. He didn't suppose that any woman could differentiate accurately between a lance-corporal and a major-general. She wondered if he really thought that she didn't know the signs of a captain's rank, and why men were so carelessly inaccurate in their memories of whom they met. After-wards they were both to blame themselves unduly for their own ob-tuseness. At the moment, Rigby's next remark that he understood that the incoming Fusiliers would be more numerous by an extra twenty than the departing Highlanders, drove the earlier thought from Miss Preston's mind.

"Then," she said, with an unusual sharpness, "they'll have to sleep on the floor." Captain Callover might be plump or lean as he pleased, but nothing excused his omission to mention this numerical difference. Now the staff were gone home, except a few trusted members whom the closing of Norchester House had enabled her to recruit from that source, and whom she allowed to stay on the prem-ises.

"They won't want to sleep tonight," Rigby endeavoured to con-sole her, "they'll all sit up waiting for Candleton to call round with a few bombs, or whatever they think's going to happen that they'd be useful to stop."

Miss Preston declined consolation. "Of course, no one'll come. Men *are* fools," she said in the tone of an unmistakable sincerity.

Rigby had sufficient discretion to say no more.

CHAPTER FORTY

IT was about one A.M. when the telephone bell rang at the side of Stanley's bed. He was restless, and though he had retired to that room, he was still up, and writing, when the sudden sound startled him in the stillness.

He walked over to the bed, and noticed that the alarm came from the instrument which was connected with Jehane's room. An-other, to be used in emergencies, or in her absence only, communi-cated direct with the main switchboard on the ground-floor.

He heard Jehane's voice: "Stanley, are you dressed?"

"Yes, more or less. Why?"

"I'm coming to your room. I don't want to come in. I want you to come to mine. Please be ready. I'll explain when I come."

She cut off without waiting for his reply.

A few minutes later Selby Ditchfield, who had undertaken the duty of keeping guard outside Stanley's rooms, and found it a very boring occupation in the midnight hours, drew his long legs inward and rose quickly from the chair on which he had been sprawling in a somewhat ungainly attitude, at the apparition of Lady Jehane Norchester coming toward him in a blue dressing-gown from the fur collar of which her head rose in a very attractive manner.

"Selby," she said, without preliminary explanations, "I wish you'd go down for me. I've left my handbag in the lounge. I must get it somehow, and I don't want to go down like this."

"Of course," he said, and then more doubtfully, "but I'm not supposed to leave here. Why not ring down for someone to find it for you?"

"Because I prefer to know who handles it. Don't be silly, Selby. You can get the lift round the corner, and be back in three minutes. I'll wait here the while. You don't suppose I'm Professor Candleton in disguise?"

Smiling at the absurdity, and glad to stretch his legs on the errand, Selby Ditchfield went.

Jehane knocked on Stanley's bedroom door, and it opened immediately.

"What's the matter?"

"Would you go to my room—it's the very end one on the right, if you keep to the left along the south corridor—the end one on the right—and wait for me there? I'll explain afterwards."

"I like to know what I'm doing."

"There isn't time now. Stanley, I'm...I'm not a fool."

Stanley looked along the empty corridor. "Where's Selby?"

"He's gone down to look for a handbag that isn't there. He'll be back any minute. I want your door to be locked, and you gone by then."

"I'm afraid I can't consent without knowing why."

"Can't you trust me that far? If you'd rather I explain here, instead of where we can talk safely, Molly says there isn't a Fusilier in the place. They're all fakes. If Selby going down makes them suspicious...."

"I see. They're to think I'm inside here. Wait a minute. There are some papers I must have."

Having decided, he acted quickly, though he was still in some doubt of the wisdom of the course of action which was being forced upon him. He liked to make his own plans. He was less than convinced that it was anything more than a silly scare. Still, if it were not, there would be time to get at the facts with less likelihood of interruption in Jehane's room. It seemed a sensible thing to do. He did not suppose that her plans went beyond that.

He was outside the room again by now, locking the door. He had ascertained that the two doors of the adjoining room, which he occupied during the day, were locked also.

"Go on quickly," she said, "I can hear the lift now…to the left along the south corridor…the end one on the right."

"I suppose Molly's there?"

"Molly's room's next to mine. You can go there if you like."

"I beg your pardon," he said, as he realised the irritation—or was it anger?—in her voice. "I don't like being bustled."

The next moment Selby appeared, but Stanley had already turned the corner in the opposite direction.

"I'm so sorry," Jehane said, before Selby could commence the history of his futile search. "I remembered almost as soon as you'd gone. I'm nearly certain I left it in Molly's room."

"No trouble. Nobody tried breaking in while I was downstairs?"

"No," she laughed. "No one's tried except I. Well, good night, and thanks."

She disappeared, and Selby resumed his watch.

It was about an hour later that the young lady who was on night duty at the telephone switchboard on the ground-floor, took a call for Captain Callover. She reported this, in the first place, to Rigby, who was playing poker with two companions in the adjoining room, which had been previously allocated to the hotel manager.

"General Trent wants to speak to Captain Callover. He says it's most urgent."

"Wants to make sure he isn't asleep, in their fussy way," Rigby remarked rather to his companions than the girl—. "All right, you go back to the board. I'll find Captain Callover." He remembered his intention of renewing acquaintance with that officer. Perhaps his ideas of duty would not prevent him joining the game.

He found the Captain easily, with a sergeant's help. The Fusiliers seemed to be a numerous and very wakeful guard. The Captain was not far away, but the sergeant's help had been useful. Thin men often become fat, but it is unusual for them to lose about ten inches in height during the autumn months. A very singular change.

Showing no surprise at this alteration, and omitting to remind the Captain of their previous meeting, Lord Rigby Stilton said politely that he would show him the way to the telephone. Captain Callover made no objection. They went together to learn why General Trent should desire to engage in conversation at two A.M., when good generals are almost always in bed.

It appeared that the reason was sufficiently serious. A report had reached Scotland Yard, from a source that could not be ignored, and had been passed on to the Military Authorities, that an attempt was to be made to destroy the Rafton during the night. How? It was not known, but it was not a risk to be continued for an avoidable moment. Captain Callover must evacuate the Rafton immediately, bringing Mr. Maitland to a place of safety, according to the sealed instructions with which he had been supplied to deal with such an emergency. Mr. Maitland's secretary, Lady Jehane Norchester, must also be taken care of. As to others in the hotel, they must be warned, and could please themselves.

Captain Callover addressed the telephone operator. "Ring up Mr. Maitland at once." The young lady had heard enough to lead her to the conclusion that she was in an unhealthy place. Her thoughts went to her hat, but she kept her place, putting the Captain through to Mr. Maitland's room on the direct wire. Then she rose in some haste, not seeing why she should wait while the conversation proceeded.

Captain Callover gave her a glance. He said: "No one will leave the premises till the safety of Mr. Maitland has been assured." That would not only prevent any premature alarm in the street: it might arouse a general willingness to expedite Mr. Maitland's departure.

Rigby surveyed the back of the gallant officer's head (if an officer he really were) as it bent over the telephone. It was slightly bald. It looked thin. He thought it might be broken quite easily. It would have been a pleasant task, but of its wisdom he was less sure. He became aware that conversation did not commence.

The Captain looked up. He looked worried. He said: "I can't get any reply."

"Oh, well, perhaps he's asleep," Rigby suggested easily. "We don't often phone him at this hour." If Stanley were awake to the position, or had made escape already, there was no need to hurry matters. Let Captain Callover continue to try.

But that gentleman was of a limited patience. He put down the receiver. "I'm afraid something's wrong," he said. "I'll go up." There could be no doubt that he was a genuinely worried man.

"All right," Rigby said cheerfully. "Come along."

Captain Callover may not have welcomed his company, but it would have been difficult to make a plausible objection. Besides, he might be useful to show the way. They went up in the lift together, a sergeant and a dozen privates following by the stairs.

They found the dimly-lighted corridor quiet outside Mr. Maitland's rooms. Selby Ditchfield controlled a yawn to assure them that there had been no disturbance there. Mr. Maitland in his room? Yes. Where did they suppose? He spoke with conviction, and was believed.

But if Mr. Maitland were in his room, it appeared that no knocking would bring him out. Rigby, never an adept in deception, had difficulty in deciding what expression it would be most natural to assume. He believed that the alarm was faked with no innocent purpose, and if Stanley had suspected it, and had found some means of escape, it was a good thing. But he must continue to show confidence in Captain Callover, and concern that Stanley did not reply. He wished that his sister Muriel had got the job.

Fortunately, a belated thought that Stanley might not have got away, and there might be some fatal tragedy behind that silent door, assisted him to an appropriate facial expression.

Selby Ditchfield suffered from no corresponding difficulty. He was no fool, and he had not taken long to connect that unexpected silence with his abortive descent for a handbag which was not there. He had no reason to doubt the genuineness of the alarm which was now raised. In imagination he saw the search continuing till it should be revealed to a score of onlookers that Stanley Maitland spent the night in his sister-in-law's bedroom.

He looked at Rigby in desperation; if he could have spoken to him alone! Have given him some hint to call off the search! And yet—apart from the difficulty of a private word—what could he say? He knew Rigby's feelings toward Jehane. Everyone did. He was the last man to whom he could give a hint that Maitland spent his nights in her room. And again—if the danger were near and real, ought he not to direct the search in the right way?

Being more vague even than Rigby as to what the danger might be, it fortunately occurred to him that if Stanley's friends could not find him, his enemies might be unlikely to do so. Delay was the best chance. Any moment he might appear, to give what explanation he would of where he had been. That was up to him. Perhaps none might be asked. Meanwhile, let them bang as long as they would on the door of an empty room.

But they were tiring of that. Captain Callover had given instructions to break it in. Rigby gained the delay of a moment's discussion by suggesting that there might be duplicate keys. But, if so, where were they to be found? No. The door must be forced.

So it was, with some delay, for it was stoutly constructed. After that, an intervening door had to be forced before the second room

could be entered. Captain Callover had the barren satisfaction of assuring himself that no one was there.

He came back into the passage to find that a young lass, short
and plump, with china-blue eyes, and an innocent, rather startled
expression, as though roused from a recent sleep, had joined the
group. She was clothed in a dressing-gown of crimson silk, rather
low at the neck, and added a note of colour to the drab group of uniforms that crowded round the door.

Rigby stood immediately behind her, but it was to Selby Ditchfield she spoke, as he came out of the room, having been one of
those who had assisted the search, perhaps all the more zealously
because he could contribute no more than a simulated curiosity.

"Selby, whatever's the matter?"

"Mr. Maitland's not in his room."

"I don't see why—." She ended the sentence with a glance at
the smashed door.

"He's very urgently wanted. We couldn't make him hear, so we
had to break in."

Captain Callover interposed. "If you can tell us where we can
find Mr. Maitland, madam—."

"I could have told you without making all this mess."

Rigby, standing behind her, gave her a poke in the back. He received her answer in the form of a backward kick from a sharp-
edged heel. Private as these motions were, they did not entirely escape the suspicion of Captain Callover. If they decreased his confidence in Lord Rigby Stilton, they added to his assurance that this
daughter of Eve would prove a simple and veracious witness.

The china-blue eyes met his own as in a personal confidence.
"It isn't Mr. Ditchfield's fault that he didn't know. I asked him to go
down for a moment for a handbag that I thought I'd left in the
lounge, and while I was waiting here, Mr. Maitland came out."

She paused a moment, and the Captain asked impatiently: "Yes.
Where did he go?"

"I can't tell you which room, but he went along that way, and
down the stairs at the end. He went to one of the Gadarenes."

"The Gadarenes?"

"Gadarenes," Rigby interposed to explain, "are stenographers of
the best brand."

By this time the whole party were moving in the direction she
had indicated, which was directly opposite to that which would have
led them to Jehane's room. The Gadarenes were lodged on the floor
below that on which they now were. The natural way to reach it

would be by the lift, but anyone, wishing to do so without attracting notice, might use the emergency stairs at the end of the corridor.

Rigby followed in silence. It seemed to him an unlikely, though not an impossible tale, and why she had told it he could not tell. But he knew that Molly was less simple than her appearance might suggest to the masculine mind, and his first attempt at interposition had received the lesson of a well-bruised shin. Miss Preston might be wearing a dressing-gown—but she had not come on the scene in her bedroom slippers.

Selby had listened to the mendacious narrative in an equal silence. He was of a natural obedience when Molly indicated her will, and, beyond that, he thought he understood.

He did not doubt that Stanley was in Jehane's room. Roused by the noise of those bursting doors, and aware of the compromising position in which they might be discovered, they had resorted to this device, of sending Molly to mislead the chase with a tale that was parallel to the truth it was designed to hide. It might easily mean an hour's delay while the rooms of those innocent young women would be unceremoniously ransacked. He found a moment's leisure to reflect that it was rather hard on the Gadarenes. He wondered whether this diversion would enable Stanley, if not to leave the hotel, at least to remove to some part of it where his presence could be more innocently explained. But it seemed that that was not to be. Captain Callover took the precaution of ordering that sentries should be posted on every floor. Having done that, he proceeded to an energetic search where it is needless, and would therefore be inexcusable, for us to follow, knowing, as we do, that Mr. Maitland was not there.

It was a full hour later when Captain Callover finally realised that he had drawn a blank on the floor of the Gadarenes. It did not follow that Miss Preston's tale was untrue. He recognised that Stanley had had ample opportunity of leaving whatever room he might have occupied before the search commenced in that direction, but he was confident that he could not have left the hotel. The exits were too well guarded for that.

He was anxious and hurried, for he should have been far out of London by this hour with his victim in the closed van which was waiting two streets away, and with the reward of £10,000 for his safe delivery well in sight. But he made dispositions for a complete search of the hotel from basement upwards, and might have been another two or three hours before he had come to Jehane's door had not the young lady who controlled the switchboard assisted the search with a suggestion for which she had not been asked.

It was very naturally and innocently done. She had heard nothing to indicate that the alarm was not genuine. She stood beside the private who had been placed in charge of the switchboard, in a continual wonder that she had not turned to ashes during the previous half-minute. It was an experience of which anyone might tire. Her thoughts were still on her hat.

Now that Captain Callover returned to the ground-floor to make fresh dispositions after two abortive hours in the upper regions, she altered his programme instantly by one innocent and pregnant sentence: "I wonder whether Lady Jehane knows."

Captain Callover remembered his charge concerning that lady, which had been absent from a harassed mind. Where or which was she? All the inhabitants of the hotel, including the Gadarenes in various intermediate stages of their usual toilets, were now following and impeding his movements. Could Lady Jehane tell him anything? And which was she? Enquiry quickly made it clear that she was not there. No one had seen her. Where was her room? On Mr. Maitland's floor. That she had slept through the noise of those bursting doors was not a probable thing.

Captain Callover, cheered by a new hope, led the way upstairs again. He rattled on a locked door. It appeared that Lady Jehane was inside. She called: "What's the matter? Well, don't make that noise. I'll come out as soon as I've got something on."

He put his ear to the door. He said: "There are two people in that room." Satisfaction spread good-humour over his face as he added: "Might have guessed he'd have picked the best."

Selby stood in the rear of the group with Molly beside him. He was not surprised. It was what he had known all along. Molly looked anxious and worried. "If only," she said, "we could have kept them away a bit longer."

Rigby was close behind them. He heard Captain Callover's remark. He was white with anger, which other feelings complicated. He pushed forward, intending to give the Captain an unexpected diversion. Molly held on to his arm. "Rigby," she said sharply, "don't be an utter fool."

No one took notice of what they might say or do. All eyes were fixed on the door, from the other side of which there came the sound of a heavy fall.

Captain Callover said: "Break it in." The door was not as strong as had been those of Mr. Maitland's suite. The panel split from the lock. They entered a room that Lady Jehane and Stanley had just left. A large hole in the masonry of the opposite wall sufficiently indicated the way by which they had gone. Captain Callover, standing amid a rubble of fallen plaster and bricks, looked through the hole. "I wonder where this leads," he remarked, as his head went through.

"I think he'll find it's next door," Molly remarked happily, but he did not hear her. Strong hands had been inserted under his arm-pits on either side, and he was dragged through the hole.

Lord Rigby's opportunity of breaking that egg-like head was over for several years.

The Captain's followers hesitated. A distribution of uniforms among them a few days previously, and some very meagre instructions in military demeanour and etiquette, had not been sufficient to supply the confidence which the situation required. They had been feeling increasingly, as the night-hours passed, that things were not going according to plan. Unless it have confidence in its leader, any lawless organisation will quickly fall apart. Neither confidence nor respect were engendered by the manner in which Captain Callover had disappeared from view.

The next moment their hesitation ended. *"Hands up!"* The voice sounded behind them in sharp command. They turned to see the muzzles of rifles levelled in their direction, and the picturesque uniforms of the Banffshire Highlanders.

CHAPTER FORTY-ONE

THE incidents of the night could not have been easily kept from the publicity of the daily press, and, in fact, it was not attempted. They disputed prominence with the arrests of the scientists, and caused many to suppose that these gentlemen were suspected of complicity in the attempted abduction. Others, better informed, looked with a confident suspicion toward the group of politicians who had been driven by Stanley Maitland's coming into the wilderness of opposition, or who may be said, more accurately, to have exiled themselves through one of those political miscalculations which are more bitter in memory than a defeat in the open field.

In Mr. Goldstone's office there was little doubt, and in his own mind there was none, that the Hon. James Shackston could have supplied full information concerning, even if he had not contrived and financed, it. But many things may be believed which it is impossible to prove, and may be foolish to say.

The arrested leader could not be Captain Callover, as that gentleman was fulfilling his military duties as a gallant member of the Gibraltar garrison. The police suggested William Turner to be a name with which he had been associated for a longer time, though, it might be, with no better right. He admitted this very readily, and appeared willing to supply any further information within his power. He even gave the impression that, if he could have betrayed those who had induced him to attempt his disastrous enterprise, it would have been a pleasure to do so. But, in fact, he knew little. He had been paid a sum of £5,000 to cover the expenses of organising the raid. This considerable sum had been delivered to him in bundles of one-pound notes, and its value had encouraged him to condone its bulk. The detailed typescript instructions which he had received were found to be on a variety of paper too common to form a clue. The forged order which had withdrawn the Banffshires had been the most promising document, but was not sufficient to be the basis of any definite process. Had the kidnapping succeeded, Mr. Turner's van was to have been met by another at a lonely spot near Gerald's Cross, where he would have handed over his victim for a cash payment of £10,000 which would have increased his already considerable profit, and which was to have been guineas if Lady Jehane Norchester had been included in the bag. But of that van no trace could be found.

The purpose of the attempted abduction, the possible fate of the man who had been for a few weeks the actual ruler of England, were food for a speculation to which there could be no certain solution. But it was a simple supposition that he would have been coerced by privation or torture to disclose the secret of William Feltham's invention, though the use to which that knowledge would have been put, whether merely to his own undoing, or for the substitution of another, perhaps less tolerable, tyranny, was less easy to say.

As is usual in such circumstances, the newspapers offered a plausible solution of the admitted fact that Mr. Maitland had been discovered in and escaped from Lady Jehane's bedroom, which simple-minded people believed, and the sophisticated understood without difficulty.

She received a full measure of credit for the bold device of piercing the wall which divided her room from the adjoining premises. In some versions she tore it down from floor to ceiling with bleeding hands, while her lover held the doorway gallantly against their crowding foes. In others there was a tendency to reverse these occupations, and Jehane exposed the naked breast of womanhood in Amazonian defence of her lover's life.

The truth (which is of very little importance) was that the idea of making a hole in the wall had been easily thought of, but the operation itself had proved harder to perform.

It would certainly not have succeeded within the available time had it not received vigorous assistance on the other side from the military guard in the adjoining building, who had responded to the efforts of the labourers at an early stage, and had also secured the street against any possible success of Mr. Turner's enterprise some time before the return of the Banffshire Highlanders gave them sufficient force to re-enter the hotel and resume possession.

It resulted from one of those curious contradictions in English character which are so much easier to observe than to interpret, that the adventure enormously increased the popularity both of Stanley and Jehane. Their names became romantically linked in the public mind, and it may be doubted whether anyone could have done him a. greater injury than to produce conclusive evidence that he cared less for his reputed mistress than for the wife who had deserted him at the time of crisis.

CHAPTER FORTY-TWO

MR. HENRY SIMPSON was an intelligent man, as most farmers are. He was keenly alert to the possible consequences of the changing order around him, and with much of the impersonal interest which is common to many men, but which few women can understand. Yet he looked first at the immediate consequences to himself and to those things for which he was responsible, as is natural, and perhaps right.

He was a thoughtful man as he rode up to the Home Farm to see how Timms was getting on with the spring ploughing, which he had failed to oversee as he knew that a master should.

It was a morning of cold spring sunshine, and a bitter wind from the northeast, which met him as he came to the crest of the hedge-side path, and reined up to survey the land which fell away upon either side. He looked round to the grey horizons thinking of snow. It would be bad for the lambs if it should come now. Last week it had seemed that the spring was here, but in this climate you could never tell.

He rode on again oblivious in his own thoughts to the surrounding scene—so oblivious that he found himself pulling shut a field gate with his whipstock after he had ridden through it, almost in the face of Lady Crystal, who came riding toward it.

The frown which had been born of her own reflections passed too quickly for him to see it. When he raised his eyes and spoke with an easy apology, she was what her training and character required that she should be to him, and to such as he. Serene, and friendly, and remote.

"Good morning, Simpson," she said pleasantly. "We haven't seen much of you up here during the last fortnight. "

She meant no rudeness by the familiarity of her address. It was how she had been taught to speak of and to the tenants of the estate. In his heart he thought it a rather impudent mannerism, but be knew that there was no conscious rudeness, and he gave his attention to more serious things. On her side she had been conscious at times of a little—well, lack of proper respect in Simpson's manner of address—but it had not blinded her to the fact that he was the best farmer on the estate, and the only one who still met his obligations punctually, without cavil or complaint. Without wasting time in useless grumbling, he had bent his mind to overcome successfully the economic problems which the bad faith and indifference of post-war governments had inflicted upon him. No one but himself—and perhaps his wife—knew what measure of success he had reached, or what his losses had been.

"No," he said, "I've been over in the next county watching the Screen there. It's a queer thing to see them farming this very land, it may be three hundred and fifty years back, and to see how little change there's been in the land itself. There's one corner where it might still be the same hedge."

There was a ten-second silence, while the horses moved impatiently. He could not ride on unless she should rein aside, which she made no motion to do. He was in a mood to talk to someone from a full mind, but only on the subjects with which it had been concerned. She was restless and empty of motive, glad of anything which would divert her from her own thoughts.

She said idly: "You must have seen something more than an old hedge to keep you there at this time of the year."

"Yes," he answered, "I saw more than that." He looked at her with a sudden keenness in the puckered grey eyes, which only revealed his age, for in his fiftieth year he still had the spare activity of a younger man. "I haven't seen Mr. Maitland down here lately. I suppose he's too busy to come."

"Yes," she said tonelessly. "I expect he is." She wondered how much he knew or supposed, as she turned the subject in a natural manner by asking if Mrs. Simpson were well, and if Cyril had been able to return to school.

He said that Mrs. Simpson was well, and that Cyril went back last week, but he held to the thought in his own mind, adding: "I wasn't sure at first what it all meant, but I'm getting to think it's the best hour that England's had for a long day. I was wondering what to do about this." He took a paper from his coat-pocket as he spoke, and then added: "But I expect you've heard about it already."

"Perhaps," Lady Crystal said non-committally, "I could tell better when I've seen what it is." She held out her hand.

She observed that the document was an intimation from an unemployment bureau that Mr. Simpson could have the benefit of the services of any number of available men that he might require for four hours daily without any obligation to remunerate them for the service rendered.

She read it, and was aware, as she so often was in these days, that she did not know what to think. She had known her own world so well, as her class had, but now she was in a sea of continual doubt. Everyone argued about everything, and everything had a different effect from what people supposed it would.

But she spoke her thought from an honest mind: "Isn't it rather like slavery? I shouldn't think any man would work well under such conditions as that.

"Yes," he said. "It seemed that way to me at first, but I'm not sure. Perhaps a parasite's as bad as a slave. I reckon I've worked for these men for the last five years—I'm not blaming them—but it might be the way to get their self-respect back, if they see it right. You see, it's only for four hours a day. They'll be paid fully by what they draw. And how much better it'll be for them than just standing about! And if they're doing some good work, it's all helping to get the country back to prosperity, and that's the way to get them jobs in the end, if anything is."

"Do you think they'll be any use to you, if they come?"

"I'm not oversure about that," he said doubtfully. "They'll know more about looms and lathes than how to lay a hedge, or bed a horse down, when they first come. And they'll have a four-mile walk each way from the town, unless they're to be carted out."

"I can tell you that," Lady Crystal interposed. "I heard about it last night. They're to be distributed in the municipal motor-cars. Most of the councils and corporations have a few dozens or hundreds, and they're to be used for this scheme. I suppose the town clerks will be getting about on their own legs."

"Well, that's so much to the good. But I thought at first that I wouldn't touch it at all. It seemed like taking farm pupils with no premiums, and I've had enough of them even when they've paid a price at the start. But they'll be a poor lot if I can't get them to kill some thistles…and I thought it was a thing that I ought to help, like it or not. You don't know what it'll do for some of these men, when they're weeded out. Besides, I've seen how this land used to be worked, and I can't get it out of my mind."

"You think it was better then, Honestly, Simpson, would you back if you could?"

"I wouldn't have things just as they were then, if you mean that. I'm not fool enough to think any time was perfect, because it didn't make all our mistakes…and I've seen a good many things as I've sat in the Pastograph Cinema during the last fortnight that we don't want again. There were the pigeons, for one. There must have been dovecotes that held thousands on the south side of the Hall. It was that way that they always flew."

"Yes," she said. "They're on the old maps."

"Well, those pigeons wouldn't do here, but I suppose they didn't grow roots then as we do now. Maybe they scared them off the corn when it got ripe. They weren't short of boys then. Or maybe they thought they got it back with the birds they'd kill in the winter days:"

"Yes," she said, "it was having no imported foods. It must have been rather a monotonous diet."

"I don't know as to that," he answered doubtfully. "They didn't look starved." In fact, they had looked rather the other way. Even the animals were rather fatter than we are used to seeing today. The standards of rotundity seemed to have changed, not only for men and women, but for horses and milking cows. He had been reminded of some old prints that had been in his family for generations. The animals in them had the same generous contours. He went on:

"There were things to see that we wouldn't want again, but I couldn't help thinking that you can't have a much better product than English men and women—and English horses—from English land."

"You mean the country population was larger?"

"It was, on this land." He looked upon the empty landscape where no men moved, and on the few remaining cottages which were worth no man's while to repair. "Yes," he said, "about twenty times. They were hay-making in May, or in early June."

"It seems early for that."

"It seems early to us. They wouldn't get the weight that they might have had in another three or four weeks, but they'd get a lot better hay. The seed hadn't begun to fall."

"Well," she said, "I'm afraid there's no bringing the old times back."

She reined her horse aside as she spoke, and he took the hint. He raised his hat, and rode on.

As he turned leftward toward the higher plough land which was his goal, he looked down on the Long Meadow, on which he had seen men mowing three hundred and fifty years ago.

Each somewhat more advanced than his right-hand neighbour, the line of scythe men had stretched across the meadow, from hedge to hedge. Regularly, rhythmically, the scythes had swung, and the left-hand swathes of summer grass had lengthened behind them. How rapidly, how equally, they had worked! How often they had drunk from the jugs—were they of home-brewed ale?—that the women brought! How heartily they had eaten at the noon-hour rest! There was no space for a laggard in that slanting line. A man could not shirk without its regularity giving way. They moved with one purpose, even in the pauses when they would whet their scythes.

Once the farmer had walked watchfully across the field. He was a fleshy jovial man of the back-slapping kind. For no very clear reason, Mr. Simpson detested him uselessly over that gulf of years.

But he did not doubt that he knew his job.

He watched him stop by one of the younger women, saying something that seemed like a jest. He pulled her up by the ear from the grass over which she stooped. He spoke again, giving her some errand, at which she ran away with lifted skirts over the new-mown grass.

He went on watchfully behind the mowers. He stopped behind one who seemed to be of poorer physique than the others. He looked with contempt on the strip behind him, which was somewhat narrower and less regularly cleared than were those on either side. With an opprobrious gesture he jerked his thumb as a sign for the man to go. With evident protest the scythe was surrendered. It was a rough world for weaklings, of which Mr. Simpson had observed other signs before that. A rough, robust world.

The farmer took the vacated place in the line. The men to right and left gave him sour glances, which he did not heed, if he saw them. Perhaps they did not relish that he should come freshly to set the pace. But for an hour he went on, and then the young woman came back and a man with her to whom he handed over the scythe in turn.

Mr. Simpson, watching the grass fall, and reading by a score of signs of sunlight and leaf and herbage that May was scarcely over, had recalled a clause in one of his older leases which forbade the tenant to take more than one crop of hay annually from the land he farmed without the landlord's consent. He had never felt tempted in that direction. It had become the custom to defer mowing till the undergrowth should be sufficiently thick to assure a heavy crop. Quality had become a secondary consideration. And after that—well, though he managed better himself, he knew of more than one farm where the hay was cut field by field, lasting over a month from first to last as the machines were available, and taking its chance of the weather.

But he had watched a different standard of farming, carried on without artificial manures or imported foodstuffs. The hay crop, in quality as well as quantity, had been a vital need. If, in spite of many hands to make it quickly in sunny hours, and to gather it instantly into protective haycocks if the dark clouds gathered, the crop should be ruined by persistent rain, there would still be time to mow again in the short, hot August days.

He recalled a passage which he had read recently in a daily paper about what it called the optimum population of the world. It was much concerned lest there should be a larger population at some future period than the earth could feed. Reflecting that the earth had never been even half-populated within historical times, and that one of its present economic difficulties was the over-production of food, he had doubted whether he were reading anything better than a claptrap cry. But one statement had remained in his mind. "Even the supply of artificial fertilisers is not unlimited. The nitrates—." It didn't matter particularly what was or would be wrong with the nitrates. The important point was the assumption that cultivation must decline as the supply of artificial fertilisers should fail. But there had been no thought of such aids in the farming which he had witnessed, and the crops were good. He saw that the earth might still be fertile, though such aids should be discarded or exhausted expedients. Might, indeed, show a fairer front if men should once more prefer organic to inorganic alliance: should prefer life to death: "The point is," he said aloud with the coarseness of Nature herself, "the point is that you get no dung from a steam-plough."

Even Mr. H. G. Wells didn't seem to have thought of that.

What a fine girl Lady Crystal was! And brains, of her own kind. Breeding also. He admired good breeding, as farmers do. But he thought that a wife should stand at her husband's side. That was a natural law, so fundamental that it needed no reason to make it good. Bertha would have been at his side, though the heavens fell. He would hardly have praised her for that. She would have been in her own place.

He supposed that Lady Crystal was betrayed by the pride of her own power. It was in her orbit that she had expected Maitland to find his strength. He rode on, his mind turning to his own limited monarchy of the land around him.

Crystal rode her own way, which had no purpose or goal. She stirred to sudden gallops. Her horse looked round at her with a nervous, sensitive eye. What was wrong in Olympian heights?

She took a fence with a recklessness that she rarely showed, and came down on the other side with a few bruises, escaping lightly by the saddle-wisdom of one who had ridden almost since she could walk, and the skill of a well-trained horse.

She remounted, shaken by the fall, and rode on in a quieter mood. "The best hour in a long day." That was how it might seem to him. It looked different to her.

She was looking down now on the solid dignity of Norchester Towers. That was where the dovecotes had stood. Over near where the swan pool had been made in a later day. They had been good in their time, but it did not follow that they would be good now. You can't mix the centuries. Stanley was clever, no doubt, but he hadn't sense enough to see that.

Yet he seemed to be succeeding. That was a strange thing. Succeeding in marvellous unbelievable ways. And yet she felt instinctively that there could be but one end. You can't take three or four fences a day—and such fences!—without a broken neck in the end.

No, she had been right. She had never doubted that. She did not doubt it now. But being right was a bitter thing. Not that she thought that all was right with the land. Its depopulation was deplorable. She knew that, to her father, it had been a continual grief. Who could thatch a rick now? Old men climbed ladders on rheumatic legs rather than see the work botched by those who had no training and no pride in what they did. An old hedger-and-ditcher, whose scraggy muscles could still wield a bill-hook with a wizard's skill, was borrowed from farm to farm.

The urban population might be larger, but it was afraid of adventure, afraid of life. The old fecund hard-reared race that the land had bred had gone forth and peopled the world: that was what her father had said. He had never been tired of saying that the town-bred people were doomed. That when they could no longer have their virility recruited from the countryside which they were taxing out of existence, they would die out in the end, "Whining like rats in their own trap." That had been one of his phrases in a bitter moment when he had realised what the death-duties meant to such as he: that they could have but one issue. That the town-dweller would take his land, though he might have no wisdom to rule it

She did not look at things quite in her father's way. She was of a later generation. She saw with clearer eyes that the spirit of England still lives in the town-dweller, though it be differently ruled.

Her mind wandered to the conversation she had had last week with Mrs. Prestwick—General Prestwick's widow, who had lost her husband and both sons in the war. She had always liked and respected the older woman, had been confidential with her at times, as she seldom was with one of her own age. Mrs. Prestwick had been sympathetic, had understood so easily, had agreed so plainly with her own feelings about these abortive efforts to change the currents of modern life, and then had said at last, so inconsequently, with such a quiet finality: "My dear, you will be sorry in the end."

What had she meant by that? Crystal understood well enough. Indeed, there was no need to wait for the end. She was sorry now. But, for any sorrow, she could not change.

Everyone knew that she had parted with Stanley when this wild adventure was at its birth. The whole world knew. Mr. Goldstone had taken care of that. She supposed that it was his revenge for a rebuff which, in fact, had been impulsed by loyalty to the husband she would not support in more open ways. But, without him, it would have been known. It was an unconcealable thing.

Could she go back to him, as one who had stood aside when the battle joined, and came now to enjoy the spoils? He might refuse any reconciliation, making her doubly contemptible. For there was the fact of that unanswered letter, of which no one knew. Even Mrs. Prestwick had not been told of that. She might have judged differently had she known. But Crystal's pride was too great, the humiliation of that rejected overture was still too keen, for it to be mentioned to any.

Had Jehane known of it? Had she counselled that it should be ignored? She could imagine Jehane saying in her airy way: "I shouldn't go to her. It's like her cheek, asking you to do that. Just tear it up and you'll soon have her running round." But she didn't really think that. She didn't think that Stanley would talk of that letter, even to Jehane. It was not his way. It was more probable that he was too indignant, too deeply hurt to respond. No. She could take what consolation remained in the confidence that no one would ever know that that letter had been written. No one but she and he.

So she thought, but she was wrong about that. Mr. Goldstone had had that letter in his possession ever since it had been sorted out of a mass of waste paper which some diplomacy and a considerable sum of money had secured from the basement of the Rafton Hotel. Most of it had been of a singularly worthless kind. Letters to Maitland from half the fools in the country, which had evidently been consigned to destruction without reply. But this letter had been worth all the expense incurred.

Of course, the *Morning Standard* couldn't publish it. There was a law of copyright. And, besides, it was a respectable morning paper, which didn't do things like that. But there were ways. The time had come when Maitland was to be attacked in earnest. Mr. Goldstone would have nothing to do with that. He had been firm, even against the sneering contempt in Jimmy Shackston's eyes. "I don't want even to know," he said definitely. But, in other ways he was willing to help.

He was particularly willing to humiliate Lady Crystal. The letter found its way on to the table of the Editor of the *West End Tatler*. That enterprising gentleman published it with a few dashes, a few asterisks, and a few jocular comments. Lady Crystal was unaware that it had been published two days ago.

What she did know was that she had alienated herself from her husband by a gulf which it seemed that nothing but his ruin could ever bridge. And though she might expect that ruin, she did not desire it, either for his sake or her own. She knew, too, that her defection had weakened his position from the first, so that, should he fail at last, from whatever cause, it might be hard to say that it had not turned the scale against him. She may have exaggerated the importance of the support that she could have given. Stanley ruling England from the prestige, the political importance of Norchester House, seemed so much more natural, more precedented than that he should attempt to do it from the Rafton Hotel.

She wondered how the position was complicated in the minds of those who looked on by the fact that Jehane was still with him, and was said to be ordering his new establishment. She was almost incapable of a vulgar physical jealousy, and the popular view of, the popular reaction to, the tale of the night escape had made little impression upon her. She had neither shared it, nor realised what it was. She knew the pride of her race. She knew Jehane. But she saw with a bitter anger that people might look at it in various ways.

She remembered Dora Flinthead's jest at Lady Valentine's last Tuesday. Dora had been staying at Merton-Ash, and had brought back Muriel's gossip about the happenings at the Rafton, which she had visited on the pretext of taking Rigby some things he needed.

Muriel had speculated as to when Mr. Maitland would turn his attention to the marriage laws. She was reported to have said that it was about time that he spared a thought for the surplus women, and gave the weekenders a square deal. It was not clear what Muriel had meant. Muriel's meanings were often obscure, and those who tried to clear them might sometimes wish afterwards that they had been less enterprising. But there had been something else that she had heard Dora repeating, though not to her. Something about scrapping the first word in the Deceased Wife's Sister's Act, and Stanley being the law of the land now, and could do what he liked.

She had not heeded it then. She was not of the disposition that overhears and suspects, but the words came to her with the possibility of a new meaning now. Was it that they had been aimed at Jehane and her? She knew that Jehane's treatment of Rigby was one of Muriel's continual grievances. What an impudent cat Muriel was!

CHAPTER FORTY-THREE

THE following morning Lady Crystal received anonymously by post two separate copies of the number of the *West End Tatler* which contained her letter.

Had that been all, it is doubtful whether she would have read the offending paragraph. She did not belong to the class of English people who are hypersensitive to the printed word. She knew that she was the subject of frequent press references in Court and Society columns, and that they were often inaccurate. They would announce her arrival in Edinburgh the day after she left for Ballater. But who cared about that? She knew that there is a lower class of paper which repeats or invents scandalous gossip which it attaches to well-known names. Now and then someone, annoyed or injured by too persistent attacks of this kind, would bring an action for libel; but it was not a very dignified thing to do. Of course, if damaging attacks should appear in a respectable paper, it might be a different matter. But for the rest—well, servants gossip and lie. Everyone knows that. If a bad case were forced upon your notice, dismissal might be a necessary consequence, but you do not listen at the door of the servants' hall.

The papers might have gone into the waste-paper basket unopened, but there was a letter from Lady Stillburn, with a cutting enclosed, which could not escape attention in the same way.

Lady Stillburn was indignant and sympathetic. She was eloquent upon the baseness of men (meaning Stanley), and reasonable upon the possible innocence of those who act with culpable indiscretion (meaning Jehane). Her dear Crystal's attitude had won the sympathy of all her friends, but was it not a mistake to hide herself in the country, as though she were inconsolable for one of such character, who had ceased to care for her, and had now allowed her to be publicly insulted as no *gentleman* would have stooped to do?

Crystal read the letter with astonished and angry eyes. The infernal insolence of the woman! That was her first reaction. She took a sheet of note-paper across which she wrote: *Lady Crystal Maitland returns an impertinent letter.* When this communication was in the post-rack, she dismissed the writer from her thoughts, as a trivial thing. She had dealt with her. She knew that Stanley's vagaries had not shaken her social power, which was one of those intangible things which would be forever beyond his reach. The houses where Lady Stillburn would be received next season would be fewer than in the past. She would understand that when she opened her letters tomorrow morning.

Having finished with her, Crystal took up the cutting. Anger, as she read it, gave way to incredulity, and then indignation and injured pride. It seemed an incredible thing that her letter to Stanley, a letter so personal, so intimate in its occasion and subject, should be printed there, with a jest above and a sneer beneath it. She had supposed that Stanley had been too hurt, too obstinate to reply. She had wished a hundred times that that letter had not been written: that she had gone to him instead. She might have won with the spoken word. She could surely have done so with eyes and lips; with the softened mood to which he would always yield.

She knew that this separation had not merely been an unhappiness: it had been a mistake. It had shown to others the differences that should have been known only to themselves. She had not only failed to guide the man she had married to her own ends, she had advertised her failure for all to see. And it was that letter which had made the gulf uncrossable. She could not make another overture while it was ignored so contemptuously, and the fact that it was so ignored showed that it had been a blunder to write it. Its failure condemned itself.

But all the time, in her heart, she had anticipated reconciliation. She had been watchful for a moment when Stanley might be threatened with serious difficulty or disaster, so that she might have shown her willingness, and perhaps her power to aid. And the moment had come in an unexpected way, as such moments do, and it was Jehane, not she, who had been there to aid, with a woman's courage, and a woman's finesse. Jehane had been in her place, and had taken the opportunity that should have been hers of right.

She had not doubted in her heart that with Stanley, as with herself; the bonds of honour and love had loosened, but had not snapped. Stanley might be angry, be unforgiving still, but anger is not indifference. She had thought it the anger of injured love. But this—.

And then she looked at the next paragraph. Lady Stillburn had not meant her to miss that. There was a sentence marked in blue ink, as was the main paragraph above it. But for that marking, she would not have read, and might not have understood had she done so. Beneath the dividing asterisks. there was nothing but surmise to bracket these disconnected sentences, in which there was no mention of any name. But *"a fresher cherry from the same bunch"?* Why should Lady Stillburn have marked that? Crystal was not dense. Absurd though it might be, the reference was to Jehane.

It was absurd from every angle. She was as fresh as Jehane. Only three years older, and far more beautiful. She did not think overmuch of Jehane's looks, though she knew she attracted men with her vivacity, and perhaps by her aloofness also.

But that Stanley should expose herself—that he should expose Jehane—to this! If it were done without his knowledge, without his authority, which seemed an incredible thing—well, he had the power now. It would be quickly shown, and there would be apologies to herself. If he were not lost to all sense of decency, all considerations of honour....

And she would return to Norchester House tomorrow. She had not come down here to nurse a foolish grief. It had been a device of the brain, not the heart. To render her separation from Stanley less quickly apparent, less clearly significant, than it would have been had she remained in town. She would go back now. The Norchester flag was not lowered because Stanley had gone off in his own way.

There are women who might have hesitated to do the thing which Lady Stillburn had advised, as though accepting her counsel. But the objection did not even enter Crystal's mind. She would have taken advice from her worst enemy or her lowest servant as readily as she wiped her feet on a mat.

So she went back to Norchester House, and waited with a growing impatience and alienation for a communication that did not come.

It was not likely to do so, for Stanley remained unconscious that the letter had been published, in the isolation that power, in whatever form, inevitably brings. It was known throughout the Rafton, except only by him.

Jehane should have brought it to his notice, but when we consider the implication of its following paragraph, we can understand that she was reluctant to do so. She dealt with it in her own way, or perhaps we should say in that which Rigby's attitude constrained her to do.

Rigby said he was going to interview the editor. He would make the rat squirm.

"Physically?" Jehane asked, and then added: "No, you mustn't do that. What is it to do with you?"

Rigby said it was a good deal.

"Well, I don't agree." Jehane thought a moment. "The point is," she asked, "that you want him whipped?" She felt that there was no objection to that. "It can't matter who does it, so long as it gets thoroughly done?"

Rigby rather sulkily half-agreed. He added: "If you want it done thoroughly, you'd better leave it to me."

"I don't see where you come in it at all." She took up the telephone receiver. "Get me through to the editor of the *West End Tatler*. Tell him I've got some more news for him."

"What are you going to do now?"

"I'm going to send him to buy the stick. I don't think he ought to expect us to pay for that."

"I don't know what you mean."

"Well, you will if you listen. No. It doesn't matter at all. Say if the editor isn't in, anyone who can give him a message will do. Is that—? Yes. Lady Jehane Norchester speaking. Mr. Butford? Miss? No, P. Yes. Miss Putford. That's quite clear. I want you to tell the editor about something that's going to happen this afternoon. You're sure you can let him know? Yes, within an hour'll do very well. Tell him he'll go out about five-thirty this afternoon and buy a really good cane. Better say two, in case one might break. Yes, say two. *He* will. The editor, of course. He'll buy them himself and come here. He's to be at the front entrance of the Rafton at six o'clock, and ask for the head porter. The porter'll know what to do with him, and he'd better have a taxi at the back entrance at six-fifteen to take him away."

Jehane heard an altercation of two female voices, and a sound of giggling. Then Miss Putford replied: "I can't possibly give him that message, and, besides, he wouldn't come."

"Oh, yes, he will. He'll be here before time, more likely than not. Tell him this. *Mr. Maitland doesn't know yet.* You remember the Gosport murder case? Yes, the man who's due to be hanged tomorrow for killing a nagging wife. Well, he won't be hanged. He's reprieved. That means the hangman's got nothing on for tomorrow. Mr. Maitland always likes people to work full time."

There was a second pause, and the half-heard conversation had a more serious tone. Then there was another voice, which sounded like that of an older woman.

"Lady Jehane," it said earnestly, "I feel sure there's a misunderstanding somewhere. We should never have allowed the publication of anything of which Mr. Maitland was understood not to approve. His own treatment of this letter...."

"I don't know anything about that. I expect it was forged."

"If you would like the editor to call this afternoon to explain personally, and to arrange for the publication of anything that...."

"But I shouldn't like it at all. I don't see men of that kind. He'll have to ask for the porter. He won't want to see anyone else after he's had a short time with him. Tell him two *strong* canes. If they don't last, we might have to ask him to call again. No, it won't be any use ringing up. Tell him it's his one chance, and it ought to give him a page of news for next week that his readers will enjoy reading. If I tell Mr. Maitland about this, he might think there's no man in England who could be more easily spared."

"Did I sound rather a pig?" Jehane asked, as she put the receiver down. She respected Rigby's codes of conduct more than she admired his intellect, and the suspicion that she might have sounded somewhat cattish (but pig was her favourite word) troubled her mind. "I should have let it go, but for you. But if I spoke at all, I'd got to let them know that I meant what I said. And I always did rather enjoy hearing myself talk."

"I should think you would," Rigby said, arriving nearer to a genuine compliment than he often did. (Such are the inspirations of love.) "You didn't put it half strong enough. Do you feel sure he'll be here?"

"Yes, Stanley's power's so absolute, it makes everyone afraid, if they've done wrong. It's not like the law. You know how gentle he is in most ways. But they're never quite sure."

"It is a bit sporting. Trust the porter to do the job right?"

"Yes. He's rather fond of me, and he was saying he doesn't get enough exercise here."

Jehane proved so far right that Mr. Jepson called punctually, with the canes in a neat parcel under his arm. There is no reason to suppose that the porter failed to use them well, in a good cause. But her suggestion that the incident should occupy a page in the next week's issue of the *West End Tatler* was not adopted, and it did not come to Lady Crystal's knowledge, whose feelings it might have influenced. Or it might not.

CHAPTER FORTY-FOUR

IT is said that the health of the human body is more likely to sustain without collapse a complete change of food and environment than a single important alteration in its established routine.

It may be that a parity of reasoning would explain the fact that the England of May 1st, 1934, had endured the bold and numerous experiments which Stanley Maitland had inflicted upon it, not merely without disaster or revolution, but with a quickening of national and individual life for which it might be difficult to find a parallel in earlier than Elizabethan times.

It was true that there were few of the great vested interests which politicians had hitherto regarded as impregnably fortified that had not suffered, but there were few also that had not experienced some compensating unexpected gain.

It was difficult even to lament the state of the motor industry, bleeding from a score of wounds, without remembering that the railways and coal-mines had found a renewed prosperity, that thousands of living English people would already have been in their hospitals or their graves had the old conditions been allowed to prevail, and that the wealth which had been wasted so excessively upon the deadly toys which it manufactured was not lost but available to recruit expenditure in a hundred other directions. There was scarcely a trade in the land which did not feel the vitalising impulse of this diverted expenditure, and as the list of unemployed in the motor industry grew, the lists in other trades diminished with even greater rapidity.

It would be beyond the capacity of a hundred volumes to record and analyse all the confusing consequences of the Orders in Council that had been issued during the three previous months.

We are only incidentally interested in these political acts of an author whose popularity was unexpected to himself as to his opponents. Beneath the surface moved undercurrents of opposition and fierce hatred, the strength of which was very difficult to measure, because they were less openly shown. For they were afraid.

For most men, life had become less secure, less certain than it had been three months before, but it was also less limited. And with the element of the unexpected, there had come a new consciousness of living, a new alertness, a recovered value in the fact of life itself. If in some ways there was more fear, in many others there was more hope, and there had been a curious decline in the number of suicides. Even gas ovens were rarely used for the insertion of a human head.

It was the uncertainty of tomorrow which, above everything else, had brought a new exhilaration to life. Formerly, it was not only that the hope and the ideal of freedom had left the world, it had been a slow and difficult process even for people to adjust their chains, a process overswept with a sea of talk. That process still continued. As though in derisive contrast to the abrupter method, Parliament still sat, and churned out its accustomed output. A faint perfunctory cheer announced that the Fleas (Regulation and Restriction) Bill had passed its third reading and gone upstairs, but no one troubled about that. They watched for the Orders in Council that were published two or three times a week, the contents of which it was impossible to foresee.

For though general outlines of policy had soon emerged, such as the determination that England should be fully cultivated, and English industries fostered, the application even of these fundamental policies had its disconcerting surprises.

The aluminium manufacturers, for instance, had rejoiced in a sudden raising of the tariff wall that protected their internal trade practically to the exclusion of competition. A month later they were confounded by the announcement that the tariff had not merely been reduced to its former level, it had been entirely removed. Who could defend or explain such arbitrary inconsistency?

A deputation waited upon Mr. Maitland at the Rafton Hotel, and was courteously received. He listened patiently to their complaints, and replied briefly.

"I gave you the entire English market. The increased output, without a corresponding rise in your overhead charges, would have enabled you to reduce your prices, with an actual increase in the net profit you would have been able to show. You don't need me to tell you that. I have evidence here under my hand that your quotations have been raised by nearly seven percent during the last month.

"You are a well-organised trade. When I freed you from foreign competition you felt strong enough to do this. But there is a power in England today which is stronger than you. Did you think that I was giving you an opportunity to abuse your position? You are not fit to control a trade. You can come back to me in a month's time, if you are still in England. It is a warning for others as well as you."

They had gone out in silence. They had not waited a month to reduce their prices, nor even a day. It was not merely that vessels were already being loaded in foreign ports with competing goods to be dumped on the English market. It was the ominous threat in the last words which affected not merely them, but caused a hasty nervous revision of price lists in many protected trades, where secret rings had been forming, and prices rising on a score of specious pretexts.

For who could forget the melancholy procession which had been walked through the streets of London a fortnight earlier on its way to the East End Docks?

Not that the new Orders increased severity of punishments. On the other hand, the huge levies taken from the public in fines at the magistrates' courts had been largely diminished. The principle that a popular activity should be allowed or suppressed is inconsistent with an income that is steadily derived year after year from such sources. They become no better than an irregular system of licensing. The only intelligent method—and the only honest one unless it be admitted that money can purchase the right to outrage law—is quietly to permit, or take steps, of whatever severity is needed, to control the offending practice.

But while Orders in Council had swept away a host of restrictive laws and all their penalties with them, others had re-established the obsolete menaces of outlawry and transportation, and it was an instance of the latter which had been brought so disconcertingly to the aluminium manufacturers' minds.

A fortnight ago, a procession of over 7,000 people hedged between the shining bayonets of a military guard had been marched through London, to be loaded upon waiting transports to a destination on the North Queensland coast.

At one sudden sweep the police had descended upon them, abortionists, birth-preventers, and dealers in instruments of condoned or illegal vices, imprisoned their bodies, confiscated their wealth, and emptied their dens, including many so-called clinics which were financed from the public purse. Headed by one notorious woman, whose name had become a byword for the prevention of human life, and who was given the invidious notoriety of walking a few paces in front of the procession, they had seen the last of the land which had given them the birth which they would have denied to others.

On that occasion Mr. Maitland had made one of his rare appearances in Parliament to defend, or explain his action, and the committee stages of the flea-controlling measure had been suspended to hear him.

"The birth-preventionists," he said, "I will not call them the birth-contollers, for no one can control birth, as many a woman has discovered in the unnatural barrenness which has followed her belief in a devil's lie—made one mistake. They are an appearance as natural to a decaying nation as the vulture which descends to batten on the bones of the dying lion, but their mistake was that the lion of England was asleep, and it will not die.

"In the desire to exercise clemency toward the individual, and faced with the necessity of drastic action, it has appeared that transportation is the only effectual remedy. Had it not been available, I should not have shrunk from the extermination of people who hold human life so lightly that they could not have opposed any substantial objection to the infliction of such a penalty.

"As it is, they have been loud in proclaiming that this country is overcrowded. They will be removed to a less crowded land.

"They have been eloquent in asserting that our economic difficulties are such that we cannot afford our children. A part of the enormous wealth which some of them have accumulated will be used to reduce this difficulty, as it will be distributed among the mothers of large families with limited incomes. They can hardly object to its allocation to relieve an evil which they have recognised so acutely and deplored so much.

"The remainder of their gains will be used to finance their going and to settle them in an empty land."

Mr. Sampson Lynes rose, and Mr. Maitland resumed his seat. This gentleman had developed a personal animosity against the country's Dictator, since his ignominious rejection from the office of Minister of Education, for which it would be unreasonable to blame him. He asked:

"As most of these people, apart from some convicted or suspected abortionists, have done nothing illegal, would it not have been fairer to warn them before inflicting this terrible penalty?"

"There are several replies," Mr. Maitland answered, "to that question.

"In the first place, it is not a terrible penalty. It is giving them a chance of decent living—probably the last and only chance that most of them could ever have.

"In the second, the criminality of their conduct does not disappear because it has been legally condoned or neglected.

"In the third, the vital consideration has been the health and increase of the nation against which they worked.

"Finally, it is kindest to themselves, because experience shows that even imprisonment does not deter such people from a repetition of the practices or vending by which they live. The profits are too large, and the difficulty of changing into an innocent occupation is too great.

"In view of the nature of the penalty which will be inflicted after this date on anyone engaging in such traffic, or distributing knowledge concerning it, it is the truest kindness to remove these people to a place where they must practise upon each other, or not at all."

"May I ask," Mr. Lynes persisted, "what that penalty is intended to be?"

"Up to the end of this year," Mr. Maitland replied pleasantly, "they will be promptly hanged."

"I thought, from other evidences..."—it was the Hon. James Shackston who had risen this time—"...that under our present tutelage capital punishment is not approved."

"It is necessary..."—Mr. Maitland turned to his new questioner with a more smiling courtesy than before—"...to distinguish between those who murder by sudden violence under stress of emotion, many of whom would neither be deterred by the fear of any penalty—in fact, they are not so deterred—nor would they be likely to commit a further offence, even if they were not punished at all—it is necessary to distinguish between such cases and those of more serious and more persistent crime."

"We have but to learn," Mr. Shackston answered. "May I enquire further what the Queensland Government has to say to this proposed dumping of seven thousand persons of questionable character upon her territory?"

"Australia," Mr. Maitland answered, "cannot logically question their character, as the vices on which they have lived have been as widely practised and condoned in that continent as in almost any part of the world. But the question does not arise. The new immigrants, being unable to live by preying upon each other, will be obliged to engage in more reputable occupations, and may soon become decent citizens. Meanwhile they will be entirely isolated in a part of the country which was previously untenanted."

"The Commonwealth of Australia," Mr. Shackston persisted, "has restricted immigration very severely during recent years. It is difficult to suppose that they will welcome the influx of so large a number of people of this peculiar type. "

"I have already explained," Mr. Maitland answered, "that they will be landed in unpopulated territory. An Englishman has as good a right to occupy any vacant land on the Australian Continent as on the day when the English flag was first planted there."

"It would be interesting," Mr. Shackston retorted, "to hear what the Australian Government has to say to that theory."

"The Australian Government," Mr. Maitland answered, "has notified me of its entire acceptance of that formula."

The silence of a great astonishment fell upon the House at this announcement. He added in explanation: "I had occasion to make it clear, in the course of a very friendly exchange of cables, that the English Navy could not consider itself responsible for the coasts of a continent on which English people are not allowed to land."

"Is this House to understand," Mr. Shackston persisted, "that the Right Honourable Member considers himself entitled to impose his will even at the opposite ends of the earth?"

"The House will understand," Mr. Maitland answered, with a manner that was invincibly affable, "that I imposed nothing. I merely negotiated a little additional freedom."

With those words Mr. Maitland had left the House.

CHAPTER FORTY-FIVE

WHATEVER conflicting results might have followed from the incidents narrated in the last chapter, and a hundred others which have been left unmentioned, as affecting Mr. Maitland's precarious popularity, it was generally admitted that it was the budget on which it was most securely based.

It may not have been—indeed, it certainly was not—an equitable budget. But, perhaps for the first time in the history of England, it was a budget that attempted equity. Out of the precedents of the hundred impositions which the tricks and thievings of a score of previous chancellors have imposed, it attempted to arrive at some equitable basis on which the necessary revenue could be collected.

The fact that long use had dulled or deadened the annoyance occasioned by many arbitrary impositions was, for the first time in recorded history, considered insufficient reason for their retention. For the first time, honesty replaced expediency as the moral standard to be applied.

The application of this principle swept away a host of taxes, stamp duties, and licences as inequitable as the window-tax of unholy memory, but which had come to be considered as inevitable as the operation of a natural law. For years to come there would be feeble-minded citizens who would doubt the efficacy of a receipt which was not fortified with two-pennyworth of cancelled stamps, or the value of a cheque which did not bear its red insignia of financial servitude.

This budget had not been imposed upon a reluctant House unfamiliarised with its provisions. Aided by the majority which Sir Bardsley Clinton's support assured, Stanley had taken it through, clause by clause, against an opposition which only weakened as it realised the enthusiasm which it had aroused in their own constituencies.

In the spirit of a large simplicity the main sources of revenue had been reduced to two: indirect taxation upon imported articles of general consumption, which was revised to an attempted justice, and somewhat decreased in some directions, in view of the extent to which these taxes fall upon the poorer citizens; and direct taxation, which was reduced to a single levy of income-tax, the death-duties being swept away. Fortuitous revenue from the imposition of tariffs which were intended to exclude or hinder the entrance of foreign goods was to be applied entirely to the reduction of existing debt.

Every individual was entitled to a free income of £100, and all surplus was taxed at a level rate. This right was shared by every child from a date six months prior to its birth. A man with an income of £1,000, having a wife and four children, would therefore have an exemption figure of £600, which would be increased to £700 if he kept a servant whom he did not occupy in any profitable industry, unless that servant had a separate income, which must be taken into account. A single man with the same income would pay tax on £900. He would not be allowed to claim for an unprofitable servant, which he could not need.

There were numerous adjustments, and some unavoidable anomalies under this system; there were some questions as to its application which only experience could resolve, but its complications, at the most, were a hundred times less than those of the system which it swept away.

No longer could it be said that a man and woman might live loosely together and be more lightly taxed than if they should contract a legal marriage; no longer was there the convenient impudence of collecting tax at the source, much of which was not owing at all, and leaving the owners of the money to get it back if they had the expert advice and incurred the expense and trouble which the process of recovery required.

The tax was fixed at twenty-five percent of the unexempted income. Its future amount would depend upon the continuity of national policy. If the reforms which were being introduced were supported, the huge diminution of national expenditure which would follow would reduce this figure within four or five years to a shilling or even sixpence in the pound. The taxpayers would have a clear issue before them. Did they wish to spend their own money, or have bureaucrats spend it for them? They would know that every new expenditure they encouraged would increase the rate of this tax, and every economy would reduce it.

The anomalous position of the Post Office Department, in which the existence of a government monopoly had been misused for taxation purposes, was dealt with in a simple and what might easily be accepted as a final way. The Department was to pay an annual fee of £1,000,000 for the monopolies it controlled. Beyond that, its charges were to be reduced to the cost of the services they provided, after the distribution of a moiety of revenue among its staff, as an encouragement to efficiency, and a reward of zealous and courteous service.

A short separate Bill provided for the winding up of the whole system of unemployment benefit, with the financial adjustments which it entailed, before the close of the year. The idleness of an able-bodied man before every need of every individual is supplied, so far as such needs can be supplied from the internal resources of the land, should be as intolerable to the state as it must be to the individual concerned. It is an absurdity in itself, and, if persistent, must be an evidence of industrial disease which no operation could cut too deep to cure.

Clause by clause, Stanley fought this revolutionary budget through a clamorous contentious House to its triumphant end. He was aware—he had to remind himself in humility at the hour of triumph—that he could never have done this by his own abilities. The credit might not be precisely due to William Feltham, but the power came from the little levers in the locked room at Dawlish Mansions. He realised that; but even so, he felt more satisfaction at this success than at all the reforms that he had imposed by the mere threat of the power he held. For in this thing, however it might be that he was in a position to introduce a budget at all, or to do it in the name of the strongest party in the House, he had fought it at last on its own merits, and he might also claim that he had sustained it upon his own. During the time that it was in committee he had little leisure for thought or action on any separate issue. The reforms he had started must develop to what ends they would, the waiting deputations must be refused, even his personal life must be in suspense, an almost forgotten thing.

But the simplicity of the budget, in spite of its originality, shortened as well as sharpened the conflict which it entailed. On the First of May it was a finished thing.

CHAPTER FORTY-SIX

IT was early in May, and shortly after the passage of the budget through the House of Commons had been completed, that Lady Crystal found herself seated at dinner beside Viscount Okehampton for the second time within ten days, and was faintly puzzled as to whether this repetition were the result of contrivance or unhindered chance. The doubt died almost as it rose, like a seed in a shallow soil, for she saw that it might be a quite natural thing.

Since she had returned to London, she had been careful to avoid giving any impression that she had retired from the political and social arenas that she had once ambitioned to influence, if not to rule, but she discriminated in the invitations which she accepted with a very difficult care. She did not wish it to appear that she chose to confine her appearances to those houses where Stanley's opponents—who were also the opponents of Sir Bardsley Clinton's government—were accustomed to congregate. Neither did she wish to go where she might meet Sir Bardsley himself, or those of his most intimate supporters with whom she had been familiar in the past, and to whom it would be difficult, without offence, to maintain the mask of silence with which she confronted the curiosity of the world.

She therefore preferred to accept invitations to gatherings in which the political element was neither predominant nor of any pronounced complexion. At such dinner-tables, politicians from opposite camps may confer at what is outwardly a casual unexpected meeting. At such tables a careful hostess will place together those of differing political interests. On both these occasions, Lady Crystal had recognised that she and Viscount Okehampton were the most important guests. It was natural that they should be side by side.

But the doubt had been natural too. They were old acquaintances. Their estates had joined for four generations. During that time there had been repeated attempts to unite by marriage those contiguous acres. It had been the dream—and expectation—of her father's life. More or less, also, it had been her own.

There had been no doubt of Viscount Okehampton's willingness. He had formally proposed on two occasions, and been rebuffed by a doubtful answer. In a cool brain she had weighed the advantages that he could offer, and they had been nearly sufficient to turn the scale in his favour. Nearly, but not quite. She had decided that she could make a success of Stanley Maitland—could make the substantial success of life which she had been young and foolish enough to value, and yet follow the inclination which was so hard to deny.

Resolving this, she had resolved also that her marriage should be so circumspectly arranged, Stanley's career so certainly established, that none should call her a fool. In particular, she was determined that she should never be the victim of the flicker of sarcasm that came so easily, sometimes so maddeningly, into Viscount Okehampton's eyes.

So that gentleman, contemplating a third, and expecting it to be a decisive proposal, had read the announcement of her engagement to Stanley Maitland, and that he had had no love for him since that date was a likely thing.

Was there contrivance, she had wondered, behind the fact that, for the second time, he was sitting beside her? There was no substantial reason to think it. Anyway, he would learn nothing. She had resolved to let no one know her own thoughts, to understand her own feelings, even if she understood them herself, of which she was not sure. If the year should end without disaster (all things are possible), and Stanley should emerge from the isolation of the Rafton Hotel, and they should take up their lives together again as though no interval had occurred, she intended to act as though it might have been an agreed thing. If she had other thoughts—if she looked to other possibilities—they were private to her own mind.

On the first occasion he had not been an uncongenial companion. They had some common topics of conversation which were discreetly and lightly touched. Subtly, inoffensively, he had conveyed the knowledge that his own feelings were not changed toward her. His voice was deferential. His eyes admired. He paid compliments in the way that she most approved, using words with economy (as he always did), and with a careful selection. There were few men who could convey more, while they said less.

He had avoided (she thought deliberately) any channel of conversation which might embarrass her with references to the Dictator of England, or the changes which he had enforced upon a half-reluctant, half-bewildered world. And that had not been easy to do. They were topics of which the papers were full, of which all England talked. The endless, often unexpected adjustments, always involving others, that each alteration in the national life would bring, formed subjects of conversation which were beyond avoidance. There was little that could be said which would not end in such references—in admiration, in resentment, or in dispute.

On this second occasion, it was a question from herself which first led the conversation in the direction of Stanley's activities, prompted by a half-heard allusion from the other side of the table to some trouble with the navy, or among naval men.

Briefly, lightly, never using a word when a pause or gesture would indicate it sufficiently, he had told her what had occurred.

The provision for the needs of the navy in Mr. Maitland's budget had dissatisfied the heads of the Greater Navy League. There was nothing new about that. They had asked him to receive a deputation regarding the retarded rate of naval construction. There was nothing new about that either. It was as normal as the morning's milk.

But the reception he had given them had been of an unexpected kind.

When the seven members of the deputation had been formally introduced, he had addressed them briefly:

"Gentlemen, you are all of mature years. You profess patriotism. You are all men of considerable means, if not of great wealth. I have had your records looked up, and not more than one of you has a reasonable right to have come here. The seven of you have been the fathers of ten children, of which two are dead. A nation of such as you would not deserve a navy. A gravedigger would fulfil its last requirements adequately. If you had been a deputation from Hoxton or Whitechapel, I would have told you regarding the navy all that is in my mind, for you would have asked with a good right.

"If your League would have a different reply, you must send a deputation of men whose wives have been allowed or beaten to breed. I say 'allowed or beaten,' because I know that in such cases as yours the fault is not always on the man's or the woman's side.

"I hope none of you will answer me with hypocritical nonsense about not having been able to afford your children. You have afforded your cars.

"Even if it were so, there are hundreds of poor families which would have adopted them to a life of hardship for a payment which you could easily have made, and which would have given them a chance of existence."

He had dismissed them with the quotation of a verse by a Victorian clergyman, which Viscount Okehampton felt unwilling to repeat, though he remembered it from his schoolboy days. "Vain those all-shattering guns." Rhetorical, almost sentimental. Written at a time when poetry was expected to be comprehensible, and in forms absurdly difficult to construct.

In fact, it was outmoded by the intervening change in the conditions of the lives of men. It had been written at a time when the struggle for supremacy between man and machinery was undecided, before men had lost the battle, if not the war.

Something, Viscount Okehampton said vaguely, by a man named Doyle. No, not Conan. Before him.

Lady Crystal produced a memory. Wasn't it the poem about which there was a fuss at the time, because the West Kents said it suggested that they were all, if not always, drunk?

"Yes, that was it."

Crystal also remembered the verse. It is curious how this old poetry (which we know isn't literature) will remain in the mind, and how hard it is to recall the modern masterpieces after a night's sleep.

"Yes," she said. "'Vain mightiest fleets.' Rather apposite, wasn't it?" The words approved, but in a cold tone. A consciousness of her own unopened womb may have entered her mind. But she was not one who showed her feelings, unless in a deliberate confidence.

Viscount Okehampton, watching with a concealed keenness, owned that she baffled his attempts to probe her. But he did not desist. He was the unsuccessful lover of Lady Crystal, and of all the land that was hers. That unsuccess was Stanley Maitland's doing. Okehampton was the ex-Minister for War. That "ex" was Maitland's doing again. And—as it had been said very forcibly at the secret meeting which had been held last Monday at the National Club— this was not one of the ordinary alternations between office and opposition which politicians expect to experience. If Stanley Maitland should succeed in establishing himself as the Dictator of England, as they did not doubt that he aimed to do, there would be no returning for them.

Worse even than that, if they were active in opposition, they could not tell what grotesque and lawless penalty might fall upon them at any moment, without appeal or redress.

To save London from its overhanging menace, to save a settled civilisation from wild and irresponsible experiment, to save menaced industries from a threatened ruin—in short, variously, to save ourselves—what extremity would be too great to be defensible? Against one whose own actions were so clearly lawless, what could be accounted crime?

But Mr. Maitland's life—at least while the secret of Dawlish Mansions remained his own—must not be attempted. Whether easily or reluctantly, they had all agreed upon that. The secret must be wrested from him, and that was impossible so long as he remained within the guarded portals of the Rafton Hotel, or moved out only in formal procession with an escort of armoured cars. They had to lure him apart, they had to seize him alone.

The crude attempt which had been frustrated already did not make their task easier, but it warned them against the folly of an ill-planned attempt. A second time they could not afford to fail.

Facing this difficulty, they had very wisely sought professional advice and assistance. A detective agency of worldwide repute had undertaken to deliver the goods, if its advice were taken. Its principal, Mr. Rinkwater, after a night's reflection, had suggested that they should seek the co-operation of Lady Crystal. You cannot lay a trap for any man with a better bait than his own wife.

The suggestion had been rather coldly received. Mr. Maitland was understood to have quarrelled with his wife, and to have established her sister in the vacated place. The contempt with which he had treated her effort at reconciliation was now a public tale.

But Mr. Rinkwater had held his ground. He did not know everything, but he was able to inform them of the condition of Mr. Jepson's hindquarters when he had left the Rafton by the back door. Attributing this to Mr. Maitland's orders, he concluded that his feelings might still retain some affection for the wife who (he surmised accurately again) had parted from her husband rather than he with her.

Of Mr. Maitland's relations with Lady Jehane, he spoke with the non-committal discretion of a man who has learnt that the obvious is not always true.

Still, there was ground for jealousy. There might very probably be ground for divorce. Lady Crystal Maitland had a reputation for pride. In a most difficult position, she had acted with dignity and independence. She might well be prepared to co-operate in such steps as would release her country from political experiments of which she had shown her disapproval, and herself from a husband who had publicly humiliated her and disgraced her name.

But it would not be an easy matter to negotiate. Lady Crystal must not be approached in a vulgar way. Mr. Rinkwater was explicit on that point, and his opinion was undisputed. The first step would be to ascertain her feelings, which must be done without her suspicions being excited as to any object in the enquiry.

At this point eyes had been turned toward Viscount Okehampton, who was known to have her acquaintance, but he had remained unresponsive. Mr. Shackston had said, leave it to him. After that, the two had had a conversation of a more private kind, at the end of which, without a spoken word but with a slight nod, Viscount Okehampton had given his consent.

Accustomed to listen more than he talked, he received confidences more often than he gave them to others. He did not tell anyone now that he had his private object, which went beyond any interest of theirs. He aimed not only to overthrow Maitland's political authority, but to win back the woman and the land which he had calculated to be his own.

At this second meeting, he was aware that some progress must be made, or the opportunity would be worse than lost. He could not continue to arrange these seemingly casual meetings indefinitely, could not do so at all without a measure of consent from her.

Having been invited to narrate the anecdote of the naval deputation, he felt that he could safely continue the subject of Lady Crystal's husband by a general reflection.

"I always thought Stanley was a clever fellow," he said, with the tone of one on a secure height who can be generous to another, struggling below. "No one can say he didn't take his chance when it came his way. Though we mightn't all have seen the opportunity quite in the same light, I'm afraid his trouble will be that he won't know when to stop."

She made no answer to that, and he took such satisfaction from her silence as he fairly could, and perhaps more. A wife should defend her husband from such a suggestion. Or, if she agreed, it should be with alarm or regret. Did she not imply that he had ceased to matter to her?

He left the subject of Maitland, to resume the subtle wooing which he had practised before. When they parted, he had said little, but he had told much.

Lady Crystal knew, not merely that he would still be glad to marry her if the ground were clear, which she would have supposed without additional evidence, but that he regarded it as a matter of practical politics, if not to plan or propose it anew, at least to reopen the possibility in their own minds. He had a gift of implying more than he said, and Lady Crystal was by no means backward in understanding the verbal short-hands of social and political intercourse. At this moment she was particularly alert behind the barrier of her guarded words.

Thinking over the interview after she had returned to her own home, she did not suppose that there was any conspiracy in which she was to take even a passive part, for Viscount Okehampton had been far too adroit, too cautious, to allow such an implication to appear; but she felt that he would not have spoken as he did, that he would not have been seeking her out at all, had he not had some assurance, beyond anything publicly known, or indicated by the outward course of events, that Stanley's fall was a near and certain thing.

Unless—was he hoping that she would divorce him, and so clear the way for a second marriage? And, if so, what ground could there be?

She had been forced by outward suggestion to familiarity with the idea that Jehane was Stanley's mistress now. She looked back on her memory of earlier days, interpreting everything in the light of later events, and she saw that Jehane might, all along, have had an inclination toward him which pride and honour would make it very sure that she would not show. It would explain her readiness to accept Stanley's programmes at his own value, her prompt decision to follow him when he left the house.

If she had joined him with such emotions below the surface, however well controlled they might be, the subsequent companionship, at a time when he might feel that he had good cause for resentment against herself, might well have resulted in a spiritual infidelity, even if it had not been followed by the physical familiarities which are considered so much more important in English law. The way—the almost incredible way—in which Stanley had treated her letter, as she still believed him to have done, gave support to such possibilities.

The kind of contemporary fiction which is most favoured by women readers had familiarised her mind with the idea that physical passion is an irresistible force before which any bond must break, and can be broken, with glory rather than shame. Of the strength of such passion she had her own knowledge, and she could imagine more. Yet the thought that it might have conquered Jehane to the ignoring of her own code might torment her feelings, but did not convince her mind. In defiance of her own self-torture, and of the common opinion around her, she still thought that Jehane might regard honour as the better thing.

It was against Stanley rather than Jehane that her indignation hardened. It was he who had treated her advance toward reconciliation with insult. It was he to whom she had once given her love. The memory of the moments of spiritual and physical unity which they had experienced at times, however seldom, should have been sufficient to make such a sequel as impossible as they made it an unforgivable thing.

And now, Stanley's fall was near. Viscount Okehampton's opinion on that was an almost final evidence, for the shrewdness of his judgments had been proved so often before. Indeed, to many observers—and the thought had not been absent from her own mind—

the fact that he had left Sir Bardsley Clinton's government had been as ominous of the end of Stanley's adventure as the finger of a pointing fate. The Hon. James Shackston was shrewd enough, but he tried to rule his own destiny, to control the event which should confound his foes. He might sink or rise. In fact, alternately, it was almost sure that he would do both, but Viscount Okehampton did not try to alter the course of fate, so much as to foresee it, and adapt himself.

She was not of a disposition easily to admit a blunder, but should she do so, she would be resolute to face its consequences, and to cut loose from a foolish past. Had her marriage been a mistake?

CHAPTER FORTY-SEVEN

SIR BARDSLEY CLINTON warned. He looked a tired man. He had aged visibly in the last four months. But his thoughts were not on his own health. He said: "It isn't only that you can't keep on experimenting like this without a crash somewhere. Your health won't stand it. You'll have a breakdown yourself. Why not stop it now, while you can?

"You've done some wonderful things. You've done more for England than any man could without the chance that came into your hands, and what very few would have tried even then. I don't say you haven't made some mistakes. I don't say..." (with his disarming smile) "...that you wouldn't have done better once or twice if you'd been willing to listen to me. But you've done things that have brought a new life to the land, and, if you stop now, the country couldn't go back. I don't see how it could.

"Why not switch this ghastly thing of Feltham's off, without waiting till the year ends, and go away for the change you need?"

Jehane asked: "Do you think he could, even then?"

Sir Bardsley's reply paused. Stanley had made many friends, but he had bitter foes also, ruined men who would not forgive merely because he had ceased the activities which had caused their fall, outlawed men who had been engaged in various anti-social occupations, and who now, while they remained in England, were at the mercy of any who might take their property or end their lives.

"It might be wise," Sir Bardsley admitted, "to take some precautions at first."

With a gesture of irritation, Stanley rose from his seat. He began restless walking across the room.

"It isn't that," he said, "though I should be rather surprised if I were alive in a week's time. I know you're right. I know the state I'm in, and it's getting worse. I'm giving freedom to England, and I've made a gaol for myself that I can't break. No, don't go...don't go."

The last words were to Jehane, who had answered a telephone call with the reply that she would come down.

He looked at her almost plaintively, as she was accustomed to his doing during recent days. He would have her always with him. The months when he had preferred to spend most of the day in solitude, his mind isolated in its constructive dreams, were over now. He did not like to be left alone.

When he saw that she was not going, he controlled himself with a visible mental effort, and resumed in a quieter tone.

"The real trouble is that I can't sleep, and if I sleep, I dream in a bad way. I'd throw it up tomorrow if I could. You don't think I want to live forever in this room. I've lost everything that I had. I'm not sure what I've done for others, but I know what it's done for me. I know I ought to stop Feltham's devilish trick. I lie awake sometimes and wonder whether he may have overlooked something in its construction—if some attention were needed which he didn't think it necessary to tell me, and if it might go off before its time. Well, I came where I should be in the soup with the rest. There's one thing we should never know. It would be too sudden for that. But the point is that, for myself, I don't care. I feel I'd rather like it than not. If I were the only one concerned, it wouldn't be a fear. It would be the one hope."

"What you need," Sir Bardsley repeated, "is a sea voyage. Any doctor would tell you that. I suppose you've had some advice?"

"No, I haven't. What's the good? I know what's wrong well enough, and he might poison me as like as not, and think he'd done the world a good turn."

"You know he wouldn't do that."

"No, I forgot. I'm a valuable life while I keep one little fact in my own head. Do you know what I dreamed last night? *I dreamed I forgot.* There was ten minutes left to think, and I sat there with the switchboard under my hand, and the minutes went, and I knew if I touched it at all I should move it wrong. No, there's no cause for alarm. It's a simple thing. All you say's true enough, but I can't do it. I've got to stay where I am."

Sir Bardsley had come prepared for a patient argument. He did not mind sitting there all day, if he could prevail at the end. He did not dispute the repeated decision. He simply asked: "Why?"

"Because I can't loose the steering wheel at the pace that we're going now. I don't mean that I've got all the sense in the world. There may be thousands who could do better than I, in the place where I am. It isn't I, it's the *power*. I can't loose that. We're trying a new road, and if the car swerves you can't have a committee talking over how far you shall turn the wheel. There hasn't only got to be the resolution or the wisdom to act at once, there's got to be the power too."

Sir Bardsley was slow to reply, for his mind had been puzzled by the same doubt. Perhaps Maitland was right. Perhaps to compromise the position might be better than to surrender it as it stood now. He said tentatively: "But you've got to stop in the end."

"Yes. I've thought of that, but we've got to slow down first. I mean to stop on the straight. I shan't start anything fresh now, or not much anyway. I shan't get up speed again."

That was the compromise for which Sir Bardsley had hoped. He was glad it had not been necessary that the suggestion should come from him. He felt that, if there should be a public assurance that no further revolutionary changes were contemplated, it would do much to quieten a growing element of opposition, the signs of which were clear to his experienced pilot's eyes, though they might be questioned by one less expert in the perilous whirlpools of public life.

His own reason was different from the one he had just heard. He regarded each fresh experiment as an added danger, both to the country and to the man who forced them upon it. He had heard rumours of changes more revolutionary than anything that had been attempted yet. He did not know whether they held any truth. It was hard to tell how these rumours rose, but they were causing disquiet in quarters which had endured or even approved the previous innovations: high quarters of international finance of an incalculable power. He feared that Maitland had succeeded so far that he was self-doomed to go on to his own disaster. He would be sorry for that. He would be sorrier for his own fall, which he expected that it would involve. But it is bare justice to recognise that he thought of England first. What might be the national consequences of a blunder of the magnitude which he felt that Maitland might have it in him to make? If he would only stop while he still could! But he saw that Maitland's reason was good too. To inaugurate some revolutionary change as December waned, and then to resign the power he held, as he had promised to do, would be an added peril. For its consequences could not be promptly controlled or altered, as was now happening to more than one of the new orders of living which were being developed throughout the land. Proceedings would revert to the old argumentative parliamentary methods, and the steering wheel might not be turned before the crash would come. Now, it could be turned in an hour. He said: "I'm sure that would be a wise plan. You've done some great things. If you can steer them in the right way, it's about as big a task as most men would care to face…if we could make a statement that there's nothing more in the way of change that the public have got to fear."

An infrequent smile crossed Stanley's face for a moment as he answered: "You think fear's the right word? No, I understand. I'm not offended at that. 'Out of the fullness of the heart—'. You don't understand what I mean to do. I'm slowing up now, but I won't have any public proclamation of that. It's an intention, not a pledge."

"As you like, of course," Sir Bardsley answered reluctantly. "But there are rumours going about of things you're supposed to be about to do that it might be well to deny. Finance has kept steady so far. Fairly steady, that is, since the Stock Exchange reopened. There've been flurries and scares and, of course, there are stocks that are worthless now, and others that have gone up out of sight. But on the whole it's wonderful how confidence has held up."

"I don't quite see that. I think it's what anyone might have expected. A virile country, where every man's expected to work, is more likely to be a good investment than one where millions are idle, and population discouraged. Yes, I know the arguments about our overpopulation and insufficient work, but the real disease wasn't there. Half Suffolk wasn't being cultivated at all twelve months ago. A kind of madness, while we paid men to stand about, and bought food from abroad. But I didn't want to talk about that. Whatever the rumours are, what harm are they going to do, and where?"

"If international finance loses its head…."

"It hasn't got much to lose. It's shown that often enough in the last ten years. But why should it lose anything now? Unemployment's practically ceased. We've stopped sinking money by the million in roads that we don't need. We've lessened the waste on the production of endless cars that are beginning to wear out before the varnish dries. The land's being cultivated. The railways are prosperous. And we're buying no more from foreigners than we sell to them. There's more cause for confidence than there's been any time in the last twenty years. And all done in about four months! There must be worse records than that."

"It isn't what's done. It's what they're afraid you mean to do any ay now."

"And what's that?"

"There are so many rumours about. Reynolds tells me, for one, that the Insurance Companies are half scared to death at a report that you're going to confiscate them."

"Then they're wrong. I did make some enquiries with a view to transferring them all to one government department. The economic waste of the present methods almost passes belief. And the hundreds of millions withdrawn from the pockets of those who need it, many years before there's any occasion for its use. And there's something rather repulsive about scores of thousands of people making a living out of their neighbours' dread of sickness and death."

"I hadn't thought of it quite in that light."

"No?" Stanley smiled again. He had recovered something of his old animation, as he forgot himself in the conversation. "I don't suppose you do now, if you said all that you think. But we needn't trouble about that. It's too complicated for a mere Order to start it on the right lines, and I'm...I suppose I'm too tired. You might manage a Bill yourself next year. You'll find, if you look into it, that it's worthwhile. You'd make the National Debt look silly with all the reserves that the great companies have stored away, and you might suspend premiums altogether for a few years, and then begin on a lower scale, with a levy that would meet all claims, and a bit more. You don't believe me, of course. A new idea in this country's always been such a frightening thing."

Sir Bardsley made no reply to that. He did not suppose that, even if he should be in office next year, he could bring in a Bill on such a subject with the slightest chance of success, and every trained political instinct recoiled from the idea. There was no popular agitation; indeed, there were enormous vested interests which would fight madly for their threatened lives. Two utterly conclusive arguments.

"Well," he said, "if you don't intend to do anything now, it will be easy to let them know. The future can take care of itself. But that isn't the main trouble. It's the rumour that you're going to make it illegal to recover commercial debts. I don't mean that I believed that. I told Reynolds it wasn't a likely thing."

"So they've got that too, have they? I suppose you think that'd be the maddest thing that I've tried yet?"

"It would destroy credit and paralyse commerce. I suppose you would agree that those results would be rather serious," Sir Bardsley answered mildly.

"Yes, everyone'd say that. But I'm not sure that it would. So many things aren't as bad as we expect them to be. Suppose anyone'd asked Gladstone or Goschen what would happen if we went off the gold standard? They'd have gone off in a dead faint at the idea: death from heart seizure more likely than not. But if we knocked all the legal debt-collecting processes on the head, you'd find people would still want to deal. I expect they'd give credit much as they do now. And they'd make bad debts, though perhaps not so many. They'd discriminate differently, and people would pay from honour instead of fear. Credit betting goes on, though you can't sue for the cash. Do you think that betting people are more honest than the rest of the world? But some put a betting debt first, and settle that, if they have to let the rest go, just because it's a debt of honour and not of law. And think of the thousands of men—judges and clerks and debt-collectors, and process servers, and bailiffs, and auctioneers, and I don't know how many others—that it would release for some honest work."

"And everyone," Sir Bardsley commented, "another enemy, as though you hadn't got enough already without them."

"It mightn't make any difference. I daresay I've got enough for a few thousand more not to count. You can't turn a scale when it's bang down."

"I don't think that's how you stand," Sir Bardsley answered with an unexpected warmth in his tone. "You've done too much good for that, though it has been in surprising and—if you won't mind me saying it—sometimes in rather ruthless ways. But some people always seem to benefit. I suppose even this idea would make some people happier than they are now. But you couldn't think of it seriously. Foreign credit would stop like a clock that had run down, and we might be starving in a month's time."

"I think you're wrong about that, about three times over. Wrong about facts and effects too. But I don't want to argue that.

"I'll tell you how I always think these things out. I can't tackle a complicated problem. I haven't got the right kind of brains. So I reduce it to its lowest terms.

"Suppose I were chief of a village, with just ten families in ten huts. And the man in number one hut comes to me, and says. 'I made a fish spear for the man in number two hut, and he hasn't paid me. What can I do?' And I should say: 'Take it back.' And the man might reply: 'I can't do that because he's broken it. Let me take the things out of his hut and sell them till I've got the price of the spear.' Do you think I should allow that?"

"Well," Sir Bardsley answered, "the man wouldn't be asking more than was just."

"Are you quite sure? If I were such a chief, I think my mind would work in this way.

"First, I should think that I am the chief of ten families in ten furnished huts, and that's better than being the chief of nine, and of one that's starving in empty walls. And secondly, I should think— suppose the other eight didn't want the things in number two's hut. You can't force them to buy. If the sale's forced, the prices may be less than the things are worth—perhaps much less. There's no justice in that. The value of ten fish spears might be taken for the price of one.

"But the fundamental fact is that the man's things are needed in his own hut, and mayn't be needed in the others' at all. There'd be no getting over that to me. I should have allowed one thing to be put right at the cost of a far greater wrong, and I should be the poorer chief of a poorer tribe, as I should deserve to be."

"But modern life," Sir Bardsley remarked, "is a more complicated thing." He didn't think this reflection to be profound or conclusive, and he was relieved when Stanley added: "But you needn't worry about that. I've told you I'm going slow."

"As an academic question," Sir Bardsley conceded, in a relieved voice, "as a purely academic question, I don't say there isn't a good deal in your point of view. But as practical politics...."

"You'd call it a dud? Well, if I let it go, I suppose it will be. Till the tail stops wagging the dog, anyway; and perhaps a bit longer than that." He added: "I don't know what I shall do yet. It's no use pressing me now. But I'm glad you came. I think the talk's done me good.

"I'm going over to Dawlish Mansions tomorrow, to see that everything's all right there."

CHAPTER FORTY-EIGHT

LUCIDLY and in detail, Mr. Rinkwater unfolded his plot. Viscount Okehampton, who had found himself cast for a leading part in the first act, listened to it with faintly contemptuous eyes. He did not interrupt till the detective's confident voice ceased with the words, "And after that you can let him go if you like, but I should think he'd be best in a good jail. Might be best for himself too."

In the atmosphere of that room, it was easy to agree that if Stanley Maitland lost the power that he now had, he would be safest in a good jail, for it represented all that his work had injured, all the hatred that the events of the last four months had aroused, all the fears of what he might be about to do.

It represented more than that. Baron Michelson himself—the finance of Europe—was in the chair. The leading politicians, the greatest lawyers, of six months ago, sat with the captains of the ruined industries that had drugged the souls or poisoned the bodies of their countrymen, and that no previous politician had dared to check. Only yesterday a representative of the great insurance companies, bringing a credit of a quarter of a million pounds to be used at his own discretion, had joined their committee. All the power in England that was not in Stanley Maitland's hands was represented here.

Mr. Rinkwater's confident voice ceased, and Viscount Okehampton said, with a brief finality: "That's no good. Lady Crystal wouldn't do it. Too much breed."

A silence of consternation fell upon the room. As Mr. Rinkwater had unfolded his plans, the Viscount's active co-operation had been a vital thing, and they all knew that Okehampton was hard to move when he had once made up his own mind.

More than that, his decided judgment found an echo of assent in other minds. Those who knew her best were far from certain that Lady Crystal would.

Mr. Rinkwater was unperturbed. With a sustained confidence he quoted verse. The furies of Hell, it appeared, were no better (or worse) than understudies to a woman scorned. Mr. Rinkwater had learnt much of humanity from the dramatic poets. He had even penetrated the rich wisdom of Chaucer. He found that when he followed the signposts of such axioms, he was rarely wrong.

It might be thought that he had failed to be guided by the right quotation for Viscount Okehampton, for that gentleman remained unmoved by his argument. He did not condescend to reply. He only said, in a low but audible voice to the Hon. James Shackston, who was seated beside him, as he rose to leave the table: "Well, Jimmy, you brought me into this. You can count me out."

He walked from a silent room.

He went away wishing them every success, and well pleased with himself also.

Rinkwater's folly had given him the chance for which he had watched. He had seen from the first that the best road to a happy marriage with Crystal was not that of being linked with her in a plot to destroy her husband. All the same, Maitland had got to go. It had suited him to probe her feelings, and to prepare her mind, but he had not intended to go further than that.

Now the detective's plan had given him the genuine occasion which he had anticipated. For his contempt was a real thing. Lady Crystal wouldn't do it. A gentleman would have understood. It was equally true that he wouldn't have been a party to it himself, but he had not felt it necessary to mention that. The words he wasted were few.

He left a room in which the only man who looked unconcerned was the insulted Rinkwater. "Gentlemen, that's the best thing that could happen. I rather counted on that."

Baron Michelson, fingering his pen clumsily in swollen gouty fingers, turned a coldly impartial glance upon the detective. He was used to the judging of men. He asked: "You're sure that's the best plan?"

"It's practically the only one—in outline, not in detail, of course. We can't try getting him out by force. It's failed once. It's a clumsy way. It might fail again. We've got to get him to walk out of his own free will."

"You think he will?"

"He won't walk. He'll run."

"And we may conclude that Viscount Okehampton's assistance is not essential?"

"Not in the way I proposed. Mr. Shackston'll do that a lot better than he. But he'll go on helping us in his own way."

The Baron observed that Mr. Rinkwater smiled slightly, as though inwardly amused at some unconscious part that Viscount Okehampton was expected to take in the approaching drama. He did not rashly conclude that there was sufficient substance for that smile. He knew enough of the Viscount to judge that it would be very difficult to guide him along a path where he did not intend to go.

But he was satisfied that, so far, Mr. Rinkwater had anticipated the course of events, rather than received a disconcerting rebuff. He concluded from that that he was a man worth backing in this emergency. He said: "Mr. Rinkwater, you haven't yet mentioned your fee."

The detective was cautious. "I wondered how high you'd be willing to go."

The Baron looked round. No one spoke. "I don't think we should name a limit, if you succeed."

"No limit?"

"None."

Mr. Rinkwater remembered a pied piper, more generally known than was anyone in that room. He said: "I'd rather have a figure clear from the first." (Even that hadn't saved the piper from a good deal of after-trouble, and a bad debt of a thousand guilders.)

The Baron fumbled for a cheque-book. He wrote a signature surprisingly small and neat to come from those gouty fingers. He tore it out, and passed it down the table.

Mr. Rinkwater gazed upon a blank cheque signed by one of the three richest men in the world. He surveyed it without enthusiasm. He remembered something about a white elephant. If he should fill it up for a fantastic amount (who, in such a position, could be sure of controlling his own greed?) and be told by a polite clerk at the counter that payment had unfortunately been stopped, it might be a very difficult amount to collect. The power of those for whom he was acting was too great. Next week they might be almost omnipotent in England by his own act. No, it must be clearly arranged. Such a cheque should be filled up by the hand that signs it. He said: "I think, if you don't mind, I'd rather have an agreed amount."

Baron Michelson's eyes approved. He felt that they had got the right man. The cheque was passed back. The Baron paused a moment with a raised pen. His glance moved round the table as though making a silent assessment upon those who were seated around it. Then, neatly and carefully, he filled up the form. Mr. Rinkwater, receiving it again, observed that it was dated a week ahead, and draw to self or bearer for £137,006 4s. 2d. Reading these figures he felt that he was not being treated in a niggardly way. The six pounds tended curiously to emphasise the substantial nature of the preceding figures. He wondered whether the odd money had been added with that object, or whether the Baron had made a lightning calculation of various contributions which he was to ask from his associates, of which this was the sum. Or perhaps it was done with no further object than to make the cheque look more like the record of some legitimate commercial transaction. Certainly, it had a greater effect of actuality than would have been the case had it been drawn for a round amount.

Mr. Rinkwater liked the cheque, as he had been expected to do. But, to Baron Michelson's surprise, he held it in a hesitating hand. He said doubtfully: "It's dated...I'm afraid I can't get this through in a week's time."

Mr. Lynes spoke impatiently: "It oughtn't to take more than three days, if you can do it at all. We want it done now."

Mr. Cherrington, the Insurance Companies' representative, supported him. "Time," he said, "is of the essence of the contract." He had a habit of speaking platitudes in a portentous voice, as from the heights of an Olympian wisdom which the ordinary policy holder was not created to attain; but there was a note of more natural human apprehension in his voice as he added: "We don't know what may happen from day to day."

But Mr. Rinkwater was firm. "He is rather iconoclastic," he agreed. (The word pleased him. Half the men there wouldn't understand it, and the others would admire him for being able to use it.) Everyone knew whom he meant. Maitland was continually in all their minds. "All the same," he said, "I can't get to work before Monday next. I want the help of a man who comes out of jail on that day." He let the cheque lie on the table before him.

The Chairman spoke again. "Mr. Rinkwater, we don't want to question your judgment. We have great confidence in you. I feel that, when I say that, I am speaking for all. But our friend, Mr. Cherrington, is quite right when he says that we don't know what may happen from day to day.

"In a madman's hands, a country may be ruined within a week. Mr. Maitland has shown that he has no regard for individuals, or for property's most sacred rights. He has no regard for the institutions of centuries or for constitutional law. When we think of what he has done already, and of the further confusion that may fall upon us on any day—."

Mr. Goldstone, more inclined to observe than to interpose, as a journalist is inclined to be, and thinking facts more important than rhetoric, spoke for the first time. "Who's the man you want out of jail, Mr. Rinkwater?"

"I want Starchy Gates."

Mr. Goldstone said "Oh," in a thoughtful voice. Of course, he remembered about Gates—Patrick Gates, better known as Starchy in the criminal world, who had had seven years' penal (which meant about five in reality) about five years ago. Mr. Goldstone concluded that there must be rather more in Mr. Rinkwater's plan than he had disclosed in his first ingenuous narrative. He had thought that all along. He had the pleasure of a man who can congratulate himself on an unusual insight. He asked: "Can't we get him released?"

Mr. Tomplin felt sure that we could. He spoke with some knowledge of Home Office procedure, and from the depths of a bitter heart. He had sent his only son to Oxford with an allowance of £500 a year. Last week, under the new educational system, the boy had been sent down. It was no question of misconduct or idleness. Thomas Tomplin was not vicious nor rowdy. He worked hard. He was good at sports, which appeared to be about the only feature of modern life, except religion, which Mr. Maitland had left alone.

But he had been told that he was wasting his time, and must make way for those who could take fuller advantage of the opportunities of college life. It had been suggested to him that he would make a successful agricultural labourer, and the amazing, maddening thing was that Thomas had agreed. With a sigh of relief he had made a second-hand sale of the books which he had tried to like, and offered his services to a market-gardener.

Mr. Tomplin had an added cause for irritation in the fact that he had supposed his son's position to be secure, where many of his friends had already suffered. For those who had been at the Universities simply because their parents thought it to be their proper place had been cleared out two months earlier.

The idea that the Universities should exclude all, from whatever stratum of the community, except such as wished and were able to learn, had been a very popular feature of the new system of education; but it could not be expected that it would be approved by those whose sons had been requested to leave to make space for students of higher moral and intellectual types.

Mr. Ricardo Tomplin, ex-president of the Board of Trade, once an assistant-secretary at the Home Office, and now father of a market-gardener, felt sure that Plumpton-Marshall could be prevailed upon to let the required convict loose a few days earlier than the routine date that should permit him to resume his peculiar methods of livelihood. The idea of Plumpton-Marshall's humanity being utilised to provide ammunition for Stanley Maitland's downfall appealed to his sense of humour. What about a sick wife, or a dying child? A confidence which the event would justify inspired him to say: "I'll get Marshall to do that." With a subtle knowledge of human nature in general, and of that in particular of Mr. Plumpton-Marshall, he saw that a request made in the name of humanity would be the more difficult to resist when it would come from a political enemy, and one who had not acquired a character for sentimentality.

With the aid of some information which Mr. Rinkwater supplied, he was able on the next day to send a telegram to Mr. Plumpton-Marshall regarding the health of Alfred Edward, Starchy Gates' second son, of such an urgent and affecting character that the Home Secretary wired for the convict to be released immediately, without delaying to ascertain its truth.

Starchy Gates, leaving the prison, was met by a gentleman who had no connection with the Discharged Prisoners' Aid Society, but yet was able to offer him immediate and congenial work.

CHAPTER FORTY-NINE

"Do you mind," Jehane asked, "if I see the letter?"

Stanley hesitated a moment. Then he passed it across the table.

Jehane read it with care, and a bitten lip. "I can't believe," she said, "that Crystal ever wrote that. It's not her style."

"It's her handwriting, isn't it?"

"Yes," reluctantly. "It's her writing."

"Then—"

"Yes, that's how it seems. I should like to ask her, all the same." She passed the letter back with a puzzled frown. "You won't go?"

"Yes. I think I shall."

Stanley knew that he had meant to go from the first minute that he had read the letter. He had recognised Crystal's writing in a moment, before he had opened it. Perhaps (he thought) he was more conscious of it than her sister was. Not that it had any conspicuous beauty. It was of that rarer kind which is said to be hardest to imitate because it has no decided difference from the normal. It was exact, regular, well-formed, and well spaced. In fact, it was Crystal herself. Equally free from any natural baseness, or extravagance of ideality. Sane, normal, assured. It may be unlikely that character can be told from the markings of a man's palms, or that more than capacity for development of character (if even that) can be learnt from his skull's shape; but his writing is his own work. It is self-expression of a revealing kind, though its meaning may not always be easy to reach.

Crystal's writing was that of one who will walk with the crowd, but who will walk well. She would have been a good cook or a good queen. Serene and self-sufficient at either occupation, certain to endure it with honour, slow to quarrel or plead, and well able to hold her own.

Jehane spoke with decision. "I think it's a silly thing to do." She was secretly aware that she trod thin ice, though Stanley might be unconscious of it, as she hoped he was.

He looked surprised at the word. He asked: "Why?"

"Because she could let you know so much more easily—more safely—in other ways. Besides, it wouldn't be easy for you to leave here without being seen. She doesn't seem to have thought of that. She seems to have lost her head."

Stanley felt the force of these criticisms. They had been striving for attention in his own mind, and had been rebuffed already. He read the letter again.

MY DEAR STANLEY,

I have learnt of a plot which is being formed against you, which is much more serious than the previous attempt, because it is being organised in a different way, and the people behind it are much more important.

I know how you feel about me, but my own feelings haven't changed, and whether you ever come back to me or not, I can't stand by and see you in danger.

I can't write all that I know, it wouldn't be safe, and I mustn't come to the Rafton, or you come here, because they would notice, and I couldn't find out anything more.

What I want you to do is to come to 37, John Henry Street, S.W.7—you know, behind Chandler's Mews—to be there at ten P.M. on Thursday night, and I'll tell you all that I can. You can be back before midnight. I promise I won't talk about anything except the above, which believe me is serious and *urgent*.

Stanley, for your own sake, don't fail.

Your loving wife,

CRYSTAL

P.S. If you value *my* safety, don't tell anyone about this letter. They wouldn't stick at anything if they guessed. There will be a taxi, No. CX37, at the corner of Hartley Street that you can use if you like. You will know that that one is safe, but of course if you think it would be better to walk, it only means starting a bit earlier.

When he had finished it, he looked up, saying: "I suppose I oughtn't to have shown it even to you. You see how the envelope's marked." It bore the legend MOST PRIVATE *Personal and Urgent.* Jehane regarded it without respect.

"We get lots like that. If I hadn't thought I recognised Crystal's handwriting it mightn't have come up at all. Certainly not unopened. Your staff's too good for that."

"But you do recognise that it's Crystal's handwriting?"

"If I know Crystal's handwriting, it's there, and so's her signature too. But if she wrote that letter she's gone cracked. Not that we need be extra startled at that, if you come to think."

"Why don't you think it's her style?"

"Because it wanders about. Crystal would have said all that in half the words. And she doesn't underline and she wouldn't say 'the above.' Not like it's done there. And she wouldn't propose that you should meet her behind a mews. If there's any real danger, there must be a hundred better ways of letting you know it than that.

"Why shouldn't she tell Sir Bardsley? She knows him, and she knows he can be trusted. If he couldn't deal with it himself, he could come here. It's not like Crystal at all."

"There's a good deal in what you say. But I think the writing's final. There may be reasons why I should meet her like that that we can't guess in advance."

"Yes, or snow in June. Do you mind if I ring her up, and find out?"

"No…but yes, I should. She might think I ought not to have mentioned it. Besides, there might be danger for her. Who knows that the wires aren't being tapped?"

"Not round this quarter," Jehane answered with conviction. One or two such incidents had been discovered and dealt with in a way to discourage others. "They may be in Norchester House."

But she said no more, seeing that no consent was to be obtained.

Stanley went to his own room, and his own thoughts. Probably whatever was puzzling now would be explained when he saw her. The construction of the letter was rather bad. It was confused and diffuse. But agitation might explain that.

Of course, there was another possible explanation. Crystal might have gone over to his enemies. It might be a trap. If might not even have been composed by her at all. It might have been written to dictation or to a draft. But if Crystal could do *that*…. He felt that he would still go, not caring what the event might be.

Jehane stood as he had left her, in a frowning indecision. She said aloud: "He can't do worse than skin me alive." She considered that telephoning to only sister's has never been a felony, nor even a misdemeanour, by English law. That was one point on which Stanley had made no change.

She rang down to the switchboard, and gave instructions that she was to be put through to the exchange direct. Then she asked for Norchester House.

After that she said no more about Crystal not having written the letter. She had heard the truth from her own lips.

CHAPTER FIFTY

IT was on Wednesday afternoon that Stanley received the letter. He did not mention it to anyone except Jehane, nor allude to it again until the afternoon of the following day, when he said that he should like dinner to be punctual at seven P.M., which was somewhat earlier than his usual hour.

"I told Molly you'd probably like it rather earlier than that. I said six-forty-five," Jehane answered, and he agreed easily. He had been restless all day with the expectation of meeting Crystal again after their months of estrangement, speculating as to what could be the nature of the plot against his life or authority which could only be conveyed to him by such an interview, and excited by the adventure of escaping, though only for a few hours, from the place of security which had become his jail.

He went over the letter, sentence by sentence, again and again. Was it a hypersensitive imagination that it rang flatly and false, like a base coin? Or was it that Jehane's suggestion had poisoned his mind? Or that the increasing morbidity of recent weeks inclined him to hesitation and distrust?

But he was not morbid now. He was inclined to put his doubts aside. He was only restless for the time to arrive. His mind dwelt on one sentence of that somewhat commonplace letter. Her feelings had not changed. Was it an advance to reconciliation, to reunion of their separated strength, a new assertion of the reality of the love of which they were both aware, but which had never risen to unhindered heights?

If that were so, might he not take up with a new energy, a new hope, the task at which he knew that he was faltering now? Beside that hope, the question of a plot to be overcome seemed no more than a trivial thing. The thought that Crystal might be leagued with his foes, might be calling him to his own destruction, was a treason to their love which it would be baseness to entertain, and, if it were so, the tragedy would be in the fact itself, rather than in its consequences to himself.

He dined, as had become habitual, with Jehane and Rigby and Molly Preston. He had come to be equally dissatisfied with solitude or with the company of those before whom he must weigh every word before it was uttered. Of these three, he was sure that they were his friends, and he could be confident in advance that they had nothing to obtain from him, even information, which he could not afford to give.

He found himself disinclined to eat, and the others seemed to be of the same mood, for the courses were quickly passed. It was only at the end of the meal that he mentioned that he would be going out.

"I know," he said to Molly, "that some of the kitchen staff sleep away. About what time do they leave?"

"It depends upon when I can let them go. Usually about nine."

"Could you let them go at eight-thirty tonight? I want to go out without being noticed, and to do so with them from the back entrance seems the best chance. Are they checked out and in?"

"They're checked in very carefully in the morning. I don't think there's quite so much care at night. Not with the military guard. Of course, going out isn't quite the same thing as coming in. And, of course, their faces are known. I think if you walked out behind the others in a confident way it might not be noticed particularly. The street won't be very light at that hour."

Rigby said: "I don't think anyone will look twice, if you ask me. It isn't the soldiers, it's we who held the real supervision, back and front, as to who goes in and out. The soldiers get changed so often. They trust to us to know who's who, and they're there if we want help to throw anyone out. I'll tell Selby to take the guard at the back tonight, and not to worry as to who walks out, so long as the wrong people don't walk in."

Stanley was back in his room before half-past seven. There was still more than an hour to wait. He read the letter again, though he had known it by heart since yesterday. Should he take the offered vehicle, or show his distrust by walking, or entering another? Did not the fact that the choice was left to him show that there was no trap to fear? Or was that no more than a subtle subterfuge to disarm his doubt? Well, if he were trusting at all, there was no use in stopping halfway. He would take the taxi, if it were there.

He put a light automatic pistol into his pocket, and then threw it aside. It would be a poor chance if it came to that. If he were walking into a trap, it would not be so weak in the jaws that a pistol would set him free.

With the returning doubt, he took from his pockets various private papers, including some of Feltham's notes and formulæ, which he had partly learnt to understand, and which might mean more to others than to him. He put them into the security of his private desk, and paused over that little deadly phial which had been William Feltham's end. He had hesitated to destroy it, and feared to leave it anywhere about. His pocket had always seemed the best place for that. Well, it was a small thing. Let it stay where it had been. It was safe there from his friends, and if his enemies should seize it, it was at their own risk.

How should he re-enter the hotel? He ought to have arranged that with Jehane before now. It was a difficult matter, not knowing how long he would be away. But it ought not to be very long.

He phoned for her, and found that she had gone out. Then for Rigby, with the same result. Then for Molly, who could say nothing as to where they had gone, or whether together or separately, or when they would return. But she would arrange with Selby that there should be no difficulty about re-entering—if possible, without observation.

He had a passing thought that they might have remained at call at such a time. But they had had little leisure of late. As they knew he was going out, it was natural that they should take the same opportunity.

CHAPTER FIFTY-ONE

It is of the perversity of women that they are courageous over great, and timid over very trifling things. Yet there are many them who would have hesitated to invite a man to accompany them at eight P.M. on a mysterious and probably dangerous excursion, the nature of which they were not prepared to disclose, about three hours after rejecting his proposal of marriage.

Yet Jehane did this...without wasting a thought or an atom of nervous energy upon any aspect of the matter, beyond the obvious one that he might be useful, and would be glad to come. Perhaps the fact that the proposal was the seventh which she had received from the same direction, being of a serial kind—and a serial which might not have reached its concluding episode—may have influenced her decision. Perhaps it was only that her mind was on more important things.

She had actually resolved upon this course of action before the seventh proposal had supervened, and been dealt with as it deserved.

In fact, ever since she had learnt from Crystal that she had actually written the letter which had been meant for Stanley's eyes alone, and expressed her opinion upon Crystal's sanity and other cognate matters with the vigour and picturesqueness of phrase to which she was always inspired by her sister's rectitudes. That the pearls of speech which had been produced by the irritation of Crystal's replies had been less informative than Jehane's objective sentences usually were, arose from the fact that she had felt it necessary to avoid disclosing that she had read the letter, which, as Stanley had objected to her speaking upon the subject to Crystal at all, she had felt obliged to do. But to enquire concerning the genuineness of a letter which appeared to be in Crystal's writing, and intended to be passed to Stanley unopened, was a natural thing.

Recognising afterwards how much of trouble and disaster might have been avoided by a more frank exposure of their sisterly minds, she said that it showed what rot all diplomacy really is, which is a contentious subject too large to be allowed to divert us here.

But she gave some information—indeed, more than she gained—including the fact that Stanley had not known of the insertion of Crystal's letter in the *West End Tatler*. Then how had it reached the hands of the editor of that periodical? How did Crystal expect her to know that? Probably (she ventured) Stanley had never seen it at all. Perhaps Mr. Jepson had intercepted it, and been keeping it all the time till he thought he could publish it without being whipped. Had he been whipped? Yes, of course. Called by appointment, bringing his own canes. Jehane owned that she had arranged that. Not that she had cared. She had done it to save his life, which Rigby would otherwise have taken. But she thought Crystal was a silly chump. If she wanted to talk to Stanley, why hadn't she come here? She knew his address. If she were married to Rig—anybody, and he weren't doing what he was told, she wouldn't go off sulking into the country; she'd be on the spot. Crystal could bet her boots about that.

Crystal was very unlikely to bet her boots about anything, but some matter for thought she must have received, and some revision of judgment may reasonably be expected to have resulted, though whether or how far, if at all, they modified her attitude or subsequent actions must be seen in its own time.

Jehane satisfied herself that the letter had come from Crystal, and it did not enter her mind that her sister could be involved in a plot against Stanley's freedom or power. But she still thought it a silly business. She finally concluded that Crystal's aim was to resume the obligations and pleasures of marriage, and that with feminine obliquity, she was using this information about a plot (if any plot were there) to convince Stanley of her loyalty, and to get him where they could make their peace on a neutral ground. She could imagine that Crystal would prefer that to the publicity of surrender which would be implied by her entering the Rafton portals, and which would certainly be reported in the press with unforeseeable mendacities embroidered upon it.

All the same, it was a silly business; and if Crystal had gone dotty there was an increased occasion for the remaining half of the family to keep its head.

If Stanley should leave the hotel unobserved by others, no one would be likely to be excited by the fact that a two-seater car was proceeding in the same direction. If he were observed by unfriendly eyes, there was good reason that friendly ones should be used in the same way.

It was as the result of these reflections that she had ordered an even earlier dinner than Stanley's impatience would have required. She did not intend that her car should be waiting at the hotel door for him to see it as he came out, and perhaps for others to observe its action in following him.

She left half an hour before, in the company of a silent, mystified, but obedient Rigby. She drove round Hartley Street, with her lights falling for a moment upon the rear-plate of a standing taxi, and stopped quietly in the rear of the Rafton Hotel, about fifty yards from the back entrance, the lighted vestibule of which would show when the little group of employees should emerge, while she would be secured from observation by the surrounding shadows.

"It's a good thing," she said to Rigby in the interval of waiting, "that you can shoot straight, which I never could. The bird I aim at's always been the one that's quite safe from me. Apart from that, it's a good thing that babies...." She stopped rather abruptly. She had been about to mention a popular superstition that children benefit more in their intelligence from the quality of their mother's brain. This might have been taken merely as praise of herself, or of disparagement of Lord Rigby Stilton in a detached spirit. It might also be taken as having a dual application of a more intimate and prophetic kind. It is cruel to encourage groundless hope. It was much better left unsaid.

Rigby kept to the main issue that she had raised. "Who," he enquired with a natural curiosity, "am I expected to shoot?"

"I can't tell you that, because I don't know. Almost anybody's possible. You heard Stanley say that he's going out, and it's our part to see that he comes back at his own time."

"Do you know why he's going?"

"I know something which I can't say, and I wish I knew a lot more."

"Does he know that he'll be followed like this?"

"Not from me."

"Sure he won't mind?"

"He'll be glad if he needs help. If he doesn't, he needn't know."

"That's how it is, is it? Well, carry on. I think he's coming out now."

"You've got eyes! Well, no one seems to be caring particularly. I don't know what he'll do next. He may take a number thirty-eight bus, or a taxi, or he may make for that one we saw standing in Hartley Street. We'll just hang back and watch. But you can't be too ready. If anything happens about here, it'd be a quick thing."

"Yes. I've no doubt it would. But it's not likely here. Not in the least."

Rigby proved right on that point. Stanley walked quickly, but without haste, in the direction of Hartley Street. No one accosted him. No one appeared to observe who he was. If he were followed, it was done too cautiously and too skilfully for Rigby to detect it, though he watched from the advantageous position of the open car, which Jehane managed with some adroitness, not following at an equal distance, and once drawing up at the pavement for two or three minutes when the bare straightness of the side-street enabled her to do so with the assurance that they would be able to recover the trail.

Stanley did not appear to care whether he were followed or not. He neither dallied nor hastened. He did not look back. They saw him reach the taxi, and get in after a word with the driver.

They followed the taxi with an equal ease. Jehane had been prepared for signs of a struggle as Stanley would be seized by the hidden occupants, and for the excitement of a full-speed chase through the London streets. Even when she saw that he entered it without any resulting excitement, she more than half anticipated that it would drive rapidly in any direction rather than to the address which had been given in Crystal's letter. But she was wrong again. At a sober pace, and as directly as was consistent with a choice of the quieter ways, it proceeded towards John Henry Street, which it entered at the southern end, where that modest byway curves behind Chandler's Mews, which is no more than the memory of a name, as so many London mews of a past century have now become.

The curve of John Henry Street obliged them to follow somewhat closely if they were to observe what happened. To continue their course, passing the other vehicle as it drew up at No. 37, would have been the most natural thing to do, but if the driver should not regard that procedure with suspicion, that Stanley would recognise them would be an almost certain result, which Jehane preferred to avoid. Stopping twenty yards in the rear, they watched him get out, pay the driver, and knock at a door which opened promptly to let him in. Meanwhile the taxi backed into a gateway entrance, to enable it to turn in the narrow street. It came back, the driver passing them without a glance, and having put down his flag in invitation for another fare.

"What," Rigby asked, "do we do now?"

"Wait here, I suppose," Jehane answered shortly. She felt vexed, which she knew to be absurd. Had she wanted something evil to happen? Of course not. Yet the event seemed tame, and their elaborate trailing to be melodrama of a foolish kind.

Now they might sit here—for how long? If Stanley came out, it would show that they had been wasting their time, and that he needed no aid from them. If he didn't—well, how long were they to sit there waiting for him to do so?

They sat there for two hours, getting increasingly chilly in the open car. Rigby gave no sign of his thoughts, but Jehane knew that she was of an increasing irritation, to which a measure of apprehension may have contributed. What might not be going on in that silent house, as the hours passed, and they sat there, doing nothing? Yet what, in the name of common-sense, could they do?

If Stanley did not return in safety, they had gained the certain knowledge of the house to which he had come. If they sat there all night, they would have done no more, and wasn't that a very likely thing that they would have to do if they should wait for him to come out? How long is a man likely to stay who visits his wife at night after a division of several months? Jehane considered this problem in a mind which had lost something of its normal self-confidence. She did not propound it to Rigby, who might be no better authority than herself. Her immediate problem was slightly different, though of the same species. How long does a girl who has refused to marry a man at 3:30 P.M. sit with him alone in a car in a dark street during the following night? The answer to both may be that it depends on the girl. But it may depend on circumstance also. What were the circumstances of those who were within that silent, unlighted, house? How she wished she knew!

"I wish," she said fatuously, "we knew how long he's going to be."

"He may have gone out by the front door."

"He may have *what*? Rigby, you don't mean there's another way out?"

"I should think the front of these houses would be in Bray Street. It looks like it to me."

"Then why didn't you say before?"

"I didn't know, and I supposed you did. Besides, we couldn't watch both sides at once."

"Yes we could. One each. Or someone else could."

"I thought perhaps someone else was."

Jehane was backing the car.

"Perhaps," Rigby suggested, "he'd be most likely to come out the way he went in.

"And perhaps he wouldn't."

Too angry for further speech, Jehane drove savagely round, and confirmed the truth of Rigby's suggestions. There was no space for more than a single row of buildings between Bray Street and the narrower byway that curved inward behind it. Had they approached from that direction it would have been plain from the first. As it was—well, the sooner they got back the better. Jehane did not drive as recklessly as she would have done a few months earlier, because killing people had become a more serious matter than it was then. It was no longer a mere routine of referring relatives to y our insurance policy, and the possible annoyance of a court attendance where you would be exonerated by a coroner who probably had a driving licence in his own pocket. It might mean heavy penalties. You might even have to die yourself. It would certainly mean substantial compensation from your own pocket, and that you had driven for the last time.

She did not drive as recklessly as she would once have done, but it was a very few minutes before they were back at the gates of the Rafton garage.

Jehane spoke once on the way. She said: "They did look rather like backs." It was a measure of self-condemnation which Rigby appreciated at its true worth, and perhaps more.

They met Molly on the stairs. She looked enquiry. Jehane's hand indicated Rigby and herself. "Two fools," she said lightly. Molly realised that the time was not opportune for an extended conversation. Really, there was nothing more to be said.

CHAPTER FIFTY-TWO

STANLEY paid the driver, and turned to face a solid wooden door which was divided from the pavement by no more than a single step. There was no fanlight above it, and no light could shine through from that closed interior. There was no knocker nor bell, and it scarcely looked like the used approach to a dwelling, but there was a metal number-plate on the door, and a struck match enabled him to see that it was the one he sought.

He knocked on the panel, and the door opened so quickly that his pause of inspection had seemed to those who watched to be no more than a normal interval.

A tiled gas-lighted hall was bare and neutral either of welcome or warning, but the voice of the girl who opened seemed a familiar thing. Her "Please come in, sir," caused him to look at her with attention, and recollection followed. Clara was the name. Crystal's own maid. The recognition gave him a pleasant sense of familiarity, as of one who comes home.

"Well, Clara, how are things going?"

The girl hesitated on her answer. "There've been a good many changes of late, sir," she said vaguely.

The answer reminded Stanley that when Crystal had closed Norchester House, Molly had engaged a number of that suspended staff for her own service at the Rafton Hotel. Perhaps it was best not to develop the conversation further.

Clara did not appear to have any wish to do so. She was leading the way rapidly through the house. They came to a wider hall, to a larger, more solid door than that by which he had entered. She opened this, revealing a downward flight of steps, and a railed area at the side. A car stood at the kerb.

"Lady Crystal said I was to tell you that she thought it would prevent anyone following you, if you came through this way."

"You mean she isn't here? That this car's for me?"

"Yes, sir. That's what I was to say."

She spoke as one who repeats a lesson carefully learnt. Stanley, hearing her, had a premonition of danger, which his reason declined to heed. If Crystal knew of a plot against him, it was natural that she should take precautions to keep their meeting secret. If his enemies were on the watch for any time when he might leave the hotel, how natural that she should provide against the risk that he might be followed. Without that precaution, her effort to warn him might be the very cause of disaster. Once knowing where he had gone, how easy it would be to waylay him on his return! And how simple, how sufficient was the precaution that she had taken! And how thoughtful to have reassured his doubts with the presence of her own maid! Anyway, it was too late, it would be absurd, to turn back now.

Yet there was something sinister in this elaboration of precaution, and it was with an increased sense of the peril of the adventure that he went down the steps, and entered the waiting car.

As it disappeared round the corner, the lights went out in the house that it had left. Clara had lost no time. Her hat and coat had been ready to her hand, and her precious bag. There were notes to the value of £500 in that bag.

She did not like what she had done. She was puzzled and afraid. She did not understand what it was all about, but she knew that you cannot earn £500 for no more than opening and closing doors.

She had lost her position with Lady Crystal. Bill Randall, who ought to have married her any time in the last three years, had now got the excuse that Mr. Maitland had spoiled his trade. With this money in her hands, she would be able to talk to Bill in a new way.

All the same, she did not like what she had done. She was afraid, and glad that it was over now. There was some comfort in the lighted streets, and in boarding the crowded bus.

Stanley studied the car, the way it went, the driver's back.

The car was not one of Lady Crystal's. It was a venerable antique. There was a slight sound from the springs. There was one thing certain: it had not been selected to outdistance pursuit. There might be some comfort, even some illumination, in that; though not much.

As to the way it went, it soon became evident that its destination was not Norchester House. Perhaps he should not have expected that. There came a time when he recognised the Edgware Road.

The driver's back told him least of all, but it was the direction from which most might be learned. He tried conversation: "You're not going to Norchester House?"

"No, sir, not unless you wish," was the civil answer. "We're going north now."

"Going far?"

"No, sir, not very."

What could be more reassuring than that? He was almost invited to give his own instructions. And, of course, knowing that he had that freedom, he had no desire to do so. To drive to Norchester House while Crystal waited for him elsewhere—it would be an impossible absurdity. The man may have smiled inwardly, but even in the darkness he did not allow any change to break the impassive civility of his accustomed manner. Rinkwater's trusted agents were too well-trained, too competent for such lapses as that.

They were still in a northern suburban district about twenty minutes later when the car turned somewhat suddenly from the road, and entered a drive on the left-hand side. Stanley had a glimpse of a high wall and of formidable iron gates—or were his nerves at fault? Would dignified have been a more reasonable adjective?

The car stopped before a tall white-pillared Georgian entrance, and he was soon standing in a well-lighted, substantially furnished hall. A man-servant took his hat. Another said: "This way, sir, if you please." They were deferential in voice and manner, of aspects more suitable to soothe than to excite alarm. Yet he was conscious of apprehension as of a concealed hostility, or was it only the excitement of the fact that his meeting with Crystal must be so near?—Crystal whom he had not seen since he walked so abruptly out of Norchester House four or five months ago.

The man led him past several imposing doors to a smaller one at the end of the hall. He entered a room which was well appointed, but not large. Four men were seated around a table in the centre, on which dinner was laid, though it had not been served. A chair was drawn out, and his place politely indicated.

He knew he was trapped now, and with the knowledge he forgot the disquiet which had vexed his mind for the last hour. He felt cool and equal to whatever might be before him.

He laid a hand on the chair-back, but without seating himself. "I have dined already," he said. "I thought—"

He was about to say that he had expected to meet Lady Crystal, but paused in doubt as to whether he should mention her name till he understood the position better. Mr. Shackston appeared to understand his hesitation, and filled the gap.

"Lady Crystal Maitland," he said, with a smile that was half a sneer, "was kind enough to arrange this meeting for your own good."

"So I suppose," he answered easily. "For my good, but perhaps not for yours, Mr. Shackston. That may be a less likely thing."

The voice of the gentleman at the head of the table broke in. It was not loud nor rude, but had an air of unconscious authority, as of one to whom deference is an accepted circumstance. "Sit down, Mr. Maitland, sit down. It's foolish to start quarrelling before you know where you are."

"I know where I am well enough. I prefer to know with whom I sit down."

"I am Baron Michelson. Mr. Shackston you already know. This is Mr. Cherrington, and this Professor Sturgeon."

The Baron waved a gouty hand toward the gentlemen as he gave their names. Stanley recognised the name of Cherrington as that of one of the heads of the insurance world. Professor Sturgeon he had ordered to be deported. That he was here was an evidence that his power had never been as completely exercised as he had supposed. What bribery—perhaps what substitution—what boldness of authority hostile to his own was responsible for the fact that Professor Sturgeon was sitting here?

It was a question which it seemed inopportune to ask. Perhaps the answer was in the men who were before him now. He noticed that there was another place laid, as yet unoccupied. He asked: "And the vacant chair?"

"Mr. Rinkwater may join us later."

"Rinkwater? Oh, yes. It is a familiar name."

Stanley sat down, and the service of the meal commenced. But he refused to share it. "I have dined already," he repeated, and declined the soup which a waiter would have put before him.

"It must be some time ago," Mr. Shackston suggested with the same sneering good humour which he had shown before. "It's always well to take advantage of opportunity. You never know when the next will come."

Was there a threat behind that contemptuous smile?

"Sometimes," Stanley replied. "But not always."

"We're not trying to poison you, if you mean that."

"I didn't suppose you'd be such an utter fool."

"You may find that we're not fools at all."

"Gentlemen," Baron Michelson interposed, "this, at least, is folly. Mr. Maitland, we have arranged this meeting to discuss matters of supreme importance to the wealth and progress of the civilisation to which we belong. We wish to do it without heat, and I can assure you that, so far as I am concerned, it will be without hostility to yourself. We have come here as businessmen, prepared for a business deal.

"In transactions of the magnitude to which I am accustomed, I have found, for many years, that it is best to avoid subterfuge, and to state my meaning in a plain way. I propose to do so now.

"Your acts of arbitrary legislation during the past few months have been a menace to the stability of the social order to which we belong, to the progress of science, and to the security of finance, of an incalculable gravity, which is becoming intolerable. I do not propose to disguise our resolution that this menace shall cease. It shall cease at once at whatever cost. No personal interest, no individual life, can be allowed to stand in the way of that supreme necessity.

"When I tell you that we have actually considered whether it might not be necessary to resist your activities even at the price—the destruction of the heart of London—with which you threaten us, you will understand that no minor consideration will turn us from the object on which we are resolved, and which has brought you here.

"But having said that, I repeat that we are prepared to deal. It will be your own fault if the bargain which must be made tonight shall not be voluntary on your side, and generous on ours."

While this speech proceeded, Stanley had time to regain the self-control which, during his sharp exchanges with the Hon. James, had been in some danger of slipping away. He saw that the gravity of the issue which depended upon the result of this interview should outweigh any personal considerations of his own dignity or dislikes. Even his own safety could be of no ponderable seriousness in such a scale.

"You will understand," he said, "that I am not committing my-self to anything beyond the obligation of listening, when I ask if you will tell me plainly what you propose."

"That can be understood," the Baron conceded, "if you will un-derstand also that we regard you as being so absolutely in our power that it is of inclination rather than necessity that we have resolved upon the proposals which I am about to make.

"I think it best that you should first be clear as to how you stand. You said a few moments ago that you knew where you were. I wonder how literally we may accept that statement. Do you know that you are in Burfleet Private Asylum?

"If you should be entered on these books by a fictitious name, and certified as we can easily arrange for you to be, there is no mor-tal power that will enable you to leave these walls while your life shall last.

"This is a private asylum for patients whose relatives are able and willing to pay very large sums for them to be retained here. The precautions against escape are extremely thorough, and I believe that no patient has ever surmounted them. Neither, I am told, in the history of the institution, has any inmate ever been released as cured. No one knows that you have come here, but those whose in-terests would be united to conceal their knowledge. That you should assert that you are Stanley Maitland will alone be a sufficient indica-tion of the malady from which you suffer. In that, I am informed, you will not be single. A patient was admitted last week, who is equally confident of the same identity: there will only be two Stanley Maitlands in the asylum instead of one.

"Being threatened with such a fate, it may appear to you that we are conspiring in a monstrous crime. But your reason and your sense of proportion will unite m our acquittal.

"Compared with the stakes which we have in view, the liberty of a single life must be less than a feather's weight.

"You yourself have acted without mercy, as without law, when you have used the rope or exile to enforce what you believed to be for the general good.

"With greater reason, with greater legality on our side, we are proposing to do the same—but only if you should force us to that resort.

"We would first make you an offer of a quite different kind."

The Baron paused at this point, as though to allow time for the emotions of apprehension to assert themselves in his auditor's waiting mind.

The manservant who had retired after serving the soup now returned to remove the plates, and was dismissed by the Baron from further attendance till he should be recalled to serve the remainder of the meal. Stanley supposed that his refusal to join it had somewhat altered the time and method of the attack which was being made upon him. He said nothing, and the Baron resumed.

"The offer which we make you is this. In the first place, we are aware that you are not individually wealthy, and there are developments to be anticipated in which the considerable fortune of your wife may be no longer advantageous to you. We offer you any wealth that you may be disposed to desire. On that point we will meet you liberally. You may talk in millions if you will.

"We offer you an honourable continuation, should you desire it, of your political career. Mr. Shackston tells me that a defeat of Sir Bardsley Clinton's government can be arranged on a vote of confidence. He will then be prepared to form another in which he will offer you your present position. You will still be Chancellor of the Exchequer, in which there are many who consider that you have shown a conspicuous ability. There are features of your budget which are widely commended in financial circles, and which, I will freely allow, could not have become law in a more ordinary political atmosphere. Subject to the usual constitutional safeguards, you will continue in that office, and for your future beyond that you must be prepared to rely upon yourself, as we all do.

"You will see that we offer much.

"There are, of course, certain conditions. They are not onerous. But before I ask you to consider them, I may remind you that you are in our hands. Your life, your liberty, your reason, are absolutely and entirely ours. How completely that is the case I am prepared to explain in detail if you should desire it, but I hope that it may not be necessary. The power you once held is a lost thing. The power is in our hands. You must try to remember that.

"Our conditions are these. You will first explain to Professor Sturgeon the method of controlling the apparatus which William Feltham designed, and give him access thereto. You will give him all the formulæ and calculations—in fact, all papers of whatever kind—which came into your hands when Feltham died.

"That, so far as I am concerned, would be the sole condition that would be required, from which everything else which we regard as necessary would smoothly follow. But there is a detail which has become an obligation of honour, and which it is therefore necessary to make clear. Viscount Okehampton was of material assistance to us in the earlier stages of the arrangements which bring us together now. He desires to marry your wife. If you die, the ground will be cleared. If you continue to reside here, the position will be of a practical similarity, for I understand that a body will be recovered from the Thames in a few days' time which will be identified with your own. If you accept our offer, it must be a condition that you facilitate the divorce which will become necessary by that development.

"You may see the advantages of accepting our offer without requiring any lengthy interval for debating it in your own mind, or you may desire a short period for reflection upon it. There may be minor details on which explanation or discussion would not be wasted on either side. It is never my method to force a decision under any circumstances, and, in the present instance, it is no more than your own future—your own fate—which is at stake. Frankly, we are too strong to care. Mr. Maitland, will you now join us at dinner?"

With a face as devoid of expression as he could make it, Stanley answered: "Yes. I shall be pleased to do so." Before everything, he must gain time to think.

CHAPTER FIFTY-THREE

IT was not an hour ago that Stanley had told himself that the issues at stake in that room were too great for any personal consideration to be more than a triviality in such comparison. Baron Michelson had said the same thing. Yet with the minutes passing, and the necessity for vital decision becoming more imminent with every swing of the pendulum of the clock which faced him over the fire-place, Stanley found his mind concentrated upon the suggestion of Crystal's prospective infidelity. He would not deny that, in some aspects, it had a probable shape. He knew that Okehampton had courted Crystal before he himself had met her—that their marriage had been generally anticipated, and that it would have great material advantages of a mutual kind. From the moment of the sudden quarrel of months ago, he had had no communication from her—till that letter of yesterday. But that letter presented a problem which he could not solve. He remembered Jehane's resolute scepticism concerning it: his own doubts of its sincerity, which he had silenced less by reason than by a wilful effort of loyalty. Was the explanation to be found in the fact that it had been written to trap him—to bring him here?

It might well be that a letter which simulated loyalty from a mind that was contriving treason might fail in similitude. His knowledge of Crystal assured him that such a result would, in her case, be particularly probable. But the same knowledge made such baseness seem an impossible thing.

Still, there was the fact of the letter. It was useless to try to ignore its nature, or its present significance. There was the fact of the stipulation of divorce which was now made. Common sense assured him that Baron Michelson would not attach this petty private condition to the world-issues with which they dealt unless he felt in honour compelled to do so. Yet it might be Okehampton's condition, of which Crystal did not even know. But for what? The Baron would not hamper his negotiations in this way unless Okehampton had been of some essential help. Had it been his part to procure the letter which was to bait the trap? He could not easily think it. Yet the facts of the letter, and of the stipulations for divorce, were unshakable.

He resolved at last to raise the question explicitly, and see whether he could draw anything from the mouths of his enemies which would assist to resolve his doubt.

"There is one thing which puzzles me," he said, addressing Baron Michelson rather than his other antagonists. "I had a letter from my wife only yesterday, the contents of which are inconsistent with the stipulation which you now make. Can you give me any explanation of that?"

The Baron's reply paused. He knew that the letter had been forged, and it was a thing which he could not say. It was a feature of the affair, also, which be particularly disliked, forgery being, in his view, the one uncondonable crime. Beyond that, while he recognised Mr. Rinkwater's quite exceptional efficiency, it appeared to him that the whole thing could have been done in a simpler way without Okehampton's assistance, and without this divorce business encumbering the negotiation. Also, he had no intention of lying, even for the stake for which they now played. Ruthless and dominant as he might be in the financial world, the truth was the deadliest weapon which he ever used. Looking straightly at Stanley, he said: "Mr. Maitland, I can give you my word of honour that Lady Crystal did not express her true feelings in that letter, whatever it may have contained, of which I have no more than a general knowledge."

"You know, Maitland," Shackston interposed, "you're bound to give a woman a divorce if she asks for it. Every gentleman does."

Stanley repressed the discourteous retort which the remark invited. He had resolved that passion should not disarm his reason at this crisis of many fates. He asked quietly: "And what cause should you suggest?"

"There wouldn't be any difficulty about that. If you want to keep Lady Jehane's name out of it, you can get someone else for a tenner. You know that well enough."

"*Lady Jehane?* You don't really suppose—?" The incredibility of the suggestion overcame the indignation which it might otherwise have excited.

Shackston interrupted with: "It's no use exclaiming like that, Maitland. It's known everywhere."

"Then it may reasonably be considered remarkable that it was not known to me. I think, if you ask Lady Jehane herself, that you will find her to be equally ill-informed." Beyond the slight note of sarcasm in his voice, he still held his feelings under control.

Baron Michelson, watching keenly, decided that there was blundering somewhere. It confirmed his judgment that women should be kept outside all business deals. You should use them and pay them off. It had been the mistake here, and he had to see that it should make no difference in the end.

But Shackston stood to his guns. "It's no use telling me that bunkum. Think of what's been in the press. You know, Maitland, it's silly bluffing like that. You must have known it had leaked out months ago. Ever since you got through the same hole in the bedroom wall. And you knew what was in the *West End Tatler*. You don't think Lady Jehane read that, and couldn't tell what it meant? Are you going to tell me she didn't know who the cherries were? And the thrashing you gave the man, too! They say he lay in bed for ten days, and then couldn't sit comfortably."

Stanley said: "Is that so?" It seemed the less he said, the more he was likely to learn. But at this point there was a diversion of a servant's entrance, who told Baron Michelson in a low voice that Mr. Rinkwater had arrived. The Baron answered: "Ask him to wait a few minutes. I'll let him know when we're ready." He returned his attention to the table to say: "Gentlemen, I don't think we need go into all this. If Mr. Maitland says that Lady Jehane is nothing to him, we shall take his word. He's in the best position to know. We all know how these tales get about, and if one man's got whipped for spreading them, it won't have done any harm." His voice took a more serious tone as he addressed himself to Stanley directly: "Mr. Maitland, I don't know anything about these matters, and I don't want to. I'm sorry that they've been brought in at all. But I want to draw your attention to one point. There is no stipulation—there is no suggestion—that you should divorce your wife. It is no more than that you should facilitate the proceedings if she should desire to commence them against yourself. If there be any misunderstanding which you can remove when you are at liberty, and free from the restrictions of the exceptional position which you will then have vacated, you can proceed in your own way. I think that is the vital fact which should be before you now."

Stanley had had time to think. He did not suppose that Shackston had been speaking from the baseless fabric of an inventive mind. He saw that things must have been happening around him of which, though they had so intimately concerned him, he had remained ignorant, while men thought that he ruled the earth. Such are the limitations of power, and its penalty also.

He saw that whatever Crystal had done, she might have had provocation beyond anything which he had known. There might be other things of which he was ignorant still. But he felt that nothing could justify the treachery of the letter which had brought him here. It was a matter on which he would decide nothing until he was sure that he knew the truth.

Apart from the confusion caused by the intrusion of this personal issue, what ought his decision to be? He saw that they offered much. They offered things that many would take with outreaching hands. But he knew that their purpose was not merely to stop any further exercise of the arbitrary power which he now held, and which he had been in the mood to let slip, from the sheer physical and mental exhaustions of the last four months. In some perhaps vital directions they would aim to undo that which was already done. To what use, also, would they put the infernal knowledge which he was not to suppress, as he had intended, forever, but to transfer into Professor Sturgeon's hands?

How, if he should refuse the offered bargain, would they attempt to force him to the disclosure of that vital knowledge? With no clearer purpose than to gain the delay during which a plan of action might be contrived, he asked: "If I write a letter to Lady Crystal, will you undertake that it shall be delivered to her own hand, and that I shall receive her reply?"

Professor Sturgeon, a man with a high bald head and a narrow nose, spoke for the first time. "It won't be any use having letters brought here. You'll leave tonight, if you ever do."

The Baron frowned slightly, either at the request itself, or the reply which it had received. "If you think," he answered, "you will see that you are asking an impossible thing. Lady Crystal might decline to reply."

"No, Maitland, that cock won't fight," Shackston added. "You won't diddle us like that. We're going to settle this now."

Mr. Cherrington alone remained silent. He cared only for one thing: that the Insurance Companies should be left alone. He had commenced life as a door-to-door canvasser, collecting pennies. He was now individually worth about one and a quarter million pounds. There was nothing unusual in that, as the records of the Probate Office will show during almost any recent year. And about one farthing of every penny he had collected had been distributed among his customers in a very honest, systematic, and well-advertised way, so that they had it when they needed it most. If Mr. Maitland would only leave the insurance business alone, he could deport all the scientists in London, or hang them in festoons around their places of resort, and Mr. Cherrington would not lose an hour's sleep.

He had come there at the call of a great fear, and he was now in the throes of another of a different kind. He did not like his companions' methods, especially those of the Hon. James Shackston and Professor Sturgeon. Why couldn't they talk business in a friendly way? He believed in smooth speaking. It was that alone that had placed him in possession of one and a quarter million pounds. He was nearly sixty now, and he had kept clear of every kind of criminality, except income-tax evasion, and that had been so necessary in itself, and so carefully and safely contrived, that it could hardly be called a crime at all. It had been the recreation of a blameless life.

"If it could be done without risk," he began, with conciliatory voice and manner, "and we could reduce to writing the headings of the agreement into which we should then be prepared to enter—I don't see that a delay of forty-eight hours would be detrimental. It would be better to agree then than to disagree now. I've often found that a short interval brings the parties together...and, Mr. Maitland, we're prepared to pay, as Baron Michelson said at the first. We want this trouble off our minds, and if we can get that we're prepared to pay well."

"I shall want two days to think this thing over," Stanley said firmly. "I shall want to write to Lady Crystal during that time, with an assurance that the letter will be delivered, and the reply, if any, returned to my hands. At the end of that period, I will either give you a final Yes or No, or be prepared to put an alternative proposition before you."

"I've told you before," Mr. Shackston said angrily, "that that cock won't fight. If you want to get out of here, you've got the chance and you've heard the terms, and you'd better understand this: the terms won't alter, and the chance won't last."

"And if I refuse, Mr. Shackston, will you tell me with the same pellucid clarity precisely what you propose to do?"

But even the natural irritation caused by this manner of address did not blind Mr. Shackston to the fact that pellucid clarity would be of doubtful assistance here. He was aware of one weakening and one inscrutable colleague, and the confidence with which Professor Sturgeon had favoured him as to his proposed methods of persuasion, did not assure him that either the Baron or Mr. Cherrington would be pleased to hear them. He said shortly: "You'll find out soon enough, if you don't see sense first. Professor Sturgeon'll see to that."

"Why the Professor, more than Mr. Cherrington, who seems to me to be gifted with exceptional persuasive power?"

"Mr. Maitland," Baron Michelson interrupted, "this is a serious matter. Your detention, if it should be unfortunately necessary to prolong it—together with any measures which may be incidental thereto—will be in the hands of Professor Sturgeon, because he purchased this institution outright three days ago, and is now in sole control.

"But not, I suppose, with his own money?"

"That is immaterial to the present issue."

"It would be possible to question that."

"Possible, but futile."

"Yes, I suppose it would. May I amend my previous question to enquire how Professor Sturgeon proposes to obtain the information from me, should I decline to supply it?"

"You'll learn that fast enough," Shackston repeated in a last effort to prevent that question receiving a more informative answer. But the Professor, who was a precise man, felt bound to differ.

"I am not prepared to endorse that statement without important qualification. The degree of conscious knowledge with which Mr. Maitland will communicate the information which we require is, in the present state of our knowledge of such conditions, somewhat difficult to determine."

He spoke in a nervous high-pitched voice, his dull black eyes regarding his purposed victim in an impersonal yet malevolent way which Stanley found particularly hard to endure. Yet he was determined to avoid the display of useless anger, or foolish fear. He suggested with a derisive courtesy: "If you would be more explicit, Professor?"

Professor Sturgeon was not slow to answer. He addressed Stanley directly, his high-pitched voice vibrating to a note of bitterness that changed to malevolent anticipation as he explained the method by which he hoped to obtain the secret of Feltham's invention should Stanley decline to yield it to the more mercantile persuasions which had been offered already.

"Mr. Maitland," he said, "I will tell you what I propose, so that you may understand that the methods of science, even toward yourself who have destroyed with ignominy some of the noblest intellects of our time, and have driven others, as you thought that you had driven me, into an exile where they must live in ignorance and ignoble toils, will be exercised with all the humanity that the occasion allows.

"You have this great discovery, which will yet clothe the name of William Feltham with an immortal honour, which you obtained by murder, and which you hold back from those who are most competent to control it. Can there be any course toward yourself which would not be justified to recover this priceless secret for the use of those who are its natural heirs? Can there be anything which would not be justified to return our colleagues from that exile to the researches from which they have been torn away?

"I could tell you of a hundred ways by which you could be forced to give up that secret. Tortures of pain or thirst which would make you glad to relieve them at any earthly cost. We could obtain our end by no more difficult method than the refusal of the sleep without which no man's life may continue. But we shall do nothing either to hinder or break your rest. You may remain awake as long as you will, and when you sleep at last it will be too heavily to stir for a needle's prick. When you awake, you will prattle freely of the things that have been hidden deepest in your secret mind. You will think that you talk but with yourself, and that you are able to visit the scenes of the days which are behind us now. We shall know all that we will, but whether you will know that you tell it is beyond what I am prepared to say."

"And if your devilish project should go wrong, as I think it would, for reasons which you may guess if you can, the secret of Feltham's invention would be lost forever, and the execration of all that would follow would be on your head, and the heads of those who are with you here."

"Not at all," the Professor answered confidently. "We should not be connected with your disappearance in any way. It is as George Thompson that you have been entered on our books, and as George Thompson you would continue."

Stanley saw with satisfaction that Mr. Cherrington's natural healthy colour had receded as these exchanges took place. But he overlooked him to address Baron Michelson, whom he regarded as the controlling mind, and as one whose instinct and practice would incline toward a less violent and criminal solution than that which the Professor had indicated.

"I think, Baron Michelson, if any justification were needed for the course which I took to restrain the activities of some only of the research-workers in this country, we have heard it now.

"I have no doubt that this place is strongly guarded, and that I should find escape very difficult, if not impossible. To that extent you have me trapped, as you might find that you are trapped your-selves if the Professor should succumb to a temptation to enlarge his catch. Should I communicate William Feltham's secret to him (even supposing that I were able to do so while I am detained here), what confidence could there be that he would not decide to dispose of all of us in the same way, and use the power which I should have placed in his hands as Feltham had proposed to do?"

"The point," the Baron answered, "is ingenious, but does not arise. I can assure you, for any satisfaction that the knowledge may give, that I have the situation in my own hands." His face was im-mobile, and Stanley could observe no sign that he had shaken his confidence. But the eyes of the Professor were venomous. Had he surprised a secret anticipation of the sinister possibilities of power which had been hidden behind that high-domed forehead? He saw that Mr. Cherrington's hand trembled slightly, crumbling his bread. Even Shackston's truculence might be covering an uneasy doubt. The Baron went on: "You have asked for a delay of forty-eight hours, at the end of which you have promised us a definite reply. As to the nature of that reply, I do not see that you have any option at all. Whether we can concede the time for which you ask is a point on which I think it best that we should consult in private. You will excuse us for a few minutes if we leave you alone."

The four men rose without further words, and withdrew. Stanley, wondering a little that they had not preferred to ask him to retire, sat at the empty table. He hardly knew whether he wished that they should insist on an immediate decision, or grant the interval for which he had stipulated. Two days in the custody of Professor Sturgeon, which he supposed it would mean, did not appear a very attractive programme. Suppose the Professor should decide to win the game off his own bat, and try a little private coercion? He would never dare to sleep during those two days after the suggestion which had been made. But the hint he had given that he might be in some way unable to pass over Feltham's secret while they held him there, might be a useful doubt to have invaded their minds. He must, before everything, maintain the confident demeanour of one whose aces were still unplayed.

What ground had he for any remaining confidence? He thought of that little phial which his pocket held. Four drops—four tiny drops—in the half-empty wine-glasses, and there would be no more to fear from the four who were plotting against him now. But even at this extremity of personal peril, even when he thought of the national issues—even perhaps of civilisation itself—which were at stake, he still felt that it was a thing that he could not do. Perhaps, had it been the Professor alone...or, perhaps not. Actually the Professor would have been the most difficult with which to deal, for his glass was empty, and it would have been necessary to refill it from the decanter at the further end of the table. And now they were coming back, and the chance was gone.

CHAPTER FIFTY-FOUR

THERE was a fifth man in the group who re-entered the room, one whom Stanley did not know.

"This is Mr. Rinkwater," the Baron said in informal introduction. "We had expected him earlier, but it seems that he has dined already.

"I will tell you frankly, Mr. Maitland, that I was disposed to grant you the interval for reflection for which you asked, but it was necessary to consult Mr. Rinkwater first, so that we could be absolutely certain that there could be no danger from such delay.

"It now appears that you were followed to John Henry Street, but not further. Your friends waited at the door by which you entered, and may be there still. Mr. Rinkwater assures us that there is no danger from anything which they have learnt, or from enquiries which may follow.

"That being so, we are willing to allow you the period for which you ask, but we cannot come here ourselves again. There is a possibility that we might be watched after your disappearance becomes known. It is a remote risk, but it is one which we shall not take.

"Professor Sturgeon will take charge of you, and knows our minds. On the terms which have been stated, you can secure your release at an earlier hour, if you should decide to do so. It seems to me that it might be a wise thing."

Stanley wondered in one swift doubt whether his warning had caused them to resolve that they would not put themselves in the Professor's power for a second time. But there was no consolation for himself in that. There was more hope in the conviction he felt that they would not leave the Professor in control without some sufficient hold upon him to protect themselves. Very certainly, the Baron was not a fool.

Stanley was conscious of a cowardly impulse to say that he would surrender now—at least, that he would discuss terms, rather than that he should be left in those asylum walls, in the power of one who represented the sinister evil that threatens to rule the world, and against which he had shown himself as its open, and perhaps its only powerful foe. They would go, and he would be left there—George Thompson, the lunatic. Perhaps soon to be so in fact, as well as in name.

Scarcely knowing what he would say when he began, he asked: "I can write to Lady Crystal, as was understood?"

He had no clear idea of what purpose it would serve, nor even of what he would say. But behind the outward calmness which he maintained, he had the urge for action of a trapped rat, that runs backwards and forwards against the bars.

The Baron took this request as implying a willingness to arrive at an ultimate agreement, which he greatly desired. However ruthless he might be if he thought the occasion required it, he was not naturally criminal. He saw, also, that such a settlement would be the safer and more certain course to the goal he sought.

"If Mr. Rinkwater can guarantee that such a letter can be delivered and answered without risk," he answered, "we have no objection to that."

Mr. Rinkwater was not quick to reply. In his private mind he knew that he ought to have eliminated Lady Crystal entirely when first he knew from Viscount Okehampton's report, as well as that gentleman's personal attitude, that his plan of using her as a deliberate decoy was impracticable. It was then that he had resolved to utilise the unequalled ability of Starchy Gates to forge the letter which would draw Stanley into the trap. It was at that point that he should have dropped Lady Crystal from the counters with which he played. But it had seemed then that to do so would be to admit an earlier error, and professional pride had supported arguments which would not have been sufficient of their own weight to induce him to persuade Mr. Shackston to continue the attempt to use her.

Now he thought that the forged letter would have been all-sufficient if neither Lady Crystal nor Viscount Okehampton had been used at all, either as agent or tool, and he had some reason to suppose that the Baron took the same view. So he did, and so most men would; and yet, ironically enough, it was not the case. Mr. Rinkwater's calculations had gone wrong at another point. He had relied upon the supposition that Stanley would show the letter to no one, whereas he had allowed Jehane to see it. This error might have wrecked the whole elaborate trap which he had constructed, when Jehane rang through to her sister to ask her confirmation. That it did not do so was entirely owing to the fact that she had written another, and as Jehane avoided mentioning that she had seen more than its envelope, it appeared that Crystal had confirmed the forgery when she accepted responsibility for an intercepted letter.

Secretly blaming himself for that which had saved him from egregious failure, Mr. Rinkwater had no further use for Lady Crystal Maitland, nor desire to hear her name again. He had done his part, and (he thought) done it well, with which opinion we may be disposed to agree. The results were in their own hands, and no longer concerned him. But he was not going to say that his organisation could not deliver a letter and obtain a reply without exposing the channels of communication. "Yes," he said, reluctantly, "we can do that, if it's important. Of course, I can't guarantee that we shall get any reply.

Baron Michelson added: "I must see the letter first. I can give you twenty minutes to write it before we leave."

"Very well. I will write it now."

"There is a writing-table in the next room."

Stanley found himself there, apparently alone and unwatched. He reflected that the security of this place must be very great for so much freedom to be allowed to one placed in the dreadful jeopardy which Professor Sturgeon's threats had indicated. But he was not inclined to the folly of an abortive attempt at escape from those strong and doubtless well guarded walls. If this battle were to be won, it must be by other methods than that. And the moments were passing—what should he write to Crystal, whom he had loved and trusted, as he believed that she had loved and knew that she had trusted him, till that fatal moment of quarrel had separated them for all these months, and perhaps forever? Crystal, who was said to desire that he should give her some legal grounds of divorce, who was said to believe (but what incredible nonsense!) that Jehane had taken her place. If she did not know him, she must surely know her sister better than to believe such a tale. Why, Jehane was certain to marry Lord Rigby Stilton. If she didn't admit that herself, it was plain to anyone else who watched them together.

But what should he write to Crystal?—Crystal, who it appeared on the evidence of her own handwriting, had betrayed him to the peril in which he now stood. And it was to be something that Baron Michelson and doubtless others must be allowed to read before it would reach her hand. Well, he must do that for which he had stipulated, and which had been the first pretext for the delay which he had gained. He wrote:

MY DEAR CRYSTAL,

I am told that you wish that I should give you some legal ground for divorce.

If you had credited reports that you have already such grounds, you will accept my word that they are entirely baseless, either in act or wish.

The request is one to which I cannot give any reply unless I receive it in writing in your own hand, nor credit it in advance of that evidence.

Yours,

STANLEY

He read it over with dissatisfaction, feeling it to be ill-constructed, and conscious of all that it did not say. It was the sort of letter which may be drafted many times and torn to shreds before the final version is sealed and sent. But there was no time for that, and he was constrained by the fact that it would be read by others, and a sound judgment that the prospect of its delivery would not be increased by any reference to his present circumstances. He made no allusion to Crystal's apparent treachery, for, if it were a delusion of malignant circumstance, such a suggestion would introduce a poisonous complication to the clear issue which was now between them, and, if it were true, what was there which it could be worthwhile to say?

Anyway, it was done. There had been plain paper and envelopes in the rack of the writing-table, and now he enclosed and addressed it, but without sealing. He noticed that the rack contained other stationery with the name of the institution upon it, and of Dr. James S. Lowter, with many following initials, as its Principal. It was easy to judge that Dr. Lowter was the proprietor of a few days ago, and that he had been bought out with a liberality which had prevailed upon him to make an instant exit, leaving even the personal effects with which the room was strewn. Stanley walked round, alert for anything that he might learn, but what hope was there in that?

He felt the presence of the ejected Doctor, as he looked upon the personal trifles of him who had been the jailer of the wealthy imbeciles (or those who had been so certified) who were imprisoned like himself behind these sombre walls. Dr. Lowter had ruled them with the power of peace or torture, the power even of life or death. He had represented the most potentially terrible of all tyrannies, the power of scientific knowledge, the power that throws an advancing shadow of servitude over the earth today. He was conscious that he himself also represented that power, insofar as it was with one of its own most dreadful weapons that he had challenged its dominion. Had it turned upon him to defeat him here? It seemed a very probable thing.

But it was not the power of science alone that had snared him, it was the power of wealth, which was still a separate kingdom with which science must negotiate, often with humble eyes, as one begging for bread. How long would that last? How long would it be before wealth would become the open vassal of the greater power?

It was the power of wealth, as well as that of science, which was displayed even by this institution of Dr. Lowter's. Wealth had bought the use of the knowledge which it did not itself possess. So it was wealth and science in combination—Baron Michelson as much as, perhaps more than, Professor Sturgeon—which had brought him here. Whatever might be the relative power of these monarchies, were they not invincible in combination? Should he not have seen that, if he were to contend with either, he must make alliance with the separate power? Had he not assaulted the citadels of evil with an impetuosity which had failed to count his forces with sufficient accuracy, or marshal them with sufficient skill? But while he analysed (as his mind had grown into a constant habit of doing during the last months, until it would rebel at a toil which it could not cease), he saw that there was a further power which might be as potent as those others which showed more formidably to the physical eye. The old power of wealth, arrogant and dominating, had been exerted against him. So had the new power of science, more arrogant and more ruthless than that which it threatened to overthrow. But there was a third power which had joined them to his undoing in most unnatural alliance: the power of love. And it was that power that had turned the scale. He saw it as a power that was defeated continually, but that was ever ready to be defeated again. Would it always turn the scale at the last?

Was it there that the explanation lay of all the evils which have pursued the feet of men, and which they have been merciless to pass on to their fellow-creatures? The worst horrors of continental laboratories had been watched by a silent God, while the intervention of men had been stayed by the appeal of science to their basest instincts. "Let us work these abominations, and in the end we will relieve you from your own diseases." The ultimate responsibility must be His. Was it that He could afford to wait, because the last word would be His also? Wealth would be a shrivelled thing, and science, cowering afraid, would have forgotten its boast that it could take control from a Creator's blundering hand, and love would triumph, the one reality in a world of shadows and lies?

These thoughts, taking minutes to read, were of a moment's space. They broke before the sharp remembrance that whatever powers might triumph, Stanley Maitland had failed. He had not even used his brief period of authority to a tithe of its possibilities. There was this legal filthiness which was the recognised portal of divorce, to which Shackston had alluded: how easily he could have ended that! Well, he had his own troubles to think of now. *He saved others, himself he cannot save.* The words drifted into his mind. He remembered when and of whom they had been spoken, and he saw himself for a moment in his actual size. Baron Michelson entered the room.

He took the letter, opened and read it without excuse, and put it back without remark. Being a shrewd man, he concluded that Viscount Okehampton had a disappointment to face.

"I wish," he said, "that we could have settled the matter now. If the main point were agreed, I would take your word, Mr. Maitland, for its fulfilment, and you should return with me to my own house. No? I am afraid you will have an uncomfortable time here. I have done what I could. Of your safety during the next two days you need be under no apprehension whatever. We wish to settle this matter by agreement, not violence. I regard it as the only satisfactory way for ourselves—and, of course, for you. But Professor Sturgeon insists that you cannot remain except under the name and with the description in which you are entered here. You must expect, with some possible alleviations, to be treated as George Thompson while you remain, but instructions will be given that you can communicate with Professor Sturgeon at any hour. It is improbable that the routine of such an establishment will allow of the retention of any personal effects without examination. If there should be any papers or other things of which you would like me to take charge during this interval of negotiation, I can assure you that their privacy will be respected."

Stanley hesitated. There might be other things that his pockets held that he would not wish to be handled by an asylum attendant, apart from the little phial the investigation of which might have such disconcerting consequences to a too-curious enquirer. But they were not things that he wished to pass over to the Baron's eyes. He said: "Baron, you seem too respectable for your present profession. But if you want to act decently you could easily tell them to leave me alone." It was uncertain how the remark would be received, or whether it would secure the favour for which it asked, but it was a chance worth trying. Baron Michelson merely answered: "As you will."

He went out without further words, and a few minutes later, he was seated in the comfort of his ample car, with Messrs. Shackston, Cherrington, and Rinkwater around him. "I wish," Mr. Shackston said, "we could have got it settled now. A little more pressure might have brought it off."

"There's no time like the present," Mr. Rinkwater, to whom the remark was addressed, conceded readily. He was inclined to Mr. Shackston's opinion, but felt that he had done his part, and the gentlemen must please themselves.

"I doubt," the Baron interposed, "whether you realise the supreme importance of a voluntary agreement if possible with a feeling of some goodwill remaining on either side. Mr. Maitland is of a considerable and untested popularity. The power which will remain in his hands if he should surrender his present advantage is very difficult to assess. If we pursue the path of coercion, we do not even know to what extent it may be in his hands to give us the satisfaction at which we aim, while he is confined in his present quarters. He may say that the secret is in Feltham's papers, and that they are at the Rafton, where only he can obtain them. He may say that he can do nothing without visiting Dawlish Mansions. His reticence and the appearance of confidence which he maintains are warning of caution. This is no ordinary antagonist, and no ordinary position which we are facing now.

"If he gives us what purports to be the required information, how and how soon should we be able to test its accuracy? We cannot tell. The shortest delay, as well as the most satisfactory result, must depend upon a bargain such as will be observed among businessmen."

Mr. Cherrington murmured agreement with this sentiment. Like the Baron, he believed in deliberate business bargains with a reasonable element of mutuality. The advantages which you sought would be matters of abstruse calculation. They would often be far ahead. And you did not break laws. You studied them expertly that they might become your servants, and help you to victory.

Mr. Shackston also believed in bargains, but in a different way. The Baron and Mr. Cherrington used their excellent brains to devise such, the keeping of which would be to their ultimate advantage; but, bad or good, they would abide by them in a legal way. But Mr. Shackston's bargains were rarely kept. He made them as the moment asked, and the detailed ingenuities of his mind were afterwards applied to avoid their fulfilment. He observed the political rather than the business code.

"You will see that this letter reaches Lady Crystal, and that any reply there may be is promptly in my own hands," the Baron said to Mr. Rinkwater, rather curtly. He had a suspicion that that gentleman might think that Starchy Gates would be the readiest source from which a satisfactory reply could be obtained, and, looking further ahead than some of his associates, he saw that it would not do. Their one difficulty in the way of that desirable treaty of peace, which he still thought that it would be possible to secure, and which would free the financial world from the rumblings of subterranean earthquake over which its mighty pillars had trembled, was that forged letter which had baited the trap, the falsity of which, if he were ever to emerge from those asylum walls, Stanley must surely learn.

And he had no confidence in Professor Sturgeon's methods, from which his instincts recoiled, as David from the armour of Saul. It was criminal, and his successes were won with the law as his most potent ally. It was because the stability of the law had been shaken that he was concerned in this matter at all. His mind gravitated ever toward the refuge of legality as a river runs to the sea. He saw the ultimates of Stanley's policies more clearly than he himself had per-ceived them. Gradually perhaps, but surely also, they would not only increase individual freedoms, they would substitute personal authorities for coded laws. It was in such atmospheres that financier's teeth may suddenly leave his head.

It was peace by treaty he sought, and might have obtained but for one little thing of which he did not and could not know. And he regarded that forged letter as the one obstacle which would arise at a later stage, with consequences which were hard to foresee. It was the blunder of an inferior mind. It would always enable Mr. Maitland to break faith at a future date, and to point to that document as his justification.

It was largely from an anxiety to know where that letter was that he had made the offer to take charge of Stanley's papers, to avoid them passing into other hands. Not that he would have broken his word concerning them. Rather, he would have used the opportunity to demonstrate that he was of a personal integrity in such pledges, and perhaps for reminder afterwards that he could have destroyed the document had he been of a nature to do so.

Meanwhile, he would have known where it was. He had a restless consciousness of that forgery which none of his companions shared, and only Mr. Cherrington would have understood.

The car had left by the back entrance of the extensive asylum premises, which was in another road from that by which it had entered. The approach from this side was a private cul-de-sac which Dr. Lowter had preferred to leave unlighted. The car had waited within the shadows of this dark approach till the road was empty, and then, under the guidance of the Baron's discreet and silent chauffeur, it had slid smoothly and swiftly along the lamp-lit road.

With the openness which avoids remark, it set down its several occupants at points suitable to their convenience, and went on to deposit Baron Michelson at his own door. It was still barely midnight, and they had passed unnoticed through the crowded streets.

CHAPTER FIFTY-FIVE

"IS that you, Crystal?"

"Yes."

"Well, I'm Jehane. I suppose you know my voice well enough. Have you got any news about anything that I might like to hear?"

"I don't know what you mean."

"You don't know any reason why I might want to ring you up? No, I can't explain. I'm coming over."

"It's no good coming now. I'm going out."

"Then stay in."

Crystal heard the receiver put back. She hesitated a moment, and then cancelled her car.

It was barely twenty minutes later that Jehane appeared.

The sisters looked at one another in the uncertainty of an affection which had its roots in the traditions of family and the recollections of a common childhood, and across a gulf of recent separation of the depth or shallowness of which they were both unsure.

They stood a moment without greeting of hands or lips, and then forgot themselves as the directness of Jehane's first question struck to the centre of that which was in both their thoughts.

"Where's Stanley?"

"How should I know? I thought you were looking after him now."

"Don't be silly. Where did he go after you met him last night? He hasn't come back yet. I couldn't say that on the phone."

"I didn't meet him last night."

"Not in John Henry Street?"

"Not anywhere. Where did you suppose?"

"But you know what you wrote. You said...."

"Did Stanley show you my letter?"

"Yes, he wasn't sure that it...*Crystal, what did you write?*"

"If you saw the letter...."

"I don't know that I did. Crystal, don't waste time. What did you write?"

Crystal stood silent a moment, facing the angry impatience in her sister's eyes. Then she said quietly: "There's no reason you shouldn't see it." She went to her desk, and unlocked it. As she opened it, she saw a letter on the blotting-pad addressed to herself in Stanley's writing. It bore no stamp. It must have been delivered by hand. How had it come there?

She looked at it with an inward bewilderment, and then at Jehane. Were these two things part of some plot against her—this letter, and her sister's presence when it was found? Jehane looked unperturbed by a pause and glance which she could not understand. She could not see the letter from where she stood by the fireplace.

Crystal's face showed the reserve which it had learnt when Jehane had teased her in childhood days. Whatever position she might be about to face, she was resolved that her own dignity should not go down in the fight. She left the letter untouched, and took out a copy of her own from the little drawer which had held it.

"It's not exact," she explained, as she handed it to Jehane, "it's a draft. But it's near enough. It's all there."

Jehane read:

MY DEAR STANLEY,

There are things of matters of importance which I should like to discuss with you. I feel sure that you will not refuse me this.

I will come to the Rafton you at any time, if you will say when it will be convenient to you.

Yours sincerely always,

CRYSTAL

"He didn't get this letter."

"Then what did he get?"

"He got one that was faked."

"Stanley ought to know my writing by now."

"So ought I. I'd have sworn you'd written it, though I thought you must have gone cracked. It was the cleverest forgery I ever saw. The question is: who knew you were writing to Stanley? If you know that, you'll know how to start on the right track."

Crystal looked doubtfully down upon the unopened letter, trying to probe the nature of the snare into which she had fallen. Should she open it now, or should she leave it till Jehane had gone? Were they foes or allies? If she had been a fool, as she was inclined to think—though she was not yet sure how—was it to be confessed to Jehane, or could it remain forever concealed in her own mind?

Jehane's voice broke the silence sharply: "Crystal, don't be a mule. Didn't anyone know you were writing that?"

Crystal fought down the inclination to refuse to reply. If Stanley were in danger through her—. But she had done nothing except to try to warn him—. But if he were—. She answered candidly: "Jimmy Shackston knew."

"*Jimmy Shackston!* And why on earth should he want you to write that?"

"He didn't. He wanted me to write something different…. He wanted me to ask Stanley to come here."

"Why?"

"To warn him about a plot."

"And why didn't you?"

"I wasn't sure who to trust. Besides, I thought he might refuse, as he did before."

"Are you quite sure he did? He mayn't have got that letter, if he didn't get this."

"But he let it be published afterwards."

"Of course he didn't. He doesn't know about that to this day. If he'd ever had the letter, it wouldn't have ended there. You ought to have thought of that."

"But the editor was punished for printing it? So I was told."

"Yes. I fixed that. Rigby wanted to murder him, and I thought he'd better be left alive to think it over after he'd got hurt. But we're wasting time. The question is where Stanley went last night, and where he is now." She went on to tell of the contents of the forged letter, and how Rigby and she had waited vainly at a door which would not open again.

Crystal listened with a whitening face, as she realised the nature and character of the forces against which they were left to fight. She said: "We must let Sir Bardsley know." And then: "But there's a letter from Stanley here. He must be somewhere where he can write."

She tore it open, and read it silently. She passed it to Jehane saying: "Perhaps you know what it means. I never had such a thought."

Jehane read it in an almost equal bewilderment. "If you know anyone who wants to marry you," she said, "you ought to be near the kill."

"There's Viscount Okehampton," Crystal answered doubtfully, "I think he must be in it somehow. He's been hanging round me till the last few days. But I can't really think—".

"No, of course not. He hasn't the pluck, nor the brains. But he's one of the same gang. How you could have all Stanley's enemies swarming round, when you might have—but I'm not going to quarrel now. I thought of what I'd do as I came here. I only wanted to know who it was."

"If I can do anything to help," Crystal answered, "you know I will. I do think we ought to let Sir Bardsley know first."

"And I don't. He'd run clucking round like an old hen, and everyone'd know something was up. But you've helped a lot.

"You see, no one knows Stanley's gone except me, and Rigby and Molly—which means Selby Ditchfield—and of course those who've got him and won't tell. I've had everything carried on as usual till I came over here. I even promised to marry Rigby if he'd eat Stanley's breakfast after he'd just finished his own. You can tell I wasn't sticking at anything when I said that. Yes, of course he did.

Ate it up like a bird, and talked to Stanley in the next room while they were clearing away. Well, I'm not the power behind the throne, I'm the power in front, which may turn out to be a lot more useful now. I only wanted someone to go at, and Jimmy sounds like the one. Anyway, it's worth trying."

She went to the telephone, and asked for Embankment 7000. When she gave her name, she was put through to the Assistant-Commissioner with great celerity.

"That you, Sir Henry? Well, there's a job this morning after your own heart. Mr. Maitland wants Jumping Jimmy laid by the heels—yes, of course, who else could I mean?—ready for a hanging tomorrow. There ought to be quite a row of them ready for that by then, but I daresay Mr. Maitland will be content with sending them to Tibet, or somewhere a bit further. You know how easygoing he is, especially when it's something against himself. Yes, rather. It's high treason, or whatever you call it to try to take Mr. Maitland's life. I expect medium treason's the word. And forging Lady Crystal Maitland's name, and a few little trifles like that. Yes, he's in it up to the neck. No. Mr. Maitland doesn't blame you about that. He doesn't see how you could, the way it's been planned. But he'll blame you if you don't get Jimmy in the next hour. You'll find him trying to look innocent in the National Club, more likely than not. You're to run him in, and not let him say anything. Mr. Maitland says you can tell him that he's to get ready for being hanged tomorrow—I think compose his mind's the right thing to say—and if he wants to talk, I'm to come round and see him myself. I'll come round this afternoon anyway, and tell you the whole tale.

"And I say, Sir Henry, you might tell your men to watch his face when he knows they've come to take him. Mr. Maitland rather thinks he may believe the plot's been a success, and, if so, anything he says is likely to give him away. If he makes any trouble, tell them to tell him that I rang up Lady Crystal on Thursday afternoon to know whether the letter was genuine, and after he's thought that over you'll find he'll come like a lamb.

"Well, I thought you'd say that. Perhaps we ought to have let you know. But there's never been any danger, and you know Mr. Maitland likes to do these things his own way. Perhaps he just wanted to wait for a full net. But, Sir Henry, there's one thing you ought to know, in case Mr. Maitland rings you up himself later in the day. He walked out of the back entrance of the Rafton at 8:30 P.M. last night, behind the staff servants that sleep out. We don't expect the military to be any good till it comes to a row, but don't you think some of your bright young things ought to have noticed that?

And I don't believe a living soul saw him come in again during the night. No, he hasn't said a word, but I thought you'd just like to know. He isn't worrying about that, but you won't find there's much blue sky left if you let Mr. Shackston slip."

She put down the receiver. "I shall feel a bit better when I know Sir Henry's made that arrest. But it's come off so far. I don't believe there are many who could lie better than that. You never know till you try."

But Crystal did not respond to the nervous energy of Jehane's flippant mood. Like Baron Michelson, she had more confidence in the established order and the invocation of lawful powers. She felt that Stanley's disappearance ought to have been communicated to Sir Bardsley Clinton without delay, and, of course, to Sir Henry, as representing the detective force, and to a score of other friendly authorities whose combined resources would have concentrated to trace and rescue. But she had a shaken confidence in herself, and she only said: "Do you really think it will come off like that? I should have thought he would have insisted on speaking to Stanley himself."

"Well, it looks like coming off, and I thought it would. You see, I always speak through the telephone for Stanley to Scotland Yard. They've had instructions like that before. Of course, they wouldn't really hang anybody without everything going through in the regular way. But arrest's a different thing. And I rather counted on Sir Henry feeling that he'll have the blame for not having been awake to what's been going on. He isn't worrying over whether I've given him Stanley's instructions properly, but only lest Jimmy should slip under the ropes."

"I hope you're right. But, oh, Jehane, why didn't you make it plain what you meant when you rang me up the first time? If you'd only said the letter didn't read like mine!"

"Yes, I know. I've been telling myself what a fool I was ever since last night, and wondering how long it would be before anyone else noticed it. It was just cowardice. I didn't know whether you'd mind my having read the letter, if it were really yours."

"I daresay I might," Crystal said generously. "Anyway, it's done now. Do you think this is Stanley's letter, or another forgery?"

"It isn't easy to say. It's more his style than the other was like yours. I don't see how they thought they'd get the answer. You'd naturally write to the Rafton, if you didn't know what had happened—unless they could intercept it in the post, or after it had been delivered."

"If they could get it put into this desk—".

"Yes, we haven't won yet." A sense of the hidden strength of the forces that were arrayed against them oppressed Jehane's mind for a moment from its usual buoyancy, and her tone reacted on her sister's less confident, if not less courageous temperament.

"Jehane—you don't think Stanley's really in danger? They wouldn't dare—?"

"I'd give a lot to know that. But it's no thanks to you, if he's alive now. If they hadn't thought you were willing to throw him over, they wouldn't ever have tried—Crystal, you're not *crying*? I didn't think you could. What a pig I am. Of course, he isn't in any danger. There isn't a man in England that would dare to harm him while that thing in Feltham's flat stands as it does. You know I don't mean half I say, and the rest isn't worth hearing. I told Rigby I'd marry him if he ate the bacon, but I didn't say when. I'll make it three weeks after Stanley's back safe, and see what he'll do then. Crystal, I've got another idea. We might use the press a bit after all. I know you'll feel better if you think we're doing things in an orthodox way."

Jehane withdrew an arm which had been round her sister's neck in a demonstration of affection which it would be hard to equal since they had slept as children in the same bed, and went back to the telephone.

"Miss Vera Hastings in? No, nobody else. It's Lady Jehane Norchester ringing up with some news you'll be sorry to miss. I thought that might make a difference. Yes, I'll hold on. Mr. Goldstone? Yes. Good morning. I want Miss Hastings. Yes. I know you're the editor, but I want her. But Mr. Goldstone, I'll just say this. I gave you the straight tip once before, and I'm going to now. But it's Miss Hastings's scoop. I liked her when I saw her before, and I'm going to give her a leg up.

"You'll be a bit surprised when you know what it is, but you'll know it's true, or I shouldn't give it to Miss Hastings to ruin her.

"And just one thing more. There've been some queer things happening in the last two days. I don't know how much you've been in them, but you'll be safe if you stand out now. But you'll have to publish just what you're told and when. No, of course you haven't. You wouldn't. Anyway, *don't*…don't put any other reporters on this job. Stand right away, and leave it to what I give Miss Hastings, and you'll be glad afterwards. Yes, I'll hold on."

A few minutes later Miss Hastings realised that it was indeed the scoop of her life which she was taking down with a rapid pencil, while she listened to Jehane's voice through the receiver at her left ear.

Mr. Goldstone, sitting opposite in a hardly controlled impatience, was soon listening to her translation of the shorthand notes she had made:

"A warrant," she read, "has been issued for the arrest of the Hon. James Shackston on charges of forgery and attempting the life of Mr. Stanley Maitland. It is anticipated that this arrest will lead to the disclosure of a widespread conspiracy, particulars of which have been known to Mr. Maitland for the last two days, but which he allowed to develop until the culprits had fully revealed their hands.

"It is rumoured that Mr. Maitland left the Rafton Hotel last evening, alone and without recognition, and was away for several hours in pursuance of a plan to obtain final evidence of the conspirators' intentions as directed against himself. The incident, when the full facts are known, is likely to provide one of the most romantic episodes of modern times.

"We understand that Mr. Maitland is anxious to act with particular clemency toward those who have been associated in this conspiracy, and we are able to state on the highest authority that any who surrender at the Rafton Hotel before eight P.M. tonight, without attempting any previous communication with their fellow-criminals, are guaranteed exemption from the extreme sentences of death, exile, outlawry, or prolonged imprisonment, which their misconduct has merited. Those who do not avail themselves of this opportunity must abide the consequences without expectation of any further mercy."

Miss Hastings read these paragraphs over a second time at Mr. Goldstone's request. "She wants us to publish it in those words?" he asked doubtfully.

"Yes, Lady Jehane was very definite about that."

Mr. Goldstone looked puzzled, and far from satisfied. Lady Jehane was not a journalist. He could have displayed the facts contained in what would be a mere half column of print in such a different way! Still, there was no restriction on the size of type, or the headlines that he might use. If his afternoon edition were alone in having this news, it would be one of the greatest scoops of his career.

But, apart from that, he had an instinctive feeling that he was being used; that he had not had all the truth. Had he had it at all? The same instinct told him that some at least of those startling statements could be believed. He felt convinced that Lady Jehane would not have announced the impending arrest of the Hon. James without a solid foundation for the news she gave. If that were true, the rest was of a probable kind. Beyond that, he had his own peril to consider. Too cautious to go too far, he was yet of the party among whom he knew that such a conspiracy was in gestation. There had been a note of warning from Lady Jehane which he would do well to heed.

"Yes," he said, "let it go. You'd better be round at the Rafton a bit later, and see what you can learn. She seems to cotton to you."

As he spoke, there were two interruptions. The telephone rang, with the information that Lady Jehane Norchester wanted to speak to Miss Hastings again, and Miss Rimington stood at the door in an attitude of deferential urgency, with a short typescript in her hand.

"One moment, Miss Rimington." Mr. Goldstone waved her down with a plump hand, preferring the additional information that might be coming through to that which he saw that she had already, of whatever quality it might be.

"There's just one thing that I forgot to mention," Jehane was saying, "you can announce that from Monday next Mr. Maitland's headquarters will be at Norchester House."

"Now, Miss Rimington." Mr. Goldstone invited her narrative a few minutes later when he had digested the information which he had last received, which seemed in some illogical way to give an additional stamp of verity to that which he had doubted before. He had directed its extension to about twice the number of words which Jehane had considered necessary. ("On and after, Miss Hastings, not from.") He was ready to turn his mind to another of the excitements on which it thrived.

"We've just had the news that Mr. Shackston has been arrested at the National Club. I thought it was sufficiently important to interrupt almost anything. It's quite authentic. Mr. Walford saw it all, and telephoned from the Club. Yes, J. S. Walford, the member for Brantwood. He says," she read out from the script which was in her hand, "'he was taken in the smoking-room by three plainclothes men from the Yard. Inspector Courtfield was one. He seemed to lose his head at first, and knocked one of them over a chair. There was a struggle after that, and a lot of shouting, and some of the members of his own party crowded into the room, and wanted to know what it was about, and he called to them to throw the detectives out And Inspector Courtfield said: "I shouldn't interfere, gentlemen, if I were you. We've got Mr. Maitland's own orders, and we've got plenty of force outside." They looked out of the windows, and there were police all about the street, and mounted men round the van, and they stood back. And then the Inspector said something to Mr. Shackston about a letter, in a low voice that I couldn't hear, but he seemed to collapse a bit when he heard it, and after that he went quiet.'

"There's another report," Miss Rimington added, "that came in from someone in the street. It only says that Mr. Shackston was hurried into the van, looking very white, with a streak of blood down one side of his face, and his coat half torn off his back."

"Very well, Miss Rimington, have it spread out a bit. In two minutes we ought to have it on the machines."

It had all happened within half an hour of Jehane ringing up the Assistant Commissioner. Certainly, Sir Henry had lost no time.

CHAPTER FIFTY-SIX

THE paragraph which Jehane had dictated in imitation journalese was published unaltered by Mr. Goldstone's periodical, and read with various degrees of perturbation by those who had been concerned in the conspiracy. Several who had been in its outer circle, supporting it financially, or attending its secret conclaves, would spend the remainder of the afternoon in useless pacing of their private rooms, as they debated whether they were sufficiently unimportant to escape discovery, or whether they might regret the loss of this dangerous opportunity of a lenient hearing as they should climb the steps of the gallows, the victims of one of Mr. Maitland's swift and ruthless acts of justice, on the following day.

But their actions do not concern us. If they attended at the Rafton to be interviewed by one of Mr. Maitland's friends, it would be found that they had nothing vital to communicate, and if they stayed away the event would show that they had nothing vital to fear.

Of the three who had left the asylum together in Baron Michelson's car, the Baron read the column without outward emotion, or any great inward surprise. He did not conclude that its contents were true, but he had no doubt that something had gone wrong with Mr. Rinkwater's scheme. Sooner or later he would know what it was, and that would be time enough. It was a clumsy, criminal business with which he should not have associated himself, even under the abnormal danger to the financial structure of Europe which arose from Mr. Maitland's eccentric activities. Forgery is a fool's game. It did not enter his mind that he might secure his safety by attending at the Rafton Hotel. If Mr. Maitland were retaining his power, which appeared a likely, though not a certain thing, he must make terms with the civil authority, as finance has done a hundred times before, and always with the knowledge that it will remain when the political power to which it must be respectful is a fallen thing.

He called in a confidential secretary, and for twenty minutes he dictated an abstruse argument setting up the interesting proposition that as England had abandoned the gold standard, the reserve bullion lying in the vaults of the Bank, and then amounting to about one hundred and thirty million pounds, was of no practical value, being held there by a financial superstition rather than any continuing necessity. Why should it not be realised on the markets of the world and the proceeds devoted to one of those great schemes of emigration that Mr. Maitland was known to favour?

To facilitate this operation, and to steady the exchanges at the time of its first announcement, he offered the aid of the vast resources of his own financial house, and of his continental allies.

We need not follow his argument into all the intricacies with which it dealt, which would be of interest only to those few who are competent to understand or dispute them.

He directed that the proposal should be sent to Mr. Maitland by registered post.

He debated in a scrupulous mind whether he should stop the cheque which he had drawn in Mr. Rinkwater's favour, and decided that, on his present information, it would be unjust. There would be time to cable from Paris.

He sent for other secretaries, and gave various instructions in his unhurried, methodical way.

Then, with a physical reluctance of which he allowed no sign to appear, he committed his gouty body to the unstable comforts of his private plane.

Mr. Rinkwater also read the news without any intention of visiting the Rafton Hotel resulting from that perusal. Professional etiquette was the one point of conduct on which his code was inflexibly high. He simply gave instructions for the truth of these reports to be tested, and went on with the work of a busy office.

Mr. Cherrington read the news, and fell forward across his desk. When he recovered, he ordered his car, and descended the stairs, holding hard on the banister with a trembling hand.

Of others who read the same news with more than an impersonal interest, we may observe Mr. Starchy Gates, immaculately dressed, and lunching late in a Piccadilly restaurant, who promptly took a taxi to the Rafton, and gave everyone away as far as he was able, which was a limited matter, for Mr. Rinkwater had trusted him as far as was unavoidable, but no more.

Viscount Okehampton read the same news with a slight sardonic smile. He was not sure that he was not rather pleased than otherwise. It is satisfactory to find that your judgment has been right as usual. He had no doubt that Maitland would come a cropper in the end, when he would be in a better position with Crystal because he had declined to be drawn into this discreditable affair.

He looked somewhat less complacent when he read in another evening paper that Sir Bardsley Clinton and Lady Crystal Maitland had lunched with Mr. Stanley Maitland that day at the Rafton Hotel. And what was this which he had overlooked before about Maitland moving to Norchester House? But we know how unreliable these newspaper reports usually are.

Sir Bardsley Clinton and Lady Crystal, it may be needless to say, had not lunched with Mr. Maitland, who was still in the Burfleet Institution, enduring the name and attributes of George Thompson. But the report was so far true that Crystal had actually returned with Jehane to the Rafton Hotel, and had so far persuaded her sister of the folly of attempting to win the game by her single efforts that an invitation to Sir Bardsley to come to lunch had been issued in Stanley's name, and with an urgency which had caused him to cancel a prior engagement, and lose no time in proceeding to the Rafton Hotel.

Sir Bardsley, whose feelings were usually under good control, arrived in a state of hardly-repressed agitation, for a report had reached him, just as he was entering his car, that there had been a widespread conspiracy against Mr. Maitland's life, and that Mr. Shackston had been arrested after a desperate fight at the National Club, in the course of which two of its members and one policeman had been killed outright, and seven others taken to hospital.

He did not doubt that this was the subject on which Mr. Maitland now desired to see him, but he felt that he deserved that he should have been consulted at an earlier stage. He had had an uncomfortable feeling for some time past that Mr. Maitland was becoming more perfunctory in his recognition of the distinguished position which he held, as well as wanting in memory of the friendly services which he had rendered at the first establishing of his singular authority. Perhaps, he told himself, it was no more than the sensitiveness of an old man, but, all the same, he meant to make his resentment clear on this occasion. If Mr. Maitland did not require his help, let him manage things in his own way. If he did, let him inform and consult him before the course of events had gone too far for any counsel to turn it. But how seldom do we say what we have planned beforehand! Sir Bardsley sat down to a cold lunch at which there was a somewhat larger party than he had anticipated meeting. It was a pleasant and most complete surprise to find Lady Crystal presiding: it was puzzling to observe that Mr. Maitland's place was un-filled.

"I'm afraid, Sir Bardsley," Lady Crystal explained, "we're not offering you a very good lunch, but it has been necessary to have everything on the buffet, so that we shall not be disturbed till it is over, as I understand Stanley sometimes does, when he is meeting someone with whom he wishes to have an uninterrupted talk of a specially private kind."

Sir Bardsley looked round the table. He saw Lady Jehane and Miss Preston, Lord Rigby Stilton and Selby Ditchfield. All, no doubt, in Mr. Maitland's confidence so far as their own spheres were concerned, but hardly a gathering at which the conversation would be so private that table service must be entirely excluded.

Lady Crystal's presence suggested that the occasion might be of some domestic importance, and this, added to the rumour of plots, and of Shackston's arrest, certainly foreshadowed some interesting revelations, but Sir Bardsley had a strong preference for a hot lunch properly served. Well, no doubt Mr. Maitland would be here in a moment, and would explain.

"I'm afraid," Jehane began, "you won't see Stanley, Sir Bardsley. We had to ask you in his name, because we felt that we ought to consult you without delay, and, among those of us who are here, we've kept the secret so far, but Stanley went out last night in reply to a forged letter that Crystal was supposed to have written, and he's not come back yet."

"But," Sir Bardsley interposed, "I heard a report just before I came here that Mr. Maitland had had Shackston arrested this morning."

"I did that in his name, because Jimmy's mixed up with the letter in some way, and he's the only one we're on the track of at all who may be able to tell where Stanley is. I told Sir Henry to let him know that he'd get hanged in the morning more likely than not, and that, if he'd got anything to say against it, he could ask for me, and I'd see him on Stanley's behalf."

"Has he asked for you?"

"No, not so far. They were to telephone me at once if he did."

"And he was arrested two or three hours ago. Well, there's time yet. I think you'd better tell me the whole tale."

Sir Bardsley's voice was grave, and Jehane felt some sinking of heart as she recognised how promptly he had uncovered the secret worry of her own mind. Jimmy Shackston was evidently in no haste to pour his confidences into her willing ear. Suppose his silence continued, what was she to do next? Perhaps, after all, Sir Bardsley's advice might be worth having.

She found him a good listener. Beyond two or three questions to elucidate minor points in her narrative, he did not interrupt her at all.

When she had finished, he said only, with his usual mildness: "I think, Jehane, you might have consulted me a few hours earlier. And yet the course you have taken may prove successful, as the bolder one often is. It has succeeded to a point already. But it was not one that I could have approved in advance."

He became silent again, and then added: "Before I say one or two words in criticism, I will tell you that I have decided to adopt the position as it now stands, and so far as my influence or authority goes, in the exercising in his absence of Mr. Maitland's peculiar powers, you can rely upon that support.

"Having given you that assurance, I will tell you what I think to be the special dangers we have to face.

"In the first place, I am not as yet greatly concerned for Mr. Maitland's personal safety. His enemies desire to control the power that is in his hands, rather than to execute any personal vengeance. The method you have adopted may succeed in tracing him, in which case it will have justified itself. But, should it fail, its disadvantage is that it has delayed the use of the more obvious methods, and we cannot, even now, put them in operation without a public confession which should now be avoided except as an absolutely last resort.

"I believe the forces which will be found to have united in this attempt are extremely powerful, and they may not collapse, even before the disconcerting attack which you have made upon them.

"You may have been disposed to underestimate the value of publicity in such a position, or the difficulty of concealing anyone in this country against his will, if there be a general determination to find him.

"You will see that there can now be no completely satisfactory termination of the affair unless Mr. Maitland can return before his absence becomes known, and, if possible, without it being known afterwards.

"I confess that I can see nothing more that can be done for the moment. We have only to await the possible results of Mr. Shackston's arrest, and of the offer of amnesty which has been made. Of course, a single confession may be enough to give us all we require."

There was an uncomfortable silence as Sir Bardsley ceased. He had not addressed Jehane personally after the first remarks. His eyes were now upon the pear he was peeling. But the whole strategy had been hers. It was she who had followed Stanley last night to that futile waiting. It was she who had insisted that his absence should not be disclosed while there was a possibility of his returning unnoticed. That expectation she had not entirely abandoned until her interview with Crystal had revealed something of the elaboration of the plot which had trapped him, and the probability that Shackston was among its contrivers.

Then, with a swift audacity, she had used her position as Mr. Maitland's secretary and most frequent medium of communication, to strike, as she had hoped, a paralysing confusion among his foes. Now, if that stroke should fail.... She saw Crystal's anxious eyes on Sir Bardsley's face. She felt that she would be too generous to say any word of criticism, but they both knew that Crystal's way would have been to inform Sir Bardsley at once, to use the organisation of the police in an instant search. Perhaps an authority might have been found for arresting Shackston in a more regular, and even a more effectual, way. Jehane felt that the same doubt was in all their minds.

It was a doubt that was not relieved when Sir Bardsley spoke again.

"As I have said, the course which has been taken may justify itself. It may even prove to be successful as no other would have been likely to be. But it may have another consequence, which it is well that we should consider beforehand.

"Should we learn of Mr. Maitland's present location, whether from Mr. Shackston or another, and should he be in any danger, or strongly held by those who may be disposed to resist his surrender, we have precluded ourselves from requisitioning police or military help unless we would make public denial of the position which we have already set up.

"You needn't worry anyone about that," Rigby said shortly. "Let us know where he is, and there's a dozen fellows here that'll have him out, and be glad of the job. Ay, Selby?"

Selby said: "Damned glad," in a tone that left no doubt of its sincerity. It had been no easy matter to keep their sporting friends together, as the months had gone, and no incident had relieved the monotony of the passing days. But for that little matter of Captain Callover, it would have been an impossible thing.

Jehane was conscious of the loyalty with which Rigby had taken his first opportunity of coming to her defence, but it did nothing to raise her spirits. "Worry anyone"—of course, that meant worry her. Everyone must understand Sir Bardsley's criticism—his condemnation—in the same way. And she was not sure he was wrong.

The broadside she had fired into the ranks of Stanley's enemies had already shut up Jimmy Shackston, a maddened man pacing a felon's cell in a turmoil of mind which could not resolve on the course of action which the occasion required; it would spread wider consternation with the reading of the newspapers which were even now being distributed through the streets. But she could not know this. In the atmosphere of that room she could only feel an uncomfortable sympathy which was itself condemnation.

She rose up, saying: "Well, I'm sorry, Crystal, if I've been a fool. You know that. But I told Sir Henry I'd see him this afternoon, and even if Jimmy won't squeal, I'd better keep my word about that. We've got to carry it through on the lines I started, if there's any way that we can. We all seem agreed about that. Rigby, you might make a mess about Stanley's plate before you ring, and one or two of you go into his room, as though he's got a conference there. Tell them to serve coffee here for the lot when they come back. I think I'll go now."

The telephone bell rang sharply. Miss Trentham reported that she had taken a call from the Assistant-Commissioner, but he desired to speak to Lady Jehane herself. Jehane heard Sir Henry's voice. She listened for some moments while her companions waited in an almost breathless silence. They heard her ask: "Then he doesn't seem frightened?" and then: "Well, tell him I'll come, but he'll have to alter his tone if he wants to come out of this with his neck like it is now." She put down the receiver with something that sounded like a muttered curse in the silence. She looked round, saying: "Jimmy seems to be on his hind legs. It's no use saying anything more now. It's up to me. I know that. I'll do what I can."

Sir Bardsley said kindly: "I'm sure you'll do that, my dear."

Crystal caught her hand and held it a second as she passed her chair.

With such encouragements, she went to a battle of wits and bluff with the Hon James Shackston, with Stanley Maitland's life, and perhaps with a few more important matters, as the stakes for which they played.

CHAPTER FIFTY-SEVEN

THE HON. JAMES SHACKSTON was a successful politician, which may not be synonymous with saying that he was an expert liar, but it may be generally conceded that there is no inherent improbability in the two descriptions being applicable to the same man.

He was used to lies, both in act and word. He expected them to appear, and he believed himself to be skilful in their detection.

In considering the probable consequences of the disappearance of Mr. Maitland, he had concluded that his immediate followers would either run about in confusion, as aimlessly as a hen that has lost her head, or that, if they should retain sufficient self-control, they would inform Sir Bardsley Clinton, who would deal with the situation in his own way, and with the propriety of the head of His Majesty's Government.

He had anticipated excitement at Scotland Yard, with instant military and police activity, and much spectacular motion of flying squads. There would be radio and press appeals, worded in the different manners of these two mediums of publicity.

But of all these they had been assured by Mr. Rinkwater that they need have no dread. No consumption of petrol nor printers' ink, no bellowing of loud speakers, would result in the disturbance of the Burfleet Institution, or the removal of Mr. George Thompson from its embracing walls.

In an acute and active brain, Mr. Shackston had also considered the possibility of efforts being made to identify the kidnappers, and had seen the possibility that Lady Crystal's letter (or rather its substitute) might be discovered, and this line of investigation lead back to himself. But he had little fear of this, for he considered that if it were traced at all (which was doubtful), and if Lady Crystal were disposed to assist the search (which he thought unlikely), and if she should direct enquiry towards himself (for which there could be no support but her own word, with a very vague accusation at most), the time which these enquiries would take would probably be a matter of days, and the whole episode would be brought to finality at an earlier hour.

At the worst, he anticipated that he might be questioned by the police, and he prepared his reply. That being done, he turned his mind to more important and more probable things.

He had no thought of being in any personal danger. The combination of political, social, commercial, and financial forces which had united to secure the overthrow of the Maitland autocracy was too powerful for the security of those who represented it to be lightly menaced. With Maitland himself removed, what head of opposition would remain to face them? Sir Bardsley Clinton! Well, they would know how to deal with him. The old dodderer would be shaking in those absurdly old-fashioned carpet-slippers which he was known to wear in his own home.

When the morning came without any alarm being raised, Mr. Shackston, stretching his legs before the comfort of the smoking-room fire (for the morning was chilly, though the season was that of the later spring), concluded either that Mr. Maitland had announced last night that he was going out for an uncertain time, and left instructions that no fuss was to be made if he did not return till the next day, or else that Sir Bardsley Clinton had been informed, and was in too great a funk to make public announcement of the catastrophe.

After the unexpected excitement of his arrest, and on recovering some measure of self-control in the privacy of a police cell, he turned his thoughts from the folly of his own behaviour in losing his temper and head together, and considered the position with sufficient acuteness to come to the conclusion that Maitland had not escaped. He had (he thought) underestimated the courage and decision of Sir Bardsley Clinton. He recalled that that elderly gentleman, in the course of a long political career, had usually come out on top, and that there had been a previous occasion when he had confounded his enemies by a prompt audacity which his established character had given them no reason to anticipate.

He saw that if the forgery of Lady Crystal's letter had been discovered yesterday, according to the disconcerting hint which Inspector Courtland had given, the subsequent procedure would have had some almost certain differences. On the other hand, a partial disclosure of the truth, arising in the course of the first hurried investigations following the discovery of Maitland's disappearance, would be likely to point suspicion in his direction, while giving no clue to those who were associated with him. In fact, apart from the difference that he attributed too much to Sir Bardsley, and too little to Jehane's part in the matter, he guessed very near to the truth.

What, he asked himself, should he do or say in such circumstances? Obviously as little, and that as late, as he possibly could.

Time was the one thing required, the one essential of victory, time for Maitland to give way, or be coerced into surrender, time for the powerful interests which were associated with him to assert their strength. To betray them, or to embarrass them by an individual capitulation, would be to betray himself also. Lady Jehane would see him, if he wished? No doubt she would. No doubt she would be glad to do so. A very clumsy trap.

So far, his mind was confident, and his course clear. But with the dismissal of the idea that he was in any personal danger, the enormity of the outrage which had been directed upon him, and the annoyance of this confinement, reasserted themselves. He had an important social engagement at home tonight. He had promised his wife that he would not fail to be back in time. He ought to be starting in a couple of hours from now. He could not delay some explanation. What would that energetic American woman do when she learnt that he was jailed like this?

On an impulse to break the net, if a sufficient protest could do it, he asked to see the Assistant-Commissioner, and Sir Henry very promptly came.

Mr. Shackston did not attempt to placate his jailer with any aspect of courtesy. He commenced in his more truculent manner: "I'd just like to hear from your own mouth by what right you think you can hold me here." He added, with a threat which was scarcely veiled: "I want to know who'll have the job of paying for this when I get out."

Sir Henry Ballard was a man of a stiff formality. He was as unlikely to submit to browbeating as to attempt it himself. He answered with a direct precision. "You have already been informed of the authority under which I am acting. You were arrested on the order of Mr. Stanley Maitland. My present instructions are that you will be hanged tomorrow."

"You daren't do such a thing as that."

"I shall, of course, do nothing without the necessary legal authority."

"Which you won't get."

"Then you have nothing to fear."

Mr. Shackston would have liked to say that he had excellent reason for believing that Mr. Maitland could not have issued any instruction for his arrest that morning, but a vein of caution which controlled even his more bellicose moods forbade him to do so. How could he tell to what purpose such an admission might not be used against him? For if he were innocent of complicity in Mr. Maitland's abduction, what reason could he have for asserting his absence now?

He went as near the truth as he dared when he said: "I don't believe there is any plot, except the one that's landed me here, and I mean to make those concerned feel more than a bit sick about that before they're through. I'd bet you an even tenner that you're being pulled on a string. How do you know that the order isn't forged?"

"I am fully satisfied of the authority on which I am acting."

"Well, you'll look a bit worse than silly, if it turns out that you've been had. Why not ring up Maitland himself, and make sure?

I'll bet you any sum you like you'll be put off with a tale that he's out somewhere."

"As Mr. Maitland seldom leaves the Rafton, that is entirely improbable."

"I thought your man said you'd arrested me for luring him out."

Sir Henry Ballard looked at his prisoner with a silent keenness before which the assurance of Mr. Shackston's manner suffered some diminution. He answered drily: "We are aware when Mr. Maitland leaves the hotel. He went out shortly before nine o'clock last night, and returned at about six-thirty. He has not been out since."

Mr. Shackston had a good ear for the truth, as liars often have. He recognised the note of sincerity in Sir Henry's voice, and his confidence fell. Sir Henry spoke as one who has the assurance of a personal knowledge. If it were true, Mr. Shackston felt that he was in a jeopardy such as he had not imagined until that moment. Yet, if it were true, why were not others arrested beside himself? Why did Lady Jehane offer that transparent interview?

Sir Henry Ballard watched his discomfiture. It amounted, in his judgment, to little less than a proof of guilt.

"I think, Mr. Shackston," he said, with a grave formality, "you will do well to take your position seriously. Very seriously indeed."

He was in the act of withdrawing when his prisoner called after him "You can send Maitland's bitch in, if she wants to come."

Sir Henry turned back. He was aware of the popular idea respecting Mr. Maitland's relations with his sister-in-law. The noun which Mr. Shackston had used was a favourite with him. We have heard him use it before. But it is one which, for some occult reason (it being entirely inoffensive) no woman likes to have applied to herself. Sir Henry replied, with sincerity: "I can take no message in such a form."

"I will see Lady Jehane Maitland," Mr. Shackston said, rather sulkily, and Sir Henry went without further words.

CHAPTER FIFTY-EIGHT

JEHANE'S two-seater ran with a defiant swiftness through the diminished congestion of the London traffic. She had no fear of being stopped officially in this era of recovered freedom. It was merely the duty of the police to take the number of every car which moved to the common danger, and a formal notification would be received on the following day. The receipt of three such notices, unless formal appeal were made against them, meant that the delinquent would not drive in England again, and even a single one would be an almost automatic verdict of manslaughter if he should be the cause of any subsequent fatality. The absurdity of suspending a licence for a few months, and then exposing the lives of pedestrians once again to the sporting chance that a man's character might change, his drinking cease, or his driving capacity improve with lack of practice, was gone, it may be hoped forever; as was the fining system which allowed the wealthy to endanger the peace of their fellows for a moderate tariff, which did not even go into the pockets of those whom they might annoy, but into the unbottomed folly and waste of the public purse.

More than one watchful constable pulled out his notebook as he noticed the swift rush and listened to the impatient hoot of the approaching car, and one was already writing down its number before he recognised who its driver was, and put a thickly obliterating pencil across a foolish note. For the superstition that all men are equal, or should be equally treated, which had never been logically observed, was now also a fading dream.

Should they report Mr. Maitland's secretary for the dangerous folly of rushing at more than fifteen miles an hour through the busy London streets, it was a reasonable supposition that she would be able to reply with a statement of such urgent business as would justify the risk she took. They gave her the same consideration that they would have shown to the red cross on a surgeon's car.

Giving no thought to such questions, Jehane found herself very quickly shaking hands with Sir Henry Ballard, and remarking, in as confident a tone as she could control, that she was afraid she had given him a rather difficult prisoner.

But Sir Henry's mind was on another matter. He put her remark aside with an indifferent, "Oh, we're used to all sorts. That kind of bluster doesn't cut any ice here." And went on to say, "I think, Lady Jehane, it's only due to my Department to put this report before you. It seems that Mr. Maitland was seen both to leave the Rafton last night, and to return early this morning. I will admit that the report should have come rather more quickly to my own hand. But its importance was not sufficiently understood. I'm afraid I have to admit also that Mr. Maitland's identity was not recognised. Probably that was how he wished it to be. You see, he does not often make any public appearance, and photographs are a poor substitute for familiarity with walk and figure."

"Yes," Jehane said vaguely, "I can understand that. I'm sure your men didn't overlook anything." The truth appeared to go even further than that. They could see people who were not there.

"Thank you," Sir Henry replied, with a faint note of gratification in his formal tones. "I should be obliged if you would inform Mr. Maitland that that report has been laid before you."

"Yes, yes, of course." She wondered whether she were asleep or awake. Yet the explanation was a very simple thing. A young and vigilant officer had actually observed that there was one more than usual in the little group of servants who left the hotel. When he was subjected that morning to a sharp interrogation from a worried superior, he had replied to that effect, and when the unfortunate man who had succeeded him on duty during the night had understood that the unknown figure was that of Mr. Maitland, and that he had returned to the hotel in the early morning, he had lacked the moral courage to say that he had not observed the additional figure in the morning group. From this interrogation had resulted the definitely worded report which had been rushed on to Sir Henry's table with such celerity that it had appeared to have been already on the way when his first sharp queries had startled his subordinates with the fear of one of those departmental enquiries which all peace-and-pension-loving officers have the sense to dread.

Sir Henry had some reason for the confidence with which he had assured Mr. Shackston that Mr. Maitland had returned in safety.

"Mr. Maitland," Jehane said, "asked me to say that he wished me to interrogate Mr. Shackston absolutely alone. He doesn't wish that I should be overheard at all. He thinks that is the only way in which Mr. Shackston is likely to make the confession which it may be of national importance to obtain."

Sir Henry looked his dissent, and she wondered uncomfortably whether those who are accustomed to tell the truth really do make the most convincing liars (as she remembered reading somewhere) when they put their backs into it.

But Sir Henry did not doubt that she spoke with Mr. Maitland's authority. He only felt that he would have been glad to have had it done in another way.

"He's in a rough mood," he said doubtfully.

"I'm not afraid of him."

"No, I shouldn't say that you are. But, you know, Lady Jehane, it's wonderful what we can persuade them to say when we get round them for a few hours, and they get flurried, and start contradicting themselves."

Jehane had a moment's doubt—which was not the first—as to whether it might not have been better to take Sir Henry into an earlier and completer confidence. His tone did not suggest any particular affection for the man of whom they were talking. But she could not suppose that he would have arrested him in such circumstances, and, if he had, he would have incurred a responsibility which might have proved his ruin—no, it would not have been fair to him. Anyway, it was too late for regret now.

"I dare say that's how it will end," she said hopefully. "Mr. Maitland's giving him this chance as he's asked for it, and if he hasn't the sense to use it in the right way, I've no doubt he'll come into your hands, and you'll turn him inside out. We know he substituted a forged letter for one he got Lady Crystal to write, and that ought to give you a good start."

Sir Henry looked more cheerful at this conditional promise, and Jehane, conscious that the last remark went somewhat beyond anything of which they had certain knowledge, realised that the path of mendacity is a very slippery one, and had the sense to say no more till she found herself face to face with Mr. Shackston, and was assured that she was alone with that gentleman.

"Well," he said, "a nice mess you've made of it now."

"Have I?" she said cheerfully. "You don't look as though you've had a very pleasant morning yourself."

Mr. Shackston scowled at this allusion to his somewhat dishevelled appearance, and the fact that one side of his coat was torn about a foot down from the collar.

"Now look here, Lady Jehane," he said angrily, "you know who's responsible for this outrage, and you know the bluff's failed, and he'd give his ears to get out of it now."

"Who do you mean?"

"Clinton, of course."

"He had nothing to do with it at all."

"Then who had?"

"Didn't they read the warrant to you, or something? They ought to have told you that."

"They told me a lot of lies. You don't suppose I really think it's Maitland that's done this?"

"If you don't, it only shows that you knew all about what happened last night, and that you're in the right place now."

"It doesn't show anything of the kind. Suppose I did hear something about it, it's not my business to protect him." He watched her keenly as he said this, and then laughed derisively. "I tell you Maitland's gone, and he isn't back now, let Ballard say what he will."

"If you'd seen the report on Sir Henry's table, you'd have seen that the police saw Mr. Maitland leave the hotel last night, and return early today."

"And if that were true, you'd know a lot more than you do now."

The suspicion which had been in his mind from the first had become a certainty as he had watched her reaction to the idea that he might have knowledge of what was happening without actual complicity. If Maitland had escaped, there could be no doubt about that. She would not have been sent to interview him here without being told that he was one of the little party last night. And as he looked at her, another idea entered his mind, to be received with incredulity, and then with a dawning recognition of a startling truth.

"So it isn't Clinton? You damned young vixen," he said savagely. "I believe you've done this off your own bat."

"You can think what you like," she answered, with a rising anger that faced his own without fear, "but if you hope to get out of here alive, you'd better talk rather differently."

"You needn't worry about me," he answered, with more confidence than he felt; "when this game's played, I'll be out of here, and if you're not doing five years' hard, it'll be because you've begged off in the right way."

She controlled her temper to the realisation that the interview was not going as she had meant it to do. Would it not be better to admit the truth, and argue frankly from the actual power which was in her hands, now that she had Sir Bardsley's support? And while she hesitated, he began again, having checked his own temper in a similar mood.

"Now just listen to me, Lady Jehane, and you'll hear more sense than you'll ever get out of your own head. I'm not asking what Maitland is to you. Everyone knows that. I suppose you were bound to put up a bit of fight, but this thing's too big for that, and you may be doing him more harm than good, and something you'll get no thanks for, even from him.

"I'm not going to admit anything. We'll say we both know he's at the Rafton now, and he sent you here. But if we're both wrong, and he's somewhere else, where you don't want him to stay, then he's got just one chance, and that is for me to see what I can do to make peace before anything worse happens, and I can't do that while I'm shut up here. Suppose they heard of what's happened to me, and got a bit rattled, and thought it would be safest to do him in? You couldn't blame me for that."

"I should kill you for that," she answered, with a quiet determination, "if I had to do it with my own hands. Crystal would, if I didn't."

He answered her with a short laugh. "You'd find you're wrong about that. It's all silly talk about forging letters. I couldn't do such a thing if I tried all night. Lady Crystal's in this as deep as anyone." He added pointedly: "You can't wonder at that."

It was a shot at random which might have hit, but which went badly astray. He thought that if she believed her sister to be involved in the plot, she might be more disposed to come to such terms as would set him free. How could he tell how much she might merely guess, how little she might know?

She looked at him with contempt. "If you can't think of anything better than that—! Mr. Maitland is returning to Norchester House on Monday."

He heard the accent of truth in her voice, and the answer confused and disconcerted him with the evidence of something which did not fit the facts as he supposed them to be, but he waved it aside. "Maitland can go where he likes, if he's come to terms before then, and if he hasn't he'll have lost any chance—".

She broke in swiftly: "Then you admit the whole thing?"

"I don't admit anything. I only tell you I know ways I could help if you weren't so silly as to keep me here."

"If you want to get out, there's only one way, and that's to tell all you know."

"Oh, no, it isn't. You'll get no word from me on such terms as that."

"Mr. Shackston," she said slowly, "I'll give you a last chance." (But was it a last chance, she thought, for him, or for the success of her own effort—perhaps for Stanley's life?) "If you won't talk to me, Sir Henry says he can make you in his own ways, and I think he'll be glad of the job. They don't call it the third degree here, but when they take their coats off to it in earnest I expect it comes to much the same thing."

"You damned bitch! Ballard wouldn't dare, not without an order that you know you can't get. You daren't."

"I dare do a lot more. I don't know how this is going to end, but it's going to be unpleasant for you. Sir Bardsley's promised to back us up about that. Hadn't you better tell me what I want to know? You'd be out in half an hour if you'd do that."

There was a long moment's silence. Jehane saw the hesitation in his eyes, and it seemed for one instant that the victory was to be hers. But when he spoke, he only said sullenly: "You'll get nothing from me. You'd better clear. You'll be singing a different tune before long."

She went back to Sir Henry Ballard. She might recognise defeat in her own mind, but that was no reason why she should admit it to others. She said: "You weren't far wrong about him. He keeps admitting things, and then drawing back. I expect he'll be ready to make a statement if you leave him quiet for an hour or two to think it over. If not, I'm sure you'll know how to get it in the best way. I'll send you Sir Bardsley's authority to use your own judgment how to make him talk. He knows who forged the letter, if he didn't do it himself."

Sir Henry said drily: "You can trust us to know how to deal with him." He thought she should have realised from the first that it wasn't a woman's work. With a deferential politeness to rank and youth and beauty, and perhaps most of all to Mr. Maitland's confidential secretary (and probable mistress), he walked down beside her to the pavement, and opened the door of her waiting car.

CHAPTER FIFTY-NINE

THERE was still one chance, one desperate chance, Jehane thought, as she steered her way back through the thickening traffic of the later day. Sir Bardsley must be persuaded to use such authority as he (or the Home Secretary) might have with Sir Henry Ballard, to take whatever steps might be necessary to make Jimmy Shackston open his mouth, and, in view of what they wanted to get out of it when it did open, that would involve a full disclosure to Sir Henry of the real position, and of the extent to which he had been deceived already. How would he take that?

Well, it was for Sir Bardsley to deal with as he thought best. She was less sure of herself than she had been, though she recognised the need for action as more urgent than ever as she recalled the threat that Jimmy had made that his arrest might drive his fellow-conspirators to more hurried and drastic action. She put on her brakes sharply, swerved, and skidded, and scraped the varnish from a standing car. Why didn't the man look where he was going? After all, in spite of all Stanley had done, there was still one fatal accident a day in the British Isles, and, if so, why hadn't she as much right to it as anyone else?

She knew Stanley said that even those few hundred had got to stop. But the motor trade said they weren't worth talking about. Look at the scores of thousands of people they used to bury, and nobody seemed to care in the least. The victims were dead, and their relatives had their pockets filled, and the traffic whirled ahead, and it was all very jolly indeed. And yet when Stanley had hanged two or three dozen motorists, what a fuss there had been! The value of human lives seemed to have gone up in the night.

Anyway, she couldn't stop at such a moment to bother about the varnish of that car. It wasn't her fault if the wheel skidded. It was the greasy road. She'd got to get back to Sir Bardsley the first second she could. A closed car passed her, from the interior of which someone raised his hat. It was only a moment's glimpse, but she felt sure that she had recognised Sir Bardsley Clinton, and that he looked like a man who had just had some good news.

Puzzled by that swift glimpse, and annoyed that she would not find him awaiting her return, she pressed her foot viciously on the accelerator. Two minutes later she entered the Rafton Hotel, and made her way to Stanley's room where she expected that Crystal and the others would be waiting to hear the tale of her failure. She entered to find Crystal and Rigby and Selby Ditchfield leaning over the table from which the lunch had been cleared, and on which a large map was spread open. They did not even look up as she came in.

Instinctively she felt a difference of temperature, though she could not understand it, and her voice had its natural buoyancy as she began: "When you've quite finished settling your summer holidays, perhaps you'd kindly…."

Rigby looked up apologetically: "Oh, I say…you don't know, of course. We've had a man here named Cherrington, and he just spit it all out. They've got Stanley in the Burfleet Institution. It's a lunatic asylum somewhere in London. We're just looking it up. We're going to make up a little party to fetch him out after dark."

"I suppose Sir Bardsley knows all about it?"

"Yes, he's going to have a few words with Plumpton Marshall, so that he'll have the police on the alert without telling them too much, in case Sturgeon gets the wind up, and tries to move him again."

"Who's Sturgeon?"

"Professor Sturgeon, the brain specialist. He's the man that's got him now."

"But—I thought he'd been transported. I'm sure that was—"

"So it was, but he got a substitute somehow. Cherrington half admitted that there might be other cases besides his."

"Where's this Cherrington now?"

Crystal said: "We couldn't let him go. He might have given us away in turn if they'd got at him from the other side. Selby's made him safe."

Selby looked up with a smile. "He wanted us to know that he's a good man. One of his companies lent twenty-three millions to the Government during the war. We didn't ask how much it had had back. He seemed to think it was very patriotic of him to have had it tucked away ready for such an emergency. He's in one of the pantries now, handcuffed to a Royal Scots Fusilier, who's got instructions to knock him on the head if he says anything except to ask for a drink.

"It sounds safe enough. But we mustn't lose any time getting Stanley out, all the same. Professor Sturgeon won't exactly love him, and Jimmy seemed to think that having locked him up might make the others inclined to...to...anything Jimmy says is almost sure to be wrong."

She had changed her sentence from its natural ending as she had observed the anxiety on her sister's face. But Rigby confirmed her warning: "Cherrington said much the same thing in his own way."

"I thought we ought to start at once," Crystal said, "but Sir Bardsley said we mustn't try anything till after dark. He wants Stanley got back now without anyone ever knowing that he's been away."

"It isn't only that," Selby added, "it may be safer if we can pull off a surprise. If we march up to the door with a row of bayonets, there's no knowing what a man like Sturgeon might try on, if he thought he was done for himself, and he can't expect much after a second innings like this."

"It won't be dark for three or four hours yet. It seems a long time to wait."

"It won't make so much difference really. We've got to get there, and there'll be a bit of smelling round to do before we start breaking in.

"It does seem a long time," Crystal added, "but I think they're right, all the same. You ought to let Miss Trentham know you're back; she's having calls all the time."

"What about?"

"Enquiries about Stanley, and what's happened, and wanting to speak to him or to you. There seems to be a suspicion that something's wrong, and neither of you being able to answer—".

"I see. Well, they can be switched on to me now. I'll try to give them the right talk. Mrs. Shackston been on? No, I couldn't stand her just now. Besides I shouldn't know what to say. Miss Trentham had better tell her to get some more insurance on Jimmy's life if she knows how. Perhaps Mr. Cherrington'd see to that."

"There seems to be a long drive to the back, from what looks like a quiet road," Rigby was saying. "That ought to be our way. If we could get a good ladder at that side before we were seen. A fire-escape'd be the best thing."

"How many are you meaning to take?" Jehane asked.

"About a dozen. That ought to be enough. Sir Bardsley said we aren't to stand any nonsense. The only thing that matters is that we bring Stanley off, and if there's any resistance, we're just to shoot our way through, and he'll see that we don't get into trouble for that."

"You're not going, Crystal?"

"Yes, I am."

"We shan't let Lady Crystal get into any danger," Selby assured her.

"You'll find she'll please herself about that," Jehane answered "No, I'm not coming. I wish I were, but I'm needed here. Besides, Rigby knows I can't shoot straight. Crystal's different. She's always been rather good at the birds, and if she can shoot a decent thing like a pheasant, she ought to enjoy potting Professor Sturgeon."

"I don't suppose there'll be any shooting," Rigby said. "We ought to manage better than that; and anyway, we shan't want Crystal to help."

"I don't care how you manage so that you bring Stanley back safely, and Professor Sturgeon along too. You'll need him if you want to call it a good bag."

"And if I bring both—?" Rigby asked. Their eyes met in a duel which was understood without words.

"Oh, well, if you bring both."

"That's a promise?"

"You can call it that if you like."

"I reckon that brings the Professor here," Rigby said grimly, with little foresight of how he would keep his word in the end.

Jehane watched them go with a smile and a confident word, but with an inward bitterness. She didn't want to stay, but she knew that she was more likely to be of use where she was. Besides, it was Crystal's place, not hers, and there had been enough of the sort of talk that she had ignored from Jimmy Shackston that afternoon.

It was about three hours later that Miss Trentham rang up, saying that someone wanted to speak to her very urgently, but would give no name. "It sounds like Mr. Maitland's voice," she added in a puzzled way.

"Oh, put him through—put him through," Jehane answered with an excitement in her voice which caused a look of comprehension to cross Miss Trentham's face in the room below. "So that was really it, all the while," she said, as she put the speaker through. But she was a good secretary, and no one would ever know what she had guessed, to her life's end.

"Jehane," the voice said, "is that you? I want help sent at once. You'd better phone the police-station in North London nearest to the Burfleet Institution, and tell them to break in back and front, and at any cost. They'd better come armed, and be prepared for some resistance, though it may collapse when they arrive, if nothing much has happened before then.

"I'm in a room on the first floor. Yes, I suppose you can hear. They're firing at the lock to break in the door. There'll be a row when they get in, but I may hold them off for a time. I've got a loaded revolver myself."

"Listen, Stanley. You won't have to wait long. There's Rigby and a whole lot of his boys just about due to get in by the back way; so make the time pass if you can. Crystal's with them as well. Yes, Crystal. She didn't write that letter. It was just a fake. I told you it wasn't her style. And I've got Jumping Jimmy in the lock-up, wondering what's to come next. Baron Michelson? I hadn't heard about him. I expect Crystal has, but I was out. We've got a man named Cherrington in the pantry chained to a Scots Fusilier."

She stopped with the instinctive perception, which we all know, that she had no longer an auditor. Quickly, one after the other, she heard two reports, dull, but louder than those she had heard before. After that there was silence.

It was about three hours later that Lord Rigby Stilton walked into the room, carrying a parcel of very moderate size.

With an anxious expression on his face, he laid it upon the table, and undid the string. Spreading it out, he disclosed a little pile of calcined ashes.

"Rigby," Jehane said in a puzzled expostulation, "what on earth have you got there? Why don't you say anything? Is Stanley all right?"

"Yes, *they're* all right," he said rather gloomily. "They're coming upstairs now. But I asked them to let me get this over first."

"Get what over?"

"Professor Sturgeon."

"You mean—". Horror, incredulity, and a dawning conviction followed across her face. Of course. That was how Feltham had gone. But being told isn't like seeing.

"You say that's Professor Sturgeon?"

"Yes."

"*All* of him?"

"All I could get out of the grate."

"Is it…"—Jehane wanted to be fair, but it was not the kind of wager to be too lightly decided—"…is it more than half?"

Rigby looked doubtfully at the little heap. Honestly, he was not sure. He did not wish to fail in sportsmanship, but then he expected an equal standard from her also, as they both knew. "Well, if you think that's sporting—" he said, with a note of bitterness which she lacked the heart to ignore.

"No," she said, "if you put it like that, I'm not quite sure that it is."

CHAPTER SIXTY

IT had been rather late in the day before Professor Sturgeon read of the arrest of Mr. Shackston, and the invitation to the conspirators to surrender at the Rafton, which Jehane had issued to the afternoon press.

Up to that time, he had left his new inmate alone, and had even instructed the asylum attendants that George Thompson was to be treated with some special consideration, as his mental condition had not yet been definitely ascertained.

To this measure of self-denial (for such it was), he had been persuaded by the curt and emphatic directions of Baron Michelson, who had made it clear that an exact obedience was essential to the securing of the immunities and rewards to follow.

He did not fail to observe that if he should secure the monopoly of Feltham's secret, the power at which that unfortunate scientist had aimed, and Maitland exercised, would pass into his own hands, and he was resolved to possess it. But he was not equally resolute to secure it, to the betrayal of his colleagues, for his exclusive use.

It was not that he would have been withheld by any principle of honour, arising from the fact that the Baron had saved him from a hateful exile, and the degradation of menial toils, nor that he had received the Burfleet Institution as a first munificent gift in evidence of the rewards which would be freely available to the man who could take over and understand the secret knowledge which was in Maitland's hands, but not in his mind, like a manuscript in an unknown tongue.

He knew that honour is an empty sound, without any specific gravity. Gratitude will never be precipitated in any test-tube. Such words were of the chatter of children, before scientific investigation had traced them backward to the primitive instincts from which they rise. Such emotions are for analysis only. If we observe them in ourselves, we are interested in an atavistic impulse curiously transformed. We control it firmly, recognising with humility the humble origins from which we have evolved ourselves.

But the Professor had never been seriously inconvenienced by the self-assertion of altruistic virtues. He was aware of certain instincts of cruelty, greed, and caution which might have been harder to check. But he saw no reason to attempt that difficult enterprise, recognising them as of a protective quality.

With an equal selfishness, he lacked the raw vitality which had given direction to Feltham's dreams. His strongest lust was for the exploration of bodies and brains in which the blood still beat. If the once-dancing peeress who had inflamed the crude imagination of William Feltham had come to the Professor also in some unholy vision, she would have been writhing conscious on the dissecting-table, rather than lifting arms of invitation from a couch of flowers.

The control of the five-dozen of wretched beings over whom he had now become the presiding deity, was alone sufficient to give him assurance of many pleasurable excitements. That, and much beside, was to be the reward of loyalty to the Baron and his associates. He was unlikely to take the risks of adventuring on a separate enterprise while their schemes went well.

He read the afternoon news while partaking of the weak tea and one piece of unbuttered toast which would be his sufficient sustenance till he reached the frugality of his evening meal; for like most men who work with brain rather than body, and have reduced the latter to an efficient subordination, he was of abstemious habits.

He read with some disquiet, but without panic. He had a deep contempt for politicians in general, and for the Hon. James Shackston in particular. That he should be in a mess seemed a very natural thing. Apart from that, he had exceptional reason for deciding that the reports he was reading must be largely lies. No one had disturbed him. He touched the bell, and asked for a report of George Thompson. He was soon reassured with the knowledge that he had been exercised with the less violent of his fellow-inmates, and had just been returned to his own cell.

Professor Sturgeon decided that whatever Mr. Maitland's friends might know, it didn't include the vital fact that he had got him locked up here. Doubtless Baron Michelson had the position in hand.

Having finished his toast, he returned to the study of a list of the inmates of the Institution which was now his. He considered their medical history. He referred to the circumstances in which they had been deposited, the attitude of their friends, and the amount of the remunerations which would end with their deaths. He ticked with a blue pencil the names of five on whom it might be interesting and inexpensive to operate at an early date.

But while he did this, his mind continued to dwell upon the all-important enterprise on the success of which all his pleasant dreams of exploring the recesses of the human cranium must depend. Should Mr. Maitland recover his authority, it would be exile for him, at the best. At the worst, it might be a broken neck. For an eminent scientist to die of a broken neck is a very terrible thing.

He was not rash enough to attempt to establish telephonic contact with Baron Michelson, and he assumed correctly that that gentleman would not adventure anything so transparently foolish; but it occurred to him that this unforeseen development might be held by the Baron to excuse him if he should endeavour to bring Mr. Maitland to a prompt decision, or he might even expect such a course of conduct from him. He might be blamed for a resulting failure, should he let the opportunity go by, while he knew that Mr. Maitland's friends were active upon the trail. Indeed, in such circumstances, it might matter little whether he were blamed or not. He must secure a decision for the sake of his own skin.

On arriving at this conclusion, he rang for Mr. William Broughton, the chief officer or "nurse" of the establishment, with the intention of asking that George Thompson should be brought before him.

Mr. Broughton presented himself with the announcement that he had been about to come for instructions as to how he should deal with the same inmate.

Mr. Broughton was a large, broadly-built man whose normal manner was of a bluff and jesting brutality. He could be good-humoured and even kindly to the less troublesome patients, and there were few whose insanity was sufficiently dense to render them incapable of appreciating the dangers of his robuster moments.

Mr. Broughton's present difficulty was a question of discipline. Soapy, having refused to come in when his period of exercise was ended, had been properly cuffed by one of the attendants. George Thompson had interfered, and James Thomson had been knocked down in a resulting scuffle, with indications of a broken nose. Mr.

Broughton would have dealt with the incident on the spot, but had been restrained by the instructions he had received concerning the comparative sanctity of George Thompson until further orders.

The Professor, apart from a moment's indication of anger during verbal confusion as to the Thompson or Thomson who had been removed from the scene of action in a damaged condition, received the report without emotion, and merely said at its conclusion: "I'll deal with this, Broughton. Bring George Thompson to me."

"What if he won't come?"

"I don't think you will find any difficulty about that. I don't wish you to use any violence. In the event of difficulty you must let me know." Mr. Broughton departed on his errand with more satisfaction than he would have readily admitted at the peaceful limitation of the instructions he had received. Mr. Maitland had shown a capacity for hard hitting which we have had no previous occasion to observe, and which James Thomson (who had been doing him no harm!) had found to be of an extremely disconcerting kind.

A few minutes later, George Thompson, having required no physical persuasion to secure his presence, appeared in Mr. Broughton's escort, and was requested by Professor Sturgeon to take a seat with a politeness which reduced Mr. Broughton to a puzzled wonder as to the kind of man that his new master would turn out to be.

"I shan't want you again, Broughton, until I ring. I may be some time with Mr. Thompson, and I don't want to be disturbed," the Professor said, and then rose to follow the retreating attendant into the passage, and give the further instruction: "You'd better wait by the end window. Have a couple of men with you, and come at once if I ring. You'd hear the bell from there. He might turn violent at any moment, though I don't think he will."

He came back to face the man who had cleaned out his laboratories and condemned him to ignominious exile only a few weeks ago, and who had now fallen into his power.

They looked at one another for a few minutes without speaking. The Professor was unsure how it would be best to begin, and Stanley had no intention of doing so. He waited his opponent's opening in a wary silence.

"I sent for you," the Professor said at last, "because you have now had time to consider your position, and I thought you might have something you would like to say."

Stanley would have liked to say a good deal the expediency of which would have been less than doubtful. He contented himself with replying: "I undertook to give my decision in forty-eight hours to you, and to those who are associated with you. I fail to see why I should give it to you alone in less than half the time."

"Yet there might be reasons," the Professor suggested. "Then I should like to know what they are."

Professor Sturgeon's practised vices were not those of the diplomatic service. Faced by this direct question he hardly knew what to say. But he knew what he wanted, and he knew the power that was in his hands. He took the shortest cut to his goal when he answered: "It is no longer possible to give you the time for which you asked owing to the actions of your own friends. It is necessary that we should have an immediate decision."

"So your gang are on the run already?"

"I didn't say that. While you are hidden here, the advantage is on our side, but we do not intend to run the risk of delay."

"Suppose you let Baron Michelson know that I am prepared to discuss the terms of a friendly settlement with him?"

"He wouldn't come. He might be followed. You must settle this with me now."

"Suppose I should write the formula out for you here—what assurance should I have that I should be released, and the other conditions observed?"

"You've got the Baron's promise. The terms are nothing to do with me. If we've got the formula, you don't matter to us."

Stanley was sceptical on that point. He thought that he might contrive to matter a good deal. Yet the Professor, knowing that he lacked the technical knowledge which would have enabled him to exploit Feltham's invention in any separate way, might honestly take that view. Or he might not. Stanley had no intention of letting that terrible power loose upon the world. Yet he knew that his refusal, if it were accepted as final, would place him in an instant peril. He had been threatened with insanity, the infliction of which is perhaps the most ghastly power which penetration into the secrets of creation has placed in the hands of man. Even at that cost, he felt that he must not give way. Even though he must disappear from the knowledge of men, and be no more than George Thompson the imbecile victim of Professor Sturgeon's experiments, the secret must be kept. He had good reason to know that he could not give away when in a condition of imbecility that which he withheld now. He had taken certain precautions a week ago.

"It seems to me that you are asking me to trust you a good deal."

"Really, Mr. Maitland, I don't see that you have much choice."

"I have the choice of refusal."

"Which would entail unpleasant consequences to yourself which I don't wish to mention. If you'll look at it sensibly, you'll see that you have no choice. Even if you were to make the murderous attack upon myself which you have been considering for some minutes, it would do you no good. There is a bell under my foot. In thirty seconds you would be overcome, and your fate certain."

"Suppose I go into the next room, and write out what I know of Feltham's invention, and the formula which controls its action, and bring them back here, and we talk the position over quietly? Couldn't we fix up something between ourselves, without Shackston and the rest coming into it at all?"

The Professor looked tempted, and yet afraid.

"You see, Professor, you could have all Feltham's papers—they are at the Rafton now—and they'd mean a lot more to you than they do to me. We could do more together than I can ever do alone."

The Professor was silent, in a nervous hesitation which he was unable to hide. He could not make up his mind whether he wished to be treacherous to Stanley or to his fellow-conspirators, or whether to both or neither. But the formula by some means he must get, and it began to look as though success were within his reach. He was in a trembling excitement which he controlled with difficulty.

Stanley saw his condition, and went on, without waiting for a reply.

"Suppose I write it all out, and bring it back to you here, and you give me a cup of tea—you don't overfeed your guests at this institution, Professor—and I go over it with you. There are some things that may take a bit of explaining. And suppose we strike a bargain then? And, by the way, Professor, there's one thing I ought to mention while it's on my mind. It's nothing to do with this. But there's a man shut up here who's as sane as yourself. I don't say he was when he came in. But he's been sane for three years. Of course, you've only just taken over, I understand that, and I thought you'd be glad to know."

The Professor looked interested. He asked the man's name.

"Yes," he said, "I dare say you're right. There's a very large fee being paid for that man.

"My predecessor told me in the course of a short but most interesting conversation which we had before he cleared out, that there have been investigations on two occasions as to the alleged sanity of inmates here, and in both instances he was able to show that the patients undoubtedly suffered from insane delusions.

"You see, Mr. Maitland," the Professor went on, his mind forgetting its agitation, and even the critical issue which was between them, as it was drawn into explanation of a subject with which it was normally occupied, "an insane man is almost always convinced of his own sanity, and some of them can represent such an aspect very plausibly, very plausibly indeed.

"But if a man's really sane, it's quite a different thing. He's shut up somewhere with a lot of lunatics who don't make the most congenial or the most cheerful companions—you've seen enough already I expect to appreciate that—and perhaps he knows that his money's being wasted by a faithless wife, or his business going to ruin, and he knows his relatives will move heaven and earth to get him kept where he is, and he's got just one chance, when the Commissioners look in, to make them believe he's sane, and, if that fails, his hope's gone for a good many months to come.

"And before they see him, they'll be told that he's an unfortunate case with a fixed delusion that he's hated by all his friends, even by a devoted wife, as these poor insane people are so apt to imagine—and, almost before he begins to plead, he sees them looking at him in a pitying way, and he knows what they think. And he finds himself speaking passionately and not very wisely, and they move off, saying to one another that there was a wild look in his eyes, and he might have become violent at any moment.

"When they're told afterwards that his wife's very anxious to have him back, and willing to take the risk (but do they think it would be safe?), they say, better wait for a time, anyway, and see how he goes on."

The Professor put the case so well that Stanley was inclined to think that he might have done him some previous injustice. He felt glad, even amid the acute anxieties of the moment, that he had been able to inform him that there was one of these unfortunates among the inmates of the Institution over which he had acquired control. He had anticipated that he would take it in a different way. In view of the extremity of the duel that he was compelled to fight, it was embarrassing to find that the Professor had a side to his character of an unexpected decency. And while these thoughts passed through his mind the Professor went on:

"The question I have been anxious to study is how far or how long the human mind can retain its sanity under such conditions. It might be thought that the atmosphere of a madhouse, such as this, to one who is condemned to live and die as a certified lunatic among imbeciles and madmen whose conversation and habits are often of an almost grotesque obscenity, so that to associate intimately with them must be repulsive except to the purely scientific mind (which is comparatively rare) would be sufficient to produce the condition which is supposed to exist already, and that this would especially be the case in instances where there must be acute mental agitation arising from anxiety to deal with sentimental or material interests in the outer world.

"The question is of a real scientific importance, as it may tend to show the extent to which insanity may be induced by extremities of mental disturbance, or may be independent of all but purely physical changes in the substance or structure of the brain itself, or extraneous pressure upon it.

"I put the point in a non-technical way, which I am sure that you will appreciate. A study of this man, as the years pass, may provide me with data of the greatest scientific interest, though it will, unfortunately, be impossible to publish it, unless a more enlightened public opinion shall recognise the propriety of subordinating the interest of the individual to the paramount importance of scientific investigation."

"You mean, Professor, you'll keep him here?"

Stanley had endeavoured to control his voice to an unemotional question on a matter of fact, but he could not have been entirely successful, for the Professor looked at him with a sudden recognition of all that he had forgotten for the last ten minutes, and with what Stanley felt to be a sly and latent hostility which a further word might waken to malignant action. He felt that he was regarded once again as the archenemy of the scientific hierarchy, who had sent more than one of the Professor's world-reverenced colleagues to the hangman's rope, and scores to apply their boasted knowledge to the task of sustaining life in a semi-tropical wilderness. If he should promise the Professor the secret that he sought, he might be secure in a temporary immunity until it should be handed over, but beyond that—.

With a recovered reticence, Professor Sturgeon merely answered: "I must observe the man before any conclusion would be justifiable concerning him." He returned to the main subject by asking: "Do I understand, Mr. Maitland, that you are prepared to write out a full explanation of Feltham's invention and apparatus, and then, when I have been able to see more clearly what you have to offer, to discuss the terms of a working partnership either with my colleagues or with myself alone?"

"Yes. I think, in the end, that may be the shortest method. The statement itself may be rather a long one. I should like a quiet half-hour to compose it in as concise a form as the nature of the subject permits." He added, as the Professor appeared to hesitate in a doubt which he could not read: "You know, Professor, I'm rather out of my depth in this matter. You must make some allowance for that."

Professor Sturgeon made no answer. Whatever doubt he may have had appeared to have resolved itself in his mind. He rose, and led the way to the writing-room. He walked to the window, perhaps to reassure his memory that there could be no escape by the bare wall below it. He assisted Stanley in the discovery of foolscap paper in a side-drawer of the writing-desk. He said, almost genially, as he left the room: "It will be late for tea when you have finished. Perhaps you will join me in a somewhat more adequate meal. You can ring at any time when you are ready."

He stood at the door for a moment watching Mr. Maitland as he dipped the pen which was to throw open the gates of power. He went out dreaming of a day when the wondrous revelations of the vivisection-table would no longer be retarded by the interferences of the vulgar mob. Perhaps he looked further, to a day when the last secret of the Creator's laboratory will have been probed, and the control of humanity be taken forever out of His blundering hands.

CHAPTER SIXTY-ONE

STANLEY wrote slowly. He was in no haste. Though he had been resolute that the secret power he held should never pass into the Professor's hands, yet he wrote out what he knew of Feltham's invention, from the night when he had first been brought into contact with it, and the explanations that Feltham had given, in a clear and accurate way. He was determined to keep his word.

He raised his head once or twice, looking round and listening intently, that he might be sure that he was not under observation.

After a time he paused, as though troubled by a doubt of memory. He rose, and paced silently up and down the soft-carpeted room. He stopped once at the mantelpiece, idly handling the ornaments which were upon it. He went back, and wrote slowly and steadily, filling several sheets. He stopped at last. "I should think," he said, half-aloud, "that Sturgeon must be getting rather hungry by now." He got up and rang the bell.

An hour later, he was sitting with the Professor over a bottle of wine, having assisted in the disposal of a comfortable dinner and come to an understanding by which, subject only to the uncertainties of human life (as he had been careful to observe), they would rule the world together. The power which had fallen at Feltham's death into his incompetent fumbling hands would now be wielded by his new ally, and doubtless developed till it could be used with far greater accuracy and devastation. His own sphere of political and social experiment was to be left entirely to him. As the Professor had graciously allowed, its results, though they could be of no real importance, might not be altogether unworthy of the observation of the scientific mind, but for himself, he had greater dreams.

With such a power in his hands, by which whole nations could be removed, if necessary, from the path of progress, science would rise at last to its inevitable, destined pre-eminence as the guide and shepherd and god of the human race.

Mr. Maitland, having no regard for science, nor full control of the power which had come so casually into his incompetent hands, had pledged himself to leave unmolested the strongholds of religious bigotry, which is the scientist's most obstinate and foolish foe. Professor Sturgeon, under no such restriction, would root out the obsolete superstitions of Christianity, together with the other religions that afflict mankind. Who would enter a house of prayer that was under Professor Sturgeon's ban, and might sink in sudden ashes at any moment, with those who appealed within it to a regardless god?

What race of men would be slow to obey his orders of interbreeding, or social, or physical experiment of whatever kind, when his dissatisfaction might be visited upon them in that final and dreadful way?

Slightly intoxicated, as Feltham had been, at the first realisation of the power which his hand was stretched out to grasp, though less with alcohol and more with the excitement of imagination, he saw a world subdued at last to the demands and directions of science, fed, fumigated, sterilised, segregated, glanded, inoculated, vivisected, mated or sundered, as its curiosities might suggest, or its experiments require.

As the modern prison enforces a more exact and degrading servitude than was known or imagined by the inhabitants of a mediæval jail, so would the races of men be chastened to a scientific slavery more exacting than that which they had known from the scourges of superstition, or the inexorable laws of God.

In imagination his shadow fell across the world, vast as that of the Anti-Christ of Apocalyptic vision, and it was a title from which, at that moment, he might not have shrunk, if Mr. Maitland had suggested it to him.

But though the coming of such a one, with unimagined thunderbolts of scientific discovery in his hands, may be a very probable thing, it appeared shortly that Professor Sturgeon was not the man.

After a period during which he had relieved his excitement by pacing backwards and forwards across the room, he sat down again to drain a half-empty glass.

"I think you'd do well to sit quiet for a time, Professor," Stanley remarked, as he refilled the two glasses. "If you got a stroke from excitement it wouldn't help your plans now. I wonder what you suppose would happen to London, if we should both die tonight."

The Professor said that in such circumstances it wouldn't be particularly important to either of them.

"Well, I don't look at it quite like that. I've seen the strength of the forces which were joining against me for a month past, and—I suppose it was just mental strain, and the fact that I've not been happy in my private life—but I've felt increasingly uncertain that I should be able to face and overcome them. Queerly enough, that feeling's been quite gone since I found myself shut up here. I've felt sure from the first that I should come out on top.

"But a week ago I felt so uncertain of what might be before me that I actually visited Dawlish Mansions and disconnected the apparatus entirely. As far as I can tell, it's absolutely harmless now, and I don't know that anyone but Feltham could set it going again. Except, of course, you, Professor, with the information I've given you.

"Apart from that, there was one point which no one could have told for sure, though they might have guessed. The whole thing depends upon a supply of electric current that Feltham got from the main. Cut that off (it is cut off now, by the way) and it's as harmless as an empty gun."

"Why are you telling me this, Mr. Maitland?" The Professor asked the question in a dry strained voice. He looked bewildered, troubled, suspicious. He certainly looked unwell.

"I thought I might not tell you at all, if I didn't tell you now. I wonder whether you'd guess even now why I offered to write out that long account. No, you needn't look suspicious: it's quite genuine. I had too much respect for your eminent scientific attainments to try to fake anything. I haven't sufficient knowledge to do it so that you wouldn't have seen through it. Anyway, I couldn't have been sure.

"But the fact was I'd got to get into that writing-room somehow, because of something I'd hidden in one of the mantelpiece ornaments. I knew you wouldn't leave me here, even if there'd been a writing-table, because there's a telephone in this room.

"I'd got to do something that I didn't like doing—not till you told me that you'd keep a sane man here, and then I felt just as anyone would who has a chance of making things a bit cleaner than they were before. It's no good, Professor, I know there's a gun in that drawer, but you'll never reach it now. I see you guess how it is. You're dying as Feltham died, for the same reason as he."

There was the light of a fierce determination in the Professor's stiffening face. Inch by inch his foot dragged on the floor. Clear though faint, Stanley could hear the sound of the distant bell.

Feet sounded along the passage, and Stanley sprang toward the door, only turning the key at the instant that the handle rattled from without.

Well, they might rattle. The doors of the Burfleet Institution were not built to give way to the pressure of human shoulders. Stanley went back to the Professor's shrivelling form. He pulled open the drawer that had been at his right hand, and took out the loaded revolver which he had expected to find. There was a box of cartridges also.

Feeling that his position might be worse, he decided to dispose of the Professor as rapidly as possible. If he could do this before they should break in, it would be difficult for them to understand what had occurred. They would conclude that the Professor had left the room, and that he had then decided to barricade himself within it. They would look for the Professor, and probably do nothing worse than hold him prisoner the while. In the end, there would be help from outside.

He hoped that there was no remaining consciousness in the Professor's dried and contracted body as he broke it hastily, and shook it out of the loose clothes that it had ceased to fill. But the Professor himself would have been the first to argue that hesitation in such emergency would be a primitive human weakness abhorrent to the scientific mind. The sheets of foolscap that he had written out so carefully followed the Professor into the ample grate. The clothes were a difficulty. But there was a half-empty drawer into which he inserted them with some semblance of folding. They might puzzle, but no one would understand them. No one would think that the Professor had undressed in his presence, or been undressed by him, and then left the room in a condition of nudity. Anyhow, it was the best he could do.

The banging on the door had ceased before this. They were trying more effectual methods, shooting away the lock.

Stanley went to the telephone—fortunately it was not in line with the bullets—and while he spoke to Jehane, he saw the door sway inwards.

It was no time for scruples. Regardless of his own risk he ran forward, and fired two shots at a slant through the widening gap. A scream of pain, a heavy fall, and a stampede of feet down the passage old him that there was an absence of heroes who were prepared to perish for their master's rescue.

He heard a man drag himself slowly along the passage, groaning as he did so. Then there, was a louder noise of voices. Was it Rigby who called: *Hands up, the lot of you?* He was not sure, but he had no doubt of the voice of Selby Ditchfield. "This way. There's a man hurt. No, it's not Stanley. Come along."

Stanley pulled open the broken door, and went out to meet his friends.

www.ingramcontent.com/pod-product-compliance
Lightning Source LLC
Chambersburg PA
CBHW030243030726
47493CB00023B/575